KEEPER OF STONES

MÓRDHA STONE CHRONICLES, BOOK 2

KIM ALLRED

STORM COAST PUBLISHING, LLC

KEEPER OF STONES
Mórdha Stone Chronicles, Book 2
KIM ALLRED
Published by Storm Coast Publishing, LLC
Copyright © 2018 by Kim Allred
Cover Design by Amanda Kelsey of Razzle Dazzle Design
Print edition May 2018
ISBN 9781732241138

For the Rain Dogs
Beth Schmitz, Jeff and Lisa Gossett
Thank you for your guidance and keeping me on course

"History is the nightmare from which I am trying to awake."

Ulysses by James Joyce

T he white sails, tied tight against the rigging, leaked enough flap to flutter in the light breeze. Tails of ropes swung in unison with the rolling of the waves, rocking the sloop tied to its moor. AJ Moore stared up past the sails and rigging to the sky as she watched the clouds. It was rare to see blue skies this time of year, or so she'd been told. Ireland wasn't considered the Emerald Isle because of its sunny warm days.

"Step away, AJ. Step away."

Two months, and two hundred years from her future, had seemed an eternity since the fog dissipated, leaving her disoriented, confused, and finally disbelieving. She was no longer in Baywood, Oregon. If Finn could be believed, which was not one of his strong points, she was in Ireland, and the year was 1802. The year of Napoleon, a mad king on the English throne, and continual wars—certainly no place for a twenty-first-century woman.

Finn's strong arms encircle her, warm and comforting. The light touch of his fingers skims her sweater, reaching for her stone necklace.

AJ sprawled on the deck of the ship and watched the clouds float by, her skirts spread out around her. Her daily visits to the ship had become a ritual since the day they'd arrived through the fog. It wasn't as if the ship could take her home. It had been in her future, jumping with her and Finn to this new time, and it was a link to what she knew.

Desperation fuels Ethan's voice as he calls out to her, his face struck by terror. Her brother, Adam, echoes the alarm, stretching his arm out to her. He never cared about her before.

AJ shook her head to erase the memory like an old Etch A Sketch board. With the wood slats of the deck hard and unforgiving underneath her, she turned her focus to the clouds. The images shifted, first a turtle and then a horse. A hawk marred the forms, its flight breaking her concentration.

She couldn't shake the daydreams. It was going to be one of those days. The ones that led to a bout of depression. Stella would kick her ass for feeling sorry for herself. Stella believed in one day for self-pity accompanied by as many glasses of wine required to get through the night. Then move on. AJ had to believe that her friend would consider her current plight an exception to the one-day rule.

The thickening fog distorts Ethan's shape and muffles his voice. AJ can't hear anything but a rushing sound, like holding a seashell up to her ear. Finn's warm arms grip her tight. She strains to make out Ethan's face through the haze, his alarm barely visible, a silent cry forming on his lips.

She squeezed her eyes shut and sucked in a breath of cool morning air, pulling her woolen wrap tighter. The late spring sun couldn't break through the cold winds blowing in from the sea. The flashbacks didn't come as often, but when they did, they hit her with a force as strong as the day the world as she knew it disappeared. The only way through it was to relive it and deal with the aftermath.

With his arms ensnaring her, Finn touches the stone of his medallion to the stone in AJ's necklace. Ethan and the dock fade into the whiteness of the mist.

The sounds of footsteps snapped her back, and she turned her head to find the familiar dark shape set against the morning light. She threw an arm across her forehead to cut the glare from the sun and forced the tension from her muscles.

"I didn't mean to disturb you." Finn's voice was soft and distant.

She waited, but he wouldn't say anything more, not until he could determine her mood. She rolled her head away and swallowed the thickness clogging her throat. "It's all right."

"I need to make a trip to town. I just wanted you to know where I went."

"I thought you were going tomorrow." She tried to hide the bitterness. Her body ached with the need to go with him, to see other people.

"We need oats. The horses will be expecting their grain." He shuffled his feet. "And I thought I could take some of the extra loaves with me."

She couldn't hold back the smile. When she first tried her hand at baking bread, it had been a dismal failure. Finn went to town regularly to keep them supplied in fresh baked goods. Boredom eventually set in, and she focused her attention to the task. She became so adept at baking, she couldn't see the counters or tables for the number of loaves covering it, more than the two of them could eat. Finn took them to town, either to pay back the baker who supplied them in the beginning or to trade for other goods. She never asked.

"We could use some other staples. Flour and sugar. Cinnamon if you can find it."

"All right. I'll be back before supper." He waited.

She kept her head turned, staring blankly at the rigging until she heard his footsteps recede. She tired of these days where the past wouldn't let go. The last two months had been filled with anger, depression, and then curiosity about her new surroundings. She went days without speaking to him at all. In the end, she cried, letting him hold her and soothe her and tell her it would be all right. She even fell back into bed with him, trying to find any comfort she could, remembering her life before this. After all he had put her through, her heart tugged whenever she saw him, even when they had an incredible fight and he knew to stay away.

She bolted upright when she heard the hooves hitting the dirt path leading away from the cottage by the sea. Everything he did focused on her needs, her moods. It had taken two weeks before she caught on. And then she had pushed him, tested him. He never disappointed. She knew her guilt at her own mood swings would never compare to his guilt at bringing her back in time with him. It was done, and she needed to stop punishing him for it. They must discuss the future.

Standing to watch Finn disappear from sight, she brushed her skirts that fell two inches too short and tugged at the sleeves that stopped short of her wrists. Her question of who owned the well-made dresses that hung in her wardrobe had been met with a grunt from Finn. She sighed as she turned toward the rock-edged bay that protected the cottage from winter storms. Finn promised they would leave soon, but he never mentioned a destination.

Turning her back to the sea, she walked to the vegetable garden. Chores came before her daily cataloging of discoveries within the cottage. Unique household items written down with an old quill pen on any bits of paper she could find. All antiques, in her mind. She couldn't abandon her passion for the old or the love of history her father instilled in her. She wanted to remember everything she could when she found her way back home.

She grumbled at Finn as she pulled carrots, the fresh earth settling her. Through all her anger and tantrums, particularly during the first week of being completely inconsolable, he was there. She hadn't known him very long before the time jump, as she called it, but she discovered her feelings for him still

4

remained. During the days they didn't speak, she watched him, the crease of worry on his brow with long stares out to sea. He spent infinite hours working on the old house, tending the horses and maintaining the ship. She watched him from the window, from the garden, and even from the ship, where she might magically disappear back to her own time. With all he tried to do, she couldn't help but harbor anger at what he had done. She resented him for rebuffing her questions of how they came to be where they were, a place he seemed intimately comfortable with. He refused to speak of the stones.

"You need to get settled and understand how things work here. Then we'll talk about the stones." Finn kept to this line, refusing to budge.

"You owe me more," AJ retorted with the same response, always to his retreating back, stomping her foot or kicking something for emphasis. She couldn't help herself—she was a reporter after all. Or used to be.

From the garden, she paused in picking lettuce and sat among the vegetation, letting the warmth of the sun wash over her as her hands dug into the soil, a worm inching its way over her fingers. She wasn't one for gardens, that's why she loved her apartment. No fuss, no muss. But she loved Stella's flower garden, the odd-shaped paper lanterns swaying in the evening coastal breezes, and she longed to see it again.

The day of her arrival in Ireland, when the mist had faded, her first glimpse of Ireland had been the single dock, the hillside covered with spring flowers, dotted sporadically with elm trees and oaks, and the well-tended cottage. Then she noticed nothing at all when the impact of what had happened grabbed her and threw her down the rabbit hole.

Over the next few weeks she had examined the land, the cottage, and the sea, all nestled together in its own world. She witnessed the remoteness and desolation that matched her own spirit. Eventually, she came to appreciate the beauty, the imagery, and the tranquility that softened her anger and tamed her fear.

Grabbing the lettuce and carrots she'd pulled from the garden, AJ made her way back to the cottage. It was time to leave this land and figure out how the stones worked. Whether Finn was ready or not.

"THE MEAL WAS EXCEPTIONAL." Finn refilled the wineglasses and sat back, his long legs stretched out in front of him, hands resting on his stomach.

"Thank you." AJ sipped the wine and glanced at him over the rim of the glass. She couldn't ignore the presence he made. He wore simple trousers and an old woolen shirt, and though they fit loosely, she had seen his muscles flex when he started the fire. A tightening in her core nudged her as she remembered her hands moving over his warm skin and hard muscles. He smiled at her, a slow, lazy grin softening his square jaw. As if on command, a lock of his sun-kissed brown hair slid over his emerald eyes, almost black in the low light. The tingle rose up, and she averted her gaze.

"I thought we might go for a ride tomorrow." Finn stared at his glass, his finger moving slowly around the rim as if the suggestion was nothing more than a casual thought.

"Oh." AJ lowered her head and stood, carrying the empty plates to the counter. It wasn't that she didn't like horses. They were fine as long as she stayed on the ground. Her first riding adventure required two weeks of recovery before she agreed to make a second attempt. She refused any further lessons.

"You need to know how to ride. It will be noticeable if you shy away from them." A hint of a smile creased the corners of his mouth. "You really are getting much better." He busied himself with breaking off another piece of bread.

She rolled her eyes as she swept the last of the bread away from him. "Now you're just lying."

Finn grinned at her. "Aye, I'm ashamed I had to do that, but if it works, I'll do my best not to make a habit of it."

She couldn't hold back her own grin, even as she fought the growing panic of getting back on a horse. With the table cleared, she plopped down to finish her wine and mull over Finn's suggestion. He refused to take her anywhere in the two-person carriage she had seen in the barn, forcing her to stay within walking distance of the cottage.

"I'll try. It would be easier if I could straddle it like you rather than sitting sidesaddle."

He shook his head. "That would bring more attention than not riding at all. If you would promise to ride each morning, I would be agreeable to shorter sessions."

She gazed toward the window, dusk settling over the hills shaded black against the sky. He offered a decent compromise, a way to discover what lay beyond those hills—a history she only imagined. She had decided only hours before it was time to leave. This was her opportunity to meet the challenge, to see if she could blend in. She met his waiting gaze. "All right. I can't stay here forever. I need to find a way home."

LATER THAN EVENING, AJ sat at the oak writing desk in their bedroom, hunched over bits of paper. She dipped the quill into the ink, pushing to finish the words that had bounced around in her head all day.

"Come to bed. We have a long day tomorrow." Finn pulled the covers over his broad shoulders and turned toward the wall.

She finished the last few words and extinguished the lamp. Her bare feet scurried over the cool floor the fire never seemed able to warm. She missed the bunny slippers Stella had given her last Christmas. As she jumped into bed, the idea of rubbing her cold feet against his legs was difficult to squash.

For the briefest of moments, she reached to run her hand down his back, to feel the solidness of him, to remind herself she wasn't alone. He would be accepting of her touch even though his back was to her. It was his way of giving her space. She pulled her hand back and rolled to her side, waiting for sleep to come.

FINN'S EMBRACE tightens when she shows him the old antique necklace with the odd marbled stone. One that happens to match the unique stone set in his Celtic cross medallion.

Her anxiety flares as she struggles to move out of his arms. She plucks at his hands, scratching at the arms that tighten around her like steel claws. A sheen of sweat glistens on her brow, and she strains against the restricting body. She can't breathe. If she could just break free, clear her head, and get to Ethan.

The thickening fog distorts Ethan's shape and muffles his voice, but the soft words float to her. "Step away. Step away."

With his arms still ensnaring her, Finn touches the stone of his medallion to the stone in AJ's necklace.

She tenses. Something is terribly wrong. A rushing sound fills her ears as she watches Ethan fade.

The mist consumes the ship, and the dock disappears, spiriting Ethan and Adam away. AJ's skin prickles as an invisible force reaches deep inside her, pulling her as if the hand of Kronos reached inside her, grasping her spine and ripping it out.

It couldn't be real.

The muscles of Finn's arms constrict around her. The mist smothers her like a lead blanket, heavy and unmoving. She peers through the thickness of the fog, but there's nothing there.

Blinded by a bright, impenetrable whiteness, she reaches out to steady herself, but she can't raise her arms. Her head dizzy, her stomach reeling, she wants to retch. She closes her eyes as the world drops away, her stomach spiraling with it. Her head rests against Finn, his body a rock. At least that's something. She isn't alone.

Any comfort she might feel in his embrace evaporates. She struggles but can't wrest herself from the straitjacket that binds her. Her eyes snap open.

She calls out, "Finn." The vortex consumes the word before it takes shape. Her senses scream, and when she knows she's going to vomit, the fierce tug pulling at her lightens. The mist slowly dissipates, and Finn's arms, while still around her, loosen their grip.

AJ blinks to refocus. The mist disappears to reveal the mast of the ship, the deck, and then the railing. The sun breaks through to chase away the remaining fog. Her breath escapes in a rush as the dock reappears. Something isn't right—Ethan and Adam have vanished.

A well-kept house made of wood and stone sits a few hundred yards from the dock. Finn's warm fingers circle her wrist, his thumb rubbing gently against its raging pulse. His words roll over her, soft as a gentle breeze, "Do you still trust me? I have a story to tell you sweet lass."

AJ SHOVED the covers from her, sitting up and clutching her nightgown. Her breathing was hard and fast, pounding against her ribs. She counted to ten, then repeated it two more times before her heart rate slowed. She wiped her brow, sticky with sweat.

She whipped her head toward Finn. He reached for her before he turned in his sleep. Her nightmares were either becoming quieter, or he was getting used to them. When they'd first arrived in this time period, he would shake her from them and hold her tight. Now he barely stirred.

She lay down, leaving the covers off to cool her body. After a few minutes, she dragged them back over her before turning to her side, her knees pulled up, waiting for the darkness to give way to light.

2

AJ woke in a better mood than she expected after her nightmare. She didn't think she'd go back to sleep, and was surprised to find the morning light filling the room. Finn was long gone, his spot in bed cool to her touch. The scent of coffee floated in from the kitchen, and she smiled at Finn's thoughtfulness, until she remembered the day he had planned for her. Horses. Her horse was named Mabel, but she preferred "She Devil," though Finn said she was the gentlest mare around.

He assured her she didn't need to be an expert. Many women weren't exceptional riders. Men either, for that matter. But she had to at least know how to sit a horse and appear comfortable.

As her fingers roamed through the dresses in search of her riding habit, her gaze landed on the folded garments lying like a talisman on the shelf, abandoned and alone. These were her one solid connection to remind her where she had come from, who she was, and her mission to go home. For the first couple of days, the only thing she would wear were her jeans, shirt, and sweater, until Finn convinced her she needed to put them away. She washed them thoroughly and hung them, leaving them for two days just so she could watch them flutter in the afternoon breeze.

After she took them down and carefully folded them, she placed them in the closet, laying her Skechers on top, and temporarily closed that chapter of her life.

The one thing she did like about horses was her riding habit. The sturdier fabric kept her warm, and she preferred to wear it all the time, but Finn said that wouldn't be proper. As she slid on her boots, she grumbled. How many other things besides horseback riding would she need to learn?

Her nature would make it unacceptable to be subservient to men. Yet here she was in the early years of nineteenth century Ireland, and everything she knew, everything that came as second nature, wouldn't work here. She would appear brash. She would never have the knowledge, the training, or the energy to blend in.

He mentioned a cover story to explain where she had come from, why she had a foreign accent, and why she was alone with him—quite improper. But he would need to dig deep to explain her barbaric ways of not being a proper lady, as if he just found her in the barn nestled next to the lambs and little piggies. She wrestled with her need to feel indignant about the situation she found herself in and Finn's responsibility for it. But her anger and regret wouldn't help. She had to keep her focus on the one thing that mattered most—getting home.

A flash of dark gray eyes and a tall, lean frame broke through her reverie, the force so strong she fell into the nearest chair. Tears sprang from nowhere and an intense pain sifted through her. She focused on blanking her mind to chase away the chill shooting up her spine. These episodes came less frequently but when they did, each were as intense as the last. Why had she not listened to Ethan when he tried to warn her? She hadn't known why Ethan held misgivings about Finn. His suspicions about a theft ring weren't accurate, but he'd suspected danger. She had been too stupid and too involved with Finn to give Ethan the proper respect for his business and knowledge of security. Now she was living the very horror she had seen carved on his face the last time she saw him.

She sat for several minutes and allowed the feeling of utter loss to wash over her. She needed a place to climb, to work out her pent-up frustrations. Tending the garden didn't come close to the intense workout she needed. The episode faded, and her breathing returned to normal. The pain dissolved. She pulled herself up and marched to the door. There was only way to deal with her memories.

AJ now relished the challenge of the horse. She would no longer allow her fear to prevent her from leaving this place behind and finding her way home. As she passed the window, she spied Finn staring out to sea, and her heart dropped.

Accomplishing her goal to find a way home would mean leaving this man behind, and after everything she had endured, she was disturbed to discover the thought deeply shook her.

"THAT'S MUCH BETTER. You need to remember to hold your skirts with one hand as you grab the pommel, but you did quite well." Finn fussed with moving her skirts for her as he handed her the reins. "Now keep a tight hold on the reins until I can mount. If she decides to start walking, don't panic. Just pull a little harder on the reins, and she should stop. Just don't give her too much lead. The most she'll do is walk to grass."

AJ heard his words, but she could only focus on how high she was from the ground. The mare's muscles twitched as she shifted from foot to foot, and AJ kept a white-knuckled grip on the saddle. The horse continued to move even though she pulled on the reins hard enough to strain a muscle.

Finn mounted his horse, and she marveled at his natural grace. He seemed connected to the beast with a mutual under-standing that passed between them. A trust established through time, patience, and respect for each other. That was something she understood from the pets she'd coveted through her life. She glanced down at her own horse and pried one hand from her death grip on the pommel, reaching out to touch the horse's mane. Her hand slid over its neck, and she felt the ripple of muscles as they twitched at her touch.

"Good girl, Mabel. Be good to me." AJ sat up straighter and suppressed her panic as Mabel started to walk. She prayed the horse would not flee with her across the hills, leaving her to scream and hold on for dear life. But, as Finn predicted, Mabel walked only as far as she needed to find fresh grass. AJ laughed out loud.

Finn rode up next to her, his smile wide. "You didn't believe me, did you?"

AJ shook her head. "I thought you were just trying to make me feel better."

"I was. It was also the truth."

He watched her, as if he wanted to say more. "So now what?"

"We're going to walk the horses around here for a bit, then we'll walk them down the road."

"That seems simple enough."

"Aye, it sounds simple. But you need to pay attention to every detail. Focus on how you get her to walk and take direction. Once it seems you have it mastered, we can call it a day. Agreed?"

"Aye, agreed." AJ smiled at her attempted Irish lilt, and Finn's return grin warmed her. Would they still be smiling at the end of the lesson?

"Let's start with you sitting a bit straighter and then nudging her with your heel. Loosen the reins." Finn moved his horse away to give Mabel space. "That's it. Don't give her too much rein yet, just enough to walk. There you go."

AJ concentrated on sitting straight, listening to each of Finn's commands as they rode in concentric circles around the yard. They stopped frequently, turning Mabel this way and that, never faster than a walk. She could feel her body relax with the movement of the horse. Mabel seemed to understand she had a novice on board, but she tested AJ by taking every advantage to nibble grass when AJ relaxed her attention.

Finn proved to be a patient teacher as he had the day of her sailing lesson—a lifetime ago. They spent an hour in the yard before Finn turned down the road that led to the village.

AJ's comfort with Mabel increased. She grabbed the saddle when she thought Mabel might do something unforgiving, like racing off with her, but each time was a false alarm. Mabel's twitches became predictable, and AJ grew confident, as long as they would never need to go faster than their current slow pace. "How far is the village?"

"A couple of miles."

Finn kept his horse close to hers for conversation, but AJ suspected he might be staying near to prevent a runaway horse. She trusted his quick reflexes to save her should Mabel decide to test her abilities.

They rode in silence for a mile before Finn turned them around. AJ remembered the stable horses at the beach in Baywood. When the horses knew they were on their way home, their manners vanished as the horses made a mad dash for the barn, completely ignoring the commands of the novice rider. She braced herself and was surprised when Mabel didn't change her pace.

"I've come up with a cover story for you." Finn stared at the road ahead.

"Am I going to like it?" He would be better at developing a back story that would be believable. But she wasn't going to follow along unless she felt comfortable with it. She wasn't convinced Finn would consider all the details.

Finn laughed. "I don't think it will be anything you can't handle, and it will speak to all of your, uh..." Finn's forehead creased as he searched for the right words. "All your rough edges." Finn slid a glance her way.

AJ tried to appear indignant before spitting out a laugh. "Here I am, thrown two hundred years into the past, and I'm the one with the rough edges."

"With all the modern technology, you have to admit, people of your time have lost something." Finn appeared to struggle to find the right words. "There's general politeness, for the most part. But you've lost decorum."

AJ nodded. "I understand what you're saying. With all the history I've read, I know my era has moved away from the etiquettes as you know them. But most of it was a waste and speaks more to how misaligned everyone was."

"What do you mean?" Finn appeared curious.

"The difference in classes, rich versus poor, the indignity of women as second-class citizens, or worse, property. The propriety that I must conform to is basically removing my base morals that everyone is an equal, regardless of the amount of money they may have or their gender."

Finn nodded. "Aye, I saw the change in what you would call social evolution through my months of moving through time, seeing the changes in society. I can't say it's all bad. Being Irish, I certainly understand the desire to be treated as an equal. Having less money than someone else shouldn't remove a person's rights." Finn thought about it. "But for now, you are a chattel so we must find a way for you to conform without bringing out that fiery temper of yours."

AJ's anger started to rise at his deliberate challenge until she saw the grin he couldn't hold back. "Fine. I get it. When in Rome."

"You will be a distant cousin, newly arrived from America." Finn smiled at his ingenuity.

AJ thought about it. "It would solve the issue with my accent." She laughed as she thought about it more. "And my crude ways. I would think anyone from America would be considered rather low on the refined side."

"Aye. So if we tell people right off that you're from America, they may look at you strangely, but they won't ask any questions."

"Great. I'll feel like a monkey at the zoo, just no bars."

"It won't be that difficult. You're a beautiful woman, so I'm sure you're used to the staring."

Finn's statement made AJ pause. She never thought of herself as beautiful. She knew she was above average in appearance, but never thought about it more than that. She was too thin, her nose too big for her face, and her hair uncompromising which was why she preferred it short. Finn's words brought a warm glow, and she accepted the compliment.

"So why did I come to Ireland?"

"Good point. You made a stop in Ireland because we're related. I have business in London and have agreed to escort you to other family who will introduce you into proper society."

"An escort?" AJ knew enough about the time period to know this didn't seem proper. It was sure to set tongues wagging.

Finn ignored her. "You've been a handful back home with having lost your mother at an early age and only a father and brother to raise you. That's close enough to your own story, but it makes more sense if it's your mother that was lost rather than your father."

"Okay. I can see where I could have grown too wild for a young lady."

Finn glanced away, suddenly lost in the landscape.

"Finn?" She turned to match his gaze but saw nothing that would have distracted him. "Is everything okay?"

He pushed an errant lock from his face. "Sorry, I thought I saw something."

AJ stared at him. He just lied to her. She wasn't sure how she knew, she just did. And she could see he knew it too.

He continued as if the moment meant nothing. "Everyone

knows that America is not as modern as Europe. It wouldn't have all the proper avenues for a young woman to learn true societal ways. It's too new of a country, even if you did win the war."

"So I'm being shipped off overseas like a spinster to learn how to be a proper lady."

"Aye, and hopefully catch yourself a promising husband."

AJ snorted. "You're joking, right?"

"Not at all. You wouldn't be the first woman to be sent to London for such a thing. You're a bit older than most." Finn paused, waiting for a scathing remark, but AJ's brows were knit in concentration. "Looks alone can help engineer a perfect match, although I wouldn't expect him to be too young. It's the older ones who already have a substantial income that fancy themselves a beautiful wife."

AJ rolled her eyes, truly thankful this was all a ruse, although deep down she wondered what would happen to her if they couldn't find her a way home. She couldn't imagine being bartered as a trophy wife. "Great," was all she could muster and urged Mabel on, a little surprised to find they were back at the stable. She hadn't even thought about her fear of riding.

She accepted Finn's help to dismount. Patting Mabel's neck, AJ reached into her pocket for a sliced carrot and carefully extended it to the horse, who gladly took her peace offering. AJ smiled and turned to the house, leaving Finn to care for the horses. One chore she was happy to leave to a man.

"Where are you going?"

"I need a bath. All this talk of selling me off like a shiny toaster has me feeling a bit tarnished." She turned away, unsure if he would laugh at her comment. She worried about seeing the truth of the matter in his expression, and she didn't want to know how close their cover story was to the truth of her future.

FINN WATCHED HER WALK AWAY, pleased by the progress they'd made. Whether she left the horse in his care because that was what a lady of the time would naturally do or because she was irritated by something he'd said, he didn't care. She'd acted properly whether on purpose or not. She grew comfortable with Mabel without even thinking about it, her body gently swaying with the rhythm of the horse. Even with her stalling tactics, anyone that could rock climb, as she claimed she did, could learn to handle a horse. He understood it had to do with control, and if you didn't feel you had it, everything became unsteady. He knew that better than anyone.

He marveled at how much she'd learned in the last couple of months. Through all her despair, she wouldn't stop asking about each new trinket she found. But the basics of societal niceties and standard behaviors challenged her and worked against her upbringing. She had been raised in the twenty-first century, and even the smallest of inappropriate manners would be noticed in this century. At meals, he didn't care that she left a teacup or plate for him to pick up, but if anyone else had been in the room, they would have immediately noticed her transgression. He was thankful there would be servants where they were going to cover most of her mistakes.

He should be more stern about the social protocols, but he didn't want to push. He wanted to give her time—something they didn't have. With every little success, the impatient clock buried inside him ticked louder. Juggling the time he needed to complete AJ's transformation competed with his own burning drive to continue his mission.

His gut twisted each time he thought of his plan. He knew he should leave her here at the cottage, but she would never accept that, and he had no one here to watch over her. Even though she could barely sit a horse, she would chase after him the minute he left. AJ couldn't comprehend the dangerous times they lived in, and he didn't have the heart to tell her it was a long shot at best to think they could find her a way home.

He lived through months of time travel and understood the fear of not knowing what would come next and whether he would ever see home again. He wished he had some idea of how the story would end so he could ease her burden. There were days when all he wanted to do was carry AJ onto his ship and sail away. Sail anywhere that would take them away from where they had to go and forget the world around them. But Finn could no more do that than he could wish her away, back to her own time. There was more at stake than the two of them, and that mattered above all else.

Finn's best chance of encouraging her to succeed would be to tell her a little more of the story. There couldn't be any harm in telling her what he knew of the stones, it was little enough. They would leave for England soon, and he had no desire to cross the channel while dodging thousands of questions. Finn shook his head as he removed Mabel's saddle. Of all the women to find himself tied to, it had to be a reporter. He was glad for the need to rub down the two horses. It would provide him ample time to decide how much to tell her about the stones without it interfering with his own goals.

3

A J endured another week of a sore backside and long soaks in the tub, but she mastered horseback riding. She would never claim to be proficient, but she would pass scrutiny. During the lessons, Finn questioned her relentlessly about her cover story.

She chose Cambridge as her American home simply because she had traveled there with her father and knew its history well. Anyone she met in England probably wouldn't be as familiar with Cambridge as perhaps Boston. So if someone tried to test her by asking about someone in Boston, it would make sense if she didn't know them. By the end of her riding lessons, Finn agreed her back story rang true.

Trepidation over a visit to the village complemented the week of riding lessons. When the day of travel arrived, Finn fretted over AJ's preparations. Any other time, his suffocating presence would smother her, especially over such a simple task as dressing for town. But she understood his anxiety. Her emotions jumped from excitement to downright terror at the thought of going to town. She had no idea what to expect, and no amount of reading history books would be enough to prepare her for the real thing. So she welcomed Finn's hovering.

With her dressing complete, Finn gave her a nod of approval. His gaze roamed over her, and she blushed when his eyes darkened. His lopsided grin appeared, and she realized he'd switched from mother hen to rogue in a fraction of a minute.

"Don't even think about it. It took too long to get this perfect. We're going to town. Cool off." AJ turned away from him to gather a shawl and headed out the door before he could respond.

Finn helped her mount and let his hand linger on her ankle. He stared up at her. The tingle started from where his hand rested and sizzled through her. She removed his hand by backing up her horse.

He chuckled. "It seems you've mastered several skills this week."

"I've never had a problem keeping a man in his place." She could still feel his hand on her ankle, and, for an instant, something passed between them. Everything was about to change with a simple trip to the village.

"Aye, and it's a good thing. I won't have to work so hard to keep the old lechers from you."

Finn slowed their pace as he ran AJ through her background story again. She kept it simple, not too much detail, but enough to pass in most conversations. She changed subjects with ease, and Finn added a few techniques and phrases more appropriate for the time.

"The best thing you can do is to say as little as possible." Finn relaxed in his saddle, lost in thought. "I've attended my share of parties and visited enough drawing rooms in some of the best houses in London."

AJ raised an eyebrow. "Do you have a title or something?" She couldn't picture Finn dressed for societal soirees. Since arriving in Ireland, he'd only worn work clothes.

Finn shrugged. "Or something." He shifted in his saddle and

turned the subject back to her training. "Most women like to chatter, so they'll fill the space you leave empty. It's not true for the women you'll meet in the villages, but still try to keep your talk to the business at hand. In drawing rooms or parties, however, most women won't be comfortable with silence. They'll fill in the silence by answering their own questions for you. Don't worry if they're not correct."

"I get it. Loose lips sink ships."

Finn shook his head. "Where do you get these phrases? I don't understand most of them, and I've traveled more extensively than most."

AJ laughed. "I don't think there's anyone who's traveled more than you—anywhere."

"Good point."

"I know I should stay in character, even with you, but it's impossible. I have to feel that I can be myself with someone." She ran her fingers through Mabel's mane. Her next words barely audible over the sounds of the hooves. "There's no one else but you."

Finn moved his horse closer and reached out for her hand. "You'll always have me. I need you to truly believe that. No matter what happens." Finn stopped the horses, his expression grave. "I asked once if you trusted me. I know I've stretched your faith in me more than anyone could, but I'm asking you to hold on to that trust."

She searched his earnest, handsome face, wanting to believe his words. He'd decided this path for her. One she wouldn't have chosen for herself. Her future rested in someone else's hands, leaving her no choice. She had no one else to turn to, and although her trust in him wavered, she knew that she loved him. Perhaps that would be enough. Unable to verbally commit her trust, she squeezed his hand and urged Mabel on.

A full minute passed before she heard Finn catch up with her. He urged them to a faster pace. AJ concentrated on her riding, thankful for the lack of conversation. The mood had changed, and a hard ride might be the next best thing to rock climbing to clear her head.

———

FINN SHARED details of the village during their evening meals, but in AJ's experience, expectations never fit with reality. Her first glimpse of the town proved to be no exception. Disappointment filled her. The village was no bigger than a city block, maybe a bit more.

"It's so small." AJ spied a blacksmith shop. It was something her father would have loved. She itched to stop but couldn't think of a reason that wouldn't draw attention.

"I suppose it's more of a hamlet. It grows during harvest when the farms travel in for trade."

"They're so close to the sea. Why didn't they build closer for a port?"

Finn gave her an approving nod. "Excellent question. There isn't much of a bay here. Just a few isolated inlets dotted along the coast like the one at the farm. And we're not far from Waterford, which provides an active port. So the village grew up around the crossroads."

"Where there would be more traffic." Her head swiveled, taking it all in. It might be no bigger than a postage stamp but it bustled with activity.

Several farm wagons filled with early spring harvest parked between buildings. People surrounded the carts, actively trading, arms flapping, voices raised. She itched to be among them but knew it would be a mistake on her first trip. This called for observation before opening her mouth.

AJ prepared herself for staring and pointed fingers, but most people didn't pay attention to her. Finn stopped frequently to acknowledge smiling faces and pleasant greetings, but she only received a quick glance or faint hello. Finn introduced her as his cousin from America, and true to his word, they would shake their head as if that said it all.

They stopped at a thatched house nestled between the spread of two oak trees at the edge of town. Flower pots filled with spring color surrounded the entrance, giving the impression of a florist shop. She knew that didn't make sense but couldn't fathom any other trade for what appeared to be someone's home. Finn settled the horses in a paddock next to the building and guided her toward the front door. As they drew close, she glimpsed dresses hanging near the window—a dressmaker shop. She slid a glance to Finn, but he said nothing before ducking inside.

The house welcomed her the minute she walked through the door. A mixture of aromas filled the tiny room, many she couldn't name. She had no trouble recognizing the scent of fresh baked bread, cinnamon, rosemary, and a touch of chamomile. The room overflowed with an eclectic array of fabric made of various colors and textures. Simple grays and browns for everyday dresses, a few with tiny flower patterns, and those made of richly colored muslin, satin and other material she didn't know. She wouldn't pass as a fashion maven; that was Stella's domain. But she could easily tell the expensive cloth from the rest.

AJ spun around the room, taking it all in. There were ribbons and trims, buttons and bows. In one corner, finished garments hung against the wall. Most were day dresses but she spied a few men's shirts, waist coats, and tailcoats, and a couple of overcoats. Sitting off to one side were three dresses of exquisite design, hues intense with burgundy, emerald and sapphire. AJ reached out a tentative hand and felt the fabric, afraid to damage the fragile-looking gowns.

"Go ahead and get a good feel, they won't tear." The voice was loud and gruff.

AJ jumped away as if burned.

An old woman cackled. "Go ahead, girl. They're yours. You might as well get a feel for them before trying them on."

"Mine," AJ murmured and touched them again.

"Yes, your ah, cousin, insisted you have some new gowns for London." The old woman bustled in, a cloak over her arm which she hung on a peg near the dresses. Her voice took on a stiffer tone. "You'll find they're up to snuff with what they're wearing there."

"They're beautiful." AJ turned to Finn, unsure whether to thank him or just be quiet.

"And they need to be ready in three days," Finn said.

"Three days," the old woman screeched. "It can't be done." Shaking her head she grabbed the first one while mumbling under her breath. She motioned at AJ. "Let's get this on you." Then she pointed at Finn. "Get out."

Finn ignored the old woman and turned to AJ. "I have some errands to run. I'll be back in an hour, and we'll finish up." Raising an eyebrow at the old woman, Finn finished, "Don't crow at me, Marguerite. I know what you can do, and you won't get another shilling out of me. Three days." His voice was harsh, but AJ caught Finn giving the old woman a wink before leaving.

The old woman turned AJ around and untied her gown. "That Finn Murphy is a fine one." Her tone changed to somewhere between motherly and admiring. The combination would have sounded creepy on anyone else, but it worked with Marguerite, who appeared to be a walking contradiction. "It's perfectly normal for distant cousins to wed, you know. Done all the time."

The woman's forward nature shocked AJ. She found it somewhat enchanting when she wasn't the focus of Marguerite's outbursts. "It's not like that. Between us, I mean."

Marguerite, having pushed AJ out of her day dress, gave her a long assessment before gesturing her to step into the first gown. "Right, honey, it's your business."

With the dress tied, AJ immediately felt the difference

between this gown and the dresses she had been wearing. This gown suited her proportions. The sleeves hung a touch too long, but the skirts fell perfectly. Marguerite moved her hands over the dress, making adjustments, pulling here and tugging there. AJ had never experienced a personal fitting before and found the experience a bit heady.

"I don't see many men buy such beautiful gowns for a cousin. And your new petticoats and nightgown, well, I'm not sure why they have to be so fancy if he's not going to be seeing them." Marguerite turned AJ around to face her. She worked at AJ's bustline, freely reaching in to make adjustments.

AJ blushed, unsure if it was from Marguerite's hands or the fact Finn had bought her lacy underwear.

Marguerite stood back and took it all in. AJ felt like a tomato that had been manhandled at the market, softly bruised and a bit mushy. But she had to admit, the gown felt better after the dressmaker made her adjustments. The old woman stared at her and motioned for her to turn around. She smiled as she felt the wispy skirts flow around her. When she was once again facing the dressmaker, she saw Marguerite smile and nod with approval.

"Not many adjustments. Finn gave me some very fine measurements." Marguerite turned AJ around again and started unlacing the dress. "For a cousin." She couldn't seem to help getting in the last word.

AJ ignored the comment and let the gown fall away. She silently turned to find the next one to step into. This dress required less time. Marguerite's skill was evident as her hands flew to the same spots needing adjustment.

With the last gown put away, the old woman gestured AJ into a chair by a carved side table. She disappeared for a few minutes and returned with a tray holding a teapot, cups, and biscuits. Marguerite poured the tea, adding milk and sugar to her own cup. AJ politely waved away the sugar but allowed the milk to be added, feeling a bit smug at passing her first social test.

"Have you been making clothes all your life?" AJ sagged into the chair. The deep wrinkles at the corners of Marguerite's eyes and the graying hair suited her. She reminded AJ of her grandmother.

"Oh, aye, since I was a young child. My father was a tailor, and he taught me. There isn't much call for it here, but a few wives of the landlords seek me out. I think I have Finn to thank for keeping me busy." Marguerite bit into a biscuit and glanced at the gowns she made for AJ. "It's not often I get to make something so beautiful."

A blush reddened AJ's face, and Marguerite waved a hand at her. "Don't let the words from an old woman get you turned inside out. It's just us here. There's no judgment." She sipped her tea and patted AJ's hand. "I've watched that man grow up from an incorrigible troublemaker to a fine and responsible man."

"You've known him since he was a boy?" AJ sat upright, eager to learn about Finn through someone else's insight.

"Aye, I wasn't sure he was going to straighten out. He ran with some ruffians...street urchins." She made a face. "But his father always pulled him out of a scrape. That doesn't always bode well for their future, you know. But then the terrible accident happened. Well, that changed him. Put him on the straight and narrow."

AJ wanted to ask about the accident but wasn't sure how. It was probably a topic she would have known as a cousin. The old woman rambled on. "Now there's many a young woman in the village who would love to snare that one. No one knows why he's taking so long to make a decision. He was gone for a long time. We just assumed when he returned, he'd be married."

AJ let the statement hang between them. The thought of him marrying didn't bother her as much as knowing he might have old girlfriends in town. At least he didn't have a wife locked away somewhere. Not that she really believed he would, but it never hurt to be sure. Then she remembered the name of Finn's ship, the *Daphne Marie*. Before she could ask Marguerite if she knew where the name came from, the door opened, splashing sunshine across the room and blocking the face of the visitor. She recognized the outline of the familiar figure. His timing sucked. She blinked, trying to see past the brightness as the door closed behind him.

"I see you've finished. Is the three days going to be a problem?" Finn's tall frame seemed to shrink the room.

Marguerite nodded. "Everything will be ready." She squinted at him, a smile hovering on her lips. "Your measurements were almost perfect."

Finn ignored her comment and laid a silk pouch on the table. "I'll bring the rest when I return." He turned to AJ. "We have several more errands to attend to. Are you finished with your tea?"

AJ nodded, trying to behave as she thought she should. "Thank you, Marguerite. The dresses are beautiful. I'm sure all of London will want to know where they were made."

It was Marguerite's turn to blush, and the color deepened when Finn laid a kiss on her cheek and whispered, "Thank you, old woman."

Leaving the dressmaker, Finn dragged AJ to other shops, ordering supplies and staples for their journey. Any other time, these details would have fascinated her. But she preferred to spend more time with Marguerite, digging deeper into Finn's past. A topic he avoided as much now as he did when they first met.

Their final shop turned out to be an apothecary of sorts. Finn selected personal items for them, and after a short hesitation, added a new comb and hairpin AJ had been fondling. She protested, but Finn bought them, returning the smile of the shopkeeper who watched their domestic display. She lifted her chin and ignored them both, but inside, she shouted with joy that she'd passed another test.

Her joy diminished when she saw the money pass between Finn and the shopkeeper. Curious as to where his money came from, she frowned as she considered how much he would be paid for recovery of her stone necklace. He held back many details about his eighteen months of time travel, so she didn't know how he survived financially. Had he been paid in advance? That was possible.

Marguerite's sketchy words about his troublesome younger days nagged at her. It wasn't far-fetched to see Finn as a rebellious youth. But maybe he hadn't become as responsible as everyone thought. Was it possible he'd learned a way to cover it up so it wasn't obvious? The larger question was how to broach the subject with him.

4

Before leaving the apothecary, Finn stopped at a table and picked up a journal covered by soft brown leather. He turned it over in his hands and flipped through the blank pages. AJ almost drooled at seeing the blank linen pages. He surprised her when he bought two and requested they be wrapped separately so each packet held one journal, one ink pot, and one quill pen. Without another word, he tucked them both away and guided her to their next stop.

AJ hesitated before entering the inn, its thatched roof bare in spots. She braced herself, anticipating a dirty, smoked-filled room and unwanted stares from old men. But she found the opposite as she followed Finn through the door to an open table. It was as dark as she anticipated, but the wood floors and tables were clean. Embers glowed in the hearth, still warming the room. Several lamps reflected tables of people eating or chatting over mugs. Her stomach grumbled at the smell of food and baked bread.

Finn set down their purchases and walked to the bar to place an order. He returned with two mugs filled with cider. AJ took a sip and sank into the bench. Her feet hurt, and she wished she had her new boots to wear, but they wouldn't arrive for another day or two.

She glanced at Finn. He watched her with an expression she hadn't seen before and couldn't name. He pushed one of the packages that held a journal toward her.

"What's this?" AJ asked.

"It's been a long time since you've written anything. I've seen the notes you collect about the furniture and gadgets from this century. I thought you might want to keep everything in a journal, or maybe write something about your travels," Finn said. He turned away from her and scanned the room, his fingers fidgeting on the mug of cider. When his gaze rested on her again, his voice lowered to a gruff whisper. "I don't know. It's what you do, and I thought you'd like it." He sat back and sipped his cider.

She had never seen him wistful. First the dresses and her wardrobe for the trip, then the hair pin, and now the journal. Of everything, the journal was the best gift of all. She ran a hand over the package, genuinely touched by his gift. He seemed to be waiting but stared into his mug, avoiding her gaze.

She rested her hand on his and squeezed. "This is the best gift I've ever received. Thank you, Finn."

He squeezed her hand in response. They grew silent as the innkeeper placed bowls of stew and chunks of bread on the table.

"We travel soon?" AJ broke the silence, eager to know the plan.

"Aye, I think you're ready. And it's time to get this done."

She considered asking if he'd given thought to how she might return home, but his tone had hardened. He had given her a journal and knew she missed her home. She hoped it wasn't her consolation prize.

"And who is this man you're delivering the stone to?"

"They call him the Viscount of Waverly Manor. To me, he's just Beckworth. A brigand who bought a title."

"And he's the one who commissioned you to find the stone?"

Finn hesitated before answering. "In a fashion." His tone told AJ to leave it at that.

She readied herself to push him to explain, but he fell into his food as if he hadn't eaten in days. He might as well cool down while they ate. If it was in silence, so much the better.

As soon as Finn pushed his bowl away, she jumped at her opportunity. While she ate, she had put her questions in order and then rearranged them. She planned on using her standard interview technique: get the big picture and then drill down to details. But she worried that Finn would be evasive, so she refocused her questions on priority of her need to know.

"What's your plan with the stones? I assume you're going to turn yours over as well. And what? Get paid for your efforts?"

Finn blanched at her words. He sat back and stared at her.

"I have a right to know." She reined in her growing anger, lowering her voice and leaning into the table. "Those stones are what brought me here. Your own stone traveled through time in search of mine. They are surely what will get me home. You must know that."

Finn's temper flared in return as he leaned in, his voice barely audible over the noise of the other patrons. "I'm more than familiar with how you got here. I know how important the stones are. There's more to it than that."

"Like what? What else is there? Can't we just take the stones and figure out how they work on our own? Or is your payment foremost in your mind?" She was sorry the instant his eyes lowered. The questioning had gotten out of hand too quickly. Frustration at whatever game he played had gotten the better of her.

"I'm not getting paid for this." Finn stopped abruptly. He sneered at her. "I'm not going to talk about this here. It's time to go." He stood, dropped coins on the table, and waited for her.

AJ forgot the people around her as she picked up her package with the journal in it, trying to remember the joy it had brought her just a few minutes ago. Her anger moved into a despondency that overwhelmed her. He'd asked her to trust him, but it seemed trust didn't work both ways.

She brushed past him and focused on her path to the door. He introduced her to more townspeople as they returned to their horses. AJ nodded in response but didn't pay attention to what they said. She focused on Finn's last statement at the inn.

He wasn't getting paid for the stones. If that was true, she couldn't understand why he would take such a risky and unbelievable journey. He was keeping something from her. His actions and words mixed like oil and water.

She watched Finn stuff the wrapped journal into the saddlebag. They had a long journey ahead of them, plenty of time for her to find a way to get him to open up. She wouldn't dwell on finding a way home until they reached England. For now, she would capture details of her journey, not that she would be able to share them, but that wasn't the point. Writing would be a distraction from the answers being kept from her. She would keep notes of her life here in the early nineteenth century and everything she learned of the stones. She might be lost from her world, but it was time to put her reporter skills to work.

A MAN in dark clothing pulled his cap down low over his forehead and watched AJ and Finn mount their horses. He perched on a weathered bench at the corner of a building, a mere hundred feet from the stables. Like an old woman mending a quilt, he labored over a torn fishing net, yards of fabric gathered around him. He barely moved as his fingers worked effortlessly, completing one knot before moving to the next.

No one paid him any mind, and he never left his seat the entire time Finn and AJ were in town. He spared them a short glance as they headed out of town, their horses moving at a slow trot. Once they were out of sight, the man stood up, his long, lean body uncoiling as he stepped over the discarded netting. He made one stop at the general store before strolling to the stables to retrieve his horse, riding out of town the opposite direction from AJ.

ONCE HOME, Finn gave AJ a list of chores to help them prepare for their journey. Their silent ride home calmed their tempers, and with the focus on preparing the *Daphne Marie* for the sail to England, their discussions turned more congenial.

Finn spent most of his time at the ship, while AJ prepared staples for travel. She baked bread and dragged supplies to the ship in a cart. They collapsed at the dinner table after the second day of preparations.

AJ dipped a piece of bread in a bowl of soup. "I've been thinking. If you remember, I don't know how to sail."

Finn grinned. "You don't remember your lesson?"

AJ ignored the grin. "I remember almost drowning, not so much the lesson."

"You seemed to be picking up the finer points before the mishap."

"Well, I guess the mishap, as you call it, seemed to have erased the basics." She poked a slice of cheese into her mouth and refilled his soup bowl. "You can't possibly sail the ship on your own, and I won't be of any help. I can't pull those sails up."

Finn regarded her. "No. You probably could when you first arrived. You were strong from rock climbing." He gave her a long perusal before reaching out to feel her upper arms. "Now you wouldn't be able to hoist any sail."

AJ pouted. "I'm sorry I've gotten flabby while lying about."

Finn laughed. "You well know what I mean."

AJ wasn't mollified, but she couldn't blame Finn. She wasn't as toned as she used to be. There had been plenty of opportunity to stay in shape with something as simple as helping in the stables, but she had been too busy feeling sorry for herself. All wasted weeks now, and she couldn't wish back the time.

Finn finished his second bowl, wiping the remains with his last piece of bread. "You might not be able to hoist the sail, but there's plenty of other things you can do. And I'll teach you more about sailing. You don't have to spend all your time in the cabin."

AJ perked up. "And the charts. You can show me how you map out your course."

"Aye, I could do that."

"How long will it take to get to England?"

"A couple of days, I imagine, depending on the weather."

"And you'll be able to work all the…" AJ paused, not sure what to call everything. "The sails and ropes."

"The rigging," Finn said. "No. Not for this trip. I've hired some local boys to travel with us."

"Oh." AJ thought about it, unsure if she was ready to be in such tight quarters with strangers.

Finn stretched out his legs and cradled a cup of tea. "It's time to put your training to use. You know your way around well enough. There's no reason why you would know anything about sailing a ship. The boys won't think anything about you learning." He paused and focused on the cup of tea. "They'll assume I'm trying to curry favor with you."

"Great." AJ couldn't think of anything else to say, and a light blush pinkened her cheeks. She would be tested in ways she could never imagine, yet her first sea adventure excited her. Seasickness worried her, but she'd survived her first sailing lesson with Finn without getting sick, even if she did almost drown. But the sea between the two countries could be rough.

That evening, AJ turned melancholy about their last night in Ireland. She'd wasted most of her time here, and the feeling she wouldn't be returning permeated through her. As she undressed for bed, dim light cast shadows around the room. She absorbed the sight as if it was the first time she had seen it. So much had happened in this room—yelling, crying, and Finn's sculpted body joined with hers. The entire process of her coming to grips with her arrival occurred in this room.

Now, weeks later, she finally saw what lay in front of her. She accepted where fate led her. Without it, she would never move toward the next step. Her future rested with this man. For now, he was all she had.

She watched him sitting in bed trying to read a chart by candlelight. It held his complete focus. Brown curls hung over one eye. His bare chest bore the chill of the room. She added wood to the fire, and when she turned back, she could see the firelight play against his skin. She remembered the salty-sweet taste of him on her lips. Her body warmed and the feeling wasn't from the fire.

AJ let her dress fall to the ground. She pulled the laces of her undergarments, and they followed the same course. Each piece of clothing formed a puddle around her feet until she stood naked in front of the bed. Enough of a chill remained to harden her nipples as she waited.

It only took a minute before Finn sensed her presence. He glanced up, and his hands fell away from the chart. Her hair hung in thick wavy locks, framing her face and softening the edges. She pushed it back as she often did when she forgot to tie it. She caught the hitch in his breath. Her dresses fit more loosely than when she'd first arrived, and he had already thought her too skinny before the jump. Even though he joked about her being out of shape, she knew her muscles reflected a strong body.

AJ flushed the moment his eyes met hers. Her gaze lowered to the sheet wrapped around his waist. She smiled like a lynx that had caught her prey but was still playing with it. His lopsided grin appeared, and he shoved the chart away. He flew across the bed, catching her as she dropped into his arms, her hands running over his broad shoulders.

Their bodies merged together. Finn's hands caressed her face before he tangled his fingers in her hair, pulling her closer. His lips captured hers—molten, impatient and hungry.

They fell onto the bed, their hold on each other never breaking. AJ gasped as she felt Finn's fingers enter and explore. She arched reflexively, offering her hips to him. The intensity of their kisses deepened. She reached for him, guided him, increasing the frenzy, the urgency fueled by an unknown future.

They couldn't guess the course of their journey. The only thing they could control was this moment in time. And neither let go. Their movements were rhythmic as they became one with the tempo. They grabbed on as the tremors rocked them. And through the sweet release, and long after their bodies cooled, they held on, wrapped in each other's embrace.

Only one thought broke through AJ's sweet, satisfied languor.

How will I ever be able to leave him?

5

AJ stood at the railing and watched the cottage as it grew smaller. The green hills of Ireland swallowed the cozy inland landmark as they drew farther away. Would she see Ireland again and if she did, would it still be 1802? Or would she come back in her own time to see what had become of this quiet village with all the hardships yet to come? Someday she would discover if the cottage still stood or if it was nothing more than a stack of rocks. No one left behind who knew the stories of the people that made those rocks a home.

Wrapping her shawl around her to ward off the morning air, she turned away from Ireland and watched the activity on deck. Finn continued to shout commands to prepare and raise more sails as they moved out of the bay. His two new mates and the rest of the young crew appeared skilled to the task as they climbed the rigging and untied ropes.

Finn placed AJ in a spot where she could watch the activity without getting in the way. Her mounting questions went ignored as Finn focused on the ship. She marveled how each person knew his own task. As the boys climbed higher she didn't think they could hear Finn barking out a command. The wind picked up as the ship sensed the rising of the canvas and lurched, biting at the chance to be let loose.

She studied the two mates, trying to remember each step they took, each rope they pulled. Jamie, who was as tall as Finn but thin as a rail, didn't seem up to the task. But he surprised her with his speed and agility on the rigging as he climbed the ropes to unfurl the top sail, his fingers working deftly at the ties. The other boy, Fitzpatrick, was shorter and more compact. She could see him as a heavyweight contender or an alley bruiser, but his sweet demeanor destroyed those images. She doubted she'd ever learn his first name.

Both boys hardly seemed of age to be traveling with them, but she kept forgetting she was in a different time and place. Young boys turned to men at very early ages. The thought made her wonder at what age Finn had left home to make his way. He had chosen the life of a sailor, at least for a while, and she could see he knew his stuff. What she didn't understand was why he picked sea over land.

The *Daphne Marie* seemed to trust the man guiding her, the way Finn's horse understood and responded to its master. AJ didn't know anything about sailing, but it didn't take an expert to feel the ship yield to his commands. He gave her everything she wanted as each sail was unfurled, the canvas snapping to attention as the wind hit. The ship's speed increased, swiftly putting distance between them and their home.

Once the sails were set, AJ thought the tasks were completed. She was wrong. Each man or boy continued to work ropes, tying and retying as they worked each sail and spar. She assumed they were trimming the sails, and she silently urged them on as she felt the wind hit her face, the smell of the ocean invading her senses. The sound of the gulls transported her two hundred years and three thousand miles away, standing on the dock at the inn. The waves rolled beneath her feet. Tears blurred her vision until the wind dried them. She held her chin up, refusing to give in to the melancholy.

Moving toward the front of the ship, she stepped over rigging that had yet to be tied up or stored. The men worked around her as she leaned against the rail of the bow. The waves rose up to meet the hull, slapping against the *Daphne Marie*. What would they would find across the sea? Good weather and good fortune? AJ ignored the dull ache that rested deep inside her, an early warning beacon. She snuffed it out like a candle, diminishing its light. But she couldn't squash the embers that glowed their alarm.

An hour later, AJ stood at the railing and didn't hear Finn approach. He laid his hands on her shoulders before enclosing her in a strong embrace, his chin barely able to rest on top of her head. She grasped his hands as they closed around her, not realizing how chilled she had become until she felt the heat of his body.

"You're damp from the spray," Finn said. "You should go below and change into something dry. You'll catch your death of cold."

AJ's teeth chattered. "I didn't realize I was cold until now."

"It's mesmerizing, isn't it?"

"I can see the spell it casts over young boys, eager for adventure."

"Aye, it certainly caught me in its net." Finn squeezed her and turned her around. "Now let's get you below. The boys have it under control. You can watch me check the charts."

Finn guided her to the stairs. Once below, she removed her sodden shawl, pleased to see it had taken the brunt of the moisture. She wrapped a blanket around her to ward off the chill and wick away the moisture from her gown.

AJ watched Finn lean over the chart table, reviewing the map, and remembered the first time she had seen the charts. It was her first time on board the *Daphne Marie*, back in Baywood while it was docked at the Westcliffe Inn. Finn had given her and Mr. Jackson a tour. Her insides tingled at the thought of the second time she had seen the charts and navigational instruments. Finn had guided her hands over the sextant as he explained how it worked. She blushed at the memory of where that lesson had ultimately led. Now she watched his hands as he moved rulers around, and her blush deepened.

He studied the chart before glancing to the compass, then back to the chart.

"Come over and see where we're headed." He stood back to review his markings, searching for any mistakes he might have made.

"Do you have time to be doing this?"

"Aye. Now that we're underway, the boys know how to keep the girl trimmed. This isn't their first sail."

"You all worked well together."

"I was pleased to see they were in town when we arrived. I've used them before on a couple of excursions, so it was an easy choice to put them to work. They are the money makers for their families and prefer sailing to farming. They want to find a good fishing vessel and try to make a go of it themselves."

"Will that ever happen?"

Finn shrugged. "It's possible, but it will be hard work to put enough aside to buy a boat. But it's been done before. Until then, they make decent wages on a ship, especially if it's running cargo."

AJ's eyebrows drew together as she studied the chart and tried to make sense of all the lines and curves flowing across the page. Finn pointed to where the village and cottage sat on the map, a south-easterly point on the larger mass of the Emerald Isle. Then he pointed to where they were headed, east and a bit south from their location in Ireland. The destination appeared to be just south of Wales, but she couldn't tell by the markings on the map. She thought back to her history but couldn't remember the political climate between Wales and England in this century. If they stayed south of it, it probably didn't matter.

"I may change our course, it depends if the weather holds. I'd rather stay south so we'll be closer to Beckworth's manor."

"When will you know?"

"Tonight or first light tomorrow. We'll keep an eye on the clouds and the character of the sea." Finn picked up the sextant and headed for the stairs. "Let's go, and I'll show you the sextant to shoot the noon sun. Assuming you remember your first lesson." Finn's last words held a double meaning, and when he looked back at her, his eyes warming, she wondered which first lesson he meant.

"I remember," AJ said. She raced past him and up the stairs before he got any ideas. There were young men on board after all. She heard his soft laughter behind her as she stumbled onto the deck, thankful for the fresh sea air to clear their heads.

AJ grabbed the railing, taking a moment to gain her bearing. The coast was barely visible behind them. They had traveled farther than she would have guessed in such a short period of time. She leaned back to stare up at the tautly stretched sails catching every bit of wind. She peered over the railing and confirmed the sensation from the deck beneath her feet. The hull glided through the water, easily parting the ocean for their passage.

Finn spoke with Fitzpatrick, who nodded to some unheard command. Jamie was nowhere in sight. She scanned the deck, but he wasn't among the others. Perhaps he was below decks. Then she spied Finn, head back as he peered up, and she followed his gaze. There he was. She hadn't seen him when she first glanced at the sails. Jamie hung from the topmost sail, one leg partially woven into the rigging to hold him as his hands worked at a rope. She had no idea what he was doing up there. What an amazing view he must have.

She would dare the climb herself if she wasn't in skirts. Then, before she knew it, Jamie was halfway down the ropes, stopping to check another sail. Then he was back on deck, a smile stretched across his face as he nodded at her before scrambling to the stern for his next task.

AJ gazed up at the crow's nest when Finn leaned against the railing.

He looked up. "You want to go up, don't you?" His tone was quiet, although no one else could have heard him with the wind.

"It must be a fantastic view."

"Aye, but it's no place for a lady."

She glared at him before turning to watch the sea.

"At least not here, in this place," Finn said.

"I know. A girl can dream. At this point, I'd just wish for a decent pair of pants instead of these skirts."

Finn turned and took a step away. He lifted the sextant to the horizon and moved the arm until he found the right spot. He took note of the numbers from the instrument and handed her the tool.

She grabbed the sextant and used two hands to manage the weight. She traced the markings with her fingers and tried to recall Finn's lesson. Only a couple of months had passed since he explained the workings of the instrument, but with all that had happened, it felt as though she had lived the two hundred years that separated her from her home and that lesson.

Holding up the sextant, she peered through the eyepiece and lined up the bottom of the sun with the horizon. Confident of her assessment, she checked the markings and read the number out loud for Finn.

"Excellent. Very close to my own reading." Finn retrieved the sextant.

Her chin raised and a smile hovered on her lips, somewhat pleased with herself. She folded her arms and waited.

"I suppose you want to know what we do with this number."

"If you have to ask, then you really haven't learned anything about me."

Finn smirked and whispered into her ear, "I know enough

about you to make you cry out at night. And I know enough that if I don't keep you in those skirts, you'll be hanging off the rigging like some monkey. I think you'd agree I've learned quite a lot about you."

She blushed to her roots and swung around to make sure the boys hadn't heard. Heat raced through her, and she knew him well enough that it was no longer safe to go downstairs with him. Pulling herself up straighter, she turned toward the deck. "I think I've lost interest. We're both in need of fresh air."

FINN WATCHED her walk away and smiled. She was starting to get it—the innocent wordplay, talking her way out of a situation, everything she would need when she faced high society. Although he would have preferred it if she ignored the current threat and agreed to return to the cabin with him.

The truth was, he wanted to see her in pants, climbing the rigging with him by her side. But as he watched her walk to the bow, he pushed his selfish thoughts aside and considered his mission. And his promise to keep her safe. He glanced out to sea. These waters might appear mild, but the two of them headed toward a hornet's nest. With each mile they sailed, he second-guessed himself. The stakes were high, but now seemed doubly so. An invisible band pulled across his chest, at times constricting to the point he could barely breathe. And he felt it tighten the closer they got to England.

The thought cooled his growing passion, and he marched toward the stairs to finish plotting their course. He glanced at the sky before ducking below and noticed the soft wisps of clouds. He would plot a second course, just in case.

He made one last turn to the deck and called out, "Fitzpatrick. Come below."

THE WALK on the deck didn't take AJ long, and when she turned, Finn was gone. Probably returned to his charts. The sun blazed, warming her face. She preferred to stay and enjoy the weather, the sun so rare the last few weeks, but tanned skin would make it more difficult to fit in among the ladies. Lingering at the rail, she missed her long walks at the cottage, and they'd only been gone a few short hours. The closeness of the ship overtook her, and claustrophobia clutched her throat.

So far, she'd only seen the deck, the galley, and their cabin. Now seemed as good a time as any to explore. She found a hatch toward the stern and peered down. A ladder trailed into darkness, the sunlight too bright for her to catch any details. She glanced around and shrugged. Finn hadn't said any part of the ship was off-limits, and she had to find something to fill her time for the next two days. Perhaps she'd find an activity below she could help with.

She turned and lifted her skirts, carefully stepping down to the first rung. Holding tight, she kept her skirts up with one hand as she descended each rung. She stopped every other rung to see where she might be going but couldn't make out any details until she was halfway down.

Looking down into the shadow-filled room, she almost climbed back up, not wanting to intrude. Hammocks swung in time with the slight movement of the ship. Duffel bags and a handful of cots filled the rest of the space. This was where the boys slept and spent their free time. She finished her descent and waited for her vision to become accustomed to the darkness. Bags and boxes of supplies lined the walls, leaving the center of the room to the boys. Nothing to see here.

She moved through the door and looked both ways. Turning toward the stern, she found an expansive cargo hold. Another hatch shed light in the mostly bare room, where a few boxes took up less than a quarter of the space. She turned around and walked the narrow corridor toward the bow.

A few steps past the boys' room the corridor opened up to something she didn't expect. Her mouth hung open as she took in the sight of guns. Cannons, she remembered Mr. Jackson calling them. There were four on each side of the ship, locked in place and pointing toward the hull, each perfectly placed in front of the closed gunports. She backed up a step and heard Finn's words echo in his response to Mr. Jackson's question about guns. Finn had said there weren't any. The ship had been stripped for speed. He'd lied. She would have noticed cannons being loaded onto the ship at the cottage.

She crept closer and knelt down where the cannons were tightly tied. Dust settled around the floor and ropes. These had been here for a while. She lifted her head and sniffed. A light scent drifted toward her. Gunpowder? She moved to the front of a cannon and felt around the opening. Nothing. She surveyed the room and moved to the storage barrels against the wall. She found one she could open and turned her head quickly away when the smell of gunpowder assailed her.

Turning to a long box, she pried open the lid and stared down at cannonballs. She stepped back, caught a rope, and landed squarely on her butt. She stared at the barrel and the box and then at the cannons. The reality of where she was slammed into her, and the first slip of doubt crawled through her. Questions flashed. Was he keeping these a secret? She slowed her breathing and thought about it. He had lied to Mr. Jackson, but that she understood. These guns weren't replicas, and they would have raised questions if Mr. Jackson had seen them.

She stood up and brushed off her backside before closing the lids on the barrel and box. Finn had no reason to tell her about the cannons. He'd told her over and over these were dangerous times. She had nodded and given it no further thought. Were these here for protection on the seas or for other reasons she didn't want to know? She heard voices coming from above spurring her onward, back toward the boys' room and away from the guns.

AJ threw herself on the bed in Finn's cabin and stared at the ceiling. She wanted to ask Finn about the cannons but, after further reflection, decided against it. If the situation seemed right, she would ask. Otherwise, she had no reason to suspect anything out of the norm. With England constantly at war, a smaller ship like this was easy prey for the French. She hoped they would get to England without having to use them.

The topic was fair game for her journal. She sat at the desk and carefully opened the pot of ink and picked up the quill. She'd found the quill difficult to use, but had improved quickly by writing every day. She wrote for a half hour before she sat back, rubbing her fingers and wishing for her computer.

The writing turned laborious, and it was difficult to keep up with her thoughts. She rubbed her neck and put her journal away, selecting a book from Finn's diverse collection. Sitting on the bed, pillows stuffed behind her and the lamp positioned for better reading, she made it through two chapters of a sailor's life at sea before falling asleep.

She woke with a stiff neck and cringed when she bent to pick the book up off the floor. A strong desire to feel the sun on her face propelled her to the stairs. The hell with being a fair-skinned lady. If she was a barbarian from America, she might as well prepare for the part.

The darkness startled her when she arrived topside. The day had disappeared while she napped. It hadn't seemed that long. Then she noticed it wasn't simply the evening making an entrance. Charcoal clouds formed across the horizon, blocking the setting sun. There hadn't been a hint of them earlier. She searched for Finn and the boys and found them working the sails, pulling the spars to catch the changing winds. The ship road easily on the calm sea.

Finn met her gaze. He barked out commands that she couldn't hear, but Fitz nodded and scurried away. Finn strode to her, the wind tousling his curls more than usual.

"I'm afraid the storm is going to overtake us."

She nodded. He didn't sound panicked. Just giving her the facts in the change of weather.

"How bad?"

Finn shrugged. "You can never be sure, but it won't be an easy night."

"There's no way to go around it?"

"No. It would catch us no matter which direction we went. Even if we turned for home."

AJ nodded and looked at the clouds. "When will it be here?"

"We have a couple of hours, and we should eat before it gets here. The boys and I will be up all night until the storm passes." He stared at her, his emerald eyes like shards of glass. "And I need to know that you're below, staying put."

She craved something to do, to be helpful, but she would be in the way. "I'll put some food together for you and the boys. I was just hoping to stay up long enough to get some air."

Finn studied her, seeming to make a decision. "Maybe after dinner. I think you should stick with something light. Bread and cheese, no more. It's going to get rough."

"Okay." She returned below and inventoried the well-stocked pantry. Deciding on something warm for their bellies, she pulled out the makings for a meaty stew. After lighting the cookstove, she sliced bread and cheese while the stew cooked. The table was set with pitchers of cider and water. Satisfied with her tasks, she climbed the stairs and yelled over the wind for Finn. The boys came down first.

The boys shoveled the food down, hardly breathing between bites. It was too soon to tell if they always ate like this or if they didn't want to leave Finn alone. The wind could be heard shoving its way past the sails, and there was a noticeable change of pitch in the ship.

They swallowed their food, washed down first with cider, then followed with water. After belching their delight with the food, they turned sheepish, apologized, and thanked her for the meal. She wasn't sure if it was merely an afterthought or a simple remembrance of what their mothers had taught them. They fled up the stairs only minutes after they had sat down. Moments later Finn raced down, his face grim.

She didn't need to ask if it was getting worse. She could see the answer in his eyes.

6

"We'll be in the thick of it soon." Finn grabbed his bowl of stew, and AJ watched wide-eyed, as he gulped faster than the boys.

He swallowed the last bite of bread as the ship lurched, catching them both off guard. Dishes and ale crashed to the floor. She had no time to grab for the table before hitting the floor, sliding with her arms raised overhead to protect herself from falling debris. Finn managed to hold on and drag her from the floor. From above, a head appeared at the top of the stairs.

"Sorry, Captain. The wind changed on us. Caught us before we could change course. We've got it now." The voice yelled to be heard over the wind, but AJ couldn't detect any panic. She couldn't tell which boy had shared the news, but she was grateful no one had fallen overboard.

Finn helped AJ collect the dishes and food that had tumbled to the floor.

"I've got to go." Finn gave her a once-over, making sure she hadn't hurt herself or knocked her head.

She waved him off. "I've got this, just go." She braced her legs for another rogue wave and attended to the dishes. When she turned, Finn watched her. "Go, I'll be all right." She stared at him, trying to determine if his worried brow were for her or the ship. The latter certainly bothered her the most. "Are we going to be okay?"

Finn stared at the floor, then slid her a glance. His grin put her at ease. "Aye, we'll be fine. There's a chamber pot in the cabin next to the bed. I would sleep close to it until the storm has passed." Then he winked at her before disappearing into the night.

His words registered as she finished cleaning the mess. Her temperature rose. "Chamber pot by the bed, indeed. Like I'm some wee lass who can't deal with a storm."

She secured everything in the galley and poked her head into the storage room twice. Satisfied nothing else could be done, she returned to the cabin. Writing became impossible with the random lurches. Grabbing a book from the shelf, she crawled into bed fully clothed—in case of an emergency. She wasn't sure what an emergency would look like in this situation but it made sense to be ready. Reading didn't prove to be any easier.

When the ship dipped and rolled with the sea, she tightened her grip on the bedcover. She slid the book under the pillow and extinguished the lamp. Her eyes squeezed shut as another dip took the ship down a wave. Her stomach lurched when it came up the other side. She pulled the pillow over her head, counted to ten, and did it over and over until she fell asleep.

A loud sound like wood splintering, followed by a crash, woke AJ. The cabin was pitch black. After blinking several times, her vision adjusted to the darkness. She gripped the bed before rolling off as the ship crashed into a wave and popped back up like a cork released from a bottle. The ship lurched in the opposite direction, and she grabbed the headboard. She hung on as the ship dropped again, plunging into the ocean. Seconds seemed like minutes as she waited for the ship to rise again, even though she dreaded the roller-coaster motion.

After a few more dips and rolls, she searched frantically for the chamber pot, deciding it wouldn't hurt to heed Finn's warning. Unable to see it, she pushed the bed covers aside. Her first furtive step collapsed under her, and she found herself face-first on the floor. Her head smacked the floor boards. "Ow." The word rushing out of her. Reaching to push herself up, her hand hit the cold metal of the chamber pot. She pulled herself over and leaned into it, depositing what little she'd had for dinner. Damn him for always being right.

She barely got her legs under her when the ship slammed down again, shooting up more quickly than before. A strange sensation went through her as she felt her feet leave the floor and her stomach burst toward her throat. When she slammed back down to the ground, she hung herself over the chamber pot once again. That had to be the last of her meal. She crawled back into bed and pulled herself into a fetal position, somehow feeling safer. Then she remembered the crashing sound that had woken her and the sound of splintering wood. Fear in addition to the seasickness took hold.

She used the chamber pot two more times until bile was all that was left. By then, she didn't want to be away from the coolness of the metal that provided comfort as sweat broke over her body. She needed fresh air. The stale air of the cabin became stifling with the smell of her own vomit. Either the storm was decreasing, or she was getting used to the violent pitching. She crawled across the floor, careful to feel for sharp or broken clutter. She searched the darkness, but there wasn't enough light. The porthole, no bigger than a hubcap, offered no assistance. She didn't think it would be long before morning, but it didn't help now.

She pulled herself up by the door handle and opened it just as the ship rolled. The motion pushed her from the room into the short passage, and she stumbled into the galley. She dropped to the ground before she could be slammed down—taking a protective posture. Going topside seemed foolish, but the desire for fresh air consumed her. The galley's coolness provided some relief, but she could still catch a whiff of her regurgitated dinner. She felt the wetness on her gown and groaned. She would need to change her clothing.

Staying on her hands and knees, she crept from stair to stair, trying to time each step with the motion of the boat. She retched again, but nothing more came up. When she reached the door leading to the deck, she braced herself against the wall and pushed the door. It wouldn't open. Had Finn locked her in? Frantic, she heaved with all her might. The ship took another dive, and the door gave way, tumbling her onto the deck. A huge wave crashed over her, dousing her as if someone had turned a tub full of ice water over her. She sputtered, spitting out the salty brine, as she lost hold of the door, sending her sliding across the deck. Her lungs fought to take in air and expel the water that choked her. Coughing, she turned around to get her bearings. She'd begun her crawl back to the hatch when strong arms lifted her up, half dragging her back to the door.

The night air filled her lungs before someone pushed her through the door. She heard Finn's rough voice bark, "Stay put," just before the door slammed shut. The darkness enveloped her, and she took two more deep breathes before crawling back to the cabin. Every few feet, she stopped to steel herself for the drop and prepare her stomach for the next jolt. Water dripped from her hair, and her gown stuck to her. She didn't care. Just the few minutes of cool, clean, albeit wet, air helped.

She removed her dress and searched the room for their clothes. The first thing she found was one of Finn's shirts, and she pulled it on. The shirt was warm, dry, and held his scent. With a second shirt wrapped around her drenched hair, she climbed into bed and pulled the covers over her. Wrapped in his shirts, she rolled to her side, pulled her knees to her chest, and closed her eyes. The exertion of the vomiting and clawing her way topside and back had sapped all her strength, and she released her body to the deep rhythms of the rolling ship.

AJ OPENED her eyes and lay still, waiting for the next wave to hit. She focused on the beam above her, following each distinct grain that traveled the length of the wood. They had made it through the night. The gentle creaking of the hull seemed deafening after the raucous noise from the storm. Hours of torment had been her only world for several long hours.

The gentle motion of the ship told her it was slicing its way through the open sea. She inched her way out of bed. Her body tensed for an unexpected jolt of movement, and she strained to hear anything from the deck. She peeked out the porthole and saw nothing but blue, the sky and sea melding together. She turned her attention to the room and noticed the books that lay strewn across the floor. A broken cup rolled back and forth, its pieces hidden beneath the debris.

Unable to get anything from her trunk, tied down tight for the voyage, she turned back to the pile of clothing sprawled on the floor. She moved books out of the way and squatted, searching for her one clean dress among Finn's belongings.

She blew out a heavy sigh at the brown dress as a sound from behind made her turn. Relief flooded her when she discovered Finn leaning against the doorjamb. When she caught sight of the leer on his face, she wrapped her arms around her, feeling her nakedness under his half-opened shirt. Then she noticed the dried blood on his forehead, the heavy lids, and his weak smile— not a leer after all. He wasn't leaning against the door so much as it was keeping him upright.

She raced to him, forgetting her attire. He continued to smile as he partially collapsed into her, forcing her to struggle to keep him upright as she guided him to the bed. His clothing was soaked through. She wasn't sure whether to be worried more by his chilled skin or by the blood on his head.

"You're hurt." She peeled away his shirt and used the blanket from the bed to dry his chest and back, rubbing hard to increase his circulation.

"Aye. It's just a wee lump." His eyes closed, and he sagged, trying to lie down, but she pulled him forward.

"Just let me check your head, then you can rest." Pushing away his hair, she used his wet shirt to wipe the blood from his face. She brushed his hand away when he winced. The cut wasn't deep, but a lump had already formed.

"There's a lot of blood, but nothing that needs suturing. Which is a good thing since I can't sew." A wave of relief filled her when she felt Finn's weak attempt at a chuckle, then a grunt. She ran a finger over the bump and saw him wince again as he tried to move her arm away. A concussion was a possibility, but there was no way to keep him awake. Not after the long night he'd had.

Once she confirmed there were no other injuries, she let him fall back onto the bed. She struggled with his wet pants. His deep breaths turned to light snoring as she pushed and prodded to remove his clothes, drying him and then finishing by tugging him to the center of the bed. After pulling the blankets over him, she watched him sleep.

The lump bothered her, but there was nothing to be done. A memory of a deafening boom and splintering wood seemed more of a dream than reality. She brushed her hand over his face, moving his hair back, telling herself she only wanted one more look at his lump. He had to be exhausted from battling the storm.

She shook herself. The boys were her first priority. Her clean dress caught her attention, but she turned her back on it. She brushed at Finn's shirt, assuring the buttons were in place, and slid on her petticoats. The shirt looked odd over the undergarments, but it fell to mid-thigh and, proper or not, it would have to suffice.

The door opened slowly. AJ stepped to the end of the passage way, peered into the galley and spotted Jamie sitting at the table. He chewed, holding dry beef in one hand and a biscuit in the other. He smiled at her before swallowing hard.

"Looks like you survived the night." Jamie bit into the biscuit. "That was a wild one. Fitz and the others have eaten, but we could use some tea." He took another bite and seemed to remember some of his manners. With a mouth full of biscuit, he added, "If it isn't a bother."

She searched for a dish and mug to prepare her own meal. "It's no bother. You must be exhausted."

"Nah, I just woke up a bit ago. Finn made me get some sleep once the storm let up. We've reduced canvas, so we don't need everyone to keep us moving. I'll trade with Fitz when I'm done eating."

"I know this is a strange request, but do you have an extra pair of pants that might fit me?" AJ set the kettle in the stone hearth. She tried not to blush when he took stock of her appearance.

He shrugged. "You're about my size. I think I have a clean pair." He was up the stairs before she could stop him. He returned within minutes and tossed the pants to her. "They should fit well enough."

"You don't mind?"

Jamie took the offered mug of tea and drank it in one long gulp. He wiped his mouth on his sleeve. "Nah, my sister was always stealing my pants. She preferred them when she went riding. Hated dealing with all the skirts and petticoats, she said. But she was a wild thing. Ma never thought they'd get her married off."

AJ laughed and held the pants up to her. They were close enough.

"Aye, they'll fit fine." Jamie seemed pleased he could help.

"Take a cup of tea up to Fitz. Then make sure he gets to his bunk. Make sure all the boys come down for tea and more food. I'll be up as soon as I finish my own meal."

"Aye, ma'am. I'll tell them." Jamie grabbed the mug and scurried up the stairs.

She waited a few moments to see if anyone was coming back down, and when no one appeared, she kicked off her shoes and pulled on the pants. The length was a decent fit, and a rope cinched at the waist kept them from falling down. She felt better than she had in a very long time. She missed her jeans.

With dried meat, bread, and cheese left out for the boys, she tiptoed back to the cabin to check on Finn. His chest moved up and down in a slow rhythm—he was still alive. She smirked. He was going to have one killer of a headache when he woke. She gathered their wet clothes before leaving the cabin.

The bright glare of morning sun blinded her when she opened the door. God, she missed her sunglasses. She set down the clothes and scanned the deck, giving her eyes a moment to adjust. The sea was quiet and calm, as if last night had never happened. Glancing up, she saw only half the sails unfurled and a broken spar that hung listlessly from the mast. The sail had been furled and the entire piece tied to prevent any further damage, but it reduced the amount of available canvas. That would slow them down, but fortunately, the spar appeared to be the worst of it.

Jamie and Fitz chatted alongside the railing. She picked her way around debris that had not yet been removed from the deck. When the boys saw her, they forced smiles on their exhausted faces. Even Jamie, who had gotten an hour of rest, could easily use more.

"Did you get your tea?"

Both boys nodded.

"Aye," Jamie said. "We just want to get this last rigging repaired."

"Does it require both of you?"

"Nah, it won't take long."

"Then you don't need Fitz." She sounded like her mother.

The boys glanced at each other. They seemed to be deciding whether they should be taking orders from her. She glared at them, and that seemed to help their decision.

Jamie took the rigging from Fitz as they both mumbled, "Aye."

"Neither of you will be any good if you don't get rest." She refused to leave until Fitz shuffled off to his bunk in the forward hold. Once he'd disappeared from view, she surveyed the deck. "Now, is there a tub of some kind I can use to wash clothes?"

AJ and Jamie worked hard for the next two hours. She washed clothes while Jamie created a makeshift clothesline. Afterward, they removed debris from the deck, either tossing pieces overboard or stacking into a corner for Finn to determine their fate.

As they worked, Jamie kept an eye on the sails, occasionally shouting an order or modifying the rigging himself. He watched the sky as if he could read the wind before it arrived. He showed her how to tie the rigging when he adjusted a sail and laughed each time she got it wrong, the knot falling away in her hands.

When her knot held, he nodded enthusiastically. "Aye, that's the way of it. You've got it now." But at the next rigging, he laughed harder as the knot failed.

Eventually, he let her perform the entire task of undoing the rigging, throwing her entire weight into pulling the ropes with Jamie close behind her, helping her pull the sail tight. She tied the last knot and stood back, quite pleased with herself. They were breathing hard from their efforts and didn't hear the footsteps behind them.

They both jumped when Finn barked, "What's going on here?"

Jamie kept his head down. "Just trimming the sails, sir."

AJ scanned Finn's face to see if there was any new bleeding. He leaned against the railing, squinting from either the sun or a headache, but it didn't seem to lessen the ire he held in check. Then his face softened when his eyes raked over her.

She stood straighter, pulled her shirt down, and glared at him.

Finn blew out a breath and rubbed his head. "Aye, good job Jamie." He studied the deck, first glancing at the debris piled in a corner, the clothes drying in the sun, and then up at the broken spar, still tied in place. "I guess you didn't have time to fix the spar yet."

Jamie winked at AJ. "Nah, I thought I'd wait for Fitz before sending Miss Moore up the mast."

AJ tensed, unsure if Finn was in the mood for banter.

He slapped Jamie on the shoulder. "How about we wait until we reach port before worrying about the spar? I have other duties for Miss Moore."

Jamie blushed and refused to look at her, and AJ felt her cheeks flush. How had the talk turned against her?

"Now, why don't you get some rest before you drop," Finn said.

As Jamie turned away, AJ called out, "Thank you, Jamie. For all your help this morning." His smile lit up his blue eyes, and, nodding, he ran for the hold.

She turned to Finn. It wasn't difficult to see the weariness hang from him. He seemed to use the railing as a crutch. "You need more rest."

"I'm fine, at least until Fitz gets back." He scanned the deck, the sails, and then out to sea. He also seemed able to read the sky. "I guess I shouldn't have worried. You seem to have everything in order."

She shrugged. "I needed to do something. And I've had enough of the cabin."

Finn reassessed her wardrobe choice. "I believe that's my shirt. And I think I remember you wearing it last night, or was it this morning?" His voice turned into a husky whisper. "But I don't remember the pants."

AJ stepped back. "Jamie loaned me the pants."

Finn stepped closer until she had no place to go. "I needed

something to wear until my dress dried, and I didn't think my new London gowns would be appropriate." She didn't like the grin that spread across his face. Perhaps he wasn't as tired as she thought. She attempted to duck under the arm that braced the railing.

He blocked her, grabbed her waist, and drew her to him before she could put up a fight. In an instant, lips brushed hers. The warmth spread through her as his kiss deepened. His arms wrapped around her, and she leaned into him. She sighed with pleasure, and when he pulled away, she could see his unleashed passion as he stared down at her.

"I'm truly a lucky man to have such a hardworking crew."

"That you are. I hope the pay is worth it."

"You can renegotiate your wages this evening."

She snorted. "In your dreams." She pulled away from him and bolted for the clothesline before Finn could pull her back. "Did you eat anything?" AJ pulled clothing off the line, and glancing back, saw him shake his head. She sighed. "Men. Give me a minute, and I'll bring something up." She waved a hand at him. "Don't bother arguing. You'd all starve given the choice."

FINN SMILED AND THEN GRIMACED. The pounding in his head wouldn't go away, and the light hurt his eyes. He checked the rigging Jamie and AJ had worked and nodded before moving to the next brace. He moved slowly, each step increasing the strike of the hammer slamming into his head. He had moved only a few feet down the port side when AJ returned. She had a bowl in one hand and a cup in the other. He was disappointed when he saw the jerky and biscuit in the bowl.

"I'll make something hot and filling for supper. This should be enough to keep you going. The tea is more important."

Finn flinched when he took a sip, almost spitting it out. "What the devil?"

"It's an herb tea from some items I found in the stores. It should help the pounding in your head."

He thought of tossing it, but it seemed pointless. "How did you know my head was pounding?"

Her smile turned devious. "I've seen enough of Stella's worst hangovers to know what a pounding head looks like."

He stared at her.

"It's all in the eyes. They squint each time you move. And you're moving slowly, like each step is painful. Of course, the big lump is somewhat obvious."

He drank the tea, refusing to grimace. The jerky and biscuit disappeared quickly, and both dishes were handed back to AJ.

"You have two hours to do what you need to do, and then back to bed." Her hand went up again when she saw him start to protest. "No. You need rest. At least an hour or two, and then you can come back up. I'm not going to argue the point. It's done." She turned and disappeared below.

Finn shook his head, which brought on tears. She was right. It had been a long time since anyone had bossed him around. Even at the cottage when she was in the worst of moods, she never ordered him about. He smiled. She was worried about him.

7

The *Daphne Marie* made port the second day after the storm. AJ stood at the bow, leaning into the railing, her head swiveling to take it all in. This was her first trip to England, and she would never have thought to see it from this perspective. Finn told her they would dock just short of Bristol, the main port on the River Avon. For being half the size of Bristol, Portishead teemed with people, horses and carts. Piles of cargo either waited for a ship to export it or for a barge to carry the larder farther up river.

The gray skies of late spring had returned, but the rain held off. The dull, muted colors cast the entire scene in front of her into a dreary landscape. The cacophony of sounds grated on her ears. She thought seeing more people would have pleased her, but she had grown accustomed to a slower pace.

Old buildings lined the waterfront, some solidly made of brick and others battered and worn, ready for the next storm to tear them down. The crowd of bodies, mostly sailors, she guessed, appeared as weatherbeaten as the buildings. Two inns sat on opposite ends of the dock with another pub or two in between, and even at midday, men wandered in and out of their doors.

At the north end, a stable signaled the edge of town. Her hand flew to her mouth as they approached the dock. The smell gagged her, and she breathed through her mouth to avoid the offensive smells. Decaying fish, human waste, and manure overtook the dock. She hoped they wouldn't be here long.

This port and what passed for civilization made her grateful for the last calm days on the ship. The sailing had been unremarkable after the storm. Good weather had blessed them, and the wind blew in their favor. After Finn and the boys recovered from their grueling night, AJ turned to her journal, documenting all that had happened since her arrival. The people, the cottage, and daily life were jotted down in her memoirs. She would never be able to share her tales except as someone else's life, but that wasn't the point. The journal and her journey grounded her, gave her roots, and made everything real. It reminded her of where she had come from and how far she had yet to travel.

"Are you ready?"

Immersed in her daydreaming, she hadn't noticed Finn approach. She took another look at the dock and the faces of people, now recognizable rather than distant figures, and shrank back against Finn. Filthy faces and torn and stained clothing foretold of unwashed bodies, and, she was sure, an aroma that added to the smell of the port.

"As much as I'll ever be. It doesn't look friendly." She stepped to the railing and lifted her head. She could do this.

"It is a bit unsavory so you'll do well to stick with me or one of the boys at all times." Finn covered her hand with his. "We won't be here long. Don't wonder off."

She nodded. "I'd just as soon get to the next phase of our journey." With one last look at the deck of the *Daphne Marie*, she squared her shoulders, ran her hands over her hair then her dress, and followed Finn down to the dock.

They'd ventured only a few steps when a portly man with ruddy cheeks and heavy jowls strode toward them. He seemed out of place with his well-tailored waistcoat and breeches, a black top hat, and equally black cane that he used more to push people out of the way than to support any physical ailment.

"Hensley," Finn called. When the rotund man drew near, they embraced each other in a bear hug, patting each other on the back.

"Finn Murphy. You're a sight for poor English eyes." The man's voice was deep with a richness that made you want to listen to him talk and tell you stories. He chuckled with delight at seeing Finn. "We heard about the storm from another ship that arrived earlier. I'm glad to see you made it."

"We hit a storm, and while it damaged the ship, it was kind enough to drive us to our destination. The wind was at our back the whole way."

"Giveth with one hand, taketh away with the other. Good to see you, old chap."

"And you as well. I see Mary has been taking good care of you."

Hensley laughed as he patted his girth. "More than I deserve." For the first time, he noticed AJ, and he gave her a partial bow. "And who do we have here?" His question was filled with mirth, and she couldn't help but smile in return.

"This is Abigail Moore, a distant relative from America."

"Hmm, is that so. America, is it?"

"Yes," AJ said. "I look forward to visiting your country, sir."

"None of that 'sir' stuff. It's Hensley, and Finn didn't tell me in his letters what a stunning beauty you are."

AJ couldn't stop the rising blush. Recalling her training with Finn, she ignored it. "Will you be traveling with us?"

The man laughed. "Oh no, I try not to do that any more than I have to. We just returned from London, for the Season you know." Hensley led them down the waterfront. "I'm simply here to make arrangements for your next stage of travel. And, of course, you'll stay with us while preparations are completed."

"We appreciate your hospitality, Hensley. I hope it's not too much of an inconvenience for Mary," Finn said.

"Oh no, she's quite excited for visitors. We don't get many this time of year. Most everyone is still in London." He turned to AJ. "You'll be catching the tail end of the Season, but there are still several parties left. The last hurrah and all." He made a motion with his hand, and a carriage appeared out of the crowd. The splendor of the carriage stood out from the other weatherbeaten coaches and was led by two giant gray steeds.

As the carriage pulled up, AJ noticed the white horse tied to the back, at least six inches taller than the one Finn rode in Ireland. The coach sat higher than she expected and required Finn to help her step up. She sank back into the seat, dismayed to find it somewhat uncomfortable. Hensley plopped his plump frame across from her, wiping his brow with a handkerchief. She gathered her skirts to make room for Finn, but the carriage door closed.

She leaned out the window. Finn mounted the steed and walked it to the carriage door. A wry grin appeared, just like a little boy with a new toy.

"Sorry, but I need to tend to a few things. Hensley will take good care of you until I catch up." He turned the horse and was gone.

Everything started moving too quickly. She hadn't given Fitz or Jamie a proper goodbye and felt sure she'd never see them again. She'd barely put a foot on land, and now she was being whisked away to who knew where.

"I'm so glad I saw you arrive. This is not a place for a young lady to be without escort. And Mary will just love you. We're quite lucky you arrived early and can spend an extra night with us. Even though we've just arrived from several months in London, Mary already misses the excitement of company. I have no doubt she's already planning invitations to the neighbors."

AJ watched the passing storefronts and the array of people going about their daily lives. A simple life—work, eat, sleep and start it all over the next day. No hobbies or entertainment except a night of drinking and perhaps a visit to a brothel. So depressing. She turned to Hensley after the town disappeared, nodding and smiling as he talked. He shared insights to the town and his perceptions of the differences between England and what little he knew of America.

"I hear you're from a small town near Boston. Daresay London will be quite a change from what you're used to." He shook his head and gave a little chuckle. "Not that it matters. Mary will be able to tell you everything you need to know to make a successful tour of London. It's a shame Finn wasn't able to give us more notice you were going that far. My Mary makes an excellent chaperone. It's all in the introductions, you know."

The rocking of the carriage reminded her of the first few hours of the storm, and her stomach reeled. She moved closer to the window and focused on the countryside. The carriage rolled through the landscape of low, green hills and lumbering trees. The swaying of the coach took over until there was nothing but the sound of Hensley and the churning of the carriage wheels.

He talked nonstop, leaving no room for her to participate in the conversation other than to continue smiling and nodding. Mostly trivial information, the chatter provided AJ with an insight into facets of society she hadn't considered. By the end of their hour-long journey, she'd become curious about Mary. Hensley obviously thought the world of her. She came to another unexpected realization—she felt safe with him.

When the coach slowed to turn down a lane, she leaned out the window and caught a glimpse of an estate etched onto the landscape. It seemed old, but what did she know? Everything in England was old, so she had nothing to compare what was considered new or modern for this age. The estate sat in the middle of a flower-filled meadow surrounded by a scattering of trees. As they drew closer, she could see it wasn't one of the grander estates she'd seen in books, but it seemed a mansion compared to the cottage she'd left in Ireland.

An immense fountain, made of granite bricks, dominated the front court and provided a focal point for the neoclassical structure. Early summer flowers softened the gray exterior, and a fleeting sense of melancholy enveloped AJ as she thought of Stella's gardens at home. The feeling was short-lived as the carriage pulled in front of the estate and the massive door swung open. A woman, no more than five foot tall, burst forth as if she had been waiting days for the door to finally open. Two younger women rushed behind her as she barked orders about baggage and rooms and fires.

AJ tried to make sense of it all but discovered she had her own dilemma on how to exit the coach without falling flat on her face. One of those details Finn had failed to prepare her for. Fortunately, Hensley went first, and she watched how simple he made it for such a stout man. She grabbed hold of her skirts, disregarding thoughts of her jeans tucked away in her trunk, and breathed a sigh of relief when Hensley turned to assist.

She didn't have long to rearrange her skirts before the woman who had blustered out of the house grabbed her hands and stood back. The woman appraised her as if determining how much AJ had changed since the last time they'd met.

"Welcome, welcome, my dear. My, aren't you a pretty one. I hope my Hensley didn't bore you with long stories. I know the trip can be positively tedious. The ride is more enjoyable when heading to London, but one must make do." The woman couldn't have been more than five feet tall, thick around the middle with her light hair gently turning with age. But her cornflower-eyes were young and filled with merriment as she smiled at AJ and hugged her close. AJ stiffened before relaxing into the woman's embrace, unsure of what to say in return. Not that the woman had given her time to talk. This had to be Mary.

"I've been waiting so long for a visitor. I know we just returned from London a fortnight ago, but it's so quiet compared to London. But Hensley enjoys the solitude, so what can I do? The neighbors visit, but not nearly as often as I would like. But now, with the season ending, I'll have to make the most of it. You'll have to tell me where you'll be staying in London."

"Mary, give the young woman some time. She just got off the ship not an hour ago. She must be exhausted from her journey." Turning to AJ, he said, "This is my wife, Mary." Then, turning back to his wife, he continued, "This is Abigail Moore, a distant relative of Finn's. Now let's get her to her room so she can rest before dinner. Then you can get all the gossip. Although between the two of us, I'm not sure when she'll find a moment to speak."

Both husband and wife had a good laugh over that. This perfectly matched couple eased AJ's obligation to fill the void, and she tried to temper her amusement as Mary ushered her into their home.

The entrance hall immersed her in the splendor of the early nineteenth century. She suppressed the antique hunter within her in order to simply enjoy the experience. Her expectations prepared her to be overwhelmed by the gaudiness of influential estates, but amazement filled her at Mary's tasteful decorating.

Rather than dark-paneled walls, colorful wallpaper reflected Mary's fashionable tastes and spoke of their wealth. The rooms were all tastefully filled with neoclassical furniture that matched the design of the building's structure. More modern pieces mixed with old. Her jaw dropped and her mouth watered when she caught sight of original Chippendales. She could spend days going through the rooms cataloging all the pieces and wished they could stay longer.

"It will be a couple more hours before dinner." Mary turned to a young woman. "This is Betsy, and she'll be your lady's maid while you're here. She'll take you to your rooms so you can rest."

Betsy curtsied and led AJ to the grand staircase.

They were halfway up the stairs when Mary called out, "Oh, and if you have time, the gardens are lovely this time of day. With our lovely weather, you might want to wander about. Our home is open to you."

Mary waved and disappeared through a door, leaving AJ to study the entry hall from a heightened advantage. What she'd give for her cell phone or camera. She'd never be able to remember all the details and inwardly thanked Finn for giving her the journal.

Betsy guided AJ into a spacious room on the second floor, which held a carved four-poster bed with linen curtains, a dressing table, a writing table, and a sitting area for two next to a fireplace where embers waited for an evening fire. The room was darker than the rooms on the lower floor, but light from two windows diminished the shadows. The window overlooked the front of the estate, and she peered down to see if Finn had arrived, but the courtyard was empty. Even the carriage had been driven away.

She wanted to accept Mary's hospitality to stroll through the house and gardens, but the excitement of making port and the swaying coach made her drowsy. The last three days on the ship had been an exhausting adventure, and she eyed the tempting bed. She shooed Betsy away with a request to return before dinner, realizing too late she should have asked for help out of her gown. The couch would suffice for a nap, but the bed was too inviting. The hell with the gown. She climbed onto the bed and arranged her dress to reduce wrinkling. A few minutes of rest was all she needed. And she was asleep as soon as her her head hit the pillow.

LOUD NOISES from the courtyard woke her. She felt groggy and couldn't find the energy to get up. The sound of muffled voices wafted up from somewhere down below, and then it grew quiet. When she woke again, the remnants of the afternoon sun told her she had slept longer than she'd planned. She stared up at the canopy. Finn must have arrived by now. The maid hadn't returned, so she had time before dinner.

AJ glanced in the dressing table mirror. Her gown looked presentable, and only a few hairpins needed replacement. She must have been so tired, she slept like a mummy. When she turned for the door, she almost tripped over her trunk. A footman must have brought it while she slept, and she hadn't heard a thing. There was only the one trunk. They would have put Finn's trunk in his own room. Things were changing now. They had entered polite society.

She peeked out her door and listened. Faint voices from downstairs led her to the dining room where footmen prepared the table for dinner. They nodded at her.

"Sorry to bother you but can you tell me the way to the gardens?" She needed fresh air to get rid of the remaining cobwebs.

"Certainly," the older man said. "Mr. Landry can escort you."

The older man returned to his duties, and the younger man nodded before leading her through the house to a long, narrow dayroom filled with plants and several couches and chairs. The afternoon sun washed the room with warm light. French doors opened to a veranda that led to gardens in the back of the estate.

Once alone, she strolled around the room, inspecting the diverse array of art on the walls: a portrait by Reynolds, a landscape by Gainsborough, and even a William Blake. The Hensleys knew their art. As she left through the garden doors, the immense landscape took her breath away, their own work of art developed from nature. Neatly trimmed hedges bordered the garden, and curved paths ran through dozens of flower beds bursting with color. The scent of roses and other flowers she couldn't name flooded her senses and she breathed deeply as she walked the graveled path. Within ten minutes, she realized her mistake of not grabbing a wrap. Chill from the late afternoon raised goose bumps and turned her back to the house.

Spying a different set of entrance doors, AJ decided to investigate. The doors led to a library the size of her room, elegantly appointed in rich browns and mahoganies. The smell of leather overwhelmed her. It was the same aroma she remembered from her father's study, and all she wanted to do was find a good book, nestle herself into an oversized chair, and spend the next few days reading and forgetting.

A bronze statue captured her attention until she heard voices coming from the next room. They were low and hushed, but she could tell they were men. Thinking it was the footmen again, she crept toward the next room then stopped. The voices came from Finn and Hensley, and by the tone, they were having a serious conversation.

Feeling guilty at eavesdropping she tiptoed closer. She hovered close to the wall, unable to see in but close enough to hear them.

"He's doubled the amount of men." The voice was Hensley's, but this was a different man—all business, no chatter. "There's no way into the manor except walking straight through the front door."

"Why the extra men?" Finn said.

There was a moment of silence. AJ leaned farther toward the door and bounced back when Hensley's voice boomed with frustration. "We don't know. There's been talk that the viscount is planning a trip. He may have chartered a ship out of Plymouth, but I haven't been able to confirm it."

Another silence, and she pictured Finn churning thoughts in his head. "We need to know one way or the other. You're thinking the extra men are for escort to the ship?"

"Best guess, yes."

The silence became deafening. They might have left, but she didn't think so.

Finn's voice broke the silence, and his words sent a chill through her. "Then we continue with the plan. Nothing and no one can be allowed to get in the way of completing this task. We take care of this now."

"Agreed. At all cost."

AJ heard the clinking of glass and movement. The men were leaving. She searched for a place to hide and backed into a corner, tucking next to a bookcase in case the men came that way. She held her breath until their steps receded. Pulling a book from the shelf, she fell into the nearest chair.

The men's words swam around in her mind as she tried to make sense of them. Her grip on the book tightened, and she wished she had either heard it all from the beginning or none of it at all. The words she heard had been out of context, but there was no other meaning. Hensley and Finn were running surveillance on the viscount—the very man Finn was traveling to meet. It had to be about the stones.

Finn told her his mission was to retrieve the larger stone for the viscount, nothing more. She couldn't see why Hensley would be involved or why they would move against this man at all cost, as Hensley had put it. Whatever it was, Finn had put her in the middle of it, and her instincts told her it involved more than just stones.

She felt disjointed and stared at the far wall as the afternoon's light faded. They had become so close over the last few weeks, survived a storm together, and now to discover Finn was keeping secrets made her question him all over again. She traced everything she remembered from the time she'd landed in Ireland. Nothing gave her any suspicion to another motive, except for his reticence to talk about the stones. What was he keeping from her?

"There you are." Finn's voice made her jump.

Her hold on the book tightened. She was ready to question him, but when she glanced up, her uneasiness grew. His grin forced crinkles at the corners of his eyes, and the warmth reflected in them made her question everything. Was this the real Finn or just the mask her wore for her?

"Are you all right? What are you doing here?" Finn gently pulled the book from her grasp and read the title. His eyebrows shot up. "*The Mechanics of Proper Livestock Management.* Are you thinking of raising sheep?"

She forced a smile. "Who knows how long I'll be here? I doubt I'll find a job at a newspaper."

He stared at her, and the seconds seemed to go on forever. "I think you need a warm meal and pleasant conversation. And with Hensley and Mary, we won't even have to utter a word."

She couldn't help but laugh and let Finn pull her up from the chair. But when he leaned in to give her a kiss, she pulled back. "Someone could be watching."

He flinched at her rejection and then nodded. "You're right, of course." Laying a hand on her elbow, he steered her out of the library. The perfect gentleman taking her to dinner.

Everything had changed so quickly from when they'd left the ship. The few inches that separated them suddenly seemed like a deep crevasse, and she didn't know if it would be possible to bridge the gap.

8

T hat same evening, AJ stood quietly and let Betsy change her from gown to night dress. Her lady's maid brushed her hair as she stared into the dressing table mirror still wearing the mask she reserved for family gatherings with her brother, Adam. It was hard to believe she missed his goading.

Dinner had been nonstop chatter from Hensley and Mary. The only thing required from her was polite interest and head nods. Finn appeared relaxed as he joined the discussions, but she noticed his tighter grip on the wineglass and the muscles flexing along his jaw. There was no indication if his mood stemmed from his plotting with Hensley or from the rift between them. His glances flashed to her at the beginning of the meal, but as the conversation wore on, his focus turned to his host, leaving her to Mary.

After the meal, AJ and Mary shuffled off to the drawing room while the men disappeared to the study. She chafed at having to comply with social etiquette with just the four of them. Mary prattled on about London. Through it all, the only thing AJ could think about was what else Finn was cooking up. The words she heard in Hensley's study wouldn't go away.

Now, sitting at her dressing table while Betsy brushed her hair, AJ ran her fingers over the bottles of lotions and perfumes Mary had put out for her guest. She opened a container and wrinkled her nose—roses—a wonderful, heady aroma on the stem, but too overpowering in a lotion. Distracted, she dabbed a bit on her hand before standing and thanking Betsy. The young girl nodded and added wood to the fire before leaving AJ alone.

Picking up a woven plaid blanket from the settee, she wrapped it around her as she sat to watch the fire. Finn had kept his distance from her as they said their good nights, simply nodding in her direction before returning to the study with Hensley. She could sneak down to eavesdrop but had no idea what her excuse would be if she were caught. Perhaps he would stop in to see her before going to his own room.

Once she had time to analyze the situation, she was sorry she'd widened the gulf between them. Finn's business was his own, but it still rankled. He had promised to help her get home and seemed to be planning it without her. But the real reason for the divide wormed its way through her gut. He might have ulterior motives that put her needs second, or else it was all a complete lie, and he had no intention of finding her a way home. All the trust they had built since her arrival was crumbling, and she had no idea how to patch it.

She pulled the blanket closer and rested her head on the sofa pillow, pulling her legs up under the blanket. She thought of Stella. The one person who could help guide her was two hundred years away. She stared at the flames and waited for an answer to appear.

THE EMBERS in the hearth glowed, shedding a suffused light through the room, providing just enough illumination for Finn to scan AJ's room. He expected her to be asleep, assumed she'd be in the bed. His stomach clenched when he saw the empty bed drawn down for the evening. Then he spied a form on the couch and breathed more easily.

Something had changed between them. At first, he thought she might be upset about being left with Hensley for the carriage ride to the estate. But she would have let that go. This was a deeper schism.

Her head rested on a sofa pillow with the blanket wrapped tightly about her. He considered moving her to the bed but decided to leave her by the warmth of the fire. He took a chair beside her and stared into the hypnotic flames. She'd been sitting in the library when he found her that afternoon, gripping a book she would never have found that interesting.

That side of the library connected with Hensley's study. She must have overheard them. Although that would explain the change in her, it didn't shed light on why she hadn't asked him about it. Whether she'd heard some of it, or all of it, wouldn't she ask? She was a reporter after all.

Turning back to her, Finn touched a soft brown curl that lay against her cheek. Her hair had grown quickly in the last couple of months. He ran his hand down the long tresses framing her face. He preferred her shorter hair, but couldn't decide if it was because it suited her, or because he missed the woman she was before the time travel. The jump had changed her. That was no surprise considering the disorientation he'd experienced during his first time jump. She hadn't quite found her footing yet.

He had no answer on how to make her life easier. He had prepared her the best he knew how. Standing abruptly, he tucked the edges of the blanket around her and crept from the room. The door shut soundlessly behind him.

AJ OPENED her eyes and tried to stretch but found her legs caught in a tangled blanket. She popped up and flinched from a stabbing pain in her neck. She had fallen asleep on the couch for the second night in a row. Betsy had drawn back the drapes, allowing the morning sun to burst into the room. Luminous sunshine dappled the room and warmed her more than the dying embers in the hearth, until she remembered the distance she had created with Finn.

Hensley had kept Finn busy the day before, and AJ and Finn only saw each other at meals. Mary took her full attention, starved for womanly companionship. In truth, she didn't mind. The woman made her laugh, and it took her mind off her worries.

They would be leaving today, and while she enjoyed the company of Hensley and Mary, she itched to feel more momentum. Her stomach rolled as she paced the room, already fretting about meeting the viscount. It would have been easier if she didn't know Finn and Hensley were cooking something up. She didn't know whether they would be welcomed, or if the man suspected Finn's hatred for him. But she had to know more about the stones, and her only choice was to follow where the stones led.

She mulled over her situation while trying to put her hair in order, and sighed with relief when Betsy returned with her travel gown.

"Oh, Betsy. The dress is perfect. You didn't have to put so much work into it."

Betsy took the hairbrush from her and quickly fixed AJ's hair. "It's no trouble. I've enjoyed helping with what little you've allowed me to do."

AJ smiled at her through the mirror but inwardly cringed. She needed to remember her station whether she agreed with it or not. "Well, you've certainly helped me feel welcome. I would have been lost without you."

The young girl blushed but seemed eager to banter as they finished the morning ritual.

By the time AJ entered the dining room, her spirits had lifted and she smiled pleasantly, catching the men in a discussion about horses. "Good morning."

She ignored Finn's questioning gaze, understanding his confusion all too well. The mercurial change in her mood almost made her feel sorry for him. She wasn't sure about his ulterior motives, but she refused to mope about it. There would be time on the next leg of their journey to ask him about his meeting with Hensley, something she should have done two nights ago.

For now, she focused on the buffet server, polished to a high silvery sheen, and smelled the rolls still warm from the oven. Her stomach grumbled so loudly, she slid a glance to the men to see if they heard it. Her light-hearted discussion with Betsy had eased the butterflies.

"Good morning, young lady. How was your evening? I hope everything has been to your liking. We always want to make sure our guests are happy." Hensley seemed earnest in his desire to be the good host.

"It was fine." AJ waited patiently as the footman poured the coffee, hardly able to restrain herself from pouncing on it. She bent her head from side to side, working out the kinks from the night before. "I didn't realize how tired I was. I'm afraid I fell asleep on the couch again."

"And you still slept well?" Hensley asked.

"Better than I would have guessed."

Hensley barked out a laugh. "That's something Mary will be pleased to hear. Even our couches are comfortable enough to sleep on."

The men fell back into their conversation about horses. AJ partially listened, preferring to focus on the food. She hadn't eaten this well since her jump. Her cooking passed for edible, and Finn had been a good sport to put up with it. He seemed to be making up for it now, eating with passion, stopping only to comment on something Hensley said. The man really couldn't stop talking, even through all the food.

Each time Finn turned her way, she offered the slightest of smiles and felt the gulf between them lessen. But the overt politeness warned of a deeper discussion once they were alone in the carriage. And she was ready for it, desperate to unravel his secret scheming.

After breakfast, they had just stepped into the hallway when Mary bustled toward them. "There you are. Just finishing breakfast, I see. I probably should have come down, but we had a problem in the kitchen." Mary's cheeks flushed, and she took a deep breath. "There was some issue with this morning's delivery. The cook usually has it under control, but I felt I had to step in. This was the second time the delivery has been out of order. I just thought it my duty to put that man straight so it won't happen again. You can't let these tradespeople get the upper hand, or it becomes the matter of course."

Mary grabbed AJ's hands and gave her a once-over. "You look beautiful this morning, and your dress is stunning. I do hope Betsy was helpful."

AJ felt the blush rising at the compliment and squeezed Mary's hands. "She was wonderful. You really must thank her for taking such good care of me. She was a very wise decision."

Mary beamed at the compliment and prattled on as she walked them out the front door. AJ felt lighter, her smile widened, and a sense of relief flooded through her until she stepped outside.

Hensley and Finn stood at the back of the carriage, their heads bent close together. Hensley ran his hands over the sleek neck of the white steed tied to the coach and nodded as Finn spoke. They could be talking about horses, but the conversation appeared more serious. AJ mentally kicked herself. She would see conspiracy in everything now—damn her eavesdropping.

Instead of worrying, she turned her focus back to Mary's chattering. Before she knew it, she was hugging Mary and being helped into the carriage. Finn moved in behind her and fell into the bench across from her. She stuck her head out the window and waved to Mary, suddenly wishing she could stay longer. The butterflies in her stomach turned to rattlers as her apprehension grew over the next leg of their journey and meeting the viscount.

Returning to her seat, she squirmed to find a comfortable position, then laid her head back and closed her eyes. She sensed Finn watching her, but she wasn't ready to face that battle yet. Maybe Finn would broach the topic and confide in her so she wouldn't have to admit to overhearing their conversation. There was time before reaching the viscount's to put this behind them.

They had barely left the estate when she heard Finn's deep sigh.

"Are you angry with me?"

She fidgeted in her seat. "I feel things changing again. Everything seems disconnected." Her words were calm, her eyes still closed.

"I want to know if everything is okay between us." Finn's words touched her. She wanted to know that as well.

She opened her eyes and met his stare. He wanted an answer, but she wasn't ready to ask about his conversation with Hensley. "Tell me about the viscount."

Finn released a deeper sigh and shook his head. He leaned back and stretched his legs as far as the coach would allow. "The viscount is an ass, but he's intelligent." His voice grew stern. "He gives off an air that he's simply a pampered aristocrat, but he's far from that. He wasn't born into wealth any more than I was. Waverly Manor, where we're now headed, was not inherited through family."

He stopped and gazed out the window, seeming to admire the countryside before turning back to her. "Some time ago, the viscount carried out special missions for another very dangerous man. As part of his reward, the viscount was given the manor and a title. I knew him as Beckworth long before he became the viscount."

"If he's so evil, why are you working for him?"

Finn's features hardened as he glanced out the window again. "Sometimes you have to do business with people you don't like. That's the long and short of it." He turned back to her and studied her. He let a partial grin slip. "After these last couple of months, it seems I've forgotten again that you're a reporter. I know you struggle without your internet. Not being able to, what do you call it, jump on line and find out everything you need to know. But in reality, all it provides is a glossy surface of information. All you need to know is that Beckworth will appear charming but—and this is vital for you to remember—underneath all that charm is a very dangerous man. Don't ever forget he has his own motives for everything he does."

AJ nodded. She hovered between being pleased with his consideration for her strife and being scared to death of the viscount. As she contemplated his words, she realized it wasn't just the internet that could gloss over truthful details. He hadn't given her specific reasons for second-guessing him, other than what she'd overheard with Hensley, but he wasn't telling her everything. She had only his word about the viscount and it should be good enough. But all she seemed left with was that she couldn't trust either the viscount or Finn, and the thought chipped at her heart.

"Wonderful. I guess we're now leaping into the fire." She sat up and rearranged her skirts, trying to find a softer spot on the bench.

"I know the carriage is difficult to get used to after all the modern transportation you grew up with. This is a far cry from your vehicle." Finn passed her his cloak. "Here, try using this to sit on. It will provide some padding."

She glowered but took the proffered item. "I can't believe how uncomfortable it is, top of the line or not. I almost wish I had a horse."

Finn laughed out loud. The unexpected sound seemed to jar them both. "I never thought I'd hear you say that. It must truly be unpleasant."

She couldn't stop from laughing in return. "I know. I can't believe I said it myself. Maybe I'm just delirious. I almost miss the ship as well." Her heart skipped a beat when she saw his grin.

"And the ship too? I'll have to talk to Hensley about updating the carriage. I admit I don't understand why Mary hasn't already done it."

"If anyone could, it would be Mary." Her laughter brought another round from Finn. She missed their small-talk, but her smile disappeared when he turned back to business.

"The travel to Beckworth's will take most of the day. Do what you can to get comfortable and get some rest. We need to review societal etiquette again. You saw most of it at Hensley's, but you'll be tested more at Waverly Manor." He sneered. "Although Beckworth wasn't raised in such wealth, he has become quite polished as the viscount. I don't think he knows much about America, but he'll grow suspicious if too many things are ignored."

"All right. But I'd rather get started now so we can go over everything a few times. I can rest later. You never mentioned his wife."

"He's not married."

"Isn't that unusual?"

Finn shrugged. "Not really. Sometimes he has distant relatives join him at the manor to help with entertaining. To be honest, I'm not sure who, if anyone, will be there when we arrive."

She rubbed her hands on her gown, knowing she was leaving sweat stains behind but not caring.

The rattlers were back.

9

The first glimpse of Waverly Manor revealed an enchanting estate nestled in an expansive green valley, framed by wooded copses and a shimmering lake. A long tree-lined road led to the manor like something straight out of a PBS series. AJ thought of her father and what treasures he would have found if he'd had a chance to explore what lay behind those stone walls. Soon she would be able to see for herself. The manor disappeared when the carriage turned, the road dark with shade from the densely covered trees.

She settled back in her seat and refused to meet Finn's gaze, focusing instead on brushing invisible wrinkles from her dress. Her skin prickled as she tried to remember everything he'd told her about the arrival. He'd drummed it into her several times in the last few hours, but she couldn't seem to recall any details. It was like studying too much. The more you read, the less it stuck. It seemed like forever, but it couldn't have been more than five minutes before the carriage finally broke out of the trees and turned again, moving around a wide, circular drive.

From a distance, the building appeared elegant, but close up, the mirage dissolved into a cold and bleak fortress. A shiver ran through her, and she pulled her cloak tighter. The gray stone walls stretched up, pushing its way into the cloudy sky with nothing to soften the edges. AJ craned her neck out the window to see the ornate filigree at the top of the building, where she half expected to see gargoyles. Dozens of windows stared with sightless eyes, and if homes had souls, this one sat void. The manor would look its best at night with lights blazing from all the windows to erase its starkness and provide the only warmth it ever witnessed.

As the coach circled to the front of the building, several people stood at the bottom steps of the immense entrance. Obviously the staff, each person was dressed in black and white. She saw no sign of who might be the viscount, unless he had decided to dress in the same colors.

When no one else appeared, she glanced to Finn for direction. His grim face softened with a pleasant smile, and he reached out to hold her hand. It was at that moment she realized how much she missed his mischievous grins, the twinkle in his eye when he was up to no good, or those emerald eyes turned molten. Especially when he had other devious intentions that involved a bedroom or, as she remembered from just a couple of weeks before, the stable.

The memory made her blush, which made Finn's smile more quizzical. She wondered if she would ever see him again as she first knew him. It wasn't that he had hardened; he was still warm to her, provided for her, but there was a distance that had developed since boarding the ship. Even though they had been close during the sail over, she'd felt the change in him the closer they got to England. What she didn't know, and was afraid to consider, was whether it was a temporary change or permanent.

When the coach pulled to a stop, AJ released his hand to peek out the window in time to see the manor door open. A tall man dressed in a frilly coat of dark burgundy stepped out. His breeches matched the color of his coat and showed off his well-muscled legs. His light, ash-blonde hair was tied back, emphasizing his high cheek bones and narrow nose. He wasn't handsome. He was beautiful. His movements as he descended the stairs were ethereal. The impressive visage evaporated as a frown marred his features when he scanned the staff. She wasn't sure if they had somehow displeased him by simply standing there, or if this was his natural disposition.

Looking back to Finn, she recoiled at the change in him. The soft smile had been replaced by narrowed lips and a tight clenching of his jaw. His fingers curled into white-knuckled fists. The green eyes that had been warm to her just seconds ago were now as hard and dark as shards of jade. If she didn't know him as well as she did, she would be terrified of the man across from her. Though she wasn't certain what his true motives were, and with everything they had been through so far, she had never been afraid of him. But the anger-filled man across from her now, had she just met him, would have been enough for her to cross the street.

She turned away from him, pretending to be fascinated by the scene outside.

The viscount said something to an older man, who nodded and marched over to a young man. He said something that made the younger man instantly straighten and raise his head, a red blotch appearing against his pale skin. She couldn't understand what the man could have done wrong just standing in line, but he must have breached some etiquette that she would never grasp.

When the viscount turned to the carriage, his entire demeanor changed from head of the estate to charming host. A broad smile appeared on his face, and for just an instant, she caught a flash of mild irritation reflected in ice-cold, blue eyes. Whether it was for the incident with his staff or with his new guests, she didn't know. She leaned back in her seat and tugged her wrap tighter.

"Are you ready?" Finn's question pulled her away from the window.

She nodded and ran her hands along her gown. "I'll feel better if I can just make it to my room without making a fool of myself."

"You'll have time to rest before dinner. Just keep your words to a minimum with the introductions. The viscount will want to get straight to business."

Her head popped up. He was talking about the stones. A light sweat broke out, the coach closed in, and she desperately needed out. Wasted time. She should have just outright asked what his plans were for the stones. Over all the miles they'd traveled, their only focus had involved dinners and servants and how not to act like an ass. The old AJ wouldn't have forgotten about the stones or wallowed in self-pity. Wouldn't have been so weak. Where was that person? Now it was too late, and the carriage door opened.

Finn stepped out and took her hand to help her down. His own hand was warm and reassuring, but the sensation evaporated as she stepped next to him to greet the viscount.

"Mr. Murphy, I'd wondered if I'd ever see you again." The viscount's voice flowed over her, soft and inviting, but she heard the touch of steel behind the words. His attention turned to the ruffled edges of his shirtsleeves, pulling on one, tugging on the other, and finishing by running his hands down his jacket before regarding his visitors. His eyebrows narrowed as he looked at Finn, as if sizing up an opponent. AJ expected a handshake or something, but the viscount's erect bearing, his glance at Finn as if he was nothing more than an intrusion on his day, made it clear that he was greeting an employee rather than a guest to his home. Before waiting for Finn's reply, the viscount focused his attention on AJ.

"And who is this lovely specimen? Welcome to Waverly." This time the viscount did extend his hand. AJ reflexively reached out and felt his cold hand boldly grasp hers as he bent his head to brush a kiss over it. The move was unexpected, but she held her ground. When he raised his head, she stared into translucent blue eyes that refused to release her. She found herself trying to decipher what he meant by specimen, pretty sure she wouldn't like the answer.

"This is my cousin from America, Miss Abigail Moore." Finn's voice carried a note of irritation.

Finn told her he had sent a letter explaining her appearance to the viscount. AJ wasn't sure if Finn was annoyed because the viscount had forgotten or because the man was still holding on to her hand.

"Oh yes, I remember now." The viscount held her hand for another beat before squeezing it and letting it drop away.

She pulled her hand back and willed herself not to wipe it on her gown.

"Well, you're quite lovely, my dear. I think you'll do fine in London."

His words rolled over her, but his expression told a different story. Red flags waved all around her. She could see the flashing lights, could hear the blaring sirens. Every instinct shouted at her to jump on the back of Finn's horse and race away. Ride like the wind to anywhere but here. The old AJ might be rolled up in a fetal position somewhere deep down, but her survival instincts were strong. She took a step back, bumping into Finn, who, for the first time, didn't seem like enough protection.

The viscount studied her, and a slow, thin smile emerged. "You must be tired after the long ride." He turned and nodded at the man standing behind him. "This is Barrington. He'll assign you servants. I assume you'll want to rest before dinner." He stepped toward the manor before turning back to Finn. "I'll see you in the study, Mr. Murphy." Then he disappeared into the house.

The whole introduction took less than five minutes. AJ stared at the door, feeling lucky they were allowed into the house rather than being given a room over the stables. She was about to say something to Finn, but he shook his head. He steered her to the front door, leaning down to whisper, "The servants have ears."

When they entered the great hall, she gasped from the garishness that greeted them and the onslaught to her senses. It was like walking into a poorly decorated antique store stuffed with too much inventory. She couldn't help compare the manor to Hensley's stately estate, where Mary filled their home with elegance and charm. The viscount's home flaunted gold trimmings, bright colors, and an eclectic array of furniture. Tapestries, gold-edged portraits and landscapes, several as tall as she, fought for space, leaving little of the wallpaper to be seen. If only she had been wearing her sunglasses when she time jumped, anything to cut the glare.

She remembered Finn telling her the viscount wasn't married which explained the lack of charm. He didn't come from wealth and hadn't inherited the estate. Then she understood. He made up for his lack of bloodlines by flaunting his personally achieved wealth, or maybe he was just lousy at decorating. She thought it best to assume the former.

"This is Letty." The voice came from Barrington, who stepped up from behind them. His pinched face peered down at her as if she were no more than a piece of lint the maid had forgotten to pick up. "She will be your lady's maid during your stay here. Your trunks are being taken to your room. Letty will show you the way. Dinner is held promptly at seven. You'll be expected in the drawing room before then."

He turned and gave Finn the same disparaging appraisal, this time like something stuck to the bottom of his shoe. "I'll show you to the study."

Finn patted AJ's arm. "I won't be long. I'll check in with you as soon as I can."

"All right." It was all she could think to say with everyone watching her. She turned to Letty, another young girl, her head bent, almost as if she wanted to melt into the floor. AJ understood the feeling. "I believe Letty will be showing me to my room."

As if on cue, Letty nodded. "This way, mum." And, without raising her head, she led the way up the wide staircase that dominated the entryway.

Halfway up, AJ stopped to stare down at the hall, hoping for a last glimpse of encouragement from Finn. But it was empty. She followed Letty up the stairs that hugged the wall as it led them to the second floor. The hall split off in two directions. Letty turned right and stopped a few doors down, entering a room brightly colored with pinks, roses, and golds. Another overly decorated room fit for a princess.

A fire had been started, masking the gloom from the window. The room was twice the size of the one she'd occupied at the Hensley's, but for all its opulence, it held a coldness that couldn't be warmed by the fire. Whether it stemmed from the indifference of their host or the continued uncertainty of her future, it didn't matter. The effect was the same.

She dropped her wrap on the closest chair and strolled to the window to see another view from yet another courtyard. Then she spotted the water pouring from two immense stone figures surrounded by a two-foot-high circular wall. The fountain must have been hidden from view by the coach. She had been so focused on the line of servants and so anxiety-ridden to meet the viscount, she hadn't heard the water. Its musical sound seeped through the windows. A vision passed over her of warm summer days, the windows thrown open to let the sound of rushing water soothe her.

A knock at the door banished the image and signaled the arrival of her trunk. The two footmen disappeared as quickly as they came. Letty pounced on the trunk to remove the clothing, laying the gowns out on the bed and placing undergarments in the dressers. She lifted out a wrapped bundle and slid a questioning glance to AJ, but something in her return stare made the young maid return the bundle to the trunk. She suggested the burgundy gown for dinner, and AJ nodded. What did she care? A good pair of jeans and sweater would have been all she needed. And they were there within arm's reach, wrapped lovingly in that bundle, the last remnants of a woman lost in time.

"Would you like me to help you out of your gown? Then you can rest before dinner. I'll wake you when it's time to dress." Letty moved as quietly as a mouse as she helped AJ out of her traveling dress.

Exhaustion overtook her desire to talk to Finn before dinner. There was no reason for her to be so tired. The stress of worrying about Finn's covert activities and where she went from here simply tired a person out. Back home in her own time, her nonstop schedules energized her. This rambling around doing nothing all day proved more tiring than she could have imagined. It must be the idleness of the wealthy. She had been active at Finn's cottage: cooking, tending the garden, and investigating her new surroundings. She had found things to keep her busy on the ship after the storm, finding a way to be relevant. Now she moved around like a chess piece, and it was becoming monotonous.

Shaking herself from her daydreaming, she noticed Letty had disappeared as silently as the footmen. All her gowns had disappeared as well, probably placed in the wardrobe. She was alone.

She stared at the monstrous four-poster bed with a double set of drapes, sheer for warmer days and a heavier linen for the colder months. After climbing onto the bed, she crawled from post to post, closing the double drapes. In this inhospitable place, she welcomed the ability to close the curtains and hide herself from this crazy, backward world.

1 0

M uffled sounds stirred AJ, and she woke to darkness broken by a single thread of light. She blinked and tried to remember where she was. Her vision adjusted to see the opening in the draped curtain. A figure passed by the open slit, and her first thought was of Finn, as the familiar tingle jolted her. But as the figure walked past again, the shadow was too short. It must be Letty.

The drape opened cautiously. "Are you awake, my lady?"

"Yes, and you could call me Abigail. My friends call me AJ."

Letty pulled the drapes back from the bed. "No, my lady, that would not be proper."

AJ sighed and pushed the covers back. If she ended up stuck here, she would never have servants. Anyone working for her would be on equal footing, whether it was proper or not. The familiar black hole developed in the pit of her stomach. Maybe she could return to America, where she belonged, in location if not in time. For now, she'd play their games.

Letty took over and pulled out the burgundy gown, the color so deep and rich, it seemed infused in ebony . She whipped AJ's hair up and curled the ends with a hot iron before standing back.

AJ turned her head from right to left and back again before rising from the vanity. Letty excelled at her job.

"You are quite beautiful."

Letty's exclamation was so simple and sincere, a warmth for this young girl spread through AJ. She'd heard the statement from men before, including Finn, but spoken by someone with nothing to gain made her feel as if jewels had been laid at her feet. She grabbed Letty's hands, surprising the girl. "That's the best thing anyone has said to me in a very long time. Thank you, Letty."

The young maid blushed and pulled her hands away. "Everyone will think so as well. You will put Lady Osborne to shame."

"Lady Osborne?"

"Yes, Lord and Lady Osborne arrived an hour ago for the evening. Then Dame Ellingsworth arrived after that with her nephew. I don't know his name. I think he's visiting from Yorkshire."

"The viscount has other visitors?" A knot formed in her belly.

"Just for the night. The viscount has guests every so often. Usually short overnights, but sometimes he has hunting parties that last for several days."

AJ hadn't anticipated other people so soon and fought the panic bubbling up. She wasn't ready for high society. Taking a deep breath, she shook it off. Her only alternative was to have Letty remove the gown so she could crawl back into bed, draw the drapes around her, and wait until Finn took her away from this place. Instead, she checked her hair in the mirror and squared her shoulders. She would pretend she was going to one of her family dinners. It couldn't possibly be more awkward than that.

Voices from several conversations could be heard before she reached the drawing room, along with tinkling glasses and an occasional laugh or snort. She stopped for a second to ratchet up her nerves, but before she took another step, a hand grabbed her, and she let out a gasp.

"I'm sorry I haven't been up to see you, but it's not considered proper."

Finn's whisper was warm against her neck and goose bumps ran up her arms.

"You didn't tell me there were going to be other guests." Her own whispered voice attempted to disguise her uneasiness but didn't quite succeed.

Finn pulled her out of the hallway into an alcove hidden behind an immense fern. "I didn't know until they arrived. I'm not exactly in the viscount's good graces, but I imagine he wanted to make sure he had other people around as witness."

Her gaze lifted, and she almost gasped at the heat that bloomed through her. She had never seen him dressed up. His hair, which had grown out and which he rarely trimmed, was pulled back for dinner, emphasizing his rugged, tanned face. Her fingers ached to smooth the angry wrinkles on his forehead in exchange for a smile and the crinkles at his eyes. He wore a deep burgundy jacket that matched her gown and she wondered how Letty knew. She found she had trouble breathing. "Witness for what?"

Finn's shrug was almost imperceptible. "In case I just decided to beat him to death."

The statement spoken so earnestly dampened the fire smoldering just below the surface. She couldn't tell if he was joking.

The wrinkles disappeared, and his eyes darkened as they roamed over her, taking in every inch of her before landing on her lips. "You're going to turn heads tonight, Miss Moore. It's a shame we're not alone." And then he pulled her closer as his lips claimed hers, his tongue darting in to meet hers, the heat of it overwhelming her.

She groaned in response, not so much from the pleasure, but from the irritation at herself for enjoying it. She pushed him back. "What was that for?" She scanned the hall through the fern to see if anyone saw them. And to avoid his mouth that made her weak in the knees.

"It's been too long." His arms held her waist.

She pushed him away, her cheeks flushed. "Get your head out of the gutter." She ran her hands along her gown and picked at nothing. "I'm really nervous about this."

He grasped her shoulders with a gentle squeeze. "I know. Let it work for you. Be timid. Watch what the ladies do and follow the lead of others. Don't try to be Stella."

A laugh bubbled up. "I'm not up for that much acting."

He grinned, and moved his hands down to hold hers. Hands that were always so warm. "That's better. Just be careful. Many behaviors and actions can be attributed to an uncouth young woman from America. Especially one in search of a husband. But words can't be explained as easily."

"Searching for a husband?" She couldn't hold back the angry whisper.

Finn pulled her close, and his breath sent a tingle down her spine. "That is why you're in England, to find a suitable marriage." He lingered for an instant and whispered, "You thought I was joking when I told you that."

She nodded.

"I didn't plan that well. I should have made you a young widow instead. Then sneaking into your rooms at night wouldn't have stirred any tongues."

She pulled her hands away and lifted her chin. "Enough. You're making it worse."

"Just remember, behaviors are one thing, your words are another. Keep your speech brief and try to focus on what words you use." Finn turned her toward the doorway and gave her a gentle nudge.

She kept her head high on her walk to the drawing room. An image of Queen Anne Boleyn walking to her fate at the block sent a shudder through her. She shook it off. It would only be one night; the women were probably harmless.

When she entered the room, it seemed that everyone was there, four strangers and the viscount. He noticed her entrance and glided over to her.

"There you are, my dear Miss Moore." He raised her hand to his lips and lingered over the kiss. "Everyone has been waiting for you." He kept hold of her hand as he drew her into the room and whispered into her ear, "You look ravishing this evening. Lady Osborne will be green-eyed with envy."

She controlled a shiver and pulled her hand back. The hot breath against her neck made her break out in a light sweat, unsure whether he was being coy or had some ulterior thoughts. She glanced to the door, but Finn hadn't joined them yet.

Her gaze locked with a stunning brunette who marched to them. This had to be Lady Osborne. She would turn heads in any century. Her dark hair, swept up and held in place by jeweled pins, revealed a long, lean neck. The royal-blue gown emphasized her ivory skin, of which there was plenty on display with her corset and plunging neckline pushing her plump breasts into easy viewing. Her well-applied makeup revealed a flawless face, and only one thing marred the vision—the ugly scowl she couldn't hide as she gave AJ the once-over.

"So, this is the urchin from America." Lady Osborne's voice was soft and melodic, even while being rude.

AJ was tempted to match wits with her but decided to heed Finn's warning for a change. She lowered her head as she nodded in agreement. She glanced up just in time to catch a flash of anger in Lady Osborne's eyes. It seemed the lady preferred a challenge. AJ held back her smile. If she could remember to hold her tongue, she just might make it through the evening.

"Now, Agatha, we are guests here." The gentleman coming to her rescue must be Lord Osborne. He had to be twice his wife's age and his eyes, cloudy with either age or alcohol, reflected a tender warmth. He reached for AJ's hand. "How nice to meet you, my dear."

"Yes, Agatha, we should at least wait until dinner to bait our visitors." The loud voice reverberated from across the room and Dame Ellingsworth strolled to them. Though she wasn't quite as old as Lord Osborne, she wasn't far behind him. Her gray hair and soft wrinkles couldn't hide the beauty of the patrician face. Her piercing blue eyes inspected AJ thoroughly, making her feel like she'd been scanned by an Xray. Then the woman nodded. "She seems like a perfectly fine young woman. And beautiful. She would have been quite the competition back in your day, Agatha."

AJ swiveled her head to catch Lady Osborne's response but the woman glared at her as if AJ had made the bold comment. She was planning her retort when Finn stepped in, handing her a glass of wine, which she clutched like a lifeline. Tempted to gulp the entire glass, she refrained to merely a sip, afraid she'd get tipsy and tell everyone what she really thought. Finn provided protection as the birds of prey circled, until Lord Osborne called him away.

"Finn, good man, I was just telling Albert here that you have a sloop. And it's probably docked not too far from here. He's quite interested in sailing. Come and let him ask his questions before he bores us with them at dinner."

Finn nodded to the women and gave AJ's elbow a squeeze that Lady Osborne didn't miss. Her eyebrows pulled together, and AJ tried not to roll her eyes. One more piece of ammunition for the hawk.

"How is it exactly you haven't found a husband yet...I'm sorry, what was your name?"

Sipping her wine, AJ racked her brain for the answer she had rehearsed with Finn until Dame Ellingsworth chimed in. "It's Abigail. Good Lord, Agatha. Teddy told us not ten minutes ago." The older woman took AJ's hand and dragged her to the sofa.

"Tell me about Boston. I was there just before the war broke out. Has it changed much since then?"

No one was going to help her with this answer. AJ scratched at her knowledge of history, trying to remember anything of significance from that time period, a touch miserable for not being more prepared. But this time, Lady Osborne unknowingly came to her aid.

"I imagine it's returned to its original native landscape now that we've left. Isn't that why our dear Abigail is here? To find a proper match?" Lady Osborne sat across from the two women and stared at AJ over the rim of her wineglass.

"You have to pardon Agatha, my dear. She took a trip to India last year, and now she thinks all the English colonies are alike. I keep telling her it's not the same at all, but what can one do?" Dame Ellingsworth chortled.

"It's not a colony anymore." The words blew out of her like the wind locked behind a storm cellar door for too long, surprising both women. AJ lowered her head to avoid Lady Osborne's penetrating perusal. "I mean, not since the war ended."

A few seconds of silence lay between them before Dame Ellingsworth startled the room with a raucous laugh. She patted AJ on the knee. "You are correct. I can't seem to remember that. You'll keep us on our toes this evening. My poor Teddy will have his hands full with the three of us."

AJ gave her best demure smile and wondered who Teddy was until she locked eyes with Dame Ellingsworth. Those ice-blue eyes, currently warmed by her good humor, reminded her of the viscount's. She couldn't help but stare across the room to where the man stood. A cold shiver ran through her when she caught him staring at her—with those same intense eyes.

She instinctively searched for Finn just to break contact with the viscount. He stood next to a young man, fully engaged in some discussion. That had to be Albert, the nephew. A strange feeling took hold of AJ as she realized who Teddy was. She couldn't quite connect the pet name with the man who continued to watch her. Nor did she understand why Dame Ellingsworth was the only one who used the endearment.

"Where exactly in London will you be staying? I don't think Finn told us." Lady Osborne lingered over Finn's name, and a satisfied smile formed when AJ snapped an irritated glare.

AJ slid on her best reporter smile, the one she held for those obstinate interviews. "I can't recall. There have been so many stops, everything is starting to blend together. Do you visit here often?" AJ turned away from Lady Osborne, hoping Dame Ellingsworth would steer the conversation elsewhere. And she did.

"Not as often as we'd like. Teddy is such a good host, but he likes his privacy. And then he's a busy man. But now that the season is coming to a close, I'm sure we'll come by more frequently."

AJ smiled at the older woman and gave her a deeper study. The longer she examined her face, the more she saw a resemblance to the viscount. Finn had told her Beckworth didn't have a titled background, which would mean he wasn't related to this woman. But there was such a striking connection. Either she was wrong on her assessment, or Finn had lied. The thought made her queasy.

"Was your dress made in America?" Lady Osborne's change of topic should have made AJ feel safer, but nothing this woman said could be taken at face value. She wasn't sure Marguerite would enjoy this woman's business, but money was money.

"No. A wonderful seamstress in Ireland made it. She does marvelous work. And she's amazingly quick."

Dame Ellingsworth touched the sleeve of AJ's gown. "We'll have to ask Finn about her. Maybe we could entice her to visit. You wouldn't believe how difficult it is to find a decent dressmaker. Especially at the start of the season." Then she stood.

"Well, it's about time. I seem to be more hungry than usual. It must be all the excitement."

AJ turned to see what had made the woman get up and heard Barrington announcing dinner. Her shoulders relaxed. Each social engagement felt like a boxing match, and she considered herself lucky to still be standing when the bell rang. Then she felt an arm slip through hers and smelled Lady Osborne's intoxicating perfume.

"Why don't we go in together? We have so much more to talk about."

The woman's smile was blinding, but AJ's appetite withered all the same. When they walked toward the door to the dining room, Finn started toward her, but AJ shook her head. She needed to keep him distant until these people were gone.

She turned when she felt someone watching her. The viscount. He stood alone watching his guests file into the dining room. Her stomach lurched. She had been looking forward to eating, but now she didn't think she could eat a cracker. He seemed to study her all evening, trying to peek under her hood and see what made her tick. She felt the sweat pop out at her temples but avoided wiping it away, hoping the astute Lady Osborne wouldn't notice. The viscount stepped in behind her as they passed through the door to dinner.

11

The next morning, foreboding gray skies pressed down like an iron and drizzled a fine cold mist. AJ peeked through her bed curtains, wilted at the gloomy vision outside the window, told Letty she felt a bit queasy, and buried herself back under the covers. An hour later, Letty returned with a serving tray on orders from the viscount. AJ frowned when she pulled the cover off the serving tray and found a bland breakfast of toast and a single poached egg. She wolfed it down, starving after eating little of the meal the night before. Thankfully, a silver pot of coffee had been provided. She could have used two more pots but contented herself with knowing she had dodged a bullet not seeing Lady Osborne again.

She watched the viscount's guests leave from her window. They were probably miffed at not having their favorite chew toy with them for breakfast, but she had no doubt she was still a topic of discussion. Through dinner, she had remained the sport of the evening with snide remarks from Lady Osborne. Her only refuge had been keeping her head down while she pushed food around on her plate. She glanced at Finn several times, hoping for some reassurance, but he seemed distracted and unfocused.

After dinner, the women strolled back to the drawing room while the men moved to the study. Weariness overtook AJ at the thought of being left alone with the women. Claiming exhaustion from her day of travel, she begged off to bed. She held a smile in check when she saw the utter disappointment in Lady Osborne's expression and a knowing nod from Dame Ellingsworth. If she had to live as the weaker sex, she might as well use it to her advantage.

Safely ensconced in her room after dinner, she found herself fully awake, a bit hungry and completely bored. Pulling a blanket around her, she sat in front of the fire and filled pages of her journal by the dim light of the lamp. She had expected a visit from Finn, if only to talk. They needed to talk. Alone in the room, she missed the feel of his arms around her. But with all the people in the house, he must have decided not to risk the impropriety.

Now, as she watched the carriage take Lady Osborne and her companions away, it was time to search for him. She saw horses being brought out and, with a sinking feeling, spotted Finn. He walked with the viscount and two other men. Behind them was another man with several dogs pulling at their leads. She sighed. They were going hunting, even in the gray drizzle.

She returned to her journal and, after finding nothing else to write, perused several books that had been left in her room. The titles and authors were unrecognizable to her, and after reading bits of them, she understood why.

When Letty returned, she shook her head at AJ. "My lady, you need to get out of your room. I know it's dreary, and everyone has left you for the day, but you should take lunch in the dining room."

AJ's head popped up. Two things immediately came to mind. She was starving, and she had the whole place to herself. After Letty quickly dressed her, she made her way to the dining room and stuffed her face with meats, cheese and bread. She accepted a glass of wine, wished she could have had a second one, and agreed to take tea in the conservatory.

Taking the long way through the manor, she marveled at the antiques. Although everything in the house was an antique to her, she discovered pieces much older than 1802. Finn never mentioned the viscount being a collector. It was possible the viscount had simply inherited the items when he'd taken over the estate.

When she reached the conservatory, she stood at the doorway and her spirits lifted. On a sunny day, the light filtering through the tall windows would make a wonderful painter's studio. Even on a day like today, with the skies casting a dull pallor over the generous gardens beyond the windows, a painter could find just enough light to work a canvas. Giant ferns filled the room, framing the exquisite artwork that hung on the walls between the tall windows. The bigger surprise was the orchids—dozens of them in differing colors and varieties filled every spare niche. This was more than adding color to the room, this was someone's passion. She took time to observe them, stopping occasionally when she caught a slight scent.

She dropped onto a sofa and pulled her arms around her. Even with the fire that smoldered in the far hearth, without the sun, this room proved cooler than the rest of the house. The forever thoughtful Letty surprised her by bringing a lace-edged linen wrap with the tray of tea. Settled in with the wrap around her and a warm cup in her hands, she stared at the gardens and let her thoughts fade. Her shoulders relaxed, and her worries seemed to drain from her until she heard the familiar voice behind her.

"There you are. I've searched everywhere for you." Finn had changed from the hunting attire she'd seen him wearing in the courtyard that morning. He must have been soaked through from the misty drizzle outside. His damp hair had been pulled back, but an errant curl dropped across his forehead.

She almost reached out to push it back.

He sat next to her and searched her face. His expression masked something deeper than the concern in finding her.

"I've just been studying the artwork. The viscount has quite the collection of fine art." The tension released from AJ's shoulders when his light scent drifted to her. "You went hunting."

"It's a favorite sport of the viscount."

AJ nodded. That made sense from what little she'd seen of the man. He'd certainly studied her as if she were prey last night. "Did you kill anything?"

"No, the deer got away."

"Somehow that makes me feel better."

"I'm sorry for last night. Are you really feeling ill?"

"No, I feel fine, if you don't count how bored I am."

Finn touched her wrap for a brief second. "You do catch on quickly. It must be your survival instincts. The women were a bit brutal."

"Just tell me I'll never see them again, and I'll consider the whole thing more of a practice run."

"No. I don't think the viscount will be having them back for a while. He doesn't appear to like them any more than you or I. He does it for the credits earned for being the polite host of the manor." Finn's tone hardened. "It's all about appearances."

"That's surprising. I noticed a resemblance between Dame Ellingsworth and the viscount. It was in the eyes, I think."

"Nothing more than a coincidence. I told you he wasn't of noble birth."

They turned silent as they gazed out the windows as if something outside would provide a better topic. She had so many things she wanted to ask him, but now that he was finally here, she savored the simpleness of his presence next to her. They'd grown comfortable with their silences, but as the tension left her body, she noticed Finn's increase. His leg muscles tightened, and he sat upright, leaning away from her.

"So what aren't you telling me?"

Finn shook his head. "What does that say that you know me so well?"

"In this case, I'm pretty sure it's telling me I'm not going to be happy about whatever it is you're not saying."

Finn sighed as he leaned back against the divan. He reached out to grasp her hand but pulled it back.

AJ sat up to pour a cup of tea and, for the first time, noticed the second cup. She poured tea into both cups and administered the milk, doing anything to postpone what he'd come to tell her. It was going to be bad.

"I have to leave for a little while."

She let the words wash over her. She wasn't sure she'd heard him correctly. "You mean we have to leave."

He reached out and gripped her hand which lay cold and limp. "No. Just me. Just for a little while."

She took long, slow breaths to control the developing tidal wave. "I don't understand."

"I know. It's one last mission for Beckworth, and then this chapter can be closed."

"Will this mission get me closer to home?"

"In a way."

AJ heard the hesitation, the inability to commit. "Can you tell me what it is?"

"It's safer if you don't know."

"As safe as you leaving me here?"

He rubbed his fingers over AJ's hands, as if this well-intentioned action was enough to warm them, but they remained stubbornly chilled. "I've worked it through a hundred different ways. This is the best course. You'll be safer here."

AJ nodded slowly and stared out the windows, the grayness piercing her heart. "You mean I'll be safer here because you haven't turned over the stones yet."

His silence spoke volumes.

"You've already turned them over. My only way home—gone. And now you're just going to leave me here as you move on. Does that pretty much sum it up?" The panic threatening to roll over her and the fear that settled into her core rose into a molten rage. She fell into a spiral of white-hot anger that blinded her to her surroundings. That raging inferno heated every inch of her. Except her hands. She gazed down. Her hands were still covered by Finn's, and she pulled them away. She rubbed them together, but they remained stone cold.

"We'll get you home, AJ. We just have to be careful how we go about this. There are other things at play here."

She turned on him. "Okay, so tell me. Break it all down for me so I'm seeing it with all the facts."

He reached out to her again, but she shrank away from him. "I just need you to trust me. Just for a few days."

"Trust you." She spat the words back at him. "Do you remember the first time you asked me to trust you?" He blanched at her words. "Next thing I know, I'm two hundred years in the past with no way back." She jumped up and stared down at him. Even through her anger, the hurt in his eyes registered with her. And something else. A conflict raged in him that he didn't seem able to share. "All the secrecy. The meetings with Hensley, whatever little war you have with the viscount and you can't seem to tell me any of it. All for my safety. I'm no further home than I was when I first arrived. I'm supposed to trust you, but the sentiment only works one way. Where's the trust you have in me?"

She raced from the room.

"AJ, wait. Just a minute."

She turned before she got to the door. "Because you're going to tell me everything? All your plans?" She didn't need to wait for a response. The answer showed plainly in his pained expression. "That's what I thought."

Flying up the stairs, she tried to slam the bedroom door—just for the satisfaction. But the damn thing had been built too well to provide the appropriate retort. Instead, she flung herself onto the bed and cried. All the rage, panic, fear, and loneliness overtook her and dragged her into a pit of misery as the sobs racked her bones.

When AJ woke, she didn't know when the crying surrendered to untroubled sleep. She was tired of crying at every little thing. It reminded her of the months after her father had died. Weeks would go by without a tear, then the slightest thing would start a crying jag. After the bouts of crying stopped, depression had set in. She hadn't just lost a father, she had lost a friend, someone to share her antiquing and her love of history. And just when she was getting her life back on track, Finn showed up and turned her world upside down. And now she felt those tentacles of despair lurking just below the surface, ready to reach out at the worst times.

She shook herself when she noticed that a few lights had been lit, although they weren't enough to chase the shadows that darkened the corners of the room. Then she saw the tiny figure walking toward her, a gown in her hands.

"It's time for dinner, my lady." Letty laid the dress on the other side of the bed and ran her hand down it. "Your gowns are so lovely. He must think a great deal of you to provide such wonderful things."

Everything from the afternoon came rushing back, and she rolled up into a ball. She didn't want to go to dinner. She didn't want to face either of the men. "It would appear so."

"He was here just a short while ago asking for you. He seemed concerned."

AJ thought about that and damned herself for the pleasure at knowing he had come. Then she stomped it down and covered it over like some dead rat she found in the field. "Is it just the three of us for dinner?"

"Yes, and you're a bit late. We need to get you dressed quickly."

"I think I'd just like something brought to the room." She

dragged herself out of bed and let Letty remove her wrinkled day gown. She shook her head at her mishandling of the gown, the second time in as many days, unthinking of the extra work for Letty.

"The viscount was very clear that you would be coming to dinner." Letty kept her head down, and AJ wondered exactly how that conversation had gone.

"Then let's get it done." She studied the emerald-green gown Letty had picked out. "I'd prefer the brown satin gown this evening." Sitting down at the vanity, she tossed her head around. "Pull my hair all the way back and pin it into a tight bun." When she saw Letty's confusion, she patted her hand. "I'll help you. Just start by grabbing it all and pulling it back tight."

"The men seem to prefer your hair like you had it yesterday."

"Yes, I know. But I think I'd like to feel a little more American tonight."

"This is how they wear it there? It's so severe."

AJ turned her head, and her smile turned dark. Letty learned very quickly. "Yes, perfect. We call it the spinster."

12

Finn found it appalling he actually missed Lord and Lady Osborne's presence. He stared at Beckworth across the drawing room as the man stared back. One thing he knew about the man, he was punctual, and AJ's tardiness would only draw his anger. When she finally made her entrance, Finn couldn't stop staring. He slid a quick glance at the viscount and found him equally shocked.

Her hair was pulled back so tightly, it left her face with sharp angles, making her mahogany, doe-like eyes enchanting. The brown dress, which he assumed was meant to make her appear dowdy, offset her pale skin and the dark tresses she hid in the bun. Her plan had backfired. He was reminded of the first time he saw her. Her short hair had been pushed back from her face by the coastal wind, and while she was a bit thinner now, it was the same stubborn woman who faced him.

His grin was involuntary, and he enjoyed the quick burst of satisfaction when her frown deepened. She hadn't expected that response.

The viscount recovered and plastered on his own smile. But

he couldn't dull the sharpness in his tone. "There you are, my dear. You're a bit tardy."

Although the words were spoken softly, everyone understood he was irritated. Finn almost laughed but didn't dare. These two needed to get along, at least for a little while.

"I'm sorry. I'm afraid I fell asleep, and Letty had a difficult time rousing me." AJ sashayed into the room and accepted the glass of wine the viscount handed to her.

"All is forgiven." The viscount stared at her. "Although I'm not sure I like what Letty did with your hair. If I may be so bold?"

AJ blushed.

Finn wondered if it was sincere or whether she could now do it on command.

"It wasn't Letty's doing. It's how I usually wear it at home." The lies rolled more easily, and Finn had mixed feelings about that.

The viscount snickered. "Well, now I know why you're having difficulties finding a husband. I suggest you take guidance from Letty's ministrations."

This time her blush from the chastisement was real. Finn's hands curled into fists, his eagerness to defend AJ surprising him. This wasn't the time. She needed to fight her own battles.

Dinner was a stilted affair with AJ as the buffer between the men. The conversation became stunted with her one-word answers, forcing the viscount to call upon Finn to help fill the silence. When the viscount called the dinner over before the last course, he knew there would be repercussions. He second-guessed his decision to leave AJ behind.

The viscount mumbled something about a business matter and left with a single bow to AJ. She stood to leave.

"I don't want to leave with this matter between us." Finn kept an even tone. Now he knew what people meant about walking on eggshells.

She turned her head and gave him a blank stare. "So you've decided to tell me what's going on?"

"Why don't we go to the conservatory rather than the drawing room? We can talk there."

Her eyes softened for a moment. He felt the tension drain away, and he ventured a smile. That was the wrong thing to do. Her defenses went up.

She set her jaw and lifted her chin, not giving him an inch. "We can talk right here, assuming there's anything to talk about. All I want to hear is what your plans are."

Finn sighed. "I just want to find some peace between us before I leave for London."

"London?" It was almost a screech. "You can't take me to London? There must be hundreds of places you could leave me."

Finn knew she was right. He had thought about it but then discarded it. He had to move fast. Leaving her alone in London wasn't any safer than leaving her here, where he had to come back. This was the center of everything.

He stepped closer but stopped when she backed away from him. "Where I have to go in London won't be safe. It will take too long to find proper lodging for you. There's a time factor."

"Well, there's always something." She turned to leave and then stopped. Keeping her head down, she whispered, "I do wish you safe travels." Then she was gone.

He dropped back into his chair and stared at the poor footman still standing, waiting to clear the table. He motioned for the man to pour more wine. "Go ahead with your work. I'll try to stay out of your way."

The man nodded.

Finn knew he should vacate the dining room and finish drowning his troubles in the drawing room or study. But that would lead to whiskey, and that wasn't a road to travel this evening. He drained his wineglass, pushed thoughts of AJ away, and changed his mind. He stalked through the drawing room, picked up a decanter of amber liquid and a glass, and stomped his way back to the solitude of his room.

TINY DOTS of rainbows shimmered in the mist of water trickling from the courtyard fountain. If AJ pressed her nose to the glass in just the right way, she could see the edge of the lake and the reflection of the foreign English countryside. This was the first she'd seen of the sun in several days, and the weather resembled Baywood's so much, it made her heartsick at the thought she'd never see it again. While the sun should be a welcome sight, it held no warmth for her this morning. She preferred the gray skies that matched her listless spirit.

She gazed down at the man who had brought her here. The man who was mounting his horse to ride away and abandon her. He asked for trust, but the well was running dry. If she couldn't go with him, where else could she go? She had no money, no transportation, and the one thing she needed to get home, the stones, were right here at Waverly. He said he would be back before she knew it, but she gazed down at him now and rubbed at the boulder-sized rock laying deep in the pit of her stomach. It told her something different.

A sudden wave of panic seized her—claustrophobic and suffocating. She almost ran for the door, hoping to get to Finn before he rode off. She grabbed the thick damask curtains to hold her sagging weight and watched him glance up at the windows. He scanned the building as if searching for her room, but didn't see her. Turning the white steed, he gave a kick, and hooves pounded the cobblestone yard before the horse flew through the gate and down the tree-lined drive, until they were hidden from view.

She eased into a nearby chair, gripping the armrests. He said he wouldn't be gone long. But what did that even mean? Everything took forever with nothing but horses and carriages for transportation. She thought she had gotten used to the slow pace of this century, but now that she was alone, she wasn't sure she had the patience.

After a few minutes of feeling sorry for herself, she gave herself a mental head slap. She wasn't completely alone. The viscount couldn't be trusted; she didn't need to understand Finn's hatred for the man to know that. But now she had time to put her investigative skills to work, and it wouldn't be the first time she'd interviewed a difficult subject. This was the time to take control of her own fate.

Empowered by her new resolve, she left her room and was halfway down the stairs when her stomach rumbled. Acting like a child, she had refused to go to breakfast and face Finn. She was sorry for that now, but she buried the regret and tried to decide between asking for breakfast or starting her private mission. Her head was down as she reached the bottom of the stairs, and she gasped when she found the viscount waiting for her.

"I didn't mean to startle you." He stood close. Close enough for the light scent of musk cologne to roll over her, cloying. With her standing on the bottom step, he was at eye level with her. He never blinked.

"No." Her heart beat like a thoroughbred's after a race. "I just didn't see you." He continued to stare, and she swore he could read her mind. "I guess I was thinking I might be too late for breakfast." She forced a smile.

His brows knit with his annoyance. "I did expect you to be down to see Mr. Murphy off."

The silence reverberated around the foyer. She considered the best way to answer and decided on a portion of the truth. "We said our goodbyes last night. Besides, he won't be gone long. Right?"

He pulled at the sleeves of his jacket. "Of course. I'll see they freshen the buffet." He turned to leave.

"Will you be joining me?" She hated saying it, but this was an opportunity. He stepped closer when he turned back, and though there wasn't anything lustful in the way his gaze raked her, she had to force herself not to run. She felt a bit sickened, and a bit cheap, at the casualness of his glance and the familiarity they didn't share.

He stepped back. "I'm afraid I have other business to attend to. But I look forward to an intimate dinner." His tone turned mocking. "For us to get to know each other better."

With a slight bow, he was halfway down the hall before she moved. When she reached the dining room, she blindly sat down, deciding whether she should continue with her plans. She inwardly shrugged as a plate and a cup of coffee were placed in front of her. The viscount might be a dangerous man, but—in for a penny.

Her stomach rumbled after a day of moping. She savored each bite as she stuffed eggs in her mouth, tossing in the last piece of warm sweet bread—and almost choked.

A young woman stood by the window. AJ hadn't noticed her when she'd walked in, too focused on the viscount. She grabbed her coffee to swallow down the lump of bread lodged in her throat.

The woman never turned away from the window, nor showed any sign that she was no longer alone. She had to know AJ was there with the footman walking around, and her stuffing her face. The woman, standing ramrod straight, was clearly in another world as she stared at some invisible place. She appeared younger than AJ, but they could be the same age. Her hair shone like wheat, tied up into a loose bun that showed off a porcelain, swan-like neck. The soft blue gown hung from a slim body, and AJ found an instant similarity. They were both too thin for their clothing.

Not wanting to disturb her, AJ took a few more bites as quietly as she could and flinched when she knocked her cup against the saucer. Then she felt foolish. She pushed her plate away, leaned her elbows on the table, and sipped her coffee as she watched the woman. She could have been a statue out of Madame Tussaud's wax museum.

There were several possibilities of who this woman might be. Finn said the viscount wasn't married, so perhaps this was his mistress. It was possible she could be a daughter from some youthful affair. Or perhaps some other relative. AJ felt torn between wanting to start her perusal of the manor and not knowing if she should say something before leaving. Maybe this was a new avenue in her arsenal of possibilities.

She took another sip from her cup. "Have you been here long?"

The woman continued to gaze out the window, and AJ wondered if she had heard the question. Then she said, "It seems like forever at times. But yes." The woman tucked an invisible hair behind her ear. "It's been almost two years."

13

AJ pushed back her plate, sorry she had eaten so much. Two years? She'd only meant to ask whether the woman had been standing in the room long. The room felt like it was closing in. Perhaps the woman was a crazed relative who had to be kept locked up in the estate, never seen and never able to hurt anyone. AJ tried to lighten the mood. "Well, at least you're living in comfort."

The woman pivoted to stare at AJ. "Were you expecting a dungeon?"

The sharpness in her tone and her quick movement surprised AJ. Now that the woman had turned toward her, she could see she was about the same age as her and possessed a classic beauty. Her sea-green eyes flashed, at odds with her calm, vulnerable exterior. Then her lips twitched. It was as if the woman was playing a game with her. And was that an Irish lilt?

AJ set down her cup and sat back. "So I guess you don't get out much."

The woman's laugh was melodic. "That's usually how it works when you're a…shall we just say a visitor of the viscount's."

AJ paled at her choice of words. The woman's face became

serious as she glided to the table to sit across from AJ. She reached out for a piece of leftover toast and nibbled the end.

"Sorry. I know it's rude, but I didn't eat well this morning. And now I'm starving." She swallowed another bite and dabbed at the crumbs on her lips. She nodded to the footman, who brought her a cup of coffee and a plate of food. After eating half the plate, she sipped her coffee and leaned back to gaze at AJ. "That's better. Have you been here long?"

An unexpected laugh burst out of AJ.

When the woman smiled with her, AJ felt a sense of relief in finding what might be a kindred spirit. "Well, certainly not as long as you. Only a couple of days."

"And are you a visitor as well?"

Those simple words forced a shiver through AJ as she thought about it. Was she a prisoner? Unable to leave as this woman seemed to believe she couldn't? "I think I'm more of a guest." But she could hear the doubt in her own voice as she spoke the words.

The woman simply nodded. "My name is Maire."

"I'm Abigail, but my friends call me AJ."

"That's an interesting nickname. Is it just the initials?"

"Yes. The J is for Jayne. With a Y."

Maire studied her until AJ squirmed. Why was it everyone studied her as if she were a bug under a glass? It had to be her speech.

"You're English?"

"In a way. I'm from America."

"Ah." And again, that seemed to explain everything.

AJ decided she should start every conversation that way. It would save time.

"So why are you here, AJ? I believe you said you were a guest. Did you come alone?" Maire asked, her voice light.

She smiled at the use of her nickname. "I came with a friend, but he had to leave on some business. He should be returning soon." Her voice dropped as she finished, hoping she was right.

"Not your husband?"

"I'm not married." As soon as the words left her mouth she realized the woman must think she was a kept woman—a mistress. She almost laughed out loud. That was exactly what she was, at least in this era of propriety. She lifted her chin. "No, not my husband."

"Well, it must be a lovely story. Perhaps you'll share it with me some day."

"We seem to both have stories to share. Some day." AJ watched Maire as she turned her focus back to the window.

Maire stood. "I was hoping to get out to the gardens today. The sun won't stay for long. Would you like to join me?"

AJ wanted to spend her time searching the manor, starting with the library. But if Maire had been here as long as she said, she might be a better source of information. AJ stood and brushed her gown. "Absolutely. I could use some exercise."

Maire led AJ through the manor and into the conservatory. A tremor of regret ran through AJ as she passed by the sofa where she had fought with Finn. She already missed him. Then she noticed Maire's light touch on the orchids as she passed them on her way to the French doors.

The covered veranda opened to another world blanketed by green sprites. A warm wind played at the hairs on AJ's neck as the scent of roses and Sweet William floated around them. The garden enlivened the English countryside with a myriad array of flower beds in full colors—reds, oranges, pinks, and white.

On the left, set off from the house, the lake shimmered with symmetric ripples made by two swans moving placidly around the center. To the right were the woods she had seen on her arrival, farther away than she had first thought. Other trees weaved through the garden. Towering oaks provided welcome shade on summer days, while shorter trees with expansive canopies sheltered private areas for quiet contemplation or more clandestine meetings. Several gravel paths meandered through the garden, leading visitors to hidden grottoes, fountains, and statues all accompanied by benches. Hours could be spent just moving from one spot to another with nothing but a good book for company.

They walked in silence as Maire guided them, stopping to smell a rose or marvel at the colors of a peony, or touch the feathery leaf of a plant AJ didn't recognize. They strolled through the main garden area before Maire walked them across a bridge and down a sun-dappled path of trees.

"So how is it that you found yourself here?" Maire's voice was soft, as if she didn't want to wake any fairies that might be living in the trees.

"To be honest, I'm not completely sure." She didn't know how much to say. She couldn't tell her about the stone or where she came from. But she thought the woman too intelligent to believe Finn's carefully prepared cover story. And for some reason, she didn't want to lie to her. "My companion doesn't tell me a lot about his business."

"I see. So you traveled with him from America, and then he left you, without friends or other companionship."

She paused in answering, trying to stay a step ahead of Maire's questions. "I don't think he meant to leave me here. Some business came up he wasn't expecting." She shrugged. "He thought I'd be more comfortable staying here." And although she realized she might be telling Maire the truth, they were the same words Finn had told her. Another pang of regret rose before she shook it off. She still deserved the whole truth from him.

"I didn't mean to upset you." Maire turned them down another path and back toward the manor.

"I'm just out of sorts. So much has happened. I haven't had time to process it."

"We should do this again. It's been a while since I've had anyone to really talk to."

AJ studied Maire. She could see the child she used to be before she turned into this stunning woman. There was a curious mix of sensitivity and bravado, and something else she couldn't put a finger on. "I would love to do this again. There's so much I need to learn."

Marie's gaze traveled over AJ's face, leaving her with that bug-under-the-glass feeling again. "All in good time."

With a soft pat on AJ's arm, Maire steered them up the veranda and back to the manor.

AFTER MAIRE DEPARTED to her wing of the manor, AJ leaned against a wall. She had learned nothing. Maire asked all the questions. AJ seemed to be out of practice for interviews, or maybe Maire was better versed in manipulation. Either way, she had lost her desire to do anything more than walk through a couple of rooms to cross them off her list. Before she knew it, she mentally cataloged a few pieces of furniture and two paintings. Some instincts never left.

Returning to her room, she spent the rest of the afternoon writing in her journal. As an afterthought, she turned to the back of the journal and jotted down some of the finer pieces of furniture and artwork she found. But her thoughts eventually returned to Maire. Why was she here?

She ignored Letty when she heard her add wood to the hearth, and finished her final notes as the fire crackled. When she finally closed the journal, she was surprised by how dark it had become.

"You'll strain your eyes without proper light." Letty placed a lamp on the desk and laid an emerald gown on the bed.

"I didn't realize how late it was." She leaned back and stretched.

"It's good you have found something to keep you busy, my lady."

AJ brightened. It might have been a slow start with Maire, but there would be a few more days before Finn returned. She needed to learn patience. "You're right. It feels better to have things to do."

She entered the drawing room, excited to see Maire again. But the only person awaiting her was the viscount, standing by a bookcase, a glass of brown liquor in his hand. His emerald jacket matched her dress, and she remembered Letty carrying her gown to the bed, already decided.

He turned as she entered and assessed her before nodding. His smile made her stomach turn, but she smiled in return and stood quietly, not sure what to do with herself under his scrutiny.

"How was your day?" The viscount refused to release his gaze.

"A little boring. I wasn't sure what to do with myself." She broke away from his stare and scanned the room, her hands played at her sleeves.

The viscount moved to a side table. "Can I get you something to drink? Some wine, perhaps."

"Yes, that would be nice." She slid a glance to the door, but it stood empty. No Maire.

"I hear you met my other houseguest today." He moved to a divan and held out an arm for her to sit.

She took her seat, keeping as much distance from him as possible without seeming rude, and mulled over his choice of words for Maire's status. "She seems quite nice."

"She has her moods but, yes, she's mostly very nice. I think she'll make a good companion while you wait for Mr. Murphy's return."

His words provided more comfort than he could know, and the air that had been trapped somewhere in her inner core released in a long slow breath. Finn would be returning. A heaviness seemed to lift, and she slid another glance at the door. "Will she be joining us for dinner?"

"Not tonight. I thought we could discuss things that don't concern her. She'll join us tomorrow."

Her stomach clenched again. She buried her roller coaster of emotions in an attempt to clamp down her worst fear—being alone with the viscount. Before she had time to ponder his words, Barrington arrived to announce dinner.

With only the two of them for dinner, the dining room carried an intimate atmosphere, the viscount at the head of the table and her at her spot to his right. Running different scenarios over and over, she tilted her head and glanced at the man next to her. Her only recourse to make it through the meal would be to treat him as an adversarial interview. In order to pull information from him, she had to be polite. She sipped her wine, preferring to gulp a glass or two, but she needed to keep her head clear.

The first course came and went without any conversation. She didn't enjoy any of the meal, sitting on pins and needles waiting for the man to say something. He was certainly a patient man, and it was all she could do not to pepper him with questions. She almost sighed with relief when the arrival of the main course broke the silence.

"I understand you saw the gardens today."

They were such innocent words, but they gave her a chill. She didn't know if Maire had told him or if he was spying on them. He could have seen them from his study or from wherever he kept himself all day. Not everything was a conspiracy. "They're beautiful. It was nice to see the sun."

"I have an extensive staff that cares for them. It costs a fortune but is well worth it. This estate is quite sought after for formal parties when the gentry leave London for the country."

"Has the estate been in your family long?"

She might have missed his slight wince if she hadn't been

watching for it. He pushed his fork around on the plate. His jaw twitched. Maybe Finn hadn't been lying about his ancestry, even with the resemblance to Dame Ellingsworth.

He drank his wine and stared at her as if trying to read the intention behind her words. "Not long. Have you had time to explore any of the rooms? I've collected some excellent pieces of art over the years. And I hear you like to read."

She didn't want to hear about the art, she wanted to know how long he'd owned the estate. She wanted to just lay it all out on the table and ask him about the stones. "I wasn't sure you would approve of me wandering through the manor."

"Absolutely. I ask only that you keep your perusals to the first floor and the west wing. The east wing houses my private quarters and I, well, not to sound rude, enjoy my privacy." He tried a smile that looked more like a leer. "The west wing has the best library and conservatory. Both rooms could keep you occupied for months."

Months? There it was again. She felt a knot forming in her gut, fraying her emotions. She had no plans to stay here for months, but now she knew where she would find information about the stone. It would all be in the east wing. At least she had permission to wander the manor.

"I have an interest in art as well as books. I'll enjoy the opportunity to explore your collection." She thought about the east wing and how to get there. That had to be where Maire was being stashed away from visitors. Maybe she was the viscount's mistress. That would explain why she didn't care that AJ was traveling alone with a man not her husband. She really hoped not, but there was no elegant way to ask.

The silence returned as they finished their meal. When dessert was placed in front of them, AJ ignored it and focused on the coffee. She spent time adding the cream and stirring until she almost made a hole in the cup. She had forgotten the man next to her while she visualized the layout of the place and how to find the east wing.

"Do you know why you're here, Miss Moore?"

The question took her by surprise. She had relaxed her guard and should have known better. "I'm waiting for Mr. Murphy to return."

The viscount waved his hand, and a footman picked up their plates and vanished, leaving them very much alone. He sat back, pulled at the ruffles of his shirt sleeves, and turned his attention to her. "Yes, and why are you with Mr. Murphy?"

She could feel the blush creeping up her neck. "I'm visiting him from America. We're going to London." The lie was getting easier to say, but he seemed to be fishing for something more. "I thought Mr. Murphy had told you this."

"Yes, that was the story he told me." He stared at her until she turned away, which seemed to satisfy him. He picked up a book the size of a slim paperback. She hadn't even noticed it. He turned it over and ran a hand over the cover. "This is Voltaire's *Candide*. I do love adventure stories. Have you read Swift's *Gulliver's Travels*? Quite the imaginative fellow. Amazing tales of far away travel. Almost as if he traveled to a different time."

A cold chill touched the back of her neck, so icy she swore she could see her own breath.

"I also find I enjoy a good mystery," he continued, as if he didn't notice her discomfort. "It piques my interest when I think I've stumbled onto one." He turned the book over and placed it between them. "Do you love mysteries, Abigail?"

Her eyes skittered around the room, and she wondered if the footman was coming back. The realization of her predicament and being alone with him deepened the coldness spreading through her. She would have to travel back a few more centuries for that knight in shining armor. Backed into a corner, her anger sparked. If she didn't show some spine, he'd walk all over her.

Her fingers played at the napkin she had placed on the table. She thought of Stella and how she made origami figures with napkins when she was deep in thought. Stella always considered herself AJ's talisman and, it seemed, even two hundred years away, she still was. She sat straighter and met the viscount's patient stare.

"Yes, I do love mysteries. In fact, I thrive on them."

He grinned delightedly. "Excellent." The boom of his voice made AJ jump. "I look forward to our time together, Miss Moore." He drained his wineglass and stood. He stepped closer, and his smile widened when AJ leaned back. "Enjoy the library. I think we'll have plenty of time to unravel some mysteries together." He held her stare for a few seconds before he bowed his head and strode out, leaving her staring at her empty table setting.

Her body melted into her chair, her head falling back, forcing her to stare at the ornate ceiling. With anyone else, her cover story would be sufficient, but she'd never considered that his knowledge of the stones and the suggestion of time travel might lead him to a different theory about her.

She sat at the table for some time before a footman arrived to clear the room. His quick glance in her direction told her she had outstayed her welcome. "Can you tell me where the library is?"

"Yes. Just down the hall on your right. Two doors past the drawing room."

Any sense of foreboding she felt from the viscount vanished when she walked into the library. Floor-to-ceiling bookcases filled most of the walls, leaving only a smattering of places to show off exquisite pieces of art, including, she was sure, an original Rembrandt. Her mouth watered as she ran her hands over a side table and then a tall cherry clock, both Chippendale's. Her father could spend weeks in here and never come out.

She turned around and studied the library as if it were an immense living creature that required dissecting. Hundreds of books filled the room, and if she was going to find anything that led to the stones, she would need to be methodical in her search.

As she scanned for a starting point, her gaze fell on an old chess set sitting on a marble table on the far side of the room.

Sitting in front of the set, she studied it from different angles to determine its age. The mahogany board stood four inches high, inlaid with marble tile. The carved ivory pieces were finely detailed, a bit ornate, but not as elaborate as other sets she had seen from this era. She picked up the bishop and rubbed her fingers along the cool, shiny finish. An image flashed of the viscount, and she quickly set the piece back as if burned. Why did she think of him? Was he the bishop in this story and not the king? Maybe all the players weren't on the board yet.

Her thoughts turned back to her search. If she only knew what she was looking for. It wasn't as if she would simply find a book called *The Time-Traveling Stones*. And he wasn't going to simply leave the stones in some drawer. He'd keep them close to him. The whole idea of searching for an unknown object seemed daunting to the point of exhaustion. The chess set would be her starting point, and she'd move clockwise around the room. Hopefully she'd know what she was looking for once she'd found it.

After an hour, she had reviewed only a handful of shelves. There were so many marvelous books she found it difficult to stay on target. Knowing Letty would be waiting for her, she selected a title to take back to her room, sliding the book next to it on its side. This would be her starting point in the morning. She hoped Maire would be at breakfast. She felt light on her feet as she glided up the staircase. The investigation was on.

14

The next morning, AJ woke before Letty arrived. The skies were gray, but they couldn't daunt her spirits. It would be a busy day between spending time with Maire and renewing her search of the library. She had hardly slept, but she hadn't suffered the typical worry-filled sleep. This was the restlessness she felt when she was on a story. The last time she'd felt this excited was when she published her article about the McDowell house. Unfortunately, that story had led her to Finn, and then to this time and place. But that was old news.

The hour was too early for anyone but the staff to be up, and though she had permission to roam, she tiptoed down to the library. She wanted to avoid the servants, even Letty. This was her time.

She found her marking place where she had slid a book on its side. After placing it upright, she spent over an hour going through the shelves. At first, the search progressed quickly, until she found *Don Quixote.* Her father bought her her first copy of the Cervantes classic when she was in grade school, but she hadn't read it in ages.

Needing a break, she sat in front of the hearth where a housemaid had slipped in earlier to start a fire. She opened the first page and read the inscription: *To My Love, may you find peace from chasing your windmills. Yours in eternity, Eleanor.* Her fingers traced the words and she thought about Eleanor and her errant knight. Perhaps he was the original owner of the estate and had lost his battle with the windmills. She flipped through the book, reading short sections, before she laid the book on her lap and stared at the flames.

Sounds from the hallway woke her, and she bolted upright, *Don Quixote* falling from her lap. Damn. She had fallen asleep and instead of being early for breakfast, she'd be late. She stuffed the book into the pocket of her gown and ran back to the shelf to mark her place. When she stood back to see how far she'd gotten her shoulders slumped. There were so many books. This would take her days.

When she drew close to the dining room, she heard muffled voices and smiled. Maire had joined them. Patting back her hair and straightening her gown from her nap, she strode in with a smile. She held it in place even when the talking ceased at her entrance.

Maire's eyes were huge and round, like those of a deer with nowhere to run, but she managed a tentative smile for AJ. Glancing at the viscount, AJ caught the flash of annoyance, but whether it was aimed at her for being late or for her untimely interruption, she couldn't tell. He pulled at his sleeves, a habit that had begun to annoy her, and waved at the footman.

"I was wondering if you'd be joining us this morning." The viscount turned a disapproving stare in her direction.

Her smile widened as she took her seat across from Maire. She knew to be careful with the viscount, but Maire emboldened her. It appeared Maire could use a reprieve from his attentions, and the desire to protect this woman surprised her.

"Sorry I'm late. I rose early and decided to spend time in your library. Then I dozed off in front of the fire."

"Excellent. Did you find anything interesting?"

She almost choked on her eggs at the viscount's veiled hint of a search, but he only meant the books. She sipped her coffee and slowed the flutter in her chest. "Yes, I found *Don Quixote*. It's one of my favorite classics." As soon as the words were out, Maire and the viscount flashed a quizzical look at her.

"It is a popular book, I agree. But I think it's a bit overstated to refer to it as a classic." The viscount leaned back as the footman removed his plate.

"Well, one person's tragedy is another person's comedy." AJ turned to Maire. "I'm glad you were able to join us."

"Me too. It can be lonely taking meals alone." Maire turned back to her plate when the viscount sighed.

"Always the martyr, our dear Maire."

The group turned silent as the women focused on their breakfast. The viscount lightly tapped his fingers on the table. The continued rapping, as soft as it was, reverberated like a wind-up clock ticking down to a final deadline, made only more nerve-racking by not knowing what type of deadline.

Maire ate sparingly, picking at pieces, moving food around like some errant child refusing her supper. AJ wasn't sure if this was Maire's attempt at fighting her captivity, or if she always ate like that. AJ had obviously walked in on something that had put the two at odds, possibly more so than usual. Whether in support of Maire or due to her own lack of appetite, she pushed her own food around and focused on her coffee.

The tapping stopped, and both women laid down their forks, their gaze flickering to each other before dropping back to their plates.

"I'm afraid I'm going to have to leave your charming company for a few days."

AJ wasn't sure whether to be excited or dismayed. With the viscount gone, she would have time to explore the east wing, but it also meant Finn wouldn't be returning for at least that many days. The viscount would want to be here for his return.

"Where are you going?" Her head bowed over her plate as she returned to playing with her food. The possibilities of learning more of the stones played tug-of-war with a touch of claustrophobia at being locked away. The silence interrupted her inner thoughts, and she raised her head to see the viscount sitting back, cup in hand, staring at her. She wanted to glance away, but refused to back down from the man.

"I'm sorry. That must have sounded rude. I didn't mean to pry." AJ forced an innocent smile before lowering her gaze.

The viscount set down his cup and waved for a refill. The man drank more coffee than she did, which would usually give him brownie points, but that would be a cold day. He waited patiently for the coffee and then contorted his face into a charming smile. With his handsome features and decent manners, one could easily be lured into his manipulations. He wore his masks well, which, to her, even without any real evidence one way or another, made her suspicious.

"It's no secret. I'm off to London for some business. I daresay the travel will be longer than the time I need to be there, but there's nothing for it. You'll have time to get better acquainted with our dear Maire."

AJ glanced at Maire, who refused to meet her eyes. For some reason, that shook her more than it should. She would have thought Maire would be happy to have the viscount leave. But why London? He had already sent Finn there. Did it have something to do with the stones?

"It seems Maire has lost her voice this morning." The viscount tossed his napkin over his coffee and stood. His face turned scarlet, and he stared at Maire. "Perhaps the two of you can work on regaining your appetites. Starvation will prove nothing and change nothing as to your circumstances. They are what they are. While I'm gone, you should have ample time to ponder that."

He strode out of the room without a glance at AJ. Bewildered by what just happened and sorry she had been late to breakfast, she slumped against the chair. She ignored his ominous parting words, not wanting to know what they meant. When she turned to Maire, her heart sank.

The young woman could have been a statue. She sat ramrod straight, hands in her lap, her eyes focused at some point above AJ's head. The only sign of being a real woman were the tears streaming down her face. After a long, torturous minute, Maire's attention returned. "I'm so sorry. I'm afraid I pushed too soon." Her posture remained stoic as she stood. With a quick glance at AJ, she started to say something but, thinking better of it, left the room without another word.

Being left alone at the dining table seemed to be a pattern at the manor. AJ waved to the footman and sat alone with her refreshed cup of coffee. She stared out a nearby window and watched the sky darken with a threatening storm.

THE RATTLE of a teacup and saucer woke AJ from her trance. Letty picked up the serving tray and left her to stare at her journal. There simply wasn't anything more to write, and she closed it, tucking it away in a drawer. She was bored. Most of her days were spent in the library, and though satisfaction filled her with how far she had gotten, she had found nothing. Another day at most was all she needed to complete her search. The odds were narrowing on finding any insight into the viscount or the stones.

Maire had disappeared after that last breakfast with the viscount, and AJ didn't know if she should try to contact her. Her only solace was her search of the library and the tiny treasures she discovered. If only she could take them home with her. But she had to be satisfied with taking the books to her room or the conservatory to read.

When the weather allowed, she spent time walking the gardens, mainly to give her eyes a break from the library and reading. She hoped to catch a glimpse of Maire but never did.

Letty insisted on AJ sticking with rituals, so she took most of her meals in the dining room, sometimes breaking for lunch in the library or conservatory. She started to fret about how she'd fill her days after she completed her search of the library. Although she felt alone, she knew the staff was watching her, which prevented her from finding a way into the east wing. And how to conquer that issue was foremost in her mind as she entered the drawing room at the end of the second day since the viscount's departure.

She stopped in her tracks the minute she spied Maire sitting on a divan, as if she had been waiting all afternoon for AJ to appear. Maire dressed in a royal-blue gown, her blond hair tied back, the soft strands flowing loosely behind her. Her impish grin seemed in stark contrast to her rigid posture.

"I'm sorry I disappeared on you. You must think me awful to leave you alone." Maire's tone sounded regretful, but something in her eyes told AJ she wasn't all that sorry.

AJ moved into the room and accepted a glass of wine from Barrington. "It's given me an appreciation of your long visit to the manor." She slid a glance to the butler before continuing. "I've spent most of my time in the library."

Maire patted the seat next to her in invitation for AJ to join her. Then she turned to the butler. "Barrington, I'm sure you have something to do other than hover over us. I assure you we'll be on our best behavior. There's only a few minutes before dinner."

AJ watched the short staring match before Barrington bowed his head and left the room with his normal disapproving frown. Maire waited for the door to close before turning her attention to AJ.

"The viscount does have an excellent library. I've been through it myself. It's much larger than the one in the east wing."

"There's a second library?" AJ's eyes widened. This could be her key to the east wing.

"It's more of an office, I think. The viscount spends a great deal of time in there, but I have limited access to the books. There's usually more time to spend in there when he hunts or has guests for longer than a day."

"Do you think it would be all right for me to see the books there?" AJ caught Maire's glance to the door. "I know there are more than enough books in the main library, but it would be a treat."

"It's possible, I suppose. Just a short visit." Maire stared at her as she said the words. There was an expression on her face as if everything she said held some double meaning, and AJ had missed the CliffsNotes.

She decided to play a hunch that Maire knew more than she was sharing. "Do you know where the viscount went?"

"I think he said London."

Maire's innocent response spoke volumes to AJ. She couldn't count how many times her interview subjects tried this same maneuver. If the woman didn't have a habit of disappearing, AJ could take a subtler approach, but she grew tired of the word games.

"It's just us two women here, Maire. I don't know why you're here, but I have no intention of being here that long. I'm just trying to figure out what's happening." Now that the words were out, AJ sat back and took a sheepish posture.

Maire didn't move, her face as undisturbed as a clear mountain lake. Without a word, she drifted to the side table, the folds of her gown clinging to her slight frame. Opening a decanter, she sniffed and poured a dark red liquid into a glass. She took a sip and nodded before pouring two generous glasses, handing one to AJ before taking her seat.

"If we're going to be coconspirators, we should get better acquainted." She took another sip and released a long, low sigh. "I was on my way to London. It was my first long trip away from home, and I had been planning it for months. My home is in Ireland, so most wouldn't travel to London unless for some business. If you need a bigger city for something, Dublin would suffice for all your needs. But London is the center of high society, high fashion, and everything modern."

"Were you traveling alone?" AJ didn't want to interrupt, but she wanted to get to the good part before Barrington returned.

"Oh no. It's not proper for an unmarried woman to travel alone. I was with a distant cousin who lives in Dublin but has occasion to travel to London once or twice a year. He was taking his sister for her second visit, and I..." Maire stopped as she thought of her next words. "I guess you could say I encouraged dear Sean into taking me along."

AJ caught the twinkle in Maire's eye as she recalled her manipulation of her cousin. A brief concern flashed through her. Was she being manipulated? It seemed under what she thought was a timid rabbit hid a hawk.

"But you never made it to London?"

"No. I never did. We had just arrived in England and traveled only a few miles before stopping at an inn for the evening. The viscount's men came while we ate dinner. It was a small village, and there was no one that could stop them from taking me."

Maire stopped. She took a deep breath and shuddered, almost splashing her wine.

AJ reached out and touched Maire's arm in encouragement. Her first days of waking up and finding herself two hundred years in the past, removed from everyone and everything she knew, rushed over her. For the first time, she understood a bit of Maire and her need to disappear.

"All I remember as I was being dragged away from my family was a letter being given to Sean. Then I was hurried into a coach and brought here." She grabbed AJ's hand and held it. "I was escorted to a room and locked away for the first couple of days. Eventually, my dungeon became by refuge."

"It's not quite a dungeon."

Maire's tone hardened. "A dungeon has many forms when you're being held against your will." AJ tried to pull back her hand, but Maire held tight. Then her face softened. "But you are correct. We could be sleeping on cold stone instead of in a warm bed, so that is something to be grateful for."

AJ shivered at the thought and hoped the woman was being overly dramatic. "Did the viscount tell you why he took you?"

Maire released AJ's hand as she relaxed against the sofa and closed her eyes. "It was two days before I was escorted to dinner. I had been given all my meals in my room, never allowed to stray." She glanced at AJ. "There are days when I wish I never left my room. And even after all this time, there are times when I still don't."

"Like the last couple of days."

"Aye."

Almost two years without knowing your future. It was no wonder Maire lapsed into bouts of depression. She was right to think of this place as a dungeon when her freedom was withheld. Giving herself an internal shake, AJ refocused. "So what happened at dinner?"

"That was when I was introduced to the viscount, and he told me I was his house guest. He said my brother owed him a great deal of money that he was refusing to pay. Until the debt was clear, I was to remain his guest."

"That's horrible. Is that legal?" AJ's eyes almost popped out of her head. She couldn't imagine someone actually being kidnapped for a debt. But the worst part was her own brother leaving her here. Not even Adam would do that.

Maire shrugged. "Legal is whatever you can get away with. We are from Ireland. The English aren't too concerned about our rights. And the viscount has friends in very high places." Maire's smile turned wicked. "Or so the man continues to tell me when I'm not on my best behavior."

Before anything more could be said, Barrington announced dinner. Their conversation turned to trivial matters with the staff so close. Maire led the discussion with the aplomb of a hostess, never speaking of herself or AJ. They drank more wine and found a common interest in books. As the wine flowed, Maire explained her need to find a hobby to keep herself busy. And AJ discovered the loving hands that grew all the orchids she had seen in the conservatory.

"They're so beautiful."

"The orchids are the closest thing I have to friends." Tears shimmered and Maire blinked them away. "Until you."

AJ nodded as she pushed her own tears away. How lonely this woman must be.

Maire stood. "Enough self-pity. And I think we've overstayed our time. The staff needs to clear the room."

Both women stumbled a bit as they stood. They held on to each other, laughing as they left the dining room with Barrington's annoyed gaze following them out.

"Should we go to the library?" Although her head swam with too much alcohol, AJ wasn't ready to be alone.

Maire shook her head. "All in good time." She left AJ at the staircase and disappeared through another room.

AJ wanted to follow but navigated the stairs instead, smiling to herself at how much she had drunk. The last time she drank this much was on Stella's patio the night she made amends for keeping Finn a secret from her. The thought had sobered her by the time she reached her room.

After Letty left her for the evening, AJ stood in front of the window. Soft shadows played against the courtyard fountain, lit like a spotlight by the full moon. Her thoughts drifted to Finn, and she wondered, wherever he was, if he gazed out his window at this same moon. She missed Ireland. She'd never thought she'd say it. Even though she worried about home, she had never felt fear.

Listening to Maire's story, AJ questioned her status here. Was she a guest or a captive? The fact the viscount didn't care how much time the two women spent together rang alarm bells. She rubbed her arms as a chill brushed against her.

The temperature in the room seemed to have dropped five degrees. She added a log to the fire Letty had started, but she knew it wouldn't warm her. She pushed the linen bed drapes aside. A folded note was tucked partway under her pillow. With her heart racing, she crawled into bed and pulled the bedside lamp closer. A shudder ran through her, but it wasn't from the cold. Her excitement built. Maybe Finn had found a way to reach her.

She tugged the covers up and rolled to her side so she could get better light. Her fingers ran over the wax seal, and bending the note into the light, she saw the filigree M stamped into it. The M had to be for Murphy. Her heart pounded as she gently pried the wax seal open. She wondered how Finn managed to sneak a letter to her and knew instantly it had to be Letty. The young girl had no love for the viscount and could probably be bribed.

She reread the short sentence several times before dropping the letter next to her. Tears sprang from nowhere, and she fell back against the pillows. She let them fall. How could she be both happy and sad at the same time? True sorrow filled her that Finn had not sent word to let her know how he was or when he would be returning. But she couldn't stop the rising knowledge that she wasn't alone. Someone else knew what she knew. She laughed out loud. Part of her secret was out there. More than just Finn and the viscount knew something of the truth.

Picking up the letter, she read it again, searching for hidden clues in the few short words. There was nothing there but the simple truth and she ran her fingers over the note: *I know about the stones.*

Five simple words that opened up new possibilities. At the same time, the note spelled out the danger the stones represented if the author didn't want to speak the words out loud. She checked the signature, just the initial *M*. That could only be one person: Maire. She extinguished the lamp, laid her head on the pillow, and smiled. Maire would be her salvation.

15

Finn stood inside the door of the dark and smoky gaming room. He smelled the money mingled with more exhilarating aromas of tobacco and perfume, and he smiled, remembering his first days in London as a younger, wilder version of himself. He'd learned many lessons in this place, and his smile broadened as one of the young hostesses sauntered by. Yes, many things. It had been months since he'd sat at a table, and he yearned to put his idleness to use. But other matters came first.

He arrived in London a few hours earlier, tired from the two-day journey from Waverly Manor. At least the weather had been on his side. After eating a quick meal in his room, he fell onto the bed. His meetings would require alertness and very late evenings.

Finn recognized many of the faces as he strode through the gaming room, even after all this time. But his singular focus remained on the door that blended into the oak paneling on the far side of the room. It was a busy night at the club, something else that never changed. As Finn merged into its depths, the comfort of the place enveloped him like an old familiar cloak. A few men beckoned him to their table. He smiled and nodded as he passed.

A big man, much larger than Finn, stood at the door, staring with an unsmiling face. He seemed out of place dressed in formal coat and breeches, chafing under the tight cravat, yet he suffered stoically. His close-cropped hair, unusual for the times, emphasized the dominant forehead and round cheeks.

Finn stopped in front of him, matching his stare as if sizing him up, wondering if he could take him—it had been years since he'd made the attempt. After a few tense seconds passed, a crease of a smile turned at the edges of the man's lips, followed by a chuckle from Finn.

"You're a bloody door monitor now?" Finn reached out to grab the man in a bear hug, but the big man beat him to it, encasing Finn with his bulging arms. They tightened to the point of breathlessness, and Finn was pleased they were on the same side.

"Security. Better pay," the big man said, stepping back and letting Finn catch his breath. There was a twinkle in his coal-black eyes. "You weren't thinking you could take me were you?"

Finn rubbed his arms, trying to get the feeling to return. "I haven't forgot the last lesson. It's good to see you, Lando."

"When I heard it was you, I didn't believe it. Ghosts don't rise from the dead, I said. But they assured me it was true."

Finn patted the man on his back as Lando opened the door to let him pass. "No ghosts here, my friend, but we may meet some before this is done."

Lando grunted as he shut the door behind Finn.

AJ PUSHED the thick drapes back from the window and blinked at the bright light that hit her. Another day full of promise and a new lead. The letter changed everything. The stress from the last few days melted away with the knowledge that someone else knew about the stones. Maire's suggestion of them becoming coconspirators made perfect sense in combination with the letter.

She dropped on to the sofa and pulled a blanket around her. What she'd give for a huge mug of coffee. She pulled up her feet and hugged her knees to her chest. There was one last portion of the library to search, but it all seemed pointless if Maire had the information she needed. The sensible course would be to wait until breakfast and find out how much Maire knew.

The biggest question was how Maire knew of the stones. An unsettling thought occurred to her. Maire had been a guest of the viscount for a long time. Maybe they were working together. She snickered at her own stupid thought. No one could miss the loathing Maire showed for the viscount. The woman might be manipulative, but the greatest actress on earth couldn't disguise the current of animosity running between them. Many people missed the subtleties—the quiet touches, the hidden glances, or the way people moved to either avoid each other or get closer.

As a child, AJ loved antiquing with her father, but she would get bored and find a place to read. Many times, she would watch people and pretend she knew what they were thinking, or what they were saying to others when they were too far away to hear. She grew adept at reading people and relied on these visual cues in her investigations and interviews. There was no question Maire despised the viscount, but that didn't answer the question of how she knew of the stones.

She continued staring into the empty hearth when Letty entered the room. "Good morning, Letty."

Letty gave a half smile. "This is the second morning you've been up before me. Do you need me here earlier to start a fire?"

"Heavens no. I can add wood to the fire. I've just been eager to get up and start my day." She turned to Letty. The girl showed no sign that she'd left the letter. It would be safer to confirm the letter came from Maire before saying anything.

Letty's smile broadened. "That's good, my lady. It should be a nice day for the gardens."

"I agree, and I'm starving. Do you think it's too early for breakfast?" Tossing the blanket aside, she popped up to get a start on her plan.

"The viscount prefers his breakfast earlier than most, so the kitchen should be ready. I can see to it when we're done here."

After dressing, AJ hurried down the staircase and thought of stopping in the library, but she was too eager to see Maire. She ignored the first hint of disappointment when she found the dining room empty. It was too early. But when she had finished her breakfast and more cups of coffee than she had drunk in weeks, she grew agitated. Maire still hadn't made an entrance. The woman was flightier than a bird.

Doubt about who'd sent the letter crept through her. It had to have been Maire. A servant wouldn't have sent it, not with the wax seal. Unless someone used Maire's seal as a cover. She shook her head at her cloak-and-dagger thoughts. If Maire was in hiding again, AJ would return to the library to complete the last of her search. Then she would find a way to get to the east wing, with or without Maire's assistance.

After an hour, the last of the library had been scoured, resulting in nothing more than three more books to add to her reading collection. Holding the books in her lap, she viewed the library from a different perspective, but if there was anything here, it was well hidden. She startled when Barrington quietly entered carrying a sliver plate. He bent slightly as he lowered the plate to her.

"A letter for you, Miss Moore."

AJ's fingers shook as she picked it up. Her first thought was of Finn, until she saw the wax seal. It must be Maire.

"Thank you." She waited for him to leave before gently breaking the seal.

She almost laughed out loud when she read the simple sentence: *Please do me the honor of sharing lunch in my sitting room, east wing.* It was signed by the single *M*. This would be a good day after all. She scampered back to her room and made notes in her journal. But that still left another hour before lunch. Unable to focus on reading, she paced the room like a caged lion.

Grabbing her wrap, she returned to the gardens, allowing the smell of honeysuckle and the variety of colors to soothe her. Finding a secluded bench, she closed her eyes and offered her face to the warmth of the sun, her body relaxing to the trill of a warbler. Her mind drifted, releasing her memories to feel the spray of the ocean on her face, the salty breeze rustling her hair, and if she turned her head just right, she could almost hear the gulls.

FINN STARED at the results of his roll of the dice—eight. A wicked grin slipped across his face as he readied for the next roll. If this had been poker, the men at the table would assume his grin was a tell. In this game of Hazards, he was sure a few of them were positive his leer gave him preternatural insight into the next roll.

The truth was he liked to smile. It came naturally to him, and sometimes he couldn't help himself. He discovered early, especially when he was young and brash, and being from Ireland, his smile could make most men uncomfortable, and he used it to his advantage.

Tonight, his grin simply reflected a man comfortable in a setting he could control. A place that provided shelter for him at the times he needed it most—and an avenue to gain some wealth. His luck with gambling helped him during his time jumps. With his expertise in the complexities of Hazards, he found the more modern and simpler version of Craps an easy way to line his pockets. The gaming room was also where he had won the *Daphne Marie*. He could care less about the sizable winnings being added to his account tonight; he was enjoying the sense of coming home.

He studied the two men still at the table with him. The man on his left was older, at least two decades his senior. A monocle enlarged the man's eye, like a mad scientist in one of the old black and white films he had seen during his travels. Finn shook his head remembering the first time he had seen a cinema, and then on his next jump, a television. Old Doc Smythe would certainly fit into one of those tales. The man no longer practiced medicine, not in the truest sense, but he was an asset when you needed someone patched up. He never had a talent for the dice, although Finn had to admit, the man had improved his luck since he'd last seen him. And he suspected Smythe had a newer monocle that made his eye appear maniacal on purpose, finding entertainment value when he turned it on an unsuspecting competitor.

Finn didn't know the man on his right, who was about his own age. From what he had learned, the man came from aristocratic lines but had spent hard time at sea and in the king's army, wanting to gain his own experience rather than hearing about it from others. That earned the man some respect, but Finn would need to see him in action to confirm the assessment, and part of that was being played out at the table. The man's winnings had been up and down all night, and he stuck with the mark of rolling sevens, a fairly safe bet. But the man showed impressive stamina. He'd been at the table as long as Finn had. The man's name was Cutworth, but his friends called him Cutty, and he would someday be an earl. Finn smiled again. It was good to make friends in all the right places.

He passed the dice to Smythe and turned his gaze to another man who had entered the room and strode toward his usual table at the back of the room. Without making any sign that he took interest in the man, Finn nodded at the bookkeeper to close his account. He slapped the backs of both men, his grin sincere.

"It's been a good night, gentlemen, but I think I need a break."

"Dammit, man, you still have no decency. Now is no time to walk away. We have a streak going." Doc Smythe growled and sneered at two other men who joined their table.

"And now the man plans to take his luck with him and leave us to fate," Cutty added, rolling the dice in his hand over and over.

"You've had all night to watch me. If you haven't learned how to tame the dice by now, there's nothing more I can do for you." Finn stood and winked at Cutty. "Besides, you've been doing well. Stick with your instincts." He nodded at the two new men and turned away.

"Always was an insufferable bastard. Glad to see you haven't changed, old man," Smythe yelled at Finn's departing back. Finn raised his hand to signal he had heard the compliment.

He stood at the bar and ordered his first Irish whiskey of the night. He drank slowly and watched the man who had settled at the back table, his two bodyguards casually playing cards next to him. His tall, lean frame, expensively tailored in black, accentuated his raven-colored hair and blanched face. When he spoke, as he did with the old man who sat at his table, his hands moved gracefully through the air as if he were conducting the string section of an orchestra.

After a few minutes, the old man nodded and bowed before leaving the table. The raven-haired man turned his gaze on the next patron and fluttered his hands, pointing to the open chair next to his guards, who continued their card playing while keeping watch on the room.

To many men, the man appeared to be a dandy who relied on his men to keep him safe from thieves. Finn knew that was a deception many men learned the hard way. This man, whom

Finn knew only as Thorn, was an expert swordsman, graceful and elegant as he sliced men down. Though useful in close-quarter fighting, the man was worthless with a musket.

A second glass of whiskey arrived, and Finn drank slowly as he waited for his turn with Thorn.

16

Following a footman, AJ discovered the way to the east wing. It wasn't as far away as she'd imagined as they weaved through a formal living room and another drawing room to arrive at a second foyer. She didn't know where the door to the outside led but made a mental note to investigate when time permitted.

Another grand staircase led to the second floor. As she ascended, she caught a glimpse of a study just off the entryway. The room was pure masculine, with burgundy chairs and a dark cherry desk—this had to be the east library. She turned her attention to the hall that greeted them on the second floor. It seemed longer than the one in the west wing, but she couldn't be sure. The estate had been built for a family with plenty of children in addition to accommodating visitors and hunting parties. She shivered, thinking of the manor full of Lady Osbornes and Dame Ellingsworths.

The footman stopped at the second door from the staircase and knocked, then moved away to let AJ wait for the reply.

"Come in."

AJ walked in and her mouth gaped open. The room could fill

half her apartment back home, and it mirrored the opulence that spread throughout the manor. The light colors of the walls and furniture softened the tone of the chamber, enhanced by the warm summer air filtering through the open French doors. A huge bed occupied a good portion of the left side of the room, the peach-and-cream gossamer drapes catching a light breeze. The delightful scent of lavender and mint tickled her nose, but she couldn't determine if the fragrance had drifted in from the garden or from carefully placed sachets.

Two light-cherry armoires, a spacious dressing table, and a tall free-standing mirror filled the space around the bed. The rest of the room centered around a spacious sitting area complete with a lounging sofa. AJ glimpsed a portion of the balcony that must overlook the gardens, and she understood how Maire could consider this room a refuge.

Maire sat at a table near the French doors, and the light from the balcony cast a glow about her. A stronger breeze wafted through the room, and the lavender was displaced by the heady scent of roses, the smell so strong, they must be planted directly below the balcony. A flash of Stella's garden dimmed AJ's enjoyment of the moment until a clatter of china dissolved the nostalgia. Food trays filled the table, and Maire poured tea before turning a smile on AJ.

"I'm sorry I missed breakfast. I was so hoping you could join me for lunch. I think the private setting is more agreeable."

AJ took her place at the table and watched Maire, unsure how to respond to her formal greeting. It was just the two of them. The thought was barely formed when the door opened and a footman entered with another tray. He set it down and positioned himself to one side of the room. She caught a flash of irritation from Maire as she fussed with the cream and sugar and rearranged plates.

"That will be all," Maire said. "I think the two of us can handle a few sandwiches and biscuits."

The man hesitated, unsure what to do, and Maire stopped her activity to raise an eyebrow at him. A second later, he nodded and retreated from the room.

Waiting another second after the door closed behind him, Maire let out a long sigh. "I wasn't sure that was going to work. The valets and footmen, along with Barrington, seem to have orders to watch us very closely."

"More so than usual?"

"Oh yes. I've seen quite the change in them since your arrival." Maire studied AJ. "You must be very important. It seems the viscount doesn't want us alone for too long." Maire uncovered the food trays and placed sandwiches onto plates. "At least not without knowing what we talk about. So we must be very careful from now on."

"Because of what we have to talk about."

"Because of what we have in common. The stones."

Dozens of questions swam through AJ's mind while she tried to put them in order. She didn't know which one to start with, then decided to remain quiet. *Let Maire tell her story, and the questions will fall into place.*

Maire picked up the finely cut sandwich. "Let's eat first. We have plenty of time. I understand it could be another day or two before the viscount returns." Taking a bite, she closed her eyes as she chewed, releasing a soft sigh. "I have been waiting for the viscount to leave so I could make my own requests for meals. He even chooses my food for me, as if I'm a child. Then he wonders why I don't eat much."

She paused to sip her tea. "I have found some friends among the staff, but only a few. Their first thought is for their job, but they have no loyalty to the viscount." Shrugging, she picked up a different sandwich. "They need the work, so they stay. I think on some level, they enjoy helping me in trivial things."

"Like letting you select your own meals, or delivering discreet letters. I assume Letty is one that can be trusted."

Maire grinned. "Exactly. Now try one of the cucumber sand-wiches. It's not so much the cucumber but the herb spread."

AJ stared at what seemed like an idiotic idea for a sandwich. But once she nibbled the end, she almost crooned as she polished off her portion. "Okay, that was better than I thought."

"Good. So try this one next. I find the cream cheese blends well with the meat."

After consuming more sandwiches than she thought possible, AJ sat back with her cup of tea. "Why can't you find a way to leave while the viscount is gone?"

Maire's face darkened. Picking up her tea and a plate of biscuits, she led AJ out to the balcony. She placed the china on a table and leaned against the rail, breathing in the scents of the garden. Standing next to her, AJ watched her features relax, but she didn't seem ready to talk.

AJ turned her face to welcome the sun as it seeped into her bones, invigorating her need to return to the subject that lay between them.

Maire didn't make her wait long. She nodded toward the garden. "Do you see that building in the far back of the gardens?"

She had seen it when they'd first walked the gardens and assumed it was used for maintenance. "What is it?"

"I call it the barracks, but I imagine it was designed as a private residence for guests when the manor was used as a hunting lodge."

The warmth of the balcony couldn't prevent the shiver that slid over AJ. "And who uses it now?"

"The viscount's guards."

AJ's face paled.

"His armed guards. He has a fair number of them. Some travel with him, while the others remain behind. They're usually well hidden, but forever watchful. All very sophisticated."

"That's why no one saw you when we first arrived?"

Maire nodded. "Take a seat. Let me get the teapot." When she returned, she placed biscuits on the plates and refilled their cups. "The men don't usually come into the manor, but if the viscount wants to ensure my silence, he places a man or two at my door." A wicked smile filled her face. "I suppose that's why he doesn't entertain as much as he'd like to. When I first arrived, I was locked in this room for weeks while he entertained. Then he allowed me access to roam the east wing."

She shrugged. "But then he had to keep his guests in the west wing, forcing only the occasional visits. It was during one of his day-long hunts when I first discovered the letter that spoke of the stones."

AJ had been ready to sip her tea, but the cup rattled in its saucer as she dropped it back to the table. "What do you know?"

Maire's eyes lit up with a hint of mischief that AJ remembered from the first morning they'd met. "I didn't start out to snoop. There wasn't any reason for me to think to. I was just horribly bored, locked up in this room for weeks, and then granted access to only a few more rooms. I was never allowed to go outside except for this balcony, but it was off-limits when guests were here." She sat back and stared out at the gardens. "I needed some form of entertainment, so I went to the east library in search of books. I sometimes wondered if the viscount even considered the fact I might read."

Her abrupt laugh startled AJ. "He provided all forms of needlework, but I'm horrible at it, always have been. No one I know would ever knowingly hand me an embroidery needle." She teared up as she turned her attention back to the garden, lost to another time. Then she reached across the table and touched AJ's hand. "I'll never take my family for granted. If I ever see them again."

AJ squeezed her hand. "You will. We'll find a way."

Maire smiled, but AJ's stomach tightened at the odds stacked against them. She steered the conversation back to the letter. "So you went to the library?"

"The viscount left for a day hunt, so I went down to the library to find a book. His desk was there. I wasn't looking for anything, really. I would never have thought to find anything. But there was a letter partially tucked under a blotter." Maire blushed slightly. "I've been known to be a bit of a snoop as a child, and not feeling any loyalty to the viscount's secrets, I opened the letter."

AJ moved her plate and cup aside and leaned over the table, not wanting to miss a word. She felt like shaking Maire to move the story along, but managed to hold her tongue.

Maire's forehead wrinkled as if she were back in the study reading the letter. "It was a short letter commissioning the viscount to find a stone. He would be paid well upon receipt of the stone. It didn't say what kind of stone but made reference to another smaller stone that must have been sent with the letter."

AJ nodded. "I know of the large stone and one smaller one. It must have said more."

"The rest is more difficult to tell." Her face seemed paler than a few minutes before.

"Why?"

"Maybe difficult isn't the right word." Maire searched for a better word. "How do you feel about magic?"

AJ startled. Magic wasn't the word she would have used, but wasn't that exactly what she was dealing with? Was time travel just some form of magic? She would have assumed some scientific answer to her dilemma, but when she really thought about it, she wasn't sure which was any more believable.

She glanced at Maire, whose stare seeped into AJ's soul. A shudder broke her trance. "I guess I believe it a bit more now than I did growing up." She squeaked out a laugh. "I know that seems backwards."

Maire nodded. "The letter told the viscount that what he had previously been told of the stones was true. He was to follow the instructions that were wrapped together with the stone." Maire held AJ's gaze with a piercing stare. "The travel through time will not be exact, and the journey will be long, but must be taken to achieve greater reward."

AJ held Maire's gaze, her mind racing, before realizing she should appear shocked. And in some ways, she was. She couldn't understand how anyone could believe in time travel—certainly not in this century. "Time travel?" AJ's hysterical laugh seemed a perfect response.

"I thought it fantastical myself, but there have been words written about such things. Growing up Irish, you hear stories of the old world, but we all believed them to be tales from the fairies."

"Did the letter say anything else?" AJ hoped for a miracle. "You said something about instructions?"

"Aye, but there was nothing with the letter. I'm afraid that was all it said."

AJ found it difficult to hold back her disappointment. She didn't know how she felt about this, so she kept her behavior stoic, not ready to divulge her own secrets.

"I searched for the instructions but never found them."

"Who sent the letter?"

Maire smiled and shook her head. "A very good question. It was only signed with the letter S. It could be anyone."

She slumped. This told her nothing. The instructions might be able to tell her how to use the stones to get back. They had to. Lost in her own thoughts, she didn't realize Maire was waiting on her. "I'm sorry. You asked me something?"

Maire watched her intently. "Where are you from, AJ?"

She sat back, not expecting that question. "A town not far from Boston."

Maire nodded and leaned closer, her voice barely above a whisper. "But where are you really from? What time is it where you're from?"

Looking down at her hands, AJ searched for an answer. In all the rehearsals with Finn, neither of them had ever discussed the possibility of someone asking this question. He'd avoided the topic as if it were cursed. Now that someone asked, she found herself at a crossroads. If she told the truth and Maire couldn't be trusted, would they think her a witch or just plain crazy? It was one thing to talk of time travel, but to actually believe it created a completely different understanding of the universe.

Maire laid her hand on AJ's arm. "If I know of the stone and its claim to cross time, what do you think the viscount believes?"

A gasp escaped AJ's lips, and the balcony seemed to shrink in size, the manor closing in on her. She just couldn't say the words —to tell Maire she was from the future. "I don't know what you mean. I'm from America. I'm being truthful in that."

She racked her brain, remembering her dinner with the viscount and the way he looked at her. Her assumptions had made him a predator, but did he have the same question as Maire? He had to believe in time travel when Finn handed him the stones. What an idiot she'd been not to press Finn more and take the danger as seriously as he had.

AJ felt Maire's steady gaze, but she focused on the rough stones of the balcony wall. Last night, she had thought Maire to be her salvation, but she couldn't take that last step. Not yet.

Maire sat back. "I believe you are from America. The rest you will tell me when you are ready." She stood and picked up two wraps from a nearby lounge. She handed one to AJ. "Take this. The chill is back."

AJ wrapped the shawl around her and noticed the goose bumps on her arms. She was pretty sure they had nothing to do with the coolness of the afternoon shadows.

"Now come. We have time for a walk through the garden. After dinner, I'll show you the book I found that talks about the stones."

AJ's head bounced up. "There's a book?"

"Ah, that's better. I haven't completely lost you. Let's walk.

We'll worry about such things after dinner. I think you need time to digest what you've heard so far."

AJ hurried to keep up with Maire as the woman strode through her room to the door. She didn't want to go for a walk. She wanted to drag Maire back out to the balcony and see the book. As much as she wasn't ready to trust her, she knew she couldn't push Maire. The woman was like Stella in that way. AJ would have to play the game and let Maire determine the pace.

A realization came to her as she followed Maire down the hall. Part of her struggle with this century was how slowly everything moved. Her century fed off instant gratification, easy answers, and immediate access to information. She thought of Finn and how he'd dealt with the change over the eighteen months he'd traveled, making leaps through the Industrial Revolution, various wars, and finally, her time. He must have welcomed the quiet upon his return, happy to have left the noise and incessant chatter of the twenty-first century behind him. It must have been just as frustrating to live with that as it was for AJ to live without it.

Her thoughts were so focused, she bumped into Maire who had stopped in front of the viscount's study.

"We'll come back here tonight to see the viscount's books. He has a lovely collection you might find of interest."

Maire's formality returned, and AJ noticed the footman standing a few feet away. She nodded, and they continued through a second, less formal conservatory. Orchids overfilled this room as well. Maire never paused as she walked through the French doors and out into the growing shadows of the afternoon.

AJ thought Maire might talk about the book out in the gardens, out of earshot of the staff, but she had changed into the frivolous young woman the servants expected. The chatter droned on, and as much as AJ tried to pay attention, one question pushed everything else aside.

What the hell was going on in London?

The gaming lasted long into the night. Wisps of fog dodged in and out of shadows, and the sound of hooves from Finn's steed echoed through the alleys. He hoped he wasn't too late for his next visit, a place delicately balanced between the outskirts of high society and the edgier side of London. Questions of law abounded on both sides, but while the bending of the law on one side of the line was seen as just that, the same offense on the other side of the line usually resulted in a dark, dank cell or the end of a rope. Such were the days of the Mad King. But even with the lopsided justice system, the location of the house gave its clientele the freedom to come and go without fear of reprisals.

As Finn turned the last corner, the grand house stood out, taking up most of a city corner. Two stories tall, the house blended with those around it except for the extended lot filled with trees and a private garden, separating it from its neighbors. He grinned, seeing the lights ablaze in several rooms, and he chided himself for thinking it was ever too late to come here. Although it had been years since he'd last visited, he learned at the gaming tables that the house was busier than ever.

Climbing the stairs, Finn remembered with fondness, and a bit of humility, the first time he'd walked these steps. He had been brash, headstrong, invincible, and the visits to this house had brought him down a few pegs before building him back up.

The front door swung open before he had time to knock. A hefty man wrapped in a riding cloak and tall hat burst through, his face partially obscured to preserve his reputation. The young girl hanging off his arm laughed with giddiness and planted an affectionate kiss on the side of the man's face. The man turned to her, but seeing Finn on the threshold, he ducked his head, murmured a few words to the girl, who laughed even louder, and sprinted down the stairs to a coach that miraculously appeared as the man hit the sidewalk.

The girl stopped laughing as soon as the man was out of earshot and pouted at the new arrival. A spark lit her eyes as she gazed up at him. He grinned at her as he removed his top hat and felt the tug at his waistcoat as he was immediately hauled inside.

He laughed at her eagerness. "Is Madam LaGrange available?"

Disappointment marred her face. "Yes." The sigh was deep and dramatic. "But she hasn't taken any new clients for quite some time."

He simply nodded. She shrugged and led him to a well-appointed parlor. The room had changed over the years. Possibly a different color, and the furnishings were new, the artwork more expensive. Things were going well for her.

"Well, if it isn't Finn Murphy, as I live and breathe. I thought I'd never see you again." The long auburn hair framed a porcelain face with deep emerald eyes and a pouty mouth that drove most men a little crazy. There had to be Irish blood coursing through those veins, but she always denied it. She carried no hint of an Irish accent and swore to be English through and through. He knew better.

"How have you been, Maude?" Finn welcomed her into his arms and gave her a kiss.

"We heard you were dead." Maude stepped back and gave him a slow perusal.

"I've been hearing that a great deal." Now that she was closer, he could see the age hidden behind the makeup, the fine lines and shadows. But it suited her, and he was pleased she'd worked her way out of taking on clients. He swept his arms around the room. "Business is good."

"Yes. But let's not spoil the reunion with that kind of talk. Let's go to my rooms, and we can catch up without so many ears."

Finn watched another man half stumble down the staircase, another lovely beside him, holding him up. Finn laughed at the sight.

Maude yelled, "You make sure the judge gets down the stairs and into his coach in one piece. You hear me, Fancy?"

"Yes, mum." The nasally voice was strained by her exertions.

Maude took Finn's arm as she lead him up the stairs. "Now tell Maude how I can help you."

THE SUN TANGLED with the fog as the carriage rolled to a stop in front of the gentleman's club. A footman jumped down and opened the door for the viscount, who stepped from the carriage like royalty. He pulled his cloak around him and surveyed the busy street, searching for anyone he might know before turning for the stairs. Halfway up, he saw a shadow cross the steps. His face pinched when Finn stopped in front of him, his expression menacing. What were the odds in all of London?

"What are you doing here?" The viscount stood taller and squared his shoulders, but nothing could compensate for being a couple of steps lower on the stairs.

"You remember. That wild-goose chase you set me on."

Finn's wicked grin sent a chill through the viscount, but he held his ground, wanting to take a step up, but the bastard blocked the path. "The information was good when I gave it to you."

"And you still can't tell me who gave you the information?"

"No." The viscount looked around. "What are you doing at the club?"

"I'm a member."

The viscount tried to hold back his surprise. "Well, that's splendid."

"What brings you to London?"

"Just a minor inconvenience. I had no choice but to tend to it personally." The viscount stared at Finn before releasing a slow smile. "We should discuss it more thoroughly when you return to Waverly. Perhaps we can start back later today. I have a few errands I must attend to."

"Yes. I'm sure Miss Moore is wondering whatever happened to me." Finn nodded toward the coach. "I'm surprised you didn't bring her to London."

"I thought I might, but we may have missed you on the road."

"Of course. That makes sense."

He slid to the left to take a step, but Finn held his place. Forcing another smile, he kept his tone light. "So, have you been a member for long?"

"For some time."

The viscount's tone hardened. "Do you gamble, Mr. Murphy?"

"I think you know I do, Beckworth. And I have a ship to prove it."

The heat rushed to his face when he heard Finn's chuckle, and he used every bit of willpower he possessed to not pull the dagger he hid under his cloak. "This evening, then, here at the club." He pushed past Finn, his new plans taking shape before he made it through the door.

ALONE IN HER ROOM, AJ had nothing but time on her hands until dinner. She paced between window and hearth, questions surrounding her like a dust storm—scattered and unrestrained. Her journal lay open on the desk, but every time she sat to write she popped back up to stare down at the courtyard fountain. Here she was, on the precipice of unraveling the mystery of the stones, and she had to wait hours to hear more.

Tired of pacing and her whirling thoughts, she forced herself to sit and jot down a few notes. There was someone else who pulled the viscount's strings, but with just an initial, it might as well be sand in a sieve. If only they had the envelope with the wax seal, that might provide some hint. She sat back and brushed the feather of the quill across her chin. The letter implied the travel would not be exact. That didn't make her feel any better, but it did suggest why Finn had traveled through several time periods for eighteen months trying to find the stone necklace.

Finn didn't know who possessed the stone, which required renewed investigation each time he jumped. And from what little he told her, he seemed unable to control the timing of his jumps. Her heart sank at the thought. If that were true, her chances of jumping back to her time period would be slim. She had to get her hands on that book. And she needed to make a decision on how much to trust Maire.

Her sigh of relief was audible when Letty arrived to light lamps and dress her for dinner. She rushed Letty through the preparations, eager to leave the room.

When she walked through the doors of the drawing room, she wasn't surprised that Maire wasn't there. She continued her pacing, stopping long enough for Barrington to hand her a glass of wine before he disappeared to whatever kept him busy. As she sipped her wine, her eyes fell on a painting of a ship at sea, and her heart lurched as she remembered her time on the *Daphne Marie*. She turned to scan the other paintings and furnishings, the first time she'd been able to do so in this room.

Every time she visited the drawing room, she perched on a chair or couch, ready to spring like an overwound toy until dinner was called, never knowing what to expect from each engagement. Now she had time to peruse the treasures, and she lost herself in mentally cataloging the pieces. She was running her hand over a marble head that had to be a Bernini based on its Baroque design when Maire entered the room.

She wore a rose-colored gown with a low bodice, her strands of light hair piled high on her head, leaving a long lean neck and plenty of pale alabaster skin. AJ doubted she ever wore the dress in the viscount's presence, just another rebellious act under Maire's control.

Maire's smile lit the room, and she surprised AJ with a quick hug. "What a splendid day we had." She accepted a glass of wine from Barrington, who had followed her in. She sat on a sofa and patted the seat next to her. "I see you've noticed the Bernini. Fabulous, isn't it? As much as I hate the viscount, you can't fault him on his taste in art. Other than his decorating skills." She almost giggled as she took a sip and glared at Barrington, taunting him with her words of derision toward his employer.

His only response was to call them to dinner, but AJ thought she caught a smirk from him as Maire passed through the doors.

After their first course, AJ turned the subject to their afternoon discussion. "I've been thinking about our day. There's more I'd like to share about my travel here."

Maire's manner remained cool as she focused on her meal. "That's lovely. Perhaps we can have lunch in my room again. If we're lucky to have another warm day, we can sit on the veranda."

"I'm also looking forward to a tour of the study and the viscount's art collection."

"Oh, you'll love some of the works in his east library. I think we'll have some time after dinner."

AJ nodded and glanced at Barrington and then at the footmen, but if they found their conversation of any interest, they didn't show it. Despite their oblivious nature, she had no doubt they followed every word. The question remained whether the staff could see through their deception.

The smell of roast pork made AJ's mouth water as the footman placed it in front of her. A loud bang from the front entry made them all jump. Loud voices echoed from the hall, the sound of boots approaching.

Her spirits rose on the hope it was Finn marching down the hall, but it didn't feel right. Maire remained motionless, but her eyes widened as she stared at the door. The footmen glanced at each other, unsure of what to do, and when AJ noticed Barrington had disappeared, she fought the urge to flee.

Her hands gripped the chair, her knuckles whitening as the boots reached the door. She turned toward Maire, who responded with a shrug. She didn't know what was happening either.

The doors flew open as four men dressed in dark clothing and flowing cloaks marched into the room. AJ's alarm grew when she saw the scabbards under their cloaks as three of the men took positions around the room. The man in the lead stopped at the table and glared down at Maire. She stared up at him, unflinching, a severe disapproval on her face. It was difficult to discern whether she knew this man or had the heart of a lioness to show such defiance.

The man towered over the table. He was as big as a tank, and it wasn't hard to imagine the thick muscles bulging under the cloak. His rangy hair had been tied back, though most fell free, framing a scar that ran across his battle-hardened face, marring his forehead from left to right. When he turned his black eyes on her, AJ resisted crawling under the table. She tried to hold his stare as Maire had done, but was ready to concede when his hot gaze flashed back to Maire.

"What is so important that you disturb us during dinner?"

Maire's tightly controlled voice refused to give the man any deference.

"Word from the viscount. His plans have been expedited. You are to pack what you can into one trunk. We leave tonight." The man's gravelly voice boomed through the room, and his leg hit the table, making the china rattle.

Maire's laugh sounded forced. "The viscount told me nothing of this. We'll wait for his return."

"The viscount is not here to pamper you. He will meet us at the ship. Until then..." The man paused and looked at AJ before sneering at Maire, the effect thoroughly chilling. "You are under my protection and my orders. I advise you finish your meal quickly. It will be some time before your next one. The men will come for your trunk in two hours."

A cold chill ran through AJ. Leaving tonight. *A ship?* This must be a mistake. She raised her voice to mimic Maire, but her voice barely scraped a whisper. "And I am to stay and wait for Mr. Murphy?"

The man stepped toward her with his harsh gaze, and this time, she flinched, falling back into the chair. "No. My orders are for both of you." Turning back to Maire, he repeated, "Two hours. If you're not ready, my men will finish the packing for you." He gave an almost imperceptible nod to his men before marching out. One followed him through the door, but the other two stayed in position, one on each side of the room.

AJ started to say something, but Maire shook her head. Her own head dropped to stare at the cooling roast pork, the gravy congealing as the plate moved in and out of focus. She had never hyperventilated before, but she couldn't seem to catch her breath. Tremors snaked through her, and her mind whirled as she cursed Finn, wherever he was. Then Maire was next to her, her hand upon hers, tightening until AJ refocused on her.

"Let's get you packed first and then me. We'll do it together." Maire stood straight, her shoulders back and her head high. She gave Barrington a haughty stare. "Have some food wrapped for travel. I think the mood has spoiled our dinner."

He gave her a short nod, oblivious to the interruption, as if this type of thing always happened at dinner.

Maire strode to the door. Before following, AJ grabbed her full wineglass and swallowed it down. She eyed the remaining decanter, but turned to follow Maire with as much composure and regal air she could muster. The hall darkened around the edges of her vision as her sight grew fuzzy again. She took a few long breaths to steady herself.

They were halfway up the stairs before she let her fears escape. "I can't leave. My friend won't know where I went."

Maire hushed her and pulled her up the stairs to her room. The fire blazed, but it couldn't penetrate AJ's frozen state. Maire turned and grabbed her by the shoulders, giving her a quick shake, forcing her back to the present.

"I knew he'd take us to the ship, but I thought we had more time. Something must have happened to force his hand." Maire shook AJ again and smiled. "This is a good thing. The viscount is on the run."

The words penetrated the fog. *The viscount is on the run.* She searched Maire's face for understanding. "On the run from what?"

"From those in search of the stones."

They turned at the sound of a light knock on the door, and Maire placed an arm around her as it crept open. Letty stuck her head in, her eyes as big as an owl's.

"Come in, Letty," Maire said. "We need to dress Miss Moore for travel and get her trunk ready."

They spent the next half hour preparing AJ and her trunk, the task simplified by the fact she had few garments. Once AJ was dressed in her travel gown and cloak, they closed the trunk to leave for the men. AJ glanced once more around the room. She'd miss nothing from her time here. She shoved the fear back in its cage, locking it down before turning to follow Maire out of the room.

Letty reached for AJ's hand. She squeezed it and pulled the young woman along. The poor thing seemed more terrified than AJ, and she wasn't going anywhere. Her mind raced as they ran through the house toward the east wing. Where was Finn? He'd been gone for almost a week. Her gut wrenched at the thought that something might have happened to him. Tears blurred her vision, and she blinked them away. Who else was after the stones? Every time she had a plan, someone ripped it away. Her survival instincts kicked in, and she called upon her rock-climbing experience. If a path seemed impassable, you reevaluated the options. There was always a path if you took the time to find it. This time, she would have to dig deep. There was nowhere to run.

Maire's personal maid laid out several gowns for her to select. Having been at the manor for almost two years, it took longer for her to decide what to fit in one trunk. Needing to stay busy, AJ assisted Letty in folding and packing while Maire dressed. Once the trunk closed, the four women huddled on the sofa before the hearth, their hands clasped together. Though Letty had added wood to the fire, they inched closer, finding warmth in each other. No one said a word as they waited for the sound of the viscount's men.

The sweat from the horse released a sweet and pungent odor, forcing Finn to slow his pace. He had no desire to run his mount into the ground, but he heard the faint ticking of the clock running down as it chimed with the heavy breathing of the horse. There were many miles yet to cover and too much time to berate himself for falling for the viscount's ruse. He let himself get cocky thinking he had been getting the upper hand, but the viscount played him. More to the point—the man had simply outfoxed him.

He should have gone with his original instincts to leave right after his run-in with the viscount. But he hadn't finished everything he needed to accomplish while in London, and admittedly, he was curious as to what the viscount was up to. Discovering the man had left town hours before their scheduled meeting enraged Finn and left him one step behind.

Recriminations added to the long ride back to Waverly Manor. As much as he kicked himself for not leaving earlier, he was still alone in this phase of the mission. The viscount would have left a contingent of men at the manor, leaving him no way to get to AJ safely. He leaned over the great beast and whispered into its ear to move them along, promising rest. The sound of the hooves churning up soft mud beat a rhythm into Finn's conscience as he fought his inner demons against actions he couldn't undo.

THE STACCATO TAP on the roof of the coach mesmerized AJ, and her eyelids grew heavy as if weighted down by the heavy drops of falling rain. The rain had been only a mist when they'd left the manor, but the tempo increased the farther they traveled. The stress of the last few hours pressed on her shoulders, forcing her to slump against the seat, wanting nothing more than to crawl under a blanket and hope for a better morning. Her only comfort came from Maire, who sat across from her, her light blonde hair a beacon in the darkness.

They had said little to each other as they waited for the viscount's men to return. Maire shared what she knew of the man who had come for them. He was called Dugan, and whether it was his first name or last, she didn't know. It was the only name she ever heard him called. He came from the north and held a strong loyalty to the viscount. Maire had never seen any of the men question his orders. And unless the men wanted to witness the wrath of the viscount, the women were quite safe from harm. That hadn't made AJ feel any better.

She remembered the mention of a ship when Dugan marched into the dining room, but Maire had said nothing more while they'd waited in her room. If Maire knew where they were going, she didn't say, and no one had felt the urge to talk, especially with the men posted outside the door. They sat, holding hands, while their maids trembled with fear.

They weren't huddled long before a loud rap signaled Dugan's entrance, and he strode in, not waiting for permission to enter.

Two men followed him to retrieve the trunk. Dugan scowled

down at the women. He pointed to the young maids. "Get out and return to your own rooms. These ladies no longer require your service."

AJ pried Letty's fingers from her own and gave her a hug, whispering in her ear. "Thank you for everything, Letty. It will be okay. Just go to your room."

Tears streamed down the faces of both young girls, and they made a wide circle around Dugan before racing from the room. Only Letty peered back over her shoulder before disappearing down the hall.

"Let's go," Dugan barked.

Maire stood and gathered her shawl and cape, taking her time to draw on her gloves.

AJ cursed Finn. It seemed the reasonable thing to do. She could feel Dugan's glare drilling a hole in her back as she searched the room for where she'd dropped her cloak. Her movements were as slow as Maire's, but for a different reason. Maire refused to be rushed by anyone, regardless of how scary they were. AJ froze, her limbs simply refusing to cooperate.

Pulling her cloak tight, she gazed around the room. She'd missed her chance to gather more information about the stones, and Finn would never know where she had gone. With a side glance at Dugan, she tried to ignore the deeply wrinkled forehead that made his scar shine with intensity. Shoving her gloves in her pocket, she squared her shoulders and nodded to Maire.

Maire led the way at her own pace, die-hard to the end as they strolled down the stairs to the east entrance. AJ felt Dugan's hot breath behind her, an attempt to move them faster, but Maire never changed her stride. She appeared oblivious to the mist that circled them as they stepped from the manor, and she held her head high until someone assisted her into the carriage.

AJ fell onto the bench across from Maire. She had been tempted to sit next to her, to draw warmth and comfort from this woman who was apparently made of steel. Instead, she opened the curtain on the side window and peered out at the estate, which she had never observed from this nighttime perspective. It was breathtaking. Flickering candlelight lit the path to the entrance, and the wall sconces added a soft glow. Lights streamed from the windows, lending a deceptive view of home and family. She could see a loving family living here, the house filled with children's laughter and well-attended parties, the guests filling the drawing and dining rooms. The warm glow hid the stark loneliness of the current inhabitants.

As the coach drove off, she leaned toward the window, keeping the manor in view until the coach turned into the lane. The darkness enveloped them, and they sat in silence, wrapped in their damp cloaks and their own thoughts. She should be grilling Maire with her questions, but with the pounding rain and the wheels churning mud, she would have to scream to be heard. The darkness and the tempo of the rain performed their magic and lulled her to sleep.

The slowing of the horses woke her to a semidark coach. The rain had stopped, and she could almost hear Maire's soft breathing as she sat motionless, either unaware of the change in the horses' pace or just uncaring. Her eyes were closed, and she seemed years younger than the woman who'd stalked out of the manor only a short time ago. AJ leaned over and pulled the curtain aside to see a handful of dark buildings, seeming abandoned in the stark moonlight.

"We're coming to a town?"

AJ jumped at Maire's words. "I thought you were sleeping."

"Perhaps a little. I've been thinking about the viscount's plans, but the rocking of the carriage got the better of me."

Before AJ could utter another word, the coach rolled to a stop. Within seconds, the door wrenched open.

"Out. We'll stay here for the evening and then start early." Dugan held out a hand to help Maire step down and turned back for AJ.

Taking a deep breath, she took his hand, surprised at his gentle assistance, but she could feel the hardness of his arm and the muscles that rippled under her touch. She swallowed the bile rising from her empty stomach.

Dugan led them through the door of an inn. They marched swiftly through a common room where embers from a fire still glowed and up the stairs to the first door. AJ ached to speak with Maire, to talk through what was happening, but Dugan stopped her from following Maire into the room. One of the men took a position in front of the door, and all she saw was the back of Maire standing ramrod straight as the door closed behind her.

AJ was pushed into a room farther down the hall, and when she turned, a second man shut the door. No doubt his feet were planted firmly in front of it. They were trapped like rats, kept separated to dwell in their own miserable thoughts.

A fire crackled in the smoke-stained hearth, and AJ laid her damp cloak on a chair to dry. She gazed out the dirt smeared window, but it was too dark to see anything other than confirming the rain had turned to a foggy mist, blanketing the town. A cup of tea would have been perfect. No, a bottle of wine would be perfect, but she'd have to settle for neither. She doubted Dugan was as efficient as Barrington in those matters. A pitcher of water sat near the bed with a wash basin and a cup. The water quenched her parched throat, and she licked her lips, wondering how they had become chapped.

She carried the cup with her as she warmed herself in front of the fire. Her thoughts raced through the events of the day. Once again, as fate had turned in her favor with Maire's knowledge of the stones, it just as quickly dashed her plans with another turn of events. For the first time, she realized she had been kidnapped. There was no other word for it. And her next thought was of Finn. His absence festered, and for the umpteenth time, she wondered what errand the viscount had sent him on.

The tiredness seeping into her bones outweighed her concern

for the future. Unwilling to disrobe with Dugan's man right outside her door, she climbed into bed fully clothed. She pulled the thin blanket over her, and although she had placed several pieces of wood on the fire, she was glad for the warmth of her own clothing. As she lay on her side to watch the flames, the weariness descended, and she released her questions and fears. Except for that one last question that dropped into her thoughts before she drifted to sleep. Had Finn ever planned to return?

THE LAST ORANGE glow of the day settled upon Waverly Manor, casting its last shadows across the meadow and lake. As Finn walked his weary horse through the line of trees to the entrance, he could tell he was too late. There was a quiet emptiness to the place, void of the men he'd seen the first day he and AJ had arrived. He doubted AJ had known they were there—but he'd known. They were the sentinels protecting their malignant liege.

Finn handed his reins to the stableboy, issuing specific instructions to give him water before rubbing him down. He turned to the front doors, tired and hungry as the internal clock haunting him from London ticked down to its last beat.

Barrington opened the door before Finn reached it. The man's expression reflected his typical disinterest, and Finn wondered if anything ever excited the man.

"I've come to collect Miss Moore." Finn strode past the butler and stood in the middle of the entrance hall. His worst fears after seeing the manor were confirmed. If she was anywhere in this house, he would know it. He would feel it. Tremors of anger and then concern battled within him.

"I'm sorry sir, but Miss Moore left last night."

"Last night?"

"Yes. After receiving an urgent note from the viscount."

His boiling rage overrode his fears. Finn tried not to take his wrath out on Barrington, although the man's cool demeanor made it difficult. "And where did she go?"

"I'm sure I couldn't tell you, my lord. Will you be staying the night?"

Finn stared at nothing as the anger drained away. The viscount had sent word ahead and moved her. He must be meeting her at the coast, probably Plymouth. Finn could easily follow them, but his horse needed rest, as did he.

"I'd like to rest a bit before dinner. Then I'm afraid I'll need to leave as well."

"As you wish, my lord. Your room is as you left it."

The stairs seemed longer as he took each labored step, fatigue rolling over him. The discouragement at finding AJ gone hit him harder than he expected. He could have himself flogged or kick holes in the wall, but none of it would change the events of the last day or the last week. He couldn't think about anything right now, and he barely hit the bed before he was lost to slumber.

Two hours later, feeling somewhat restored, he sat in the dining room eating dinner alone with only the footmen and Barrington as company. He worked over a new plan as he finished his meal and, before leaving the manor, gave instructions to Barrington to have his trunk and carriage returned to Hensley's estate.

In the stable, Finn ran his hands over his horse, whose muscles rippled in anticipation of the next journey. As he gave his saddle a last check, he heard hesitant footsteps approach. He was surprised to see a slip of a housemaid partially hidden behind a post. He gave her his best grin to encourage her to come forward.

She stepped around the post, tiptoeing to where he stood and, with her head down, lifted her hands with a wrapped offering. "Something for your travels, my lord."

"You're Letty, is that right?"

Letty's head popped up, her smile wide and her brown eyes enormous on her tiny face. She nodded vigorously. "Yes, my lord."

"You saw Miss Moore leave?"

Her smile faded, and her head dropped. "Yes, my lord."

"Did she leave alone?"

Letty glanced around before shaking her head. "No. She left with another lady, my lord. The viscount had been gone three days before his men came and took them both."

Finn froze at the mention of two women. He truly had been an idiot on a fool's mission. The only positive out of this whole fiasco was the additional resources he'd garnered while in London. He felt the nudge at his elbow and gazed down at Letty.

She took a quick glance around before offering the package again. "There's a special treat along with some food to help ease your travel, my lord."

Finn had to lean down to hear the last part of Letty's statement, and then he gave her a warm smile. "Thank you, Letty."

"I hope you find everything you seek, my lord." Then she turned and vanished from the stable.

His smile turned to a grimace as he watched her disappear. He mounted his horse and was halfway down the tree-lined lane before Letty's words came back to him. She said she hoped he would find everything he sought, and there was something about a special treat in the package. He thought about her strange words before the realization hit him so hard, he almost smacked himself. Letty was AJ's maid.

He pulled the package from his saddle bag and carefully opened it. Dried meats, cheese, and some bread, the perfect meal for taking on the road. He didn't see anything special about it and was rolling it back up when he spied something within the wrapping. Prying the sheets apart, he found a folded note tucked under the bread. After he stowed the food back in his bag, he almost laughed at his trembling fingers. He instinctively took a quick glance around before opening the letter.

It was composed of only a few words, but they were enough to make him smile and laugh out loud. He urged his horse to a trot and tucked the letter into his breast pocket to keep it close to his heart. The words flashed through him again and again, written by a hand he knew so well and wasn't sure he'd ever see again. *We are safe. We head for Southampton.*

19

The common room of the inn bustled with activity, tables filled with travelers or locals eating and talking, the decibel level loud enough to wake the entire village. AJ stopped halfway down the stairs. After their rush through the room the previous evening, she assumed the inn to be mostly vacant. The smell of food made her stomach rumble, and she leaned against the railing searching for a familiar face. The guard in front of Maire's room had been gone this morning, and, scanning the room, she spotted her friend at a table close to the hearth.

Thank God for small favors. As tired as she had been, she hadn't slept well, and the fire in her room died halfway through the evening. She hadn't found the energy to drag herself out of bed to feed the flames, and instead, had curled into a tight ball to ward off the chill. Rolling her neck, she rubbed at the kink that wouldn't go away. At least she would find some warmth before climbing into the carriage.

Her personal guard nudged her to move, and she weaved her way through the tables to Maire who welcomed her with a smile. AJ didn't know how she did it, but Maire appeared rested, her cheeks rosy, not a hair out of place. She glanced down at her own rumpled gown and accepted the truth—she wasn't cut out for this century.

"Sit and have some porridge. It will warm you." Maire's eyebrows knitted. "You didn't sleep well."

As she sat, she noticed Dugan and his men a couple of tables over, close to the door. "No. I was exhausted, but it didn't seem to help."

Two bowls of thick porridge were dropped in front of them as an older woman, short and hefty, flashed by, dropping more bowls at a nearby table. The woman returned with two mugs of tea. It tasted bitter, but AJ savored the hot brew that warmed her.

"You still seem a little disoriented." Maire stirred her porridge, her eyes darting to the door between bites.

"Are you kidding?" AJ blurted out. She reined in her voice and peered over her shoulder. No one seemed interested in them, and Dugan's men hovered over their own food, ignoring their cargo. She finished her rant in a harsh whisper. "I've been abandoned by my friend, kidnapped by some crazy lunatic, and now I'm being transported to some unknown ship to go to some unknown place by what appears to be very dangerous men." She gathered her breath, knowing she had unloaded on Maire, but she couldn't seem to stop. "I had a horrible night's sleep, I can't get warm, and all I have for breakfast is some crappy porridge." She sank into her chair and stared at the bowl of lumpy cereal. "I hate porridge."

"So you're doing as well as can be expected." Maire raised her hand to the harried woman still racing from table to table. "At least the rain has stopped."

AJ laughed, the sound so unexpected and loud, she covered her mouth. The tension she carried with her since Dugan first arrived at dinner drained from her shoulders as if carried away by a strong tide. Her shoulders dropped, and she swallowed a spoonful of porridge before pushing it aside. "You amaze me. You deal with all this as if it's just another day."

Maire shrugged. "After eighteen months, there is no other

way, unless I give in to the madness. I learned long ago that I'm stronger than that." She leaned in. "I wasn't so accommodating in the beginning, but I have learned patience." Her lips twitched. "Something my family wouldn't have thought possible." She sat back, lost in thought before a sigh escaped. "You're strong. I had no one to help me. But you have me." She looked past AJ and grinned. "Ah, this should make you feel better."

The old woman set down a plate of eggs and sausage. "There you go, loves. Sorry. Your companions didn't think you'd want something so heavy before traveling. I'm glad to see you're made of heartier stuff." She gave them a nod before rushing off to the next table.

AJ's mouth watered, and her stomach demanded immediate attention. "God love ya, Maire." They both laughed as AJ dug in.

When she pushed her empty plate away, she turned a quick gaze toward Dugan before leaning toward Maire. "Do you know where we're going? Or how long it will take?"

"I heard someone mention Southampton before we left. I'm not sure how far it is, but I think we'll be on the road for two or three more days."

AJ groaned at the thought. "Do you know where the ship is going?"

"France."

"France? Why there?" Her perfect European vacation— England and France. Not exactly as she imagined it.

Maire's voice dropped. "I believe that is where the letter came from. I think it's the origin of the stones."

"Really? You think we're heading to where they first discovered them?"

Maire shrugged. "It's my best guess."

Before she could say more, the sound of chairs scraping across wood made them both glance at Dugan. He rose with the men and nodded to Maire. The men waited by the door, scowls on their faces, as Maire and AJ took a last sip of cold tea. In her usual defiant manner, Maire led the way as she sauntered to the front door, just another day on a pleasant journey. AJ slipped Dugan a patronizing smirk as she passed by, and he met her gaze with his disgruntled demeanor.

The weather had improved from the night before. The skies were still gray, but the clouds were high and puffy. The sun might show itself by noon. The town was nothing more than a tiny hamlet, and if it weren't for the heavily traveled road, AJ doubted the inn would survive.

Halfway to the coach, one of Dugan's men called out, "You, there. What are you doing?"

AJ's head shot up in time to see a tall man in a dark cloak running from the other side of the coach. He disappeared around a building with Dugan's men in pursuit.

"Hold. Let him go," Dugan yelled and walked to the coach. "Look it over quickly. We need to move on."

The men circled the carriage then shook their heads at Dugan, seeming to find nothing wrong. Dugan opened the door, once again the perfect gentleman as he assisted the women inside. AJ settled across from Maire and leaned over to peer out the window toward the building where the dark shape had escaped. Something tugged at her memory. There was something familiar about the shape, but whatever it was faded before she could bring it to focus.

A shift in the carriage made her turn. One of Dugan's men climbed in and gestured for her to move. She quickly plopped next to Maire, who reached out and grabbed her hand, giving it a light squeeze.

Maire whispered in her ear, "They're scared of us little women. They don't trust to let us ride alone."

Under normal circumstances, that would have strengthened her resolve, but AJ didn't feel very powerful. Yet she refused to avert her eyes or appear timid. She watched the man who was slighter of build than Dugan but who still held the same fierce expression. He also carried the mark of battle, a scar not quite as deep as Dugan's. It started just under his right eye and curved toward his mouth before disappearing into his beard. His eyes were a soft meadow green, and when he turned his gaze away from hers first, she lifted her head and smiled. Maire was right. They weren't comfortable with their mission, but what that meant, she had no idea.

FOR THE FIRST HOUR, Maire spoke more of London, but even she got tired of the game and soon fell silent. AJ had planned on questioning Maire about the *Book of Stones*, as she started to call it, but the man riding in the coach with them squashed that idea. The overnight tossing caught up with her, and try as she might, she couldn't keep her eyes open. The motion of the carriage rocked her as if she were a newborn infant in a cradle. A faint sound, like a soft squeak, beat a slow rhythm and lulled her to sleep.

She woke as the carriage slowed. Her view through the window reflected the same green hills and smattering of farms.

Maire started to wake when the coach stopped.

"We stop for a rest."

The voice made AJ jump. The man hadn't said a word this whole time, and his melodic tone surprised her, almost effeminate from such a roughened man. She wondered what had made him become a hardened mercenary. Without the scar, she imagined a smiling, jovial man with those docile eyes. Then he scowled and the image crumbled.

"This will be your last stop until after the pass. Make good use of it."

The village, if it could be called that, held a livery, a general store, and a friendly inn. The meal consisted of a hearty stew and dry bread. Now she understood why people wiped their bowls with the bread: anything to soften the hard crust. They were offered wine which AJ drank with relish. With any luck, it would put her back to sleep for the rest of the day's journey.

The men ate at the table next to them, and any conversation with Maire continued to be insipid. But shortly after the completion of the meals, the men left to prepare for travel. The women were told to remain at their table until Dugan returned for them. As soon as the men left, AJ jumped at her chance.

"I can't believe they're hovering over us. What do they expect us to do? Run away without transport or money?" AJ spat the words out, tired of being under their thumbs.

"I don't know. They seem concerned about something, but I don't know what. Perhaps someone follows us."

AJ sat up, excitement growing. Maybe Finn had returned, found them gone, and pursued them. Then her excitement deflated. She didn't know what one man could do against the six Dugan had with him.

"I had hoped we could talk about the book," AJ whispered.

Maire gave a quizzical look and then shook her head. "It's too dangerous with so many ears. Perhaps I can talk Dugan into letting us share a room tonight. Or maybe we'll have the coach to ourselves this afternoon."

Before AJ could respond, Dugan burst through the door. "It's time to move."

When they reached the carriage, AJ glanced at Maire and saw her disappointment reflected back when they saw their personal guard waiting at the coach. He helped them up and followed in behind them. The terrain shifted as they departed the tiny village. The trees increased and the trail became rockier as the road twisted its way over green hills, past a river or two, with aged oaks and birch guiding their way. After a few hours, the elevation increased and the trees became sparse.

The women attempted conversation, but Maire couldn't seem to find any enjoyable topic. The squeak AJ had heard earlier in the day persisted, and she listened to its dissonant melody, deep in her own thoughts. The excitement that Finn might be following faded away, replaced by concerns of leaving England without him. She had locked away her feelings for him after his abandonment, except when she slept. He popped into her head every night before she fell asleep and was with her before she opened her eyes in the morning. As angry as she had become with him, she still missed him, and rather than examine what that meant, she threw herself into her research about the stones.

The squeak grew louder, becoming an annoyance as it pierced AJ's concentration. She glanced at Maire and the man across from them, but neither gave any indication they heard the noise. Ignoring the sound that set her teeth on edge, she scooted to the window to watch the passing terrain, the farms more sporadic at this higher elevation. Occasionally, she spied a wondering herd of sheep and sometimes spotted their herder watching over their flock. When she turned back to her seat, she found Maire asleep and their guard staring out the other window.

She fidgeted between boredom and the inability to speak freely with Maire. Resting her head against the seat, she closed her eyes. What she would give for her phone, her Bluetooth and music to listen to—even Country. The ride turned bumpier, softly jostling her. The squeak of the wheel no longer bothered her, the sound like the humming of a clock, and soon she followed Maire into slumber.

It took Maire's shaking to wake her. She had been on her cliff back in Oregon, and Finn had been climbing with her. They had just reached the summit, rolling onto the grass, breathing hard from the exertion, and she turned her head. An involuntary tingle passed through her as she gazed at him. His dark green gaze smoldered, adding intimate meaning to the mischievous grin on his tanned face.

When she opened her eyes, she found Maire staring back, and she suppressed a shudder as a heaviness tightened her chest. She shrugged it off and pulled herself upright, brushing and tugging at her skirts that had ridden up.

"I think we've stopped for the evening," Maire said. "But I don't think you're going to like the accommodations."

"What do you mean?" AJ noticed their riding companion was gone, and she scooted to the window. All she could see were a few trees, rocks, and grass. A hill ran along the side of the road and nothing else. Bunching her skirts, she jumped to the other bench and peered out the window. The same scenery—no buildings, not even a simple cottage or outbuilding. "That can't be right. There's nothing here."

"I can't believe you slept through that squeaking wheel. It kept getting worse. They need to fix it, but by then, it will be dark. I don't think they'll continue on this path at night. It's too rough. They probably thought they had time to get through the pass before nightfall."

"Why didn't they fix it at our last stop? It's been whining since we left this morning."

"Has it? I didn't hear it. They must not have noticed or thought it would last."

"So we're supposed to spend the night out here? Why didn't they just go back to the last village?"

Maire shrugged. "From what I've seen, there's not many places on this road to turn around. We're going over a pass. It's quite rocky. And they're on a time table to meet the viscount."

AJ muttered under her breath, "Of course, it's all about him."

A half hour passed as the women sat in the coach, waiting for permission to exit. AJ wanted to walk around, but the men seemed busy and wouldn't want to waste time having to watch them. As if they'd wander off in the middle of nowhere.

She jumped when the coach door banged open.

"Out." Dugan's bark pushed AJ to action, and she almost stumbled on the step. He partially dragged them from the coach, his manners all but gone. The scar on his forehead flashed a deep red, his movements quick as he pushed them toward a rocky plateau set against the hill.

"Why are we stopping here?" Maire had stopped partway up the hill and refused to budge.

Dugan swore and let out a sigh, seeming to remember his duty and responsibility. "There's a problem with the coach. We've come too far to turn back. We'll overnight here while the men fix the wheel." He stopped, and as if an afterthought, he added, "We'll try to make you as comfortable as possible."

Their suspicions confirmed, the women picked their way over rocks to the plateau. It sat against a hillside that ran up for fifty or sixty feet. The other sides were open to the road, except for a few boulder formations that blocked the light wind. The other side of the road sloped up a gentler green hill supporting a couple of oak trees and more rocky clumps. She saw no farms nor sheep.

Turning back to their campground, she saw that a campfire had been started and an animal, maybe a rabbit, roasted over the flames. She screwed up her face in disgust at the sight of the dead thing sitting on the spit, but the smell of roasting meat made her stomach growl. Squashing her hunger, she took in the rest of the rustic setting. Individual sleeping spaces had been laid out with blankets. A few around the campfire, two by the hillside, and the rest by a rock outcropping not far from the road.

After being allowed to walk around the camp to stretch their legs and find a place to relieve themselves, the women were ushered back to their bundle of blankets. Without speaking, Maire pulled the blankets apart, arranging them in a more personal setting, once again showing her adaptability. Sometimes the woman irritated the hell out of her. She seemed so calm about all this. But in truth, what else could they do? If she'd learned nothing else in the short time she had spent with Maire, she knew the woman patiently picked her battles.

Reviewing her set of blankets, she followed Maire's example and prepared herself a surprisingly comfortable spot. Her preparations complete, she sat and drew her cloak about her, the air growing chillier.

She watched one of the men add two more rabbits to the spit while the first one was taken off. The flames drew her in, mesmerizing her with their dancing tendrils, weaving in and out, erupting as another stick of wood was added.

A nudge from Maire broke the spell, and she turned to see a man holding a flat piece of wood that held freshly roasted rabbit, a couple slices of cheese, and some bread. She took the makeshift plate and nodded at the man. She turned toward Maire, who daintily pulled apart the meat, savoring her first stringy bite.

"This reminds me of my childhood. My father allowed me to go on a couple of hunts with my brother. Sometimes an uncle or two." Maire concentrated on her food as she spoke. "I remember the stories they told around the fire after a long day of stalking a stag or some other creature. The smell of the burning wood, the smoke in our eyes, the sound of the embers slowing dying."

She tore the bread apart and picked at one end. "These are the things I think about when I'm thrown into a difficult situation. They remind me of who I am, what I want from this life." She turned a smoldering gaze to AJ, catching and holding her stare. "They embolden me to adapt, to overcome any obstacle. They help me endure."

A shiver ran down AJ's spine, her skin prickling at Maire's passionate words. "I hated camping. My father took us once. I think we all hated it. It took my father two hours to get the fire started. If we hadn't been close to home, we could have died." She smiled and pulled her own piece of bread apart. "At least the rabbit is cooked through."

Maire's tinkling laugh spread across the plateau, making the men turn to watch her before continuing their tasks. Their personal guard walked over and dropped two calfskins on their blankets before moving on.

"We do make a pair." Maire grabbed a calfskin and took a

long, deep drink. A trail of dark red ran down her chin before she brushed it away.

Wine. AJ grabbed her own calfskin and took a gulp. Not the best, but beggars and all that. Perhaps enough of it would knock her out.

The sky turned dark, and the men made their way to their own blankets to eat and drink. Whether they had fixed the wheel or not, Dugan never said. He didn't appear quite as irritated as he had earlier, so AJ assumed the repairs went well. She didn't think she'd ever be happy to climb into the coach again, but a night out here would fix that.

As the darkness deepened, she wrapped a blanket around her, snips of the cool night air finding holes through the heat of the fire. Maire fell into a peaceful sleep, but AJ wasn't tired. Too much napping during the day kept her wide awake. She lay back and stared at the night sky, millions of stars stretched as far as the horizon, and not for the first time, she wondered if her mother watched the same stars. But her mother hadn't been born yet, and no one knew AJ was missing, at least not now. The thought of time travel and what people would think of her disappearance two hundred years from now made her dizzy.

Restless, she sat up and turned her gaze toward the cinder coated wood poking out from the campfire. She traced her journey since landing in England, trying to determine where they actually were. Her expertise in history didn't include an understanding of the geography. She knew how Ireland and England were laid out, but she didn't know distances, and she was familiar with only a few of the major cities. This was the first real day of travel since leaving the viscount's manor.

How far could they travel in one day? Maybe twenty-five miles? She had no clue, but they had set a fast pace. If it hadn't been for the squeaky wheel, they would be much closer to the coast and ship. Mixed feelings raged within her. As much as she didn't want to go to France, it seemed the only direction that could take her home. But a deep part of her wanted to see Finn again. Wanted to know he hadn't abandoned her.

Staring into the flames, and with no clear direction to her thoughts, she felt herself grow drowsy. Gathering the blankets around her, punching one into submission as a pillow, she breathed out and let the tension drain from her. She listened to the sparks of the dying flames, searching for her own peace.

Until the loud explosion tore her from her dreams.

20

With the next explosive sound, AJ shot upright and rubbed her eyes while trying to organize her thoughts. The percussive blasts echoed over the clearing. There was enough firelight for her to see the men scurrying around. They ducked low as they scrambled behind rocks.

Turning to reach out for Maire, she saw one of the men dragging her behind a boulder, partially shielding her. She waved to catch Maire's attention, but the man hunched between them. He loaded a rifle with powder. She had known they were armed, but she'd never given it any thought after seeing the sword under Dugan's cloak when he'd stormed into the dining room. This was 1802, and though England wasn't currently at war with France, it was dangerous times, as Finn had warned. And no one would know what happened here tonight.

Seeing the musket, she realized she made a bright target by the fire. Dropping low, AJ looked around, wondering why no one came to take her to safety. Then she saw one of Dugan's men turn for her. Before he took a second stride, dirt flew up in front of him, driving him back.

Huddled behind the woefully ineffective barricade of blankets, she prayed she wouldn't be hit by a stray bullet. She couldn't see why anyone would purposely shoot at her. But any wound, susceptible to infection, would be as good as death in this timeline. That would indeed be a lousy way to die, in a place she shouldn't be.

She lifted her head and watched the men load and shoot, load and shoot. Why would anyone be shooting at them? Maybe Finn was trying to rescue them. She pushed the thought aside. As if she could be so lucky.

The viscount could have his own enemies. If she believed what Finn said of the man, this could be something as simple as being in a very wrong place at a very wrong time. She snorted. It all came down to the time. If this wasn't about her or Maire, the situation could be more dangerous than she originally thought.

She lowered her head and closed her eyes, wishing for the persistent litany of shots to cease. In a matter of minutes, her wish was granted as silence descended. But it lasted only a couple of seconds before she heard the clash of steel on steel. She had never heard it before—except in movies. But there was no denying the sound of one blade crossing the edge of another. A bolt of fear ran through her. Would steel be more painful than a gunshot? She pictured the blade as it sliced through skin, then remembered the scars on Dugan and her guard. At least they were alive. Maybe steel was better than a gunshot after all.

The attackers must have closed in if the fight had turned to swords. Dugan and his men were pinned against the hill with nowhere to run. She couldn't tell how many there were. It seemed like dozens. But if there were that many, wouldn't they have overtaken them? The tactics of warfare baffled her, but it wasn't for lack of trying on her father's part. She understood the basics of war: why men went to war, the advantages of one town over another, why one port and not the other. But the details of the fight, the strategies and placement of men, meant nothing.

She stifled a laugh. If only she had listened. That knowledge might have proven useful now.

All she could do was watch and wait. Without thinking, she backed slowly away until the hill pressed behind her. The viscount's men acted as a wall between her and the aggressors. The man guarding Maire pushed her farther down behind him. The flash of steel caught her eye as more men entered the fire-light. She couldn't tell if the two sides were evenly matched. Swords filled the night—slashing and thrusting and sparring.

The sound deafened her as she crouched with her back against the wall. The roaring in her ears diminished the sound of clashing blades as she tried to wrap her head around the deadly play. The view of the men sharpened within a dark, tunneled focus. One of the viscount's men went down. The blood spurted, and sprayed the man who had struck the blow, the blood shiny and wet on the blade. She fought for control over her rolling stomach, sorry she had drunk the wine. This wasn't happening.

The clamor of steel never died, but somehow, through the yelling, the screaming, and the sounds of battle, she heard her name. Distant and desperate. She swiveled to Maire who was all but hidden from sight. *Let her be okay.* The man protecting her swung his sword, his blade striking and pushing back the foe. The sweat of exertion streamed from his face, but Maire's protector never faltered.

AJ heard it again. Her name—louder, closer. She peered through the smoke from the fire and saw him. He held a sword and wielded it as if he had been born with it in his hand. He lunged, then parried, forcing his opponent to match his moves, never giving the man the ability to mount an offense. With a quick glance, their eyes met, and AJ felt her body sway in relief and surprise. A sensation of homecoming flooded her. Nothing else mattered.

Ethan.

Wonderment, quickly followed by her typical array of questions, rushed through her. She pushed them away as she watched him battle with the man who separated them. Each thrust threaded a greater fear through her, no longer concerned for her own safety but for his.

Ethan. She felt like pinching herself. The last time she'd seen him was on the dock in Baywood, just before she disappeared into the fog.

She gasped as he jumped back from Dugan's thrust. Ethan, tall and lanky, was matched against Dugan's thick, muscular brawn, one light on his feet, the other powerful in strength. And for all that, seemingly an equal match as they danced and parried among the other men.

The fire cast eerie shadows, and combined with the smell of burning wood and dusky smoke, it created a mock horror show. When blood appeared on Ethan's upper arm, reality sank in. Dugan gained ground, but Ethan held him back, doling out his own slice of pain as the larger man jumped back.

Ethan shot her a quick glance, and he yelled at her, pointing up. She couldn't hear him over the fighting. His lips moved again, but all she saw was the sweat that dampened his dark hair and the dirt streaked across his glorious face. His gray eyes nothing but silver slits in the firelight.

She didn't think she'd ever seen anyone more alive. His lips moved a third time, and again he pointed up before Dugan forced him to turn away.

Climb. He wanted her to climb.

AJ twirled around to the wall behind her. She looked up. When they'd first arrived, she'd estimated it to be fifty to sixty feet to the summit. It didn't sound like much with her experience, but the pitch was steeper than a mere scramble up the side. She would be free climbing with no ropes or protection. A fall from even midway up could be fatal.

Her climbing instincts took over as she surveyed the wall with a practiced assessment, searching for the best possible route. The adrenaline pushed through her as her mind focused on the task at hand, something she could control. Fortunately, the face of the wall was filled with rocks, holes, and a few wind-blown bushes. There would be plenty of footholds, at least from what she could see from where she stood. Once she was up higher, and fully committed, the reality could be very different.

Behind her, the shouting and sound of fighting continued. She heard a guttural scream and whipped around, terrified it came from Ethan.

No. He was still there.

The strain drained his face to a light pallor, reflected as a sickening pink from the fire. He swung his sword, stepping in, lunging before stepping back, pulling his sword up to defend. A dozen men each solely focused on the fight left no one to watch her.

She searched for Maire, but she was completely hidden from view. Two of the viscount's men took position around Maire. There would be no way to get to her. And if she had doubts about the climb, Maire would never make it. Another cry, sharp and visceral, broke her indecision. The thought of leaving Maire rocked her, but she had to rely on Ethan to get her out.

If she was going to escape, this would be her only chance.

Giving Ethan a parting glance, she turned to the wall. Quickly reviewing her path one last time, she reached for a rock with her right hand and placed her left foot on a rock two feet from the ground. She pushed herself up. Her left hand found the next hold, but when she looked down to place her right foot, she couldn't see past the folds of her skirts. Damn. Jumping back down, she almost fell when her feet tangled in her troublesome attire.

She glanced back to Ethan and for an instant their eyes met. He was tiring. They all were. The viscount's men were slowly driving Ethan and his men back. A coppery fragrance hung in the air, and she refocused, trying to block the images, forcing her mind to focus.

Dragging in a deep, rattling breath, she gathered up her gown and searched the edges of the fabric. Any snag or hole would do. She found a tattered rip in a seam about midthigh and gave a hard downward yank. Taking the edge of the now open seam, she rubbed it against a rock until it started to unravel. The fabric ripped, creating a jagged border. She removed her petticoat and tossed it aside with the remnants of her gown. The beautiful gown Marguerite had so lovingly created now hung like a sloppy rag, its new edges running to midthigh at some points before dropping to just below her knee at others.

She didn't care. Her shoes were free, and her legs would be unencumbered as she climbed.

Without looking back, she grabbed for the same rock with her right hand, positioned her left foot, and pushed off. For the first twenty feet, she felt strong. She continually searched for the next logical placement of hand and foot, her mind transported back to her climbs at home. In her mind, she was back on her favorite cliff. She smelled the salt from the sea, and below her, the sounds of the fighting men morphed into the crashing of waves against rocks.

Her arms began to tire by the time she reached the midpoint of the hill. The sounds of the fight grew faint, replaced by a rushing in her ears. She strained to hear the waves again, to hear the seagulls urging her on. The chill of the air prickling as it dried the sheen of sweat on her skin. The fire cast enough light that she could see the rocks and path in front of her.

As she climbed higher, it was no longer the fire that lit her way. It was the first hint of dawn. Ethan must have struck just before first light, hoping to catch the viscount's men at their weakest, the time when sleep was the deepest.

She pushed thoughts of the battle away and focused on her breathing. This was her time of day for climbing, when she felt the strongest, but her mind games would take her only so far. It had been months since she climbed. Her muscle memory knew what it needed to do, where to place the feet, how to grip, which holds were the best, which edges she could trust, but her arms shook as she crept up the face of the hill.

Suddenly, the sounds from below changed. Men yelled, shouting orders. Explosions from muskets started again, and the acrid smell of gunpowder wafted up the hill as if escaping through a flume. Ethan must be retreating. A cry rang out, a painful wrenching scream. Someone lay dead or dying.

She couldn't wrap her head around it. Stuck in the middle of some age-old fight between life and death, and she was the cause of it. Lost in a time of revolution and lawlessness. No hospitals or medicine of real worth, where the smallest wound from gunshot or the cut of a blade could be fatal without antibiotics or proper care.

Her head dropped and pressed into the wall. She squeezed her eyes shut. She'd put her hands over her ears if it didn't mean letting go of the wall. Dragging every mental training technique from her arsenal, she continued her push, each handhold shakier than the last, her survival instincts forming a mantra: *get to Ethan.*

After a few more feet, she stopped. Her arms and thighs quaked, and she leaned against the hill to take weight off her legs. She breathed in the musty smell of dirt and rock. The morning air tickled her skin.

She willed herself to mentally be where she could no longer physically be, even if it was for just this moment. The sounds from below grew dimmer, replaced again by the sound of the waves and the encouraging guffaws of the gulls. Her breathing slowed. She shook out her limbs, one at a time, loosening the muscles and reenergizing them. Just another ten feet to go.

Her muscles sang, loud and wrenching as she neared the top. Sweat streamed down her face, blurring her vision and forcing her to trust the feel of the rock. She could no longer control her breathing, and it burst out in short, ragged puffs. Her legs shook, the pain unbearable. She had no idea what was happening below her and no longer cared. The fall from here would certainly remove any more worry.

She screamed as she pushed one last time, stretching her arm as far as she could. The top. She had made it. But every place she grabbed was nothing but dirt that crumbled in her hand. All this way and there were no more rocks? Nothing solid to hold her weight. Her arm swung wildly, but all she met was air and more dirt.

Then a hand, seemingly out of nowhere, grabbed hold of her. It was long and lean, streaked brown with what AJ immediately realized was dried blood. She had no idea whose hand it was and didn't care. A fall to her death would be stupid, regardless of the situation she might find herself in. Friend or foe, she wasn't ready to throw in the towel.

With her last bit of strength, she squeezed the hand, strong and warm. In an instant, her body was dragged over the edge, and she fell against a solid chest. She finished two ragged breaths before turning to face her rescuer.

Ethan.

His lean, hawkish face stared down at her, etched with worry. Overcome with fatigue, she felt her body melt, the tension released and the floodgate opened. Tears of happiness streaked through the drying sweat and dust on her face.

"Thank God." Ethan pulled her close, holding her tight. "I wasn't sure I was going to be able to get you out of there." He pulled back, holding her at arm's length, scanning her from head to toe. "Are you injured?"

She didn't hear his question. All she could do was stare with wonderment. Everything faded—the fight, the last couple of months. She ran her hands over his arms, ensuring he was really here. All she wanted to do was lean in and feel the strength of him, the security.

"AJ, are you okay?" Ethan's tone sharpened. His brows furrowed. "We have to get out of here. Right now."

She didn't budge. Couldn't. "Where did you come from?" She touched his chest and then remembered the blood on his sleeve. She reached for it and released a breath. The stain was already a dark brown. No new blood. She sighed as her body started to tremble.

He drew her back into his arms, holding her tight before whispering, "I'll tell you everything, or at least as much as I know. Once we're safe. And we are far from safe at this moment. Can you climb a bit more?"

She tensed and leaned away. He'd changed over these last months. He had grown leaner, his gray eyes tired. His forehead wrinkled as he searched her face. "Yes. I'm good."

"It's not far. The men are waiting with the horses." Ethan stood and pulled her up with him.

She didn't think she'd ever be grateful to hear there would be horses. It was enough to move her to action. Ethan led her across a rock-encrusted strip of land where the hill continued up at a thirty-degree angle. Her legs wobbled, and she tripped.

Ethan caught her. "Are you sure you can do this?"

"Yes." She rubbed her thighs, working the muscles, begging them to cooperate. "Let's go."

They were halfway up the last part of the hill before she remembered Maire. She turned, but with the angle of the hill, the campsite wasn't visible. The last remnants of smoke from the muskets and campfire drifted aimlessly into the morning sky. She could hear occasional bits of gunfire, nothing more.

She couldn't see Maire, couldn't know that she was all right. Maire would be searching for her. A sharp pain of guilt stabbed her, and she almost collapsed. It seemed wrong leaving her behind.

AJ was about to turn back to Ethan when something caught her eye. Toward the north, from where they had traveled the day before, a white horse shuffled on top of a treeless knoll. Although she could see it clearly, she didn't think Dugan could see it from the campsite.

A tingle went through her as the morning light caught the man's movement. He held the reins tightly as the horse pranced beneath him.

Her heart froze. Finn. He was too far away for her to see his face, but somehow, she sensed the green eyes touch her. She knew it was him by the way he sat on the horse, the way his head tilted to one side, and she could almost see the brown curls that fell over his forehead.

Why was he just sitting there? He made no move toward the camp. She didn't know how long he'd been there, but the fight had barely ended. He must have been there long enough to have joined the fight. If he wanted to. But he just sat there, looking up the hill.

"AJ, we can't linger. I only have a couple of men holding them off. They'll be in pursuit soon." Ethan's words were insistent. He was right. As soon as Dugan checked his injured men, he'd be after them. Her gaze moved back to Finn, sitting there, still staring up at her. If only she could see his face. It didn't matter. He wasn't here. He stayed out of the fight and the rescue. If he had bothered to help, they might have freed Maire. The sense of loss, like an immense lump of clay, wallowed in her belly. She brushed at her eyes and turned away to follow Ethan.

The last part of the hill was an easy jog even for her shaky legs. But she didn't feel them anymore. Leaving Maire and Finn behind shook her more than she could have imagined.

When they reached the top of the hill, four men waited for them. They were sweaty and dirty, the strain of the battle reflected on their weary faces, but they held themselves like soldiers who had seen their share of death. Except for one man, who slumped in his saddle, using his last bit of strength to stay upright on his horse. No one assisted him, but two men kept their horses on either side of him, ready to catch him if he should fall.

One horse remained without a rider, and a jolt of relief flooded her. She wouldn't have to handle her own horse. Ethan quickly rechecked the saddle and gathered the reins from another rider.

AJ turned to search for Finn once more, a flicker of hope rising that he might try to skirt the camp to catch up to her. But his mount hadn't moved. He was nothing but a statue, staring up at her. After a brief moment, he turned his horse north, back the way he had come. Then the horse broke into a gallop and, within seconds, disappeared behind a hill.

She almost crumpled to the ground, the weight of abandonment crushing her. When he'd left her at the manor, she had still believed in him. She'd questioned his motives but always trusted he'd come back for her. Their two months together had been uneasy, but there had been something deeper there. She'd been sure of it. But after these last few days, the memory of her weeks with Finn grew faint. Had it all been a scam? It didn't make sense. Yet it was clear he'd made no attempt to get to her. No signal, no wave, no attempt at communication. It was as if he was surveying the results of his handiwork.

The rustle of hooves brought her back. She pushed back the pain to some dark corner of her soul. Ethan looked down at her from atop his horse, his arm outstretched to pull her up. His warmth embraced her as she settled against his chest. She hunched down as Ethan kicked his horse, leaving Maire and Finn behind them.

21

The beleaguered band of riders rode hard for several hours, taking short breaks to rest the horses. Two men always positioned themselves to watch for Dugan. For the first hour, AJ barely took notice of her surroundings, her body numbed by all that had happened: the raid, the miraculous arrival of Ethan, leaving Maire behind, then watching Finn ride away.

At each stop, she paced in a circle, arms wrapped tightly around her, kicking at loose stones before sitting down, then popping up to do it all over again. The events replayed over and over, but everything had happened so quickly. She tried to hear what the men talked about, but they whispered among themselves.

Ethan moved easily between the men and her, making sure she had dried meat and bread to eat, followed with some water. He said little. When the numbness wore off, her reporter's mind reshaped, organized, and prioritized her thoughts, as the miles moved them farther north, away from Maire and the stones. But she held her tongue.

By the end of the day, she was bone weary and could barely hold herself upright without Ethan's assistance.

"Just a bit farther. You can do it. We'll be there soon." Ethan's words purred like a mantra each time he nudged her to stay focused.

Her body ached from the climb and the long ride. She'd be happy to fall from the horse, crawl to a tree, curl up, and sleep forever. When the sleepy village appeared around a bend she almost wept with joy, hoping this was their destination. She would prefer a warm bed, but a pallet or a clean stable would be equally welcome at this point.

She spotted the inn. Her spirits rose while her stomach grumbled. The sun had set an hour before, and they arrived by the light of a thin moon. Her shoulders sank as they passed by the building, but lifted again when they turned toward the back. They remained on the horses while one of Ethan's men, Thomas, knocked on the back door. Minutes passed until the door opened. An old man, stooped from either age or hard work, peered at them and then spoke with Thomas, who passed him a linen pouch. The man weighed it in his hand and nodded.

"Okay. We'll be safe here." Ethan dismounted and turned to AJ, who fell into his arms, her strength sapped.

Once on the ground, she found a final reserve of energy. "You have some explaining to do."

"We'll discuss everything in the morning. We have injured to care for."

AJ spun around, surveying the men. "What can I do?"

Ethan turned her back to the inn. "You can get some rest so I don't have to worry about you. The injuries are minor but need to be tended."

She remembered the first man she'd seen after her climb, his shirt covered in blood, ready to fall off his horse. He seemed to find energy the farther they traveled, spurred by adrenaline, eager to evade Dugan. Now that they'd reached relative safety, the weariness and pain would set in. These men had risked their lives for her.

"I want to help," AJ insisted, attempting to turn back to the men.

"Have you been this difficult since you arrived?" He pushed her toward the inn, and she felt his warm sigh just before the innkeeper's wife appeared.

"Let's go, child. We have a warm bath being prepared." She took AJ's arm and smiled at Ethan. "We'll take care of everything." The woman's tone was warm and gentle, like a grandmother taking in her brood.

AJ stopped struggling and let the woman lead her away. She glanced back at Ethan. His furrowed brows made her square her shoulders and straighten her spine, exactly what Maire would do. She would behave, at least until she regained her strength. Then she would find a way to repay the men who'd saved her.

When the innkeeper's wife opened the door to the room, AJ dashed to the fire. Her body shook, cold to the bone. Wrapped in Ethan's arms, she hadn't noticed the cold. It didn't escape her feeble thoughts that she might be in shock.

The shivering didn't stop until she lowered herself into the tub of warm water, submerging herself until the water ran over her head. She remained under until she couldn't hold her breath any longer. After repeating the process of dunking two more times, she leaned back and closed her eyes. When the water turned cold, she dragged herself from the tub. She was starving.

Her torn and dirty gown had just covered her body when a knock made her jump. "Yes. I'm dressed."

"And you appear quite fetching in what's left of your gown. But I think I prefer you in jeans." Ethan's warm gray eyes couldn't hide the concern.

"Did you think to bring me some?" She held out the skirt of her torn gown. It had been a favorite, and she remembered when she'd first seen it hanging in Marguerite's shop, a product of Finn's generosity. The image of Finn sitting astride his horse,

KIM ALLRED

watching them fight for their lives, banished any softness. "I could have used them earlier."

"As well as better shoes." Ethan tossed more wood into the fire. "We'll find something for you in the morning. You'll need to make do tonight."

"I just want to sleep." She placed her hands on her hips. "After I've seen that the men are okay and I've eaten."

Ethan shook his head. "The men are fine." Then he held up his hands in surrender. "You can come down to eat and see for yourself. They're not the type to warrant pampering."

She shuffled her feet in front of the hearth. "I get it. But they risked their necks for me. I feel like I owe them."

"I'm sorry we didn't know about the other woman."

A pang of guilt hit her. "She's a strong woman. She'll be okay." Then a thought struck her. "Can we help her?"

He sighed. "Let's finish worrying about you. Then we'll see where we go from there." He opened the door and waited for her to pass.

She nodded and followed the hall to the stairs. As she descended to the common room, her list of questions for Ethan intertwined with her plan to rescue Maire. They had to go back.

AFTER DINNER, AJ thanked each man personally for her rescue. Most nodded in return, others appeared embarrassed, and she almost considered her actions a mistake, just as Ethan had warned her, until she caught two of the men smiling and slapping shoulders when they thought she wasn't watching. She bent her head and ventured a glance to Ethan, who nodded. At least her instincts for gratitude hadn't left her.

Ethan walked her back to her room, entered behind her, and closed the door. He moved toward the hearth, where a makeshift bed had been created.

200

"You're sleeping here." It wasn't a question, just a confirming statement that comforted AJ.

"I'll keep the fire going."

She sat on the bed and fingered the edge of her torn gown. Dugan and his men were out there somewhere. "It seemed like you had more men at the camp."

"There were three more. They went a different direction. It will force the viscount's men to split their force."

"I guess it worked."

"We'll see. Do you have everything you need?"

"Yes." Her weariness returned, and now that she was alone with Ethan in her room, she felt a little shy. It had been months since she'd last seen him. Although most of their friendship had fallen easily into place, there was a wide gap between them. He was obviously a time traveler himself, and she needed to know his connection to the stones.

She crawled under the covers and turned to watch Ethan. He lay on his side, watching the flames. There was no better time than now, while they were alone. She had no idea how much the other men knew of the stones, but there was no question Ethan did.

"How did you get here?" She wouldn't be able to sleep without knowing.

There was a long silence, and she wondered if he understood what she was asking. He rolled over and looked up at her. She couldn't see his face well with the light from the fire glowing behind him, and for a moment, she wondered if she really wanted to know.

His voice traveled over her, low and hushed. "I have my own stone."

The words resonated through her, and she pieced together what she already knew of the stones. "And that connected you to the larger stone in the necklace? Like Finn?"

"Yes." He paused again and ran a hand through his hair. He

seemed to search for the right words, as if working out a mystery even he didn't completely understand. "It's not a precise jump. We aren't taken directly to the larger stone. We just know we're close to it, somewhere in the same town. Sometimes Finn would arrive first; sometimes it was me."

Ethan pushed his pillow around and lay down, staring at the ceiling. "The travel time between us could be days or minutes. I haven't been able to prove it, not until this last jump. The closer I am to the stone, the faster the jump takes me."

AJ absorbed what Ethan shared. It all seemed so fantastic that if she wasn't living it herself, she would have thought them both mad. Yet here she was, and it was no dream. A thought popped into her head. "My brother, Adam. You said the jump was faster this time. Just minutes."

He turned his head toward the flames, and his voice turned raspy, like words over sandpaper. "Once you disappeared, I knew I had to get away from Adam. I tried to get away, but...I think he now has three disappearances to deal with. Or will when time catches up."

She closed her eyes. Adam wouldn't take it well. He was a lawyer who lived for facts, and as she thought about it, she realized it was one of her own inherent traits. Not something she just relied on for her reporting but her antique junkets as well. Here she was, two hundred years separating her and her brother, and she'd just now found a common thread between them. She would have laughed if it wouldn't sound hysterical.

"I can't imagine what he'll think or what he'll do. No one will believe him."

"The one thing in our favor is that we have time to correct it."

"Can it be corrected?" She sat up. "Will I be able to go home?" She cringed at the sound of her own desperation.

Ethan raised on one elbow. "I tried everything I could to keep you away from this."

She thought back to the days before the jump. Ethan had

tried, several times, to keep her away from Finn, but she had refused to listen. "I know." She hung her head. How many times could she damn Finn before she cleansed him fully from her thoughts? "So why did you want my necklace?"

He half shrugged. "I don't. My employer, well, he's more a mentor, really, asked me to retrieve it. The Earl of Hereford."

That set her back. He worked for an earl. Who was this man she thought she knew? "And you just said, sure, time travel. No problem."

Ethan laughed, the sound so deep and instinctual, her own lips curved into a smile. He shook his head. "No. It wasn't quite like that. He told me the stone was powerful, but I thought it all fantasy. The words of an old religion believed by a foolish old man. Yet, he was so earnest in his request. I had to believe him." He sighed and studied his hands. "We've been through too much together to not give him the benefit of the doubt."

"Have you been back to see him?"

"No. Ethan leaned back into his blankets. "I sent word to him. But the mission isn't complete. I don't have the stone."

There was so much to know, about Ethan as well as the stones. "How did the earl know about the stones?"

When he didn't answer right away, her stomach clenched. She couldn't take any more secrets from someone who didn't think she needed to know everything. Or worse, maybe he doesn't know. "I think we've discussed enough for one night. We both need sleep."

Several moments of silence followed, and AJ nestled down in her own blankets, staring at Ethan's solid form framed by firelight.

"Ethan?" she whispered.

His answer came faster than she expected. "Yes."

"How did you find me?" She assumed he must have known about the viscount and had just waited for a time to grab her.

"I followed you from Ireland."

"Ireland? How did you know where Finn lived?"

"When I jumped back, I found myself in Ireland. I'm still attached to the proximity of the stone." He rubbed a hand over his face. "It took a bit to track you. Do you know how many Murphys there are in Ireland?" He laughed. "But not many with a ship or one who has been gone for so long."

"Why didn't you come to me then?" But she already knew the answer. She knew it when she saw Finn ride away.

His response came slowly. "I can't trust anyone with the stones. I felt it was better to watch and see where Finn went. I was lucky enough to hear from some men in town of Finn's plans to sail to England. It was clear he was heading for the viscount, so I found my own way over. Then I sent word for my men to meet me here."

"You could have just gone to England to wait."

"I needed to see you. I needed to know you were all right."

She sat up again. "When did you see me?"

He laughed. "When you rode into town and stopped at the dressmaker's."

"You saw that?"

"Yes. I'm glad to see you've improved your horse riding skills since then."

"Funny." She lay back down and stared at the ceiling. "Thank you." He'd risked his mission to protect her, and now he risked himself and his men. She would never be able to repay him.

22

Ethan was gone when AJ woke the next morning, but he had added enough wood to the fire to ward off the early morning chill. She wrapped a blanket around her shoulders, her bare feet curling on the cool wooden floor, and stared out at the street. A gray day, but at least it wasn't raining. She sat on the sofa, pulling her feet under her and hugging the blanket closer. Her face flushed from the heat, and she closed her eyes to soak it in, wishing it was a strong summer sun that warmed her. If only she could store the warmth for the next stage of the journey.

The knock at the door five minutes later broke her trance. "Come in."

Ethan strode in. A dress lay draped over one arm with shoes resting on top and a cup in his other hand.

"I thought I'd bring a cup of tea to warm you while you get ready. And the innkeeper's wife found a dress for you. It's not fashionable, but it will serve better for travel on horseback. I don't know if the shoes will fit, but they'll be more serviceable."

AJ wrapped her fingers around the cup and sniffed the strong herbal scent. "I can't thank you enough for taking care of me."

Ethan reddened. "You don't need to thank me. There's

nothing to thank me for. I should have tried harder to protect you. I was foolish."

She searched his hawkish face. His black hair was combed back and cut short for the era. Gray eyes softened under her perusal as she remembered the job he assumed before her jump. He had been in security, or that was his story at the time. "Do you work security for the earl?"

He blew out a sigh and pushed his hands through his hair, then sat next to her. "In a fashion. I'm considered more of a body-guard. I lead a contingent of men who care for his safety and that of his property and lands."

"Like the viscount's men?"

"In a manner of speaking."

"Is that why he asked you to help with the stone?"

Ethan leaned back, taking a full minute before responding. "The earl took me out of an orphanage when I was very young. He raised me as a son. For what reason, I never really knew. The simplest answer might be because he didn't have one of his own. Since I'm not family, I can't inherit, so he put me in the best position he could. And he trusts me, as I do him."

Discovering that Ethan had been an orphan seemed to explain so much about him. And she wondered what horrible circumstance had left him alone at such a young age. She laid a hand on his arm.

He covered hers with his own and then stood. "The men are eating downstairs. I should join them."

AJ stood, her blanket still wrapped tightly around her. "It won't take me long to follow. Ethan?"

"Yes?"

"How did you know to find us in the pass?"

"How do you think the carriage ended up with a squeaky wheel?" He bent with a stately bow and a slow smile before leaving the room.

She shook her head with a laugh and picked up the dress. A

petticoat, chemise, and stockings fell to the floor. The innkeeper's wife had thought of everything. While dressing, she pieced together the streams of information she had gathered from Ethan and Finn. They both carried a piece of stone that tied them to the larger stone. Were the pieces part of the same stone or of something even larger? She had to find out why someone wanted the stones in the first place. What was in the book Maire read? Her chest tightened when she thought of Maire and where she might be. Had they continued their way south? Another dagger pierced her when she thought of Finn—watching and then riding away. By the time she left the room, AJ had come to a resolution, one that she desperately needed Ethan to believe in.

THE SMELL of freshly baked bread filled the common room, masking any unpleasant aromas swirling from a room full of unwashed men. The men laughed among themselves as they finished their meal, their mood improved by sleep and sustenance. AJ received a nod from a couple of them as she wove her way through the tables to Ethan. He sat at a different table, head down in a conversation with Thomas. When she approached, Thomas stopped talking and nodded before moving to another table.

"I didn't mean to interrupt." She sat across from Ethan, who looked like his old self, other than maybe a new wrinkle or two at the creases of his alert eyes, his smile a bit tired. It felt so good to be with him after all this time.

"You didn't. We were just planning out the day."

"About that." AJ paused as a young lad laid down a plate of warm bread, sausage, eggs, and beans. She missed her bagels. Once he was gone, she played with the beans while formulating her words. "We need to go back for Maire," she blurted. So much for easing into it.

Ethan said nothing as he finished the last bite of bread and jam. He took a long, slow drink from his mug before setting it down. His words were patient with understanding. "The viscount's men were more than an equal match for us. We were only successful because of surprise. Even if his men split into search parties, he's sure to have sent for reinforcements. And they'll be more diligent."

AJ nodded. She had thought of all that. "Yes. But they wouldn't expect us to go back for Maire. We just need to stay close and wait for when their guard is down."

"That's very risky."

"But we still need the stones." She whispered the words, but she couldn't hide her desperation. "And Maire knows about the stones. She may know enough to piece together a way home for me." She had meant to present a solid plan and reason for rescuing Maire, but even she heard the whining tone.

"Do you think Maire has the stones?"

AJ shook her head and shrank back. "No. She thinks the viscount is keeping them with him. But we're supposed to meet him at the ship in Southampton." She didn't like his sympathetic expression.

"I just received word from the earl. That's what Thomas and I were discussing. He wants us to regroup back at his estate."

AJ grabbed his arm. "It will be too late. We're not sure where the viscount is headed. Maire wasn't able to find out. But she's found information about the stones. We need to get her away from him. We have to stay close."

He said nothing as his fingernail scraped at an old knot on the table, his gaze unfocused. "Tell me what happened to Finn."

AJ scowled and turned away. "He's gone."

His fingers stretched out to touch the edge of her sleeve, his voice soft. "Tell me."

She pulled back her arm and hugged herself, flashing a defiant stare, daring him to say anything more. When he did nothing but quietly watch her, she blew out a sigh. "He left me. Left me at the manor all alone with the viscount."

"Did he say why?"

Her words were passionless. "Some errand for the viscount. Supposedly to London."

"There must have been a reason he didn't take you."

Her eyes narrowed. "A reason? He was always a little shy on details."

"And the viscount moved you before he returned."

She turned her head away, scanning the room, anything to not have to look at him. She didn't want him to see her pain, her anger.

He reached out again, and when she tried to pull her arm away, he held fast. "There's more. Out with it."

The words that finally came were low and carried a bitter edge. "He was there at the pass. When you rescued me."

Ethan shook his head. "I didn't see him there."

Her gaze turned to the same knot Ethan had played with. "I saw him, when I reached the top of the cliff. He was sitting on that damned white horse." A ragged gasp released the mixed emotions she couldn't hold back. She blinked away the tears. When that wasn't sufficient, she wiped angrily at her face and stared at Ethan. "He just sat there. I know it was him. And then he turned and rode off. That's what happened to Finn." Her final words were hot enough to scorch skin.

She wanted to pull her arm away, but his grip was strong and warm. Comforting. She stared at his long, tapered fingers, wishing she didn't have to bare her soul to this man but forever grateful she could.

A minute passed before he spoke. "I understand how much Maire must mean to you. Both of you captive with no way out. But it's too dangerous to go back."

Taking a deep breath to tamp the desperation from her voice, she laid her hand over the top of his. "Every day I'm here is a risk.

Not just to me but to the future. I'm not meant to be here. If there's a way for me to get home, I have to follow that."

"This is a different era. Things don't move quickly here. Things take time. The earl can find out where the viscount is going. It's best if we have a plan."

AJ sat back. "Maire said we were being taken to France."

He sat up. "How does she know that? She must be in the viscount's confidence."

She shook her head and leaned forward. "No, I don't think so. You haven't seen them together. You can't fake that kind of disdain. The way she changes each time he walks into the room." AJ pushed her plate away, then nibbled at her thumb nail. "I'm so worried for her. I need to find a way to get her away from him. Then, if you want, we can return to the earl and make plans to retrieve the stones." She turn a sorrowful gaze to Ethan. "We have to at least try."

Ethan took a ragged breath and rubbed his thumb gently over the top of her hand. Then he ran his hand over his face and stared at the ceiling. "All right. We'll try it your way."

She bounced in her seat, eager to get moving. Before she could say anything, Ethan shushed her. "We'll follow my lead, my orders. This is more dangerous than you can know."

She tried to hide the smile, but it was impossible. "We'll be careful, right?"

"We'll have to be a great deal more than careful." Ethan stared at her until the smile vanished. "And by taking this path, we've pretty much closed the book on being smart."

ETHAN STUFFED the last of the provisions into the saddlebag and checked the girth before laying a hand on the twitching neck of the gelding, as if soothing him would calm his own apprehension. The stablemaster claimed this old boy was the gentlest of the lot, and if the eyes were the window to the soul in horses, then Ethan would have to trust his instincts. He slid a glance to Thomas, who prepared his own mount for travel, his movements stiff, his words clipped as he gave orders to the men.

Thomas turned and handed Ethan a pistol and a short-bladed dagger. "Perhaps you'll have some time to show her how to use these. The pistol is the smallest we have." He shoved past Ethan toward the inn.

He couldn't blame Thomas. His gut wailed at the decision he made, but he couldn't seem to step away from the brink. Perhaps he'd gotten too close as Thomas said. He couldn't argue that. But was saving the stones worthy of any price, regardless of the innocent lives that got in the way? He couldn't imagine the earl would have agreed if he knew the full circumstances. Yet Ethan felt unsure for the first time since starting this quest.

Ethan's heart broke to see AJ ravaged by guilt, something he well understood. It hung on him like a hair shirt, as he knew he was equally responsible for AJ being dragged back to a time not her own. And it drove him, kept him going, because after the eighteen months he'd been gone, he had lost interest in the race for the stones.

The travel and search had worn him down. He'd just wanted to go home—until AJ. But he owed a debt to the earl which left him at this crossroads. He cursed his predicament. The stones were going to get them all killed before this was through.

He patted the horse and turned to see Thomas watching him, leaning against the wall of the inn, his face still twisted with unresolved anger from their earlier disagreement. Thomas was a big man, taller than Ethan by a good six inches, and scarred from battles in the war with France. Ethan had found him under a pile of death, where he had been left for the crows.

He had taken Thomas to a healer and remained with him until he could ride, then took him home, where he was eagerly accepted into the ranks of the earl's men. Over time, he had earned the right to be Ethan's second. Ethan didn't like being at odds with Thomas but knew of no way to settle their differences.

Ethan stowed the pistol and dagger, ignoring Thomas's glare. He patted the horse's flank and turned toward the inn. He eased his back against the wall and scanned the village before turning his gaze to the sky. Another gray day, but the rain should hold.

"The innkeeper said you would make better time by staying on the road. There should be enough cover if needed," Thomas said gruffly, holding his anger in check.

"We're just two travelers journeying south. We'll be invisible."

"Hardly. Your charade won't pass close inspection. But if you stay out of sight from travelers, you may be able to shadow your party." Thomas sighed and turned an eye to an overburdened cart that approached. "If you can catch them."

Thomas had given Ethan an opening. "I'll have to do the best I can without your skills to guide me." Ethan watched the passing cart, instincts trained, or bred, into both men to take notice of even the most innocuous thing.

A long sigh escaped Thomas as he pushed off the wall. "I believe the promotion will be mine if you don't return." He walked away, never looking back before he ducked through the door of the inn.

Ethan closed his eyes. At least he left knowing their differences had been settled. Thomas would take what they knew to the earl and prepare for the next stage while Ethan scouted the viscount's party. Not ideal. As stupid as he had told AJ, but it was the best he could do.

Ethan still leaned against the wall and was running the next day or two over in his head—the path they would take, how far they could travel in a day—when AJ found him.

"There you are. For a minute, I thought you'd changed your mind and left me." AJ struggled with riding gloves that fit too tightly. She tugged and flexed her fingers, which strained against the leather. "What I'd give for one simple mall." She pouted as she ripped them off. "Just one store, really, that had everything in it."

Ethan gave her a long appraisal from head to toe. She had talked him into letting her wear pants. Her reasoning had been well prepared, and he had been too tired to fight. He had to admit, at a distance, she could pass as a young man. It might be enough for a casual inspection. She tried to convince him to let her cut her hair, but that, he insisted, was pushing too far.

At some point, she would need to be a lady again, and it was easier to hide her locks. So she had pulled her hair back and wore a torn, ratty hat the stableboy must have found for her.

Ethan followed her to the horses and reached into one of the packs. He extracted a pair of gloves.

AJ put them on and turned her hands over, then flexed her fingers. They weren't perfect either, but they would do. "I guess I don't need a store when I have you and Finn." She stopped short. "Well, you at least. Don't you leave me."

He grabbed her arms. "This is it. There's no turning back once Thomas leaves with the men. We'll be alone."

She stared back, undaunted by his stern words. "We'll be okay. We have to be." Removing Ethan's hands from her, she gave them a squeeze before heading back into the inn. "I have food being wrapped up for us. I should only be a few more minutes."

Ethan knew they could change their minds at any time, but he'd hoped to scare some sense into her. But she had set her mind to their mission, probably the first time she'd tasted a sense of control since her arrival. He wouldn't challenge her anymore. She could take control of her own fate. His duty now was to protect her as he would the earl. He would be her knight while they tracked their prey, and with a bit of luck, they wouldn't get caught in a snare.

23

Two hours into their journey, Ethan stopped as they approached what a appeared to be a quiet village. AJ's backside was sore, but she refused to complain. There was a long day ahead of them. They had started slow, giving her time to get a feel for her horse and saddle. As soon as she appeared comfortable, Ethan picked up the pace.

When they came within view of the village, Ethan glanced back at the road they traveled then searched the trees and fields around them. "Stay here, behind the tree until I return." Then he was gone before she could respond.

She turned her horse to move behind a tree and wondered if they would do this every time they came to a town. But she couldn't argue about Ethan's concern for safety when men could still be looking for her. She removed her hat and wiped at the damp strings of hair stuck to her forehead. Although the skies were still gray, the temperature had warmed. The fields were muddy from previous rains, but the road was passable.

She smiled. Her pants were streaked with splattered mud from the horse's hooves. She ran her hands over the pants and picked at a loose thread. The innkeeper's wife had only mumbled when AJ returned from the stable dressed in the stableboys clothes. Her short time on the *Daphne Marie* had paid off with this inspiration. Then her smile faded when a flash of Finn's grin appeared from nowhere. She shook her head and turned the horse to give her a better view of the road.

Her horse pranced, and she pulled hard to settle him, taking a deep breath to calm both their nerves. The minutes ticked on. She had no idea how long Ethan had been gone. Time stood still, freeing her fears to creep from their locked chambers, leaking into the recesses of her mind. Her horse took a step, wanting to move as much as she did rather than standing here like a rabbit in a trap. She considered her inability to determine time, damning herself for not picking up a timepiece somewhere in her travels, then cursing herself as an idiot for needing one. Couldn't she tell five minutes from twenty?

She was deep into her internal debate when she heard the approach of a horse from the direction of town. It sounded like a single rider. Relief flooded her when she spotted Ethan.

"What took you so long?" AJ hissed, somewhere between fear and annoyance.

"You need to learn patience," Ethan said. "Come on out, the village is clear. The viscount's men haven't been through here so we should be all right until the next village."

AJ urged her mount out of the trees and joined Ethan as they trotted back to town. "How far?"

"About twelve miles. It will be late when we arrive."

Ethan was true to his word. They stopped only to rest the horses, taking a quick opportunity to grab a snack. They said little. Ethan wore a permanent scowl, the way he did when he was deep in thought. All AJ wanted to do was lie down in the grass and sleep for a week. Her backside ached in all the wrong places, and it was all she could do to hold on. But she didn't dare complain. This had been her idea.

They reached the village past suppertime. The sun had set,

and twilight inched its way to darkness. This town was larger than the last, but they were late enough that no one seemed to be around.

"Why don't I have to hide this time? Not that I'm complaining." She didn't want to be left out in the trees, alone in the dark.

"I'd prefer you close to me where I can see you."

She inwardly thanked him and then frowned when he rode to the stable.

"Wait here." Ethan handed her the reins to his horse and disappeared into the building.

She barely had a chance to check out her surroundings before he returned.

"We'll stay here for the night. Less flapping lips, the better."

"I'm not sure I'm awake enough to care."

Ethan led her to a clean stall, a few feet down from the nearest horse. He added as much straw as he could to dampen the smell and keep them dry. Their horses were tied outside, easy to get to if needed.

AJ didn't ask any questions when he handed her a warm bowl of stew and a hunk of bread from the local inn. He passed her a pouch with water and a mug of ale he made her drink.

"It will warm your insides and soothe your aches."

"I feel fine."

"You know you don't have to play tough with me. I'm not going to make us turn around. Not yet, anyway."

"Were you able to learn anything from the innkeeper?"

"They weren't as friendly here. I'll see what I can find out from the stableman in the morning."

"How far ahead of us do you think they are?"

Ethan chewed a piece of bread as he thought about it. He took his time, washing it down with a long swig of ale before answering. "Can't be more than a day, two at the most. But I'm guessing they've holed up somewhere."

"Why?" A yawn followed the question.

"They probably hope to find you and would prefer to have the carriage. And with some luck on our side, they'll have Maire at an inn where we might have a chance to get to her."

AJ barely heard the words before drifting off to the soft chuffing of horses.

WHEN THE MORNING sun broke the cloudy restraints of the day before, it flooded the village with blinding intensity. Sunlight streamed through the slats in the barn, flashing dust particles when Ethan crunched through the straw. He bumped into a pallet, stirring AJ as he set down mugs of coffee. A surprised cry spun him around.

"What is it?"

She snorted, stretching her legs and arms. "Sorry. I just realized how sore I am. My neck is kinked."

Ethan squatted behind her and moved his hands over her shoulders before sliding them up her neck. He felt her tense. "Relax. Let me help." He moved his fingers around, kneading the muscles.

AJ leaned into his ministrations. "Hmm. Okay, I needed this. I don't remember falling asleep."

"You were probably half-asleep when we arrived last night. I'm surprised I got you to eat before passing out."

"I used to have endurance. Just one more thing I've lost."

"I see. We're going to start our day with, what did Stella call it, a pity party?"

She barked a laugh. "And I believe she said we were all entitled to one."

"Yes, I remember, as long as we didn't drag it out past happy hour."

AJ rolled her neck and straightened. "I'm starving. Do you think we could eat at the inn?" She raised her hand. "Not that

I'm complaining about the lovely accommodations you provided."

He stopped the massage and yanked on the curls that had fallen out of the pins. "There you go. Telling stories after I've brought you breakfast in bed."

"That *was* coffee I smelled." She moved faster than her sore muscles should allow and cried out again, just before her hands clasped the mug of coffee.

He laughed. "I'm glad I'm good for something." He grabbed his own mug and tossed a wrapped bundle toward her. "Not the best breakfast, but it will do for now."

She opened the paper and broke off a piece of cheese. "I'm grateful for everything you're doing." She picked at the bread.

Ethan waited, taking a sip of coffee, watching her. "Tell me about Finn."

Her head shot up. "There's nothing to tell."

"I can see that."

She dropped her gaze and rolled up the remaining cheese and bread. "As I already told you, he went off to London on some errand for the viscount. He never returned."

There was something more, but he knew the tone and he'd get little else. "You need to get packed up." Ethan stood and appraised her. "And you need to put yourself in order. But I'd leave the dirt on your face, it looks like stubble." He scratched his chin, the whiskers rough against his hand. "I'll get the horses and take the mugs back to the inn."

He watched her pull shafts of straw from her hair and run a hand over her face before checking her fingers. He turned and smiled when he heard her cry out again. A little pain would keep her focused.

When he returned with the horses, AJ had their packs ready. The straw had been fluffed, and he would never suspect someone had slept here. "You know how to hide your trail."

"I'm learning from a master." She yanked on her hat. "I even had time to stretch. I think my muscles will cooperate." She picked up a pack to hand him. "How far to the next town?"

"It will be a fair distance. There's a second road we'll take that cuts over to the main road leading south. It should save us some time, but there's no village on that road. I picked up more food in case we need to make camp."

"Great. I'm becoming quite the backcountry girl."

"If you say so."

She shrugged. "It's just a term for someone who camps out a lot. I have to say, this adventure is teaching me a great deal."

"Oh, how is that?"

"Well, I can confirm that I prefer beds to straw floors and blankets on the ground."

Ethan smirked. "So you're more like Stella than I thought."

"I'm discovering it's one of her better qualities."

They laughed as they turned their horses toward the road. Even with the aches and pain, she must have gotten a good night's sleep as she continued her chattering, jumping from one topic to another. He found it difficult to follow her and wished he had allowed himself more sleep. So he never looked back, as he usually did, to ensure no one followed them out of town.

He kept the pace slow as they settled in to the ride. Something, maybe a sound or second sight, eventually made him turn around. Nothing there. It didn't feel right. After reaching the second road, Ethan turned his horse to face the direction they'd just traveled. He spent several minutes sitting and listening.

The last time he looked, he was sure he'd seen something. His common sense told him to go back and check, but everything was quiet now. It was probably a deer, and they needed to make better time. AJ wouldn't be able to travel as far today.

He considered taking the longer route through the next village where they would be safer, but discarded the notion. It would put them further behind. He turned his steed around and, ignoring his better judgment, urged their mounts into a canter. If there was someone behind them, the pace should shake them loose.

———————

SEVERAL MILES PASSED before Ethan stopped for a rest. Every muscle in her body screamed when AJ slithered from the horse. She walked a few feet before collapsing to the ground.

"Are you all right?" Ethan called, pulling food from the bundles.

"I don't remember ever feeling like this, even when I first learned to climb. I didn't know my backside could be so sore just from sitting all day."

"I knew it would be worse today. Maybe we should find a spot deep off the road and give you a longer rest."

"No." The word came quick and fierce, and even she wasn't sure where her voice had come from. Was it for Maire or some stupid need to prove she could do this?

Ethan sat next to her and handed her food with a pouch of water.

She pulled off her hat and stretched out her legs before biting into the dried meat. "I just need a few minutes. Maybe just a short walk to work out the stiffness."

He nodded and watched the road.

She picked at a dry biscuit, sorry she'd forced him on this journey. But time slipped away, the stones moving out of her reach. A claustrophobic sensation rushed over her, and she struggled to breathe, the trees crowding her. Her only escape was to keep moving.

"You're not doing this because of Finn?"

AJ scowled. "How could this possibly be about him?"

Ethan finished his meal and stood. "Of course, how could it?" He turned to scan the area. "I think I'll take a walk myself and make sure no one is behind us. Don't walk far."

As he strode off in one direction and her in another, she thought about Finn—for about two seconds. Her actions had nothing to do with him. This was about Maire and the stones. Finn was out of the picture. He had left her, left the stones. Finis.

She kicked at a rock and winced. Even her toes hurt. When she turned back, she found Ethan waiting for her, the reins of both horses in his hands. Her body physically revolted at the thought of getting back on the horse. A day's rest would feel so good. Maybe she would relent when they made it to the next village. She grabbed her reins and swallowed the pain as Ethan hoisted her up.

They stopped once more to rest the horses. AJ's only thought as they churned through each mile was to simply hold on. Relief flooded her as the sun set, as she knew the village must be close, but they continued to ride. Another hour passed before Ethan turned off the road.

The darkness made it difficult to see Ethan in front of her, the moon a sliver in the sky. She heard the creek, and after riding a short distance following the stream, a grouping of trees shimmered in the low light. Dear God. They were only resting the horses before moving on again.

Ethan led them to the trees and dismounted. He removed the bundles of supplies from his horse and dropped them next to one of the trees before turning to AJ. He helped her off the gelding and held her up as she fell against him, her legs shaking as if she'd run the entire way.

"I'm sorry. I guess we should have found that place off the road you wanted."

Ethan's tone was soft as he walked her to a spot by a fallen tree to let her fall into the tall grass. "It's all right. This glade should provide enough cover."

"Do you think we're being followed?" AJ had noticed the continual glances over his shoulder, more frequent in the last few hours.

"I thought so early this morning. But if we were, we're not anymore. Our riding has been a bit erratic, so I'm sure I would have seen something."

She nodded and picked through her pack when Ethan dropped it at her feet. "I think I'll wash up a bit and see if I can get this grime off me."

"No. You'll need to wait until morning. I'll get a rag so you can wipe your face, but it's going to get cold tonight. You don't want to lose any body heat."

She leaned back against the trunk of a tree, grateful there was something to hold her up. "So no fire?"

"No fire."

24

AJ and Ethan took time with their dinner, avoiding any conversation of their current situation. AJ peppered him with questions about the current political climate in England. He tried to answer all he knew of King George until the questions ceased, and AJ's breathing deepened into sleep.

He lay close to her, hoping to keep her warm with shared body heat. He furrowed his brow, fighting off the foreboding he couldn't shake. Was it a deer he had seen, or had someone followed them out of town that morning?

Although he had kept a watchful eye on the road, something eluded him. After the cutoff to the village, when they had taken the other road, he no longer felt a presence. Perhaps it was nothing more than another traveler who took the road to the village. Between little sleep the night before and trying to keep up with AJ's morning chatter, he hadn't paid close attention. The more he tried to recall what he'd glimpsed on the road, the more his growing apprehension nagged at him.

AJ STARED at Finn as he sat atop the huge white steed, his face in shadows. She sensed his scowl, the penetrating gaze locked on hers, his laugh harsh and unforgiving. Then she caught sight of his dark eyes, hard as obsidian, the flashing green turned to black as he examined her. One last puzzle piece to step over on his way to complete his precious mission. Then, without a word, he turned from her and whipped his horse into a gallop.

Her eyes shot open, and she whipped her head toward Ethan. He still slept, close enough she could feel the heat of his body. Her protector. She chided herself for ever doubting him, for not listening to his warnings about Finn so long ago. His brow furrowed, and she reached out to smooth the wrinkles, but pulled back. Even in sleep, he couldn't hide his doubt about saving Maire. Maybe he was right.

She'd told him her concern was for Maire's safety, but if she was honest with herself, her first thought was Maire's knowledge of the stones. Where was her humanity when she now only thought of herself before those around her? She blamed Finn.

Moving quietly so as not to wake Ethan, she sat up and scanned the area. The sun hadn't quite broken the horizon, but it was light enough to see the horses still tied to their tree. This was her favorite time of day, her best climbing time.

She crawled from the warmth of Ethan's presence. No better time than the present to wash the grime off and be ready to ride when Ethan woke. She stood and stretched, working out the last of the remaining aches from yesterday.

Using a rag she found in one of the saddlebags, she squatted by the creek to wash her face. She opened her shirt to wipe under her arms and around her neck. It would have to do. The icy water puckered her skin, and a light shiver ran through her. She rubbed her hands over her arms and watched the water meander around the mossy rocks and twigs, pooling in a few places before continuing downstream. AJ lifted her head to catch the first rays of the morning sun when she heard a snap from behind her. Thinking it was Ethan, she turned to greet him.

THE SOUND of screaming snapped Ethan awake. He rolled for his sword and was on his feet in mere seconds. The sun lifted from the horizon, and he squinted through the glare of the blinding light. The scream came again, followed by yelling, and he spun, turning his focus to the river.

There were four of them. They dragged AJ toward their horses. She fought, kicked, and spat, her screaming growing louder.

"Ethan!"

The men's arguing almost drowned out the warning cry.

Now it all came together. They hadn't been followed, at least not since they'd turned off the main road. Whoever had followed them from the village must have ridden on to the next, knowing they could circle around and come at them from the other direction. He was so stupid. He cursed inwardly as he ran into the melee, knowing he would never be able to fight off four of them. Two would be possible, three maybe, depending on their skill, but not four.

THE MEN FANNED out around AJ as she stood to face the viscount's men. None of them was Dugan, but she recognized one of them. She reached for her pocket, where she had hidden the dagger Ethan had given her. Before she could reach it, her arms were grabbed from behind, and she released an ear-splitting scream.

She twisted, trying to wrench free, her screams growing shriller, but the man's fingers gripped like steel claws. Another closed in on her, and she kicked, forcing the man back. His face twisted into an ugly leer. She involuntarily shrank back into the hard chest of her other attacker.

"Ethan!" His name echoed through the glade as AJ tried to evade the reach of the man's long, thick arm.

The man lurched and grabbed her arm. With a man on each side of her, they dragged her away from the stream toward their horses. She tried to turn around, squirming and yanking, when her focus landed on Ethan.

He ran toward them with sword in hand, ready for battle, his face a mask of rage. But as AJ whipped her head around, she counted four men and knew the odds were against him.

The men holding her released their grip for an instant when they saw Ethan racing toward them. She didn't hesitate and pulled an arm free, turning toward one of her captors.

Her kick landed a decisive blow against an upper leg, forcing a grunt, but before she could land another, a hard slap reeled her head back. Her cheek burned as if branded, but she didn't relent. Using every ounce of strength she could muster, she tugged and kicked again. If she could keep two of them busy, maybe that would be enough to help Ethan.

And it was—for a while.

AJ never stopped screaming as Ethan brought up his sword, time and time again, fending off attacks from two men. She watched in terror when he ducked as a blade swerved toward him, but he swung as he came back up. A guttural yelp blew out from one of the men, and he grabbed his midsection, looking down as blood appeared beneath his hand.

She didn't think it was fatal, but enough to take him out of the fight. Ethan would have been able to finish the second man, but one of the men holding her released her, pulling out his own sword as he ran toward Ethan.

His release came swiftly, and with her focus on Ethan, she didn't have a chance to try to pull free from the other man before his arms were around her, holding her tight. She forced her head back to catch his chin, but he was too tall. She stomped her foot, and she heard a satisfying groan before he shook her and twirled her around. The next slap knocked her to the ground. Before she could scrabble away, he picked her up, her body limp against him. But it didn't stop her ear-piercing screaming. He could hit her all day if it kept him away from Ethan.

The sounds of blade crossing blade echoed through the glade. AJ could hear the heavy breathing and the dragging of feet on dirt, the exertion of the fight straining all of them. She kept blinking, but it wasn't enough to clear the tears that streamed down her face. She tried to kick her captor, but he'd widened his stance. All she could do was watch; even her screams betrayed her and grew hoarse.

Her champion was weakening. Sweat ran down his face, and he struggled to keep his sword arm up as his legs grew less nimble. There were just too many well-trained men against one.

Then Ethan pirouetted to the right, forcing one of the men to take a wrong step. Ethan's blade connected with the man's arm, and he cried out as his sword dropped. AJ felt a glimmer of hope. She berated herself for all that wasted time in Ireland not learning how to wield a sword. Gardening and cooking wouldn't help her now.

Ethan seemed stronger after the last man dropped his sword, but it also urged on his opponent, who found a new reservoir of energy. Ethan continued his attacks, his face never reflecting what AJ could clearly see.

Her screams turned to pleas. "No. No. Just leave him. I'll come with you."

It didn't matter. She couldn't stop the fight, or stop the ominous scrape of blades, again and again, as they connected. Until they didn't.

AJ didn't see it happen. She only heard Ethan's cry of surprise, and she stopped her struggle. Everything went silent except for the soft breeze that rustled the leaves.

Ethan stared down at his shirt before glancing up. He caught her eyes. A fleeting string of emotions ran between them before he gazed down again. The blood snaked thin tentacles over his shirt. He glanced up once more, his eyes unreadable as he fell.

He landed hard and didn't move. The man who had been forced to drop his sword now held it with his other hand as he stood over Ethan. AJ thought he was going to swing it, but instead, the man kicked the inert Ethan in the side.

He didn't stir.

The man nodded to his buddies. They turned to AJ.

"No." The sound would have pierced the soul of any man who had one. Her struggles stopped. She felt nothing. She heard nothing. Saw nothing. Her body sagged to the ground when her captor released her.

AJ had no recollection of time passing as the men retrieved her horse. One of the men kicked Ethan a last time. She offered no resistance as they lifted her into the saddle. Her reins were held by one of the men as they turned toward the road. She would never remember the journey to the village. The one Ethan had tried to make the day before.

When they arrived at the village, they had to pull her down and drag her through the inn. She never noticed the rest of the viscount's men at the tables, nor did she resist or say a word as she was led up the stairs and pushed into a room. Nor did she notice Maire who ran to her as she dropped to the floor.

It wasn't until Maire enveloped AJ in her arms and she heard the door click closed that she allowed the tears to fall for her friend. Her sobs sprang from the darkest center of her core.

The clashing of blades ripped AJ out of her nightmare, and she struggled against her captors. She moved to rise, but something held her down, and no amount of pushing at bedcovers would release her. Then she heard the soft voice at her ear.

"It's all right, love. Everything will be all right. I'm here."

An arm released her, and she felt a soft hand rub her shoulder as if comforting a small child. She felt like one. The sound of metal pounded in her head, and her feet wouldn't move, as if she were stuck in wet cement. She glanced toward the window, the blue sky mocking her, but the memory of the morning wouldn't dissipate. All she saw was Ethan falling, over and over again. She relaxed against Maire, who kept one arm over her, her warmth welcoming against the ice invading AJ's body.

"Is it morning?" AJ stretched her legs, which she had tucked up to make herself into a ball.

"Closer to afternoon. You've mostly slept since they brought you back yesterday morning. Fortunately for us, the viscount has been delayed." Maire pulled the hair back from AJ's face. "Dugan's quite upset with you but has agreed to let you rest one more day. You should get as much sleep as you can."

AJ stared vacantly at the window. She wasn't sure she would ever have another peaceful sleep without the nightmares. They weren't all about Ethan. She dreamed of Finn, astride his horse, watching her escape before turning and riding away. He was at fault. He was to blame for Ethan's death.

She pushed again at the bedcovers, and Maire's arm slid away. The blaze of the fire did nothing to cure her chill as she poured cold water into a bowl. The touch of the rag to her head made her wince.

"Do I have a bruise? I'm afraid to look."

She turned her face to Maire who nodded.

"Yes. It should be quite spectacular by tomorrow. Just one more thing to irritate Dugan and the viscount." She wasn't condemning, just stating a fact.

AJ shrugged and held the cold rag to what had to be red and puffy eyes. She stumbled to the couch, her legs and arms feeling as battered as her face. The sound of the door opening startled her until she saw Maire lean her head out before closing the door.

"I just ordered some food."

AJ relaxed into the couch and leaned her head back, keeping the rag in place. Maire sat next to her, close but not touching. They sat in silence until a soft knock forced AJ to remove the rag. Seeing it was a young woman carrying a tray, she turned back to the fire and replaced the rag.

When the door closed again, she heard Maire fiddling with plates and cups. The drifting aroma of the warm stew made her stomach growl. Betrayed by her body begging for nourishment, she sighed and joined Maire at the table.

She stuffed her mouth. As much as it hurt to think about Ethan, he would be furious with her for giving up. Within the twenty-four hours since his death, her disbelief had turned to anger. A red-hot fury she refused to let die. There would be time later to mourn her friend. Right now, she needed the rage to give her the courage she needed for her plan. And Dugan's agreement to let them remain for a day played right into it. She glanced at Maire, gauging her mood, before grabbing a chunk of cheese.

"Can you tell me what happened?" Maire sipped her tea.

AJ had been waiting for the question as if held by invisible bonds until someone said the magic words. But she didn't know what to say, how to share her ordeal, to make Maire understand how important Ethan had been, and what a tragic loss it was. Now that the question freed her, she felt the tears threaten, and she blinked them away. She blew out a long smooth breath.

"Ethan, the man who rescued me, was a very dear friend. The viscount's men killed him." The levelness of her tone surprised her, a reporter just reporting the facts.

Maire's hand trembled when she set down her cup, but she remained silent.

"He didn't know about you, or he would have tried to save you as well." AJ pushed her remaining food away. Suddenly, the food she consumed wanted to retreat, and she swallowed, forcing it to stay down. A melancholy smile formed without permission. "He was that kind of man."

Then it all spilled out. "Ethan was good and kind and smart." She slid a glance at Maire. "He knew of the stones. The Earl of Hereford, his mentor, sent him to retrieve a larger stone that was in my necklace. To keep it away from the viscount." She told Maire of where they had gone after fleeing the viscount's men. "I was the one who convinced Ethan to come back for you."

The last words almost strangled her. She couldn't seem to catch her breath. When Maire grabbed hers and squeezed, she let the tears fall. She wiped her face, searching for the anger and giving it carte blanche to bubble forth.

She squeezed Maire's hand before releasing it to pour a cup of tea. "And I was just getting rid of the puffiness." She gave a quick snort. "As if I should care who sees me like this."

"Well, I think the puffiness is quite unsightly, so I appreciate the attempt. Although it doesn't appear to be working as well as you might have hoped."

AJ stared at her friend. Maire appeared quite stoic as she waited for AJ to complete her tale. Then AJ laughed, her laughter deep and rich before it ended on a hysterical note. "I can't believe I just laughed like that. How could I laugh?" She hung her head and kneaded her knuckles on her legs.

"Laughter is just another strong emotion. Sometimes it's required to flush out what crying won't resolve." Maire picked up the empty plates. "Something I've learned over the last year."

The silence returned. The only sound in the room came from the occasional snapping and popping in the hearth. AJ fiddled with a napkin, turning corners as if she could create the origami figures her friend Stella made when she thought through a problem.

"I've been thinking." AJ let the words hang in the air, a test of the waters.

Maire said nothing for several seconds. "I knew there was something going on. Tell me."

"I've been thinking of the earl. The man Ethan worked for. Have you heard of him?"

Maire shook her head. "I don't believe so, but there's no deficiency of earls. Do you know where he lives?"

"Somewhere not far from London."

"He would be easy to find. Even having an estate close by, he probably has a residence in London." Maire shrugged. "It's off season, but the staff could get a message to him."

"Assuming we're in London." AJ walked to the window for a quick glance before settling on the sofa, doing everything she could to avoid Maire's gaze.

"Or know someone who could get him the message," Maire countered.

"Would you trust a note from a stranger about something concerning the stones?"

"But you said Ethan worked for him, and you were friends."

"I never met the earl myself. I'm not sure Ethan mentioned me. He must have, but I'm not positive." AJ pulled her legs underneath her. "I'd hate to trust something so important to someone I didn't know."

Maire sat next to AJ and stared into the orange glow of the hearth. "Assuming we could get away, how would we get to London?" She paused and turned to AJ. "And we would lose the opportunity to know where the viscount is going."

"There must be some other way to track where he goes. Wouldn't it be safer to have more men on our side? It seems more dangerous to just stay with these men."

Maire turned back to the fire. Unable to read her face, AJ fidgeted, afraid she'd lost her.

"I can't be with these men," she said, her voice barely above a whisper.

The silence continued for several long moments. Both women stared into the flames, waiting for the answer to appear. The afternoon sun cast long shadows on the floor, and AJ could almost hear the ticking of a clock counting down precious minutes.

"I know of two herbs, hops and valerian root, which may be useful to us."

AJ's head snapped up to meet Maire's eyes. She seemed resigned, going along with a plan with which she didn't completely agree. Another person willing to follow her. And would this be another mistake that would lead to more misery?

"What would it do?"

"It helps aid sleep. If the person isn't tired, it encourages the feeling. It will be helpful if the men have been drinking through the day. Which I assume they have been, with nothing else to do."

"And you have some of this herb with you?"

"No. But they may have some downstairs. The men will be sitting down to dinner soon. I can talk my way downstairs to get a headache remedy for you. I'll tell the men I need to observe the making of the concoction myself."

"Do I need to ask why you think the innkeeper or his wife will assist you?"

"No. Just trust that they will." Maire reached for her wrap and, after a quick glance at the mirror over the washstand, readjusted her hair. "You will need to determine how we get out of here."

AJ smiled. "I have a thought about that."

Maire's attempt at a smile turned into a grimace as she opened the door. After a few quiet words to the guard, she gave AJ one last questioning glance. "You're positive about this course?"

AJ waited a beat and then nodded.

Maire sighed, pressed her hands down her dress, raised her chin, and closed the door behind her.

THEY WAITED until well past midnight to check their guard, even though AJ thought she heard light snoring beyond the door an hour earlier.

"The herbs will impact the men differently. We need to be patient." Maire finished twisting her hair into a bun and picked up her wrap.

"How much did you give them?" AJ felt in her pocket for her dagger. It seemed so insignificant, but a little blade was better than none at all.

"More than enough, but it depends how much wine or ale they drank."

"You put it in both?"

Maire nodded. "Yes, the innkeeper's wife kept him busy, and I added the herbs myself to both. They're sure to drink one or the other."

Waiting as long as she could, AJ put her ear to the door and listened. The snoring sounded louder. She held her breath and pried the door open an inch. Waited. When nothing happened, she pulled the door wider until she could see the guard sitting on the floor, head back against the wall, snoring loud enough to be heard down stairs.

Closing the door behind them, the women tiptoed past the guard and inched their way down the stairs, cringing anytime they heard a tiny squeak from a misplaced foot. They stopped just short of the common room.

In the lead, AJ scanned the room for any man possibly awake but saw no one. Maire hugged in tight behind her, taking more time to study each man, eight in all. Their heads were on tables, on their chests, or leaned back against the wall like their door guard as more snoring filtered through the room.

"Are these all the men? There seemed to be more," AJ whispered.

"I think I counted ten, but they come and go. It's difficult to be sure."

AJ pointed to a man who sat near the door to the kitchen, his head on the table in front of him. "Dugan."

"Yes, and we must go by him or attempt the front door."

AJ glanced at the front door. It seemed miles away. The kitchen was the plan, and they needed to stick with it. She reached for Maire's hand as they crept down the final two steps, past one man on the floor before coming to Dugan.

Even sitting down, head on the table, he seemed massive. Taking a deep breath, she squeezed Maire's hand and slinked past the man, each step carefully planted and tested on the wood planks. She had cleared him and was almost to the opening for the kitchen when Maire's foot found a loose plank, producing a loud squeak. The sound reverberated through the room, hanging in the air for what seemed like an eternity. AJ clung to Maire, heart in her throat, as they watched the men.

Dugan's head started to rise and wavered a bit. He reached out, fingers curling before growing still. He turned his head and rested it back on the table, his shoulders slumping.

The women blew out a silent sigh, and AJ rested her head on Maire's shoulder. Waiting a few more seconds, they scanned the room one last time before stepping into the kitchen. They increased their pace as they moved through the darkness, the embers of the evening fire providing just enough light to maneuver through the room without knocking anything over.

At the door to the outside, Maire picked up two packages tied with string and handed one to AJ. When she stared down at the wrapped food, she shook her head at Maire's resourcefulness. The phrase *catch more flies with honey* flashed through her mind, and she made a promise to look it up on Google someday, because she would swear it was discovered by someone following Maire around.

As they stepped outside, Maire ran into AJ, who had stopped. "What is it?"

"Nothing. I just needed a minute to breathe in the fresh air of freedom."

"It won't be freedom long if we linger."

AJ nodded. "You're right. I think the stables are over here."

She turned left and raced to a oversized bush. They snuck from bush to bush, building to building. Each time, they stopped and waited to see if anyone spotted them. They waited for a full minute before moving on. The ten minutes they took to reach the back of the stable seemed like forever. The door on this side was closed tight for the evening.

"Stay here. Give me a couple of minutes to check it out." AJ moved before Maire could voice her opinion.

Slipping around the side of the building, she raced to a clump of bushes and squatted. Most of the street and a portion of the stable door were visible from this vantage point. She rubbed her shoulders and relaxed her muscles, breathing in the light cool air as her heart rate slowed. Her senses alert, she counted out two minutes, then decided to wait longer.

She glanced behind her before shifting her attention back to the stable doors. As she took a tentative step toward the stable, she caught movement from the door. Two men appeared. They whispered to each other, then scanned the area.

AJ jumped behind the bush before the men saw her. She closed her eyes and listened for a few racing heartbeats before bending a branch to peek through the bush. They were still there, walking back and forth, in and out of sight. Waiting until they walked out of sight, she then scrambled back to Maire. She grabbed Maire's arm and pulled her away to another building, far enough to ensure they couldn't be heard.

"What took you so long?" Maire sounded out of breath. "I was so worried."

"I wanted to make sure no one was around. Good thing I did."

"Did someone see you?"

AJ shook her head. "No. I don't think so. But there were two men at the front of the stables. They must be watching the horses. We'll never get in there."

Maire leaned her head against the building. "I guess this was all for naught."

"No. This means we move to plan B."

Maire raised an eyebrow. "You have another plan?"

"We are not going back. Not willingly. There's always another plan."

Maire shook her head. "We are a pitiful lot. As long as we keep our wits about us, perhaps we can still succeed."

"That's the spirit." A massive amount of adrenaline pumped through AJ. It happened each time she started a climb, and it always pushed her forward, never second-guessing herself. Plan each step as it comes, and if one way is blocked, there's always another. It was always about finding the next edge. "We still have a few hours before daylight and before anyone searches for us."

"Assuming no one awakes before then. As soon as they wake, they'll know something is wrong."

"Right. So we need to get as far as we can."

"On foot?"

"For now. If we stick close to the road, we might be able to find someone with a carriage or cart who can give us a lift."

"A lift?" Maire looked doubtful.

"A ride."

Maire gave AJ a sideways glance before shaking her head. "All right, we stay close to the road."

"Which direction is London?"

Maire scanned the road in both directions, forehead furrowed in thought. She shrugged. "I think back the way we came. There was a road not too far back. I think it headed east. It should eventually lead to London."

AJ studied Maire. Her decision seemed final. "Okay. I guess that makes sense. Back the way we came. We should stay on the road as long as we can until it gets lighter. If we hear someone coming, we'll duck into the bushes."

Maire nodded, and they crept through the end of town, waiting for someone to call the alert, but no alarms sounded. AJ let out a shaky breath when the town was well behind them. They picked up their pace, arm and arm as they marched down the road. AJ stifled a laugh, her mind racing to an oddly sick vision of Dorothy and the Yellow Brick Road. They were off to see the Wizard or, in their case, the earl.

Please don't let there be any flying monkeys.

26

Long days in the saddle with short, sleepless nights left Finn exhausted and short-tempered. It seemed he made one mistake after another trying to protect those he cared for, and the results of his actions did little to secure anyone's safety.

Since his youth, he'd acted first and figured the rest out later, but these last two years had taught him patience. Carefully nurtured associations with every detail scrutinized had all worked—until now. Even as he played out this final mission, his course of action set in motion, he second-guessed himself.

His instinct had been to leave AJ at the cottage, but short of having her locked in a room, sooner or later she would have left to find her own way home. She'd been safer with him, if only he'd been honest with her from the start. Then he walked her right into the viscount's hands. Anyway he played it, he would have been damned.

With his last-minute assignations in London complete, he had placed all his chips on believing his foresight was correct. Now he allowed his second nature to take over, driving his steed to keep its pace. He grimaced. All this suffering and intrigue over some ancient stones. Yet, without the stones, he would never have met AJ. And if anyone asked, he would risk it all to do it again.

After another half hour of pushing, Finn pulled his horse to a stop at a wide stream. The sound of the slow-moving water enticed him, and a heaviness settled in. He needed rest more than his horse did, but they could manage another ten miles to the next village.

He dismounted and let his horse drink while he scanned the horizon of low, rolling hills as green as his knolls of Ireland. A movement beyond a copse of trees, far enough off the road to be ignored by passing travelers, caught his eye.

A branch of a tree moved, something passing under it, and then a head pushed through. A horse. Finn pulled his own steed from the river and turned toward the trees. There was something odd about the scene. The horse came into full view, lazily grazing the tall grasses, fully saddled but without a rider.

He reached for his sword and turned around, sweeping the entire landscape in one quick motion. A warning prickled along his spine, and he picked his way through the grass, squinting to see past the trees. The only sound came from the chomping of the horse and birds trilling in the soft afternoon sun.

The horse rubbed his nose against its leg and let out a soft chuff as Finn grew near, his own horse's ears pinned forward. He reached the edge of the grove, scanning the serene glade protected within the shelter of the trees. He caught sight of something in the grass. Bits of white among the tall blades of green.

As he grew closer, he could see it was a shirt of some kind. And someone was still wearing it. Dark hair poked out from one end, and a dark red stain mingled with mud and dirt, marring the bits of whiteness that remained.

Finn sniffed the air as if he could catch a scent of what happened. All he caught was the smell of grass warming in the sun, a flower he didn't recognize, and the sweet smell of horses.

He crept toward the man, unconcerned whether he was dead or alive, simply not wanting to surprise anyone with a pistol.

His heartbeat thundering, he nudged the man with his foot and braced when he heard a light groan. Squatting, he gently turned the man over. Blood seeped from the man's side. Then his heart stopped.

Ethan.

His breath froze, forming a lump in his chest he couldn't dislodge. What had happened here? AJ had been with Ethan. As he checked the man's body for the source of bleeding, all he wanted to do was wake this fool to ask about her.

Ethan groaned louder as Finn ripped open his shirt and found the wound, crusted black and starting to fester. He bent low and sniffed. It didn't stink, so he may have caught it before any infection set in. He was never more grateful than now for the things he'd learned during his time travel.

Finn ran his hands over Ethan's legs and arms to see if there were any further wounds or broken bones, but other than conjuring a few painful groans, he found nothing else. Ethan's face paled in the bright sunshine, glistening with a light sheen of sweat. Perhaps an infection already worked through his system. Based on what had soaked into the ground, he had lost a good amount of blood. Finn whispered a thanks to whatever god made him stop to rest. Perhaps the saints watched over them after all.

"Ethan." Finn shook the man's shoulder, trying to wake him. He tried again, more urgent. "Ethan." His raised voice couldn't elicit a better response.

He left Ethan to walk through the trees in search of kindling. After finding a few dried branches, he started a campfire, the orange flames leaping and crackling as it spread its warmth. He dragged Ethan away from the bloody ground and positioned him against another tree, next to the fire. The sound of moaning encouraged Finn that Ethan might yet survive.

Finn retrieved a bag from his saddle and one from Ethan's. He removed a shirt, two blankets, a water pouch, and some leftover cheese and biscuits. Leaving everything by the firepit, he ripped the shirt in half and walked to the stream to soak it, the water dripping to the ground as he walked back to Ethan.

He hunched down and brought the water pouch to Ethan's lips as he released a few droplets. When there was no response, Finn opened Ethan's mouth to let the water drip inside. He spent several minutes nudging the water in before turning his attention to the wound.

It was crusted over, and the bleeding had stopped. Using the wet shirt, he gently scrubbed the wound before squeezing water over it to wash it clean. A fresh trickle of blood flowed, but the wound looked pink. The oozing soon subsided, revealing a long and narrow slice through Ethan's side. Only one thing could have created this wound. A cutlass.

A raging anger exploded through him at the thought of a sword fight. He didn't know if AJ had been here, but if she hadn't been with Ethan, where else would she be? Focusing on the only thing he had control over, Finn used the other half of the ripped shirt to fashion a bandage around Ethan's middle to protect the wound. It was all he could do for now.

Finn covered Ethan with a thin blanket and stood to survey the makeshift campsite and the road beyond. Ensuring they were alone, he tied both horses to trees and pulled out a bundle of rope from his saddlebag. He walked through the glade, searching for spots to place snares. They would both need more than biscuits and jerky to keep their bellies full, assuming Ethan would wake from the blood loss or infection. Finn kept his focus on placement of the snares, refusing to let his mind wander to places he didn't want to go. He had to assume AJ was safe, or he would make himself mad.

Once the snares were set, he returned to camp and dropped down by a tree not far from Ethan. He reviewed how this new event changed his plans, especially if Ethan didn't survive. If the viscount's men had caused Ethan's injury, then AJ should be safely back with them. And he knew where they were headed. That was the best-case scenario. If it was someone else, there were too many possibilities to know where to start. He would have to choose between following the viscount to complete his mission or heading out on an aimless hunt for AJ. Whoever they were, they would have traveled by road, and if they had gone north, Finn would have seen them. But, since leaving the last village, he'd met no one on the road except one old farmer and his wagon of supplies.

Finn settled back to consider the choices. When a shaft of afternoon light hit his face, he came awake with a start. He rubbed his eyes and, before standing, quietly canvassed the area. All quiet. The sun had moved closer to the horizon, casting long shadows from the trees. He'd been asleep about an hour and felt better for it. He stretched his legs and stood over Ethan. The man's chest rose and fell. Still alive.

He tossed wood onto the fire and left to check his traps. Disheartened to find the first trap empty, he smiled when he found a rabbit in the second one.

When he returned, Ethan's color appeared to have improved. Finn washed out the dirty shirt and brought more water to Ethan, dripping the cool spring water into parched lips that seemed a bit pinker than before. Perhaps the man had a chance. He checked the wound. A splotch of blood marred the torn shirt, but nothing more. They just had to wait.

The sun had set by the time the rabbit finished roasting on a makeshift spit. As Finn watched the rabbit slowly cook, he returned to his earlier musings to determine which direction to go. He silenced the internal ticking, knowing AJ moved farther away as he sat there, coddling the man who was supposed to have protected her. If Ethan wasn't already half-dead, he would have throttled him for the risk he had taken. Finn turned the rabbit over, his stomach wailing at the delay.

"How much longer must I wait for dinner?" The voice was low and raspy, each word partially slurred.

Finn jumped to the man's side. "So you're going to be harder to kill than most."

"It may be too early to tell." Each word struggled over rough lips, followed by a sharp cry as Ethan attempted to move.

"Aye, especially if you reopen the wound." Finn pushed Ethan back down. "Stay where you are until you're a bit stronger. There's nothing to see here." Finn pulled out another shirt from his bag and tucked it under Ethan's head. "I would have packed more clothing if I'd known I'd find a stupid man along the trail."

He received a low grunt and moan for a response. Ethan's face turned paler from his one vain attempt to move. Finn wanted to strangle the man, but instead he brought the water pouch to his lips. This time, Ethan eagerly lapped at the drops, raising his head to meet them.

"Is AJ alive?" Finn steeled himself for the answer.

"Last I saw, they were dragging her away." Ethan labored with each word, sucking in his breath, his eyes pinched. "She fought like the devil."

The band around Finn's chest loosened, and he bent his head with a smile. "Was it the viscount's men?"

"Yes." Ethan grimaced.

"That's enough for now. Let's get some food in you. We'll talk more in the morning."

Satisfied the rabbit had cooked long enough, Finn pulled off a hindquarter and helped Ethan choke it down. Each morsel was followed by sips of water.

After dinner, Finn checked the bandage through Ethan's grunts before collapsing on the ground. He added a branch to the fire and stirred the flames. After several moments, he glanced over to see that Ethan had fallen asleep. With the knowledge that AJ was with the viscount's men, his instinct urged him to leave Ethan and go after her. They couldn't be that far ahead. Then he pictured AJ's brown eyes circled with gold, flashing with anger and hurt to know that Finn had left Ethan on his own. There was a bond between them he didn't understand.

He studied the man who had deftly rescued AJ, and then, for some unimaginable reason, put her in harm's way. It made no sense, but he wouldn't get an answer until tomorrow. He tossed two more branches onto the fire and stretched out. His focus returned to the flames as images of mercenaries dragging a spitting-mad AJ burned through him.

The early chirping of birds woke Finn before the emergence of the sun. He scanned the area in the dim light before kneeling next to Ethan, whose chest rose and fell, slow and steady. His color had returned, but his face shimmered with a light sweat.

Unable to do anything for him, Finn strode into the glade to check and reset snares. Returning with two rabbits, he set the first one on the spit to cook while he dressed the second. Ethan woke as the second rabbit roasted.

Finn placed a piece of bark next to him filled with strips of meat and a portion of biscuit. "Do you want some water first?"

Ethan nodded. He groaned as he struggled to sit up while Finn watched him, gauging his strength. After a minute, he helped Ethan into a sitting position. Perspiration trickled down his brow, but Finn couldn't tell if it was from fever or the exertion.

"You're a bit better this morning."

"We'll see. I had a few shakes through the evening. I'm not sure I've cleared the fever."

"Aye, I noticed. But you're awake. That must count for something." Finn passed Ethan the water pouch.

He placed the pouch against his lips, but most of the water dribbled down his chin. Wincing, he laid his head back. "I think I used up my energy sitting."

Finn grabbed the rag of shirt and walked to the river to douse it in the stream. When he returned, Ethan was chewing the last of the rabbit and nibbling on the biscuit. "You have an appetite."

"Hopefully another good sign. I don't know how long I've been out, but it seems like I haven't eaten for days."

"I've been thinking about that. I found you yesterday, but it couldn't have been more than several hours after the skirmish."

Ethan nodded. "That's good. Assuming they took her back to the coach and her traveling companion, they will use inns from now on. I doubt they'll risk another night out in the open."

"Her traveling companion. There's someone other than AJ?" Finn held his breath as he waited for the confirmation.

Ethan finished the biscuit and tipped the pouch of water to his lips. "Yes, another woman called Maire. AJ was worried about her." A minute passed and he appeared to have fallen asleep until he whispered, "She was so upset we couldn't save her." He shook his head. "I didn't think they'd still be looking for her. I let AJ think we were going to try to save Maire, but I wanted to confirm where they were headed."

He fussed with his bandage and paled before leaning back. "Not the best of plans, but you know how stubborn she can be."

Hearing there was a connection between the two women forced a slow, broad grin across Finn's face. He released a long breath that he'd been holding for what seemed like forever.

"I think I can ride to the next town. I might need a bit of a rest there before continuing on."

Finn's thoughts were interrupted when he grasped Ethan's meaning. "We go nowhere until you can stand on your own without opening your wound. You need at least another day to regain more strength. Maybe two."

"We can't wait that long. Each day, they get farther away."

"Don't you think I'm keenly aware of that?" Finn erupted, already tired of being tied to the man. "Don't you think I'd prefer to leave you here and go after them?"

Ethan stared, unflinching. Then he nodded. "You're right. You should go. I won't make it to town, not in this condition. AJ is the priority."

"Aye." His rage spent, Finn sighed as he stared at Ethan, unable to sit up on his own, let alone race after AJ. "I've had time to think it through. I'll need you fully healed if we have any hope of stealing the women back. I think we might have some time yet. Besides, what do you think AJ would do if she discovered I left you out here?"

Ethan tried to laugh but blanched instead. "I wouldn't want to be in your shoes. I have no desire to be on the wrong end of her anger."

"Then you see my dilemma."

"Yes." Ethan picked at his bandage again. "Then I need to see how bad the wound is. We need to keep it clean."

Finn knelt next to him and unwrapped the bandage.

"Well, that's a good gash, but it doesn't appear too bad. Or am I delirious?" Ethan touched the area, gingerly pressing around the wound until a trickle of blood flowed with a clear fluid.

"I don't smell anything. That's a good sign."

"It confirms one thing."

"And what's that?"

"I think I have a broken or bruised rib. I don't think the wound is what's causing most of the pain."

Finn pushed Ethan's shirt up to reveal a dark bruise. "Aye, so you do. You must have gotten kicked while you were down."

Ethan closed his eyes. "If you don't mind getting another shirt out of my bag. It can be ripped in thirds so I always have a dry bandage. I can use this other piece of shirt to keep the wound clean."

"Aye."

Finn set about the tasks, first bringing the wet rag for Ethan to clean the wound. He ripped the new shirt and helped wrap it around Ethan. By the end, Ethan had fallen asleep, his head drooped over his chest.

With little else to do, Finn searched the glade for more wood while keeping watch on his snares, and waited for Ethan to wake.

ETHAN CAME awake with a start and groaned from a new pain, a kink in his neck. He couldn't remember ever feeling so wretched. He glanced down at the sting from the wound, relieved to see the bloodless shirt. Leaning his head back with a growl, he surveyed his injuries. Between the wound, the bruised ribs and the kinked neck, the ribs were the clear winner. As if needing to prove it, he braced for the pain and took a long, deep breath, barely able to hold back the tears.

In his youth, he had dealt with bruised and broken ribs, both in training with the earl's men and in battle. He didn't think they were broken, and if the wound would stay shut, he would be able to ride soon. Ignoring the pain, he took another deep breath and listened to the stream ripple over rocks, accompanied by songbirds twittering in the early shadow of the trees. The soft scent of wild rose and summer grasses drifted through the air, weaving through the smells of a dying fire. This was home. Or just a couple of days ride from it. It seemed like a lifetime since he'd seen it.

He glanced over to see Finn asleep at his tree. Fate had certainly been on his side for Finn to find him, but the man had a great deal of explaining to do. AJ had said she'd seen him at the campsite during her rescue, but he hadn't joined in. Ethan didn't understand why the man wanted to help him after all the time they'd chased each other for the stone necklace. He could hypothesize all day and find no answer. One thing he did know: they needed to get it all out in the open before they could move forward.

Out of the corner of his eye, he saw someone approaching on the road. He sat motionless, waiting to see if he needed to wake Finn. He glanced at the horses, satisfied they seemed to be hidden behind the trees, away from the road. The apparition grew in size as it approached, and he relaxed the muscles that had involuntarily grown taut. A slow-moving wagon with a single individual, head down, making his way north. If the wagon had been moving south, he would have woken Finn to see if the wagon could transport him to town. Fate only seemed to work to a point. He watched the wagon make its way down the road, never changing its snail's pace.

"Have I been out long?"

Ethan lifted a shoulder and then grimaced. "Not sure. I haven't been awake long myself."

"You look stronger."

"Maybe enough to attempt standing. In a bit. I could use some more food."

Finn doled out leftover rabbit, a slice of cheese, and bread. "Have you truly been chasing me from the beginning?"

"From the beginning? Yes, I think so." Ethan reached for the water pouch, grimaced at the movement, and drank before continuing. "I was told there was another man searching for the stone, probably a day ahead of me. I assume that was you."

"Who sent you?"

He glanced at Finn. Moments ago, he'd decided they needed to get everything out in the open, but he'd prefer to hear more from Finn before divulging all his own secrets. "The Earl of Hereford sent me. I've been in his employ for a very long time. He seemed to think I was the only one he could trust with this mission." Ethan laughed and went silent, growing pale as a bolt of pain shot through him. After the wave subsided, he finished, "I thought he was crazed when he told me of the stone and its powers. I thought it nothing more than an old man's folly from all the books he read. Books of secret societies and old sects."

"Did he know everything the stone could do?"

"The earl can appear obtuse at times. Even more so as he grows older. It's mostly a ruse, especially when the stakes are high. At the time, he said he knew very little of the stone. But now, I think he knew much more than he shared."

"Aye. I found it all to be a tall tale, until the stone was given to me with a piece of paper with words I could barely read scrawled across it. I never learned the old language like my sister did." He paused, glancing across the glade. "There was something about the stone, just by itself. Such a tiny piece, yet I could almost feel the magic within."

Ethan nodded. "I remember that. The same strange feeling when the earl handed me the stone and the incantation. He made sure I kept the stone in a different room as he taught me to read the old Celtic words." He sobered when he gazed at the man across from him, a competitor for the stone. "What made you take on such a mission? How much did the viscount pay you for such an impossible task?"

Finn's jaw clenched. Ethan had only seen the man a handful of times, and he always flashed that grin that made men want to be his chum and left women swooning. Finn glanced away, staring at the empty road. When his answer came, Ethan had to lean over to hear the words. "Everything I do, I do for the life of a woman."

Ethan sat back. "A woman? You couldn't have known about AJ before you started the mission."

"It wasn't AJ I was speaking of." Finn turned to Ethan. "It's my sister."

He stared at Finn, waiting for him to continue, but he didn't. He pinched his brows together, stepping through everything he knew. Then it came to him. "Maire." When Finn glanced to the ground, Ethan shook his head. "And you never said anything to AJ?"

Finn hung his head, pushing his boot through the dirt. "I never seemed to find the right time. I had hoped to get her and Maire out of the manor after turning over the stones." He paused, seeming to play over his decisions. "I keep making the wrong choices with AJ."

"You poor bastard."

Finn barked a laugh. "Now that I truly am."

They sat in the glade, both staring past each other, lost in the day and the weight of waiting.

"So why didn't you help?" Ethan's tone floated through the glade, but he couldn't stop the edge of the delivery.

Finn didn't respond other than to rub a boot in the dirt. "In what way am I not helping?"

"You were there when my men rescued AJ. If you had helped, we might have been able to get them both."

"You don't know that." Finn all but spat the words. "Besides." He peered at Ethan. "I truly thought you had it well in hand. Had I known you'd botch the job and need to go back to try again, I would have thought better on it."

They stared at each other for a handful of seconds before Finn turned his gaze to the glade. He stood and walked away without another word.

Ethan rubbed his side. They needed to get space between them. The sooner the better.

As if reading his thoughts, Finn returned with a long, bare branch in one hand. At the top, a secondary branch formed a natural crutch. "Come on. It's time to get you on your feet."

It took two attempts before Ethan stood. Sweat poured down his face and stained his bandage, his breathing harsh and labored as he leaned against the stick. He swayed, and Finn reached out to steady him.

"How does that feel?"

"A bit light-headed, but it's starting to fade. I just need a minute to get sorted." Ethan waited for his heartbeat to return to normal, and when his breathing matched the rhythm, he took a step.

He wobbled, and Finn grabbed his arm. He took another step and paused, giving his equilibrium time to catch up. After the next step, Finn released his arm but followed a mere step behind. They continued until Ethan had moved across the breadth of the campsite to a stump close to the river. He sat and wiped his brow before checking his bandage.

"I'm not seeing any blood. That's a good sign." Ethan touched his ribs and flinched when he found the damaged one. "Hurts like hell, though."

"I think we stay one more day. If we can get you walking without that stick, we can put you on a horse." Finn retrieved the rag shirt and dipped it in the water. "Let's get the bandage off you."

Finn removed the bandage, and they both stared at the wound, pink and leaky, but with no fresh blood. "That's looking better. I think you're past the worst of it. You can wash up while I check our snares."

Ethan grunted and removed his soiled shirt, appreciating the cool morning air against his skin. He used the rag shirt to clean the old sweat from his body before stopping to catch his breath. Turning to face the sun, he let the fresh air dry his body before returning to the wound. Once the bandage was back in place, as tight as he could make it without passing out from the exertion, he put his shirt back on, scowling when his ribs protested. Positioning his stick and using it as a brace with both hands, he heaved himself from the stump.

He swayed but caught himself before toppling over. His balance returned more quickly than the last time. He was still walking back and forth between the campfire and the stump when Finn returned.

"You're making good progress." Finn dumped two rabbits by the fire along with more wood.

Ethan nodded at the dead hares. "As are you. At least we aren't starving."

"Aye, or I would have left you to the Fates in exchange for a fair stew in the next village."

Ethan glanced at Finn, and when he saw the man's wicked slow grin cross his face, he laughed. He grabbed his side and dropped to the stump, but he couldn't stop laughing, even when it became difficult to catch his breath. The raucous sound mingled with the songbirds and the occasional cawing of a crow.

28

AJ and Maire collapsed to the ground in the middle of a grassy clearing. AJ listened to Maire's ragged breaths, louder than the staccato of her own gasps pounding in her ears. At least she had regained part of her stamina in the last couple of days, between climbing and horseback riding. Maire had been locked away for almost two years with nothing more strenuous to do than walk around the gardens.

She hadn't planned their escape as thoroughly as she'd thought. Her entire plan focused on escaping the men who had murdered Ethan. She swallowed back the sorrow. This was no time to curl into a ball. There would be plenty of time for that once they were safe.

The morning had gone well. They made good progress until first light. Sounds from someone on the road forced them into the bushes twice, but each time, it had been a sole rider. Neither appeared to be the viscount's men, and AJ doubted search parties would be composed of fewer than two men.

They hid off the road by a burbling creek to eat the breakfast the innkeeper's wife had left them. Maire doled out portions of cheese, bread, and dried meat. AJ passed the water pouch she had taken from one of the sleeping guards.

After an hour of walking, Maire urged them to use a path through the woods. AJ agreed. Her own spidey senses tingled. Not ten minutes later, four men could be seen through the trees, and she recognized one of them. The men were on the hunt. The women moved deeper into the woods until they found another trail, then they ran as if the hounds of hell were after them, every snap of a branch sounding an alarm to keep pushing.

Now they lay in the sweet-smelling grass of a tiny meadow, staring up into an azure sky dotted with puffy pillows of white. AJ listened to buzzing insects and her slowing heartbeat as she picked out shapes in the clouds. She tensed and felt Maire's hand reach for hers when she heard a snap of a twig. They lay silent and waited. A full minute passed before they felt comfortable enough to talk.

"We should keep going," Maire whispered.

"Rest a bit longer, just another five minutes. I think we have time." AJ stood and made a slow circle, peering through the trees and bushes for anything that seemed out of place. After a minute, she sat and leaned back on her elbows.

Maire lay in the grass, turning a dandelion in her fingers, a wrinkle marring her forehead. "Maybe we should try to find a different road and watch for a wagon. There must be someone heading for market or a town."

AJ played with a blade of grass and returned to staring at the clouds. "It would save our feet, and we would make better time. But there's still a danger from Dugan. They could ride up on us without us knowing." She sat up and picked a twig from a bush, removing each leaf until the twig was bare. "If we could have gotten just one stinking horse." She tossed the twig and wiped her hands on her pants. "And what do you think someone is going to think when they see me dressed like this?"

Maire smiled, her first since their dash for freedom. "We should have brought your hat."

AJ touched the ribbon around her ponytail. "I don't think that would have helped."

"No. Probably not. But I could have passed you off as my addled older sister." Her voice turned to a sophisticated air. "She's been like that since birth, poor child. We just let her do what she wants to prevent unseemly outbursts."

AJ laughed. "I think you could get by with something simpler." She sat straighter, her chin lifted to an exaggerated height. "Oh, you have to forgive her, she's from America. What can I possibly do?"

Maire smiled. "Yes, that would work as well. I was just trying to be polite."

They both laughed as they stood and stretched.

"Shall we just see where this trail leads?" AJ glanced up. "We have a few hours before dark."

Maire nodded and followed AJ. They walked for over an hour, speaking only to point something out or stop at a strange sound.

They rested by a another creek. "I don't think we're close to the main road anymore." After washing her hands, AJ wiped them on her pants before sitting back on her heels. Not hearing a response from Maire she turned.

Maire had frozen, her head cocked to one side.

"What's wrong?" AJ whispered, hairs rising on her still-damp arms as she stood and scanned the area.

"We're not alone," Maire whispered back, turning to watch the woods around them.

AJ's skin prickled down her back as she searched the trees and tall grasses to the underbrush beyond. She saw nothing. After another minute, a snap of a twig pushed the two women together as they waited.

Maire pulled herself up, her head held high, as if waiting for an unwelcome visitor to enter her drawing room. AJ felt more like a lamb waiting to see from which direction the wolf was coming.

Another branch snapped directly behind them. They whirled around. A young boy stood just beyond the first tree, partially obscured by the shrubs around him. Dirt smudged his face, and leaves stuck out from his tousled hair. His expressive eyes, dark and inquisitive, calmly surveyed his prey. He watched them for several seconds before a slight tremor curved his lips.

AJ felt Maire relax beside her, but she wasn't swayed by the urchin. Something about him raised her hackles. It was probably nothing more than nerves after the last couple of days, but she was pretty sure he wasn't alone. She slid Maire a glance.

Her grin broadened into a coaxing smile followed by an outstretched hand, encouraging the boy closer. Maybe he was from a nearby farm with friendly parents who would shelter them.

AJ's defenses shot up when the boy turned his head toward the bushes and gave an almost imperceptible nod. Slowly, the trees moved in unison all around them. She started forward, but Maire remained calm and grabbed her arm to hold her still. AJ could do nothing but turn her head to watch the forest come alive.

They materialized out of the trees and shadows like wood nymphs, at least a dozen or more, faces masked in the shadows of the late-afternoon sun. The men and women came in all shapes and sizes: tall and short, thin and round, fair skinned and dark. As they moved into the scattered sunlight, AJ immediately noticed the odd clothing—bits and pieces of this and that, finely woven cloth mixed with patched rags. Not something a common farmer would wear. A few blended back into the trees as if they were never there.

She couldn't read their guarded faces, except for that of the young boy, who still stood among them. His smile lit up the glade as he stared at Maire. AJ understood. Anyone, especially an impressionable youth, would be enchanted by Maire. She had been too, the first time she'd seen her.

They stood at an impasse for only a minute or two, but it seemed like an eternity, as if neither party could determine friend or foe by first impression. A man moved out from the rest, his dark blond hair a sharp contrast to his darker skin. His gaze, as curious as the young boys, moved over them like warm water. But the intensity of his blue-green eyes held them frozen.

"Are you lost, little birds?" His voice surprised AJ. It was deep and commanding, with an accent she couldn't place.

Maire released her grip on AJ and stepped forward before AJ could stop her. "We seem to have found ourselves separated from our traveling companions. The woods are thicker than they first appeared." Maire held her smile as she spoke.

The man appraised her for a long while before turning his gaze on AJ, giving her the same perusal. Then he nodded. "You appear to need some food and rest. You can share a meal with us before you continue the search for your companions."

His emphasis on the last word told AJ he didn't believe their story, but beggars couldn't be picky. Food and a place to lay her head outweighed any other concern. So when Maire stepped toward the man, AJ followed and tamped down her panic as the men moved around them, guiding them deeper into the woods.

The group weaved effortlessly through the forest, a natural extension of the environment. They hadn't traveled far before the trees thinned, opening to a clearing. Noises erupted from a lively camp, which filled most of the grassy field. The camp spread out in a circle from a dozen wagons. In the distance, several horses grazed next to a narrow road that meandered away from them.

Smoke from cook fires rose in narrow streams before disappearing into the light breeze. Smells of cooking food stirred AJ's stomach into a rumble. Several children of various ages played in the field of grass, and when they saw the group emerge from the trees, they raced toward them, their screams of welcome piercing the quiet. A few ran to encircle AJ and Maire, laughing and grabbing their hands, their high-pitched voices erupting into questions as they talked over each other. AJ could do nothing but laugh along with them as they pulled and tugged.

"Enough." A loud, feminine voice shouted above the din, quieting the group to soft whispers. A woman, older than herself but younger than her mother, pushed her way through the group. She stood straight and tall. Her hair, as black and shiny as a raven's wing, was tied back, emphasizing the soft brown skin stretched over high cheekbones. Eyes almost as dark as her hair, shone with an intelligence that missed nothing. She dressed in a loose blouse and mid-length skirt over pants and boots. Bold jewelry adorned her neck and wrists, the ensemble finished with red fabric tied as a belt, showing off her shapely figure.

The woman stood, hands on hips, as she appraised the women. "What little birds did Miko find on his hunt?"

AJ kept her back straight next to Maire, but she lowered her gaze and shuffled her feet. It was like standing in the principal's office for something you didn't do but had no way to prove it.

Miko, the young blond man who'd led them to the camp, held a golden-haired girl who couldn't be more than five in one arm as he slid next to the older woman. He placed a respectful kiss on the older woman's cheek and turned to AJ and Maire. "They claim to have lost their way." The tiny girl tightened her grip around Miko's neck, and he placed his other arm around her in a protective gesture.

Still intimidated by the woman who seemed to be the matriarchal leader of the camp, AJ relaxed in the familial setting. They didn't trust her or Maire, but surrounded by children, the worst they would do was turn them away. She raised her eyes to the older woman and felt the blush warm her as she prepared her lie for them. But she shouldn't have bothered. As usual, Maire had her back.

"We ask only for a bit of food and some water to help us on

our way," Maire said. A simple request that didn't require any falsehoods.

"If it's too much to ask, we understand," AJ said. And when the woman pinned her with a silent stare, AJ held her gaze and smiled.

After a few moments, the woman clucked. "You seem harmless enough." She stepped closer. "My name is Sonya. My husband is out with another hunting party, but I think he would allow you food." Her tone turned inviting, but her eyes remained black stones.

Although the sun warmed the clearing, the woman's perceptive stare made AJ pull her cloak tighter. Sonya nodded and turned, blending back into the crowd.

Miko, the girl in his arms now squirming to be let down, motioned to a young woman. As she stepped forward, the rest of the crowd melted back to whatever they had been doing. Miko released the impatient imp from his arms, and she raced with the other children to resume their playing.

"This is Caro. She will help you get clean from your travels and provide food while you rest. You'll stay for celebration tonight."

"I'm AJ, and this is my friend Maire. We can't thank you enough for your kindness." AJ smiled at Caro before turning to Miko. "What are you celebrating?"

He shrugged. "We celebrate many things. I think sometimes it's just a reason to dance and drink, no?" Then he dazzled them with an engaging smile before striding off toward a group of men working on an old wooden cart.

AJ stared at the men and cart until Caro's soft, commanding voice made her jump. "I'll take you to the river. There won't be time to wash your clothes properly, but we can remove the dust while you bathe. Follow me."

29

AJ and Maire glanced at each other. Maire shrugged and turned to follow Caro, forcing AJ to follow. Caro's long black hair rippled in the breeze as she led them through the camp, gliding past women cooking aromatic stews, crunching dried flowers and herbs, or mending clothing. No one sat idle, everyone bent to some task.

On the other side of the camp, a slow-moving river formed a shallow pond between an outcropping of rocks and a downed tree before continuing its flow downstream. Tall trees separated the pond from the camp, leaving the women in seclusion.

"You won't be bothered here. The men use the pond first thing in the morning. We have it the rest of the day." Caro stared at the women and then huffed out a breath. "English women are always so modest. Please remove your outer clothing so I can have it cleaned. I have other chores to attend to."

AJ helped Maire with her dress before removing her shirt and pants. Caro yanked them from their grasp and disappeared through the trees, leaving the women to stare after her before turning to each other, half-naked in the late afternoon sun. Then both women burst with laughter at the sight they made.

Strands of hair fell from Maire's bun, and a slight scratch marred one cheek where she must have run into a branch. AJ ran her hands through her own hair and pulled a couple of twigs and leaves from it.

She shook her head and removed the stockings she wore under the pants. "We're a mess. I'm surprised they felt safe bringing us to their camp." When Maire didn't answer, AJ raised her head and stopped what she was doing to watch her.

She had let down her hair and, with outstretched arms, slowly turned in a circle, her face to the sun. With her long blonde hair flowing behind her, she looked like Galadriel from *The Lord of the Rings* paying homage to nature.

"Are you all right?" AJ found a rock near the water and put her toes in the pond, cringing as the chill ran through her.

"I can't remember the last time I felt so free." She spun around a last time and plopped down next to AJ, giving her a hug. "No matter what happens next, I can't properly thank you for just these few minutes in the sun."

AJ blushed and turned away. "You've had sun in the gardens."

"Not like this." Maire removed her stockings and petticoat and tiptoed into the water. "And I don't think the viscount would approve if I waded in his fountain."

AJ laughed. "No. He doesn't seem the type for such abandon."

"Come join me. We both have layers of road dust to remove."

The women spent more time playing in the water than caring about hygiene, splashing each other and chasing tiny fish before helping each other wash the dirt from their hair. They fell next to their stockings to dry in the fading sun.

"Did Ethan tell you how the earl knew of the stones?" Maire whispered the words and reached for AJ's hand, her touch light as the breeze.

AJ turned her head to stare at the trees, but she didn't pull away from Maire's touch. She waited for the stab of pain to wash over her. "No. He never said."

Maire sat up and pulled on a stocking. "The earl must have someone in France who knows about the stones."

"Ethan said he had a piece of the stone. That's how he was able to travel. His piece has a connection to the larger stone." AJ slid on her own stockings before pulling on her chemise.

"Of course. That makes sense with what I read in the book."

AJ went still. After all this time, they were finally getting to the *Book of Stones*. "Are they part of the same stone? Is that why they're connected?"

Maire thought for a minute before nodding. "Partly...but it's more than that. I think they're all pieces of something larger."

The snap of a twig made them spin around. Nothing there. Maire stood and stepped a few feet to find her gown, somehow as fresh as if it had been washed and dried. She tossed AJ her old shirt and a skirt, then picked up two packages and a calfskin before settling back down.

AJ held up the skirt, not new but a fair trade for the pants. "How did they clean our clothes so quickly?"

Maire shrugged as she opened the packages of bread and dried fish. "The magic of Gypsies."

Pulling on her shirt, AJ gasped. "The Romani. It didn't even occur to me. You knew when you first saw the little boy?"

"Aye. I suspected. In Ireland, we call them Travellers or Tinkers. We were lucky they found us."

"Aren't they persecuted here?" AJ recalled everything she had read about them, but it had been a long time ago. Even in her own time.

Maire nodded before sipping from the calfskin. "It differs from place to place, but for many, they are considered dangerous outlaws. I've always found them to be quiet people who keep to themselves. Back home, they are hard workers. They've helped us with the harvest." She frowned. "But people are superstitious. The real evil is those that hold power over others."

AJ sipped from the calfskin, surprised to find watered-down

wine. She took a deeper drink before passing it back to Maire. "You're talking about the stones again."

"Men don't send other men on some fantastical journey just to gain knowledge. Not in my experience. And certainly not the men we've been with. They have only two things they seek—power and money."

"But how will a handful of stones help with that."

"You mean besides the ability to travel through time?"

AJ turned to stare at the trees again, then slid a glance toward Maire who patiently watched her. She let out a deep sigh. "There's no reason to hide it anymore. Not from you. You know I don't belong here."

Maire moved closer. "Are you from the future? Or the past? Are you really from America?"

AJ laughed. "Slow down. I am from America, but about two hundred years from now."

"No." Maire's hands flew to her mouth, her eyes wide as saucers. "You joke."

AJ shook her head. "You wanted to know. Now you know."

Maire sat back in the grass, stunned to silence. "It's really all true?"

"I'm afraid so." AJ picked at blades of grass. She thought confiding in Maire would make her feel closer to home, but it had the opposite effect. The reality of her situation knocked her back to her first day here. This woman was her only connection to retrieving the stones and figuring out how they worked. She grabbed the calfskin and emptied it in two huge gulps.

"What was it like? The travel. Tell me how it happened." Maire's voice turned soothing, her questions matter-of-fact.

AJ focused on the question. "There was a heavy mist. A fog. It moved so quickly." She shook her head. "Most of it feels like a dream. I remember feeling sick to my stomach. Like I needed to throw up. Then the fog disappeared, and I was here. Well, Ireland. Then we traveled to meet up with the viscount."

A few seconds passed before Maire spoke. "The fog must be some type of transportation medium. I don't remember anything in the book about it. But what made the fog appear?"

AJ was going to say she didn't have a clue, but stopped. She had run the whole scene through her head dozens of times when she'd first arrived. But after a month, reliving that day didn't do anything but make her homesick, so she'd tucked it all away. She hadn't even bothered to write it in her journal. Now, it took time to step back through it all.

On the deck with Finn, his arms around her, her feeling of bliss. So stupid. Then Ethan and Adam running down the dock toward her. Poor, sweet Ethan, his face full of concern. At the time, she'd assumed it was all about him not trusting Finn. That had turned out to be an understatement. Something niggled at her. She always focused on the men during those final moments, but there was something she wasn't remembering. The necklace and Finn's medallion.

She bolted up to her feet, pacing as she ran it all through her mind once more. She spun to Maire. "The stones. The fog moved in several minutes before the jump. I don't know. Maybe it was longer, as much as twenty minutes or so. But it wasn't until the two stones touched that everything went blank. And then I was here."

Maire stood and grabbed her arms. "You're sure? It happened just as you touched the stones?"

AJ bubbled with laughter, her grip on Maire's arms tightening. "Yes. Yes. What do you think that means?"

"I don't know. There was something in the book about a connection between the stones. They are somehow drawn to each other."

"Now that you're washed and fed, I think it's time for rest. No?" Caro's untimely interruption forced AJ and Maire to stumble away from each other. Caro's eyebrow went up. "If you are finished here?"

AJ blushed and lowered her head as if she'd been caught with her hand in the cookie jar. These people moved too quietly. Although she wouldn't mind learning how it was done.

"We appreciate your hospitality." Maire collected the remains of their lunch and ambled up the path to Caro.

Caro led them back to camp and stopped in front of a makeshift tent, more like a lean-to. "You can use this. The children like to sleep outside at times. When Miko returns from his tasks, he'll discuss what can be done to find your traveling companions." Caro's sharp gaze assessed each woman in turn. "Assuming you still want to find them." She walked away without waiting for an answer.

AJ and Maire exchanged glances before Maire ducked in to sit on the blankets. AJ hesitated, turning to follow Caro's movements. She stopped to talk to a group of elderly women bent over their sewing before moving on to another group around a cook fire.

AJ searched for the men, but only a handful could be seen, two sitting on the back of an old cart and a couple more standing at the edge of the encampment by the horses, talking and laughing. A glimmer of an idea sprouted as she glanced back at the old cart before she joined Maire.

All thoughts of her plan vanished when she took in the narrow shelter. Handmade objects of various sizes hung from the sides of the lean-to. Made from sticks, strings, and leaves, they covered the walls. Other items, made with glass beads, hung to spin with the lightest of breezes. These were made by children. Some were childlike in construction, while several reflected true artistic talent. All had obviously been made with great pride to be hung for others to see.

Somehow, the children's art brought her comfort and a sense of family. Kneeling on the blankets, she found it difficult to tear her eyes away, but she finally slid a glance to where Maire lay, already asleep. She sighed. Any more talk of the stones would have to wait. She collapsed next to Maire. Her thoughts moved back to the cart and the promise it held to take them to a town.

The afternoon sun warmed the shelter, and she snuggled deeper into the blankets. She thought of a cart, magical stones, men with swords, and a lone rider on a magnificent white steed, all pushing her to follow Maire into a deep, untroubled sleep.

The sound of music woke AJ, and at first, she thought she had left the radio on before her sleep-befuddled brain caught up to current events. An orange glow filtered through the side of the shelter, reflecting dancing shadows. She turned to find Maire staring back at her.

"I can't remember the last time I slept so well." Maire sat up and pulled pins from her hair to redo her bun.

AJ ran fingers through her own hair before standing. "I suppose we should see what the music is all about. And I'm hungry again."

Maire stood and pressed her hands down her dress before fluffing it. "I'm hungry as well. I believe Miko said something about a celebration this evening. Let's go see."

As soon as they left the shelter, the deep scent of burning wood and roasting meat enticed AJ, and her stomach rumbled. Maire led the way through the empty wagons toward the huge blaze in the middle of the campsite. The music drew them forward, the sound pulsating and hypnotic.

The flames reached high in the night sky, a huge bonfire fed by the children. They jumped to the sound of the music, their smiles half-macabre in the flickering light. One girl, no more than eight, stopped to pick up a branch. Her determination was etched across her tiny face as she studied the flames before tossing the branch into just the right spot. Then she turned, throwing her hands in the air as she rejoined the dancing children.

Another fire burned several yards away, where some large animal roasted. The whole camp seemed to be here. Everyone swayed and danced to the music, their bodies harmonized to the sounds emanating from four men clustered with their musical instruments.

She skirted the edge of the festivities. A young man strummed a weather-beaten lute, encouraging each note to hover in the air, while an old man bent over a violin, the haunting melody stretching out over the camp. Another man swayed to his own internal rhythm over a harpsichord. The last man, staring out into the night as if in a trance, beat with a repetitive grace against a drum, the sound deep and resonating.

Caro emerged from the dancers, tapping a tambourine as she twirled around the musicians and then back into the crowd, her long black hair flowing behind her as the jingling sound traced her path. AJ followed the sound of Caro and caught sight of Miko leading Maire into the throng of dancers. Her body undulated with the tempo, her blonde hair free of its bun, her eyes bright in the firelight as Miko spun her around, her mouth open in laughter.

The music hypnotized, reaching down to the deepest parts of AJ, before it turned, morphing into an energetic tempo. Everyone danced and flowed around the bonfire, sometimes holding hands as they moved toward the flames before prancing back, repeating the movement before circling the inferno again. Then, in a fluid motion, they broke into partners, romping with abandon.

AJ was searching for a place to sit and watch the dancing when a bear of a man, one eye scarred, his hair neatly tied back in a ponytail, grabbed her hand and dragged her toward the dancers. He smiled, revealing a missing tooth through his rangy beard as he wove and gyrated with the beat of the music, forcing a laugh from AJ as she tried to mirror his steps. He took her hand as someone grabbed her other one. She joined the circle as it moved in and out from the fire.

Her eyes closed, and she let the group guide her around the circle, first to the right, then back to the left. She leaned her head back and gazed into the night sky, marveling for an instant at the millions of stars she could make out past the light of the flames. Her hands were released as the dancers broke from the circle. The music invaded AJ, and her body responded, drifting with the melody. As her buoyant partner spun her around, Maire fell into view.

A jolt went through her as she witnessed a new Maire, as if looking into her own soul. It was gone in an instant as Miko swept her away with the other dancers. With just that one glance, something broke free inside AJ. She let the haunting, joyous melodies wash away her troubles, her sorrows, and her pain. Hands reached out to draw her back into the circle. AJ danced beneath the moon, along with the Romani, in a celebration of life.

And for one night, she let it all go—Finn, Ethan, and the stones.

30

F inn dropped the skinned bodies of two rabbits at Ethan's feet. "I'm not sure how many more rabbits we'll be lucky enough to catch."

Ethan reached for a rabbit to mount on the makeshift spit. "To be honest, that wouldn't bother me. I've never much cared for rabbit." He grunted as he leaned over to set the spit in place. "There's more cheese and dried meat in my bags. The bread's probably too hard without stew."

"I was hoping you'd say you had a skin of wine." Finn settled next to Ethan, finding a rock to lean against so he could stretch out his legs. He studied Ethan. He'd lost some of his color from the morning, but the man had been pacing around the camp all day rebuilding his strength.

Ethan chuckled, then winced. "If I had, you would have known about it when I first opened my eyes to find myself still alive."

They watched the rabbit cook as the sun set, the horizon blending into the sky. Finn felt at ease as the silence between them stretched, not like rubber bands, waiting for the tension to snap, more like a rope held taut against a sail, pulling for that

271

extra inch in the blustering wind. He'd thought this man a competitor for so long. Now there was no question they must work together — for AJ if not the stones.

After their meal, Ethan dragged his body away from the fire, soft exhalations trailing after him as he adjusted himself against a tree. With labored breaths, he ended the stillness. "Where do you think the viscount is heading?"

"After Southampton? I'm not sure. Friends have been watching Beckworth. I hope to have answers by the time the *Daphne Marie* makes port to meet us."

Ethan raised an eyebrow at him, but when Finn didn't offer any explanation, he leaned his head back and stared at the night sky. "It must be France."

"France? How did you come to that?"

"The earl. It's how he came to get a piece of the stone."

Finn tossed wood into the fire, his anger rising. "You seemed to have left that piece out yesterday."

"Did I?" Ethan rubbed at his side. "Sorry, my mind must have been on other things."

"Aye. So tell me what else you know."

"There really isn't much more. The earl has a friend, a monk, I think, who lives in an old monastery in northern France. Though the earl never confirmed it, I believe it was this friend who sent the stone. All he would tell me was that the larger stone had to be retrieved rather than fall into the wrong hands." Ethan picked at his bandage, his voice raspy. "I've never seen the earl as obsessed as he was with the stone. And I've been with him a very long time."

Finn absorbed the information and pieced it together with everything he knew or had guessed of the stones. "There's more at play here, but I haven't been able to fit all the pieces together."

"How did Maire end up as his guest?"

The back of Finn's neck turned clammy as a cold sweat spread over him, leaving an empty void where his gut used to be. "Maire wanted to go to London. But I had a commission for a delivery of cargo to Scotland. I was only going to be a fortnight, maybe a might longer."

He ran a hand through his hair and shook himself. "Maire's headstrong, and not having our parents to tame her, she devised her own plan. Our cousin in Dublin was taking his sister to London, and Maire convinced them to take her with as a companion." He kicked a piece of wood, sending it into the flames, sparks dancing before evaporating into the air.

"When I returned home, I found a note from her." The corners of his mouth turned up, and he lost himself in his memories. "She has a way of allowing you to think she's satisfied with your decision, although half the time, she's the one who steered you to it. And if not, she finds a way to make you sorry. I thought this was one of her teaching moments, telling me I was selfish."

"She's a manipulator," Ethan said, more awestruck than condemning.

"Aye, we always thought she had a bit of the fairy in her. She learned her magic early on. It came from too much fawning over her as a child, knowing everyone thought her special. And she was. Mother had lost two previous attempts, so Maire was considered a lucky child."

His grin matched the spark in his eyes. "I should have been jealous, having lost a bit of attention from my parents, but damn if I hadn't fallen under her spell as well. From the first time I saw her in her crib and she smiled at me, I knew I would be the one to always protect her."

"Did she like you as well, or were you just a bothersome big brother?"

Finn's unexpected laugh could have startled birds from the trees. "She followed me everywhere, constantly underfoot. That's how she came to be called Maire." When Ethan raised another eyebrow, Finn shook his head. "It's true. She would watch me in the stables working the horses. She was barely walking when she stomped her foot and pronounced herself Maire. It sounded like a female horse. Her birth name was Daphne Marie, but she hated the name."

He grinned at Ethan. "I knew she looked up to me, so I tried to be the very best big brother I could be." He swallowed his smile. "We had a very happy childhood until our parents died. Then it was only me and my promise to always be there for her."

"You couldn't have known."

"That's what I tell myself in the light of day. But in the early hours of the morning, I know the truth."

"So what happened?"

"I was preparing the ship to follow her when I received the letter from Beckworth, some viscount in England I'd never heard of. Maire was at his residence recovering from a minor ailment, and she wished for me to join her. I was so mad with worry, I never gave any thought to why she hadn't written the letter herself. The letter from our cousin telling of her kidnapping didn't arrive until after I had left. I had no idea of the trap that had been laid."

"There was no reason to suspect foul play, not if you didn't know this man. Why go through all this trouble to select you for the mission?"

"I had no understanding at the time, but after meeting the man, I came to believe his threats against my sister were real. So I did as he asked. Who would have thought the small stone he gave me would do anything? I thought him mad. Next thing I know, I'm in some strange port, fifty years in the future."

Ethan grimaced. "I remember that place. And I remember the feeling. Shocked by the fact that the story was true, afraid at where and how I had traveled. And the smells."

"Oh God, they were awful. I could go another two hundred years without remembering that."

"And no idea how to find the object we sought."

Finn nodded. "Those first couple of trips were more lessons

on survival than any hope of recovering the stone. Creating stories, covering trails, and discovering how much the world changed after each jump."

"It was the third jump for me."

Finn gazed into the fire as if he could see the story play out in the flames. "That's about right. It got a bit easier. Patterns formed —how to determine the year, how to find locals who could help, building a story to use with each jump." He pulled away from the blaze and turned to Ethan. "Having money seemed to be the key."

"That's one thing that never changed. Money opens doors no matter the era."

Finn slid a glance toward Ethan, who seemed to be lost in his own memories. The wall between them continued to fall, brick by brick. No one other than Ethan could understand what it was like to jump. Never knowing when the jump would come or how far into the future they would travel.

"So why you? Why did the viscount go through all the trouble?"

And there it was. The pin that held his entire plan together. Everything he'd risk to this point, including AJ. "The only thing we know for sure is that Beckworth is nothing more than an errand boy. Unfortunately, a well-armed one."

Ethan pulled himself up and then stopped, paling at the abrupt movement, and his words filtered out as his breath returned. "You're working for someone else?"

Finn let the question hang in the air. Light from the flames brushed the leaves with gold spark against the ebony sky. The sky the only connection between worlds. "Before I took the first jump, I reached out to an old friend near Bristol. A man named Hensley. He didn't believe the foolish tale any more than I, but I needed someone to know where Maire was if I never returned."

He waited for Ethan to nod his understanding before continuing. "The man has many well-placed connections. He promised to run a quiet inquiry into Beckworth while I was gone." Finn snorted. "Neither of us expected it to be real or last so long."

When Ethan said nothing, Finn reached out to pick up another branch, but instead of tossing it into the flames, he picked at the dried bark. "He was my first stop when AJ and I reached England." Finn scraped a piece of bark off the branch and tossed both into the growing blaze. "We know Beckworth gets his funds from someone, and that person is the one with interest in the stones. And we need to take the stones away from him, especially now that we know they work."

"But you turned them over."

"I had to. I needed to get Maire out of the picture." He blew out a breath. "She was supposed to be turned over as soon as I delivered the stones, but Beckworth took an interest in AJ. He told me Maire was in London, and that I could fetch her there."

"But you didn't take AJ?"

"Beckworth insisted she remain his guest while I went to London. I had no idea if Maire was truly in London, but I was outnumbered by his men. I was going to lay it all out to AJ, but she'd gotten so angry with me." He held up his hands before Ethan could chastise him. "I know. She had every right. Everything I did to try to keep her safe backfired."

"You should have left her with Hensley."

"Anyplace I would have left her, she wouldn't have stayed for long. She needed to be near the stones."

"So when you discovered that the viscount tricked you, you returned to his manor?"

Finn shrugged. "I used the time in London to gain more financing. Then yes, I returned to find I had been outmaneuvered one more time. But this time, I knew where they were headed. Maire had found a way to get a note to me. I thought I'd have time to go to Hensley and finalize our strategy." He ran his hands over his face. "When I caught up to the women, your botched rescue was underway."

Ethan snorted. "It wasn't botched. I got AJ out. We've been over this."

Finn didn't respond. Suddenly, the fire seemed too hot, and he scooted back toward his sleeping spot. He settled against the tree and let the cool night air wash over him, dampening his temper.

"Why didn't you join the fight?"

Minutes ticked away, punctuated by the hooting of a nearby owl.

Ethan tried again. "It wouldn't have changed the outcome."

Finn pushed away from the tree and rolled over, facing away from Ethan. He felt as alone as when he'd watched AJ stare down at him, knowing he'd abandoned her again.

A COLD WIND whipped through the glade, and heavy gray clouds promised rain. Ready or not, Ethan preferred a slow and painful ride toward a warm bed rather than a day of soaked clothes and soggy grass.

Finn had rekindled the fire before Ethan woke and was gone, presumably taking down his traps. Ethan hobbled to the creek and washed his wound and face before reapplying the bandage. He left his crutch at the creek and picked his way back to his makeshift bedding, stopping twice to catch his breath.

He grimaced as he packed up blankets and other belongings, stuffing his saddlebags. The more he walked, the better he felt, the ache from his ribs settling to a dull ache. But every so often, for no apparent reason, a sharp pain would shoot through him, leaving him sticky with sweat.

The more he thought of it, the less appealing the ride ahead seemed until he glanced up at the darkening sky.

"Are you sure you'd rather not wait another day?" Finn stepped out of the trees and studied the sky with Ethan.

"Would you prefer to spend a wet day here?"

"No. But you're still a bit pale, and we haven't gotten you on the horse yet."

Ethan pushed dirt over the fire. "I'd rather arrive half-dead than spend another day here."

"Fair enough." Finn stood next to Ethan's horse and waited, his stern face as bleak as the weather.

Neither spoke of AJ or Maire, but their presence hung over Ethan, and he sensed Finn's patience wore thin from inactivity and worry.

Ethan grabbed the pommel and pulled himself up, but when he tried to swing his right leg over, his body shook with a bolt of pain so intense, tears brimmed, and he almost fell back. Within seconds, Finn pushed his leg over the horse, and then grabbed his arm before he tumbled off the other side.

He leaned over the neck of his horse, waiting for the throbbing to subside. Ethan managed a tight, "Thank you."

Finn slapped his back and grinned as Ethan grasped the saddle. "Well done. Just about eight or ten miles, and we can pry you off."

Ethan turned his horse away from Finn before hearing additional words of encouragement. He kept the horse at a walk as he led them toward the road, wincing with every step until his body settled into a steady rhythm.

Finn said nothing as he caught up to Ethan and stayed a head's length behind on his left. When they reached the road, they turned south, the storm pushing them onward.

31

A light drizzle followed Finn and Ethan into the hamlet of Brookbury. Ethan managed to dismount without falling on his face and turned the reins over to Finn. He clutched at the door to the inn, steadying himself after a long day's slow and torturous ride. The warmth of the common room seeped from the other side of the door.

Finn turned away, leading the horses to the stable for a rubdown and a meal. Ethan frowned after him. They had barely spoken since leaving camp, whether from tiredness or something else, he didn't know. Turning back to the inn, he would find out soon enough.

As soon as he walked through the door, Ethan sighed with pleasure. A roaring fire crackled in the hearth, and several people filled the tables. He counted his blessings in snagging the last available room. As much as he wanted to drag himself up the stairs to fall into bed, the smell of food drew him to a table in the far corner.

Minutes later, Finn burst through the door, the steady rain following him in. After a quick glance around the room, he strode to Ethan.

"We should be grateful for our timing if nothing else." Finn brushed droplets from his overcoat and turned his chair to scan the room.

"Then it was worth the long day on horseback. Sorry I couldn't take more than a walking pace." Ethan leaned against the wall behind him, fidgeting to find the best position.

"You were able to find us rooms?"

"One."

"Aye," Finn said. "At least it's something."

The innkeeper dropped plates of roast mutton and bread in front of them, followed by two mugs of ale. The men finished the meal in minutes, and Ethan ordered a second round of both food and drink. After eating rabbit and cheese for two days, the dinner seemed a feast.

With bellies full and warm from the ale, Finn helped Ethan up the stairs. He fell on the bed as soon as he walked into the room, neither of them questioning the fact he needed it more than Finn. The housekeeper had started a fire and left extra blankets on a side table.

Finn grabbed the blankets and dropped in front of the hearth.

Ethan turned away from Finn as a sudden rush of regret hit him. AJ must think him dead. An image of him falling to the sword replayed over and over, a screaming AJ being dragged to the horses. One more thing he couldn't fix.

WHEN ETHAN WOKE the next morning, Finn was gone. The blankets for his bed were folded on the table. Ethan sighed in the warmth of the bed. Even fully clothed, he couldn't remember such a restorative sleep.

By the time he lumbered his way downstairs, his stomach grumbled at the smell of cooked meat. He sat at the same corner table as the night before where he could watch the door. He nodded to the innkeeper.

The man disappeared and, minutes later, returned with a plate of eggs and sausage. "I was to tell you your friend said he would return by nightfall."

Ethan nodded as he bit into a piece of sausage, dry but flavorful.

Left behind with nothing to do, Ethan walked through Brookbury and beyond, slowly regaining his strength. After a mid-day meal and a couple of mugs of ale, his next stop led him to the stables.

The stableboy assisted him with the saddle, but Ethan was able to mount on his own, even with the white-hot poker stabbing at his side. He waited for the pain to subside before walking his horse out of town. He rode for a couple of hours, changing the pace to find what best suited his injury. Satisfied he would be ready when Finn returned, he left his horse at the stable, rubbed down and well fed.

By late afternoon, he fell into bed. All he needed was a few minutes of rest, and he'd be ready to take on anyone who got in his way.

THE DOOR BURST OPEN. Ethan popped up, knife in hand, a deep scowl on his face, and as his eyes focused, he emitted a low grunt.

"I've been gone all day searching for a trail that wasn't days old, and you've done nothing but lay about?" Finn slammed the door behind him and leaned against it. His green eyes blazed with cheerfulness at Ethan's annoyance.

Ethan sat on the bed, holding his side. "I see a good ride was enough to improve your spirits."

"Aye. I've always enjoyed a ride on a good horse on a beautiful day." Finn watched Ethan stand and walk to the wash basin. The man wasn't completely healed, but it would be enough for now.

"Finish your ministrations, and I'll meet you downstairs. I need food and ale."

Finn left the room with Ethan's mumbles trailing in the background. He grinned. Yes, it had been a fruitful day.

He was halfway through a plate of boiled meat, potatoes, and a mug of ale by the time Ethan joined him. He shoveled in another bite of potatoes before sitting back to watch his new friend. "You seem to be faring better."

"In between lying about all day, I've been gathering my strength and working out my muscles." Ethan stopped as a young woman placed his meal down with a mug of ale. "I also enjoyed a pleasant afternoon on the back of a fine horse."

Finn responded with a grin before returning to his meal. He should have known Ethan would put the day to good use. If he'd learned nothing of him during their months chasing the stone, he'd never questioned the man's discipline and fortitude. He shook his head as he watched Ethan finish his meal. If only they'd attempted a discussion from the beginning, they could have worked together and saved themselves time and trouble. But if they had, fate might not have led him to AJ.

"Have you drunk enough ale and put enough food in your belly to share your good spirits?" Ethan drained the last of his ale before lifting it up toward the server. He sat back and waited.

"Aye, the viscount's men have taken over an inn twenty miles or so south of here in Stony Batter." He pushed his plate away and picked up his mug.

"Why haven't they moved on?" Ethan pushed his own plate away as the innkeeper dropped two fresh mugs on the table. After the man left, Ethan leaned his elbows on the table. His eyes narrowed to slits of silver.

Finn laughed. "It appears, my good man, that our ladies stole away in the middle of the night."

"They escaped? How in God's name did they pull that off?"

Finn shook his head. "The details are a bit hazy. I found an inn just north of there, where I imagine the tale will be told for quite some time." He chuckled and pushed back his hair. "It seems that after they caught AJ and left you for dead, they kept the two women together." He frowned and stared at a crack in the table, running his finger along its length. He peered at Ethan. "She was quite distraught and believes you to be dead."

A tattered breath escaped Ethan, and he wiped his face with both hands. "My worst fears confirmed. I was an idiot for letting her come with me."

"Aye, but we already agreed to that. Now listen." He leaned over and lowered his voice. "For some reason, they stayed an extra day. Believe me, the townsfolk had an array of stories. It took a few hours to sort it out."

Ethan clasped his mug, holding on tight as Finn tested his patience.

"On the second night, the men fell into a deep sleep." Finn shook his head and tried to stay earnest. "Some had noticed the men drinking most of the day and think by nightfall, it was just too much, and a few others think the women cast a spell over them."

"Now who's telling tales?"

Finn raised his hands in defense. "I'm only repeating what I heard. You know how people talk, always weaving the best story. Why do you think it took me so long?"

"So what do you think is the most plausible? The men seemed too well trained to drink themselves into a stupor."

"Aye, and I think that's where my dear sister may have had a hand in it."

"Maire?"

"She spent a great deal of time working with our local apothecary and Travellers when they passed through. I don't think there's an herb she doesn't know."

"A sleep potion? I'm beginning to like your sister."

Finn winked. "The Murphys are not a family to trifle with."

Tension seemed to ease out of Ethan, his focus shifting to some point over Finn's shoulders. "So where would they go?"

"I've been thinking that through on the ride back. AJ believes you dead, and she's none too happy with me."

"And what would Maire do? Wouldn't she try to get to you?"

Finn returned to studying the table. He just didn't have an answer for Ethan. "My sister is unpredictable at the best of times. But I think they'd try for London."

"Why London?"

"I thought maybe they'd try for Hensley, but AJ may not think him trustworthy if he's working with me. And they need a large city in which to hide from Beckworth."

Ethan nodded. A smile slid across his face as he leaned over the table. "Not London. Hereford."

"Why Hereford?"

"AJ wants to go home. She needs the stones for that, and she knows the earl has information about them. And she knows Thomas and my men went back there."

Finn slapped his hands on the table and shouted, "Yes," ignoring the stares from the other patrons. "I need a couple of hours' sleep."

"We ride tonight?"

Everything felt right. They were back in the game. Finn flashed his grin. "Aye, we ride tonight."

THE TWO MEN arrived at the edge of Stony Batter shortly after dawn. Sun pierced the thin veil of clouds and cast a preternatural glow over the scattered buildings. Several people bustled through their morning routine. The inn sat quiet.

Finn studied each person, searching for any sign that shouted mercenary, but the anxiety that grew the closer they got to town turned to a lump of disappointment lodged deep in his chest. He glanced at Ethan, who shook his head before turning hooded eyes back to their surroundings.

"One of us needs to see when they left." Finn nudged his horse before Ethan stopped him.

"We'll both go. You can check the inn. I'll check the stores."

Finn shrugged. "I'll meet you at the stables." He kicked his horse without a backward glance. They'd made good time through the night, but Ethan's injury forced them to stop frequently. He wasn't sure what difference a faster pace would have made. Finding the women before Beckworth's men did would be a miracle.

He worried for both of them, but it was AJ's face that haunted him with flat eyes of indifference. He'd made so many mistakes with her. He should berate himself for his very first error in judgment, bringing her through the time jump with him, but he didn't know how he could have left her behind. The scrap of trust he'd reestablished over the two months they were together had been shattered, leaving nothing but icy shards slicing through him. He didn't know how many times he would have to ask her for forgiveness.

Twenty minutes later, he rode to the stables, where Ethan chatted with a young stableboy. He dismounted and tossed Ethan a package of biscuit, meat and cheese.

Ethan nodded his thanks. "This is Peter. He's been tending the stables since last night."

Finn looked down at the boy. Dirt colored his cheeks, and bits of straw stuck out of his hair. He'd probably done a fair amount of sleeping as well.

"Hello, Peter." Finn gave Peter his full signature grin, and the boy smiled, eagerness to please shining in his curious brown eyes.

"Peter has been telling me about the men who have been here the last day or so. Haven't you, Peter?" Ethan handed Peter a piece of cheese.

The young lad nodded, stuffing the entire chunk into his mouth.

Finn laughed. "Well, it will be hard to tell me anything with a full mouth." He handed the boy his package of food. "Let's water the horses while you eat, and then you can share your story. How's that?"

The lad grabbed the package with one dirty hand and the reins of Finn's horse with the other. He led the men to a water trough and tied Finn's horse to a post. The men waited as Peter slowly unwrapped the package and bit off a piece of warm pork, barely chewing before swallowing the morsel. He followed it with a bite of the biscuit and then wrapped the remaining food in the paper as if it were his most precious possession.

"Do your horses need hay?" Peter asked.

"Aye, but not too much."

The boy nodded and stuffed the package of food into a pocket. "Like I told him." Peter nodded toward Ethan. "They came the day before yesterday. They needed the wheel of a carriage fixed."

Finn glanced at Ethan, who watched the boy, a lazy grin twisting his lips.

"Good. Can you remember how many men?"

Peter thought for a moment, his eyes rolling up toward the sky as if the clouds held the answer. "Hard to tell, maybe six. They kept leaving and coming back."

"And when did they leave with the carriage?"

"Real early this morning." He shrugged. "Maybe four?" It sounded like a question, but then he stood straighter. "It was four. The rooster was crowing."

Finn shot Ethan another glance, and he nodded.

"That was wonderful Peter. You've helped us quite a bit." Finn reached into a pocket and pulled out a leather pouch.

Peter's attention riveted on the pouch as Finn picked out a silver coin and two copper ones. "A shilling for the stablemaster for a couple of hours in a clean stall for us to rest and a bit of hay for the horses." Finn stopped to make sure he had Peter's attention. The lad's head bobbed once. "The copper is for you to feed the horses. And if any of the men happen to come back into town, can you wake us?"

Finn dropped the coins into the boy's open palm, and they disappeared before he could blink. He rubbed the boy's head. "Thank you, Peter." The boy untied the horses and led them away.

"What do you think?" Ethan leaned against a stall, his hand resting on his bad side.

"I think they found them."

Ethan nodded. "We shouldn't wait."

Finn turned to watch Peter feed their horses. "We both need some sleep, and I know your ribs could use a reprieve. Two hours, then we ride for Southampton."

32

The warbling of birds stretched over the flower-filled meadow and mingled with the murmur of the river. The rays of morning sun pierced the shade of trees, emitting short bursts of spotlights on the two women lying in the grass. As the sun inched higher, one of its spotlights poked AJ's shuttered eyelid like a laser.

She moaned and turned over, searching for the comfort of darkness. Instead, she rolled onto a rock and groaned when it pushed into her side. Giving up, she bolted upright. The spotlights moved from outside her head to inside. She grabbed at her hair with both hands and moaned. *Good God the pounding is intolerable.*

Flashes of the previous night darted by with visions of dancing, fire, music, and wine. The wine. That explained it all. She hadn't felt like this since Stella's last birthday bash, and that lasted two days.

"Here. Chew it for a minute before swallowing." Maire's hand lowered to show two leaves cupped in her palm.

AJ stared up to the shadow of Maire's face before glancing down to grab the short stems, giving them a brief sniff before popping them in her mouth. She prayed the effect would be immediate.

Maire sat next to her. "It will take a few minutes, but chewing breaks up the leaves to speed up the processing."

"I guess we couldn't crawl back to the shelter." The words stuck in her mouth, and she rolled her tongue around. She felt something hit her arm. Maire offered a calfskin. After taking a sip she tried again. "I don't remember drinking that much."

"We were both very tired, even after our nap. I think the last few days of travel and running has taken their toll."

"Unfortunately, that doesn't explain the headache." AJ kept one hand on her head as she turned to see how far they were from camp. It was rather quiet for being late morning.

They were gone.

Nothing remained of the Romani. The grasses covered their tracks, the campfires were doused and raked over, leaving no signs they were ever here.

AJ scrambled to her feet. "Where did they go?"

"They left a couple of hours ago. They're good at packing quickly and leaving no trace. I imagine it comes from being harassed and scorned. The Travellers have the same ability to disappear. It's their life." Maire stood and brushed off her skirt. She held a piece of fabric with a floral print tied at the ends to form a sack. "They left us food that should last a day or so if we're careful. And they filled our calfskin. It will hold enough until we find another water source."

"They had a cart. I thought they could get us to the next town." AJ's voice caught. "Every time something seems to go our way..." She didn't finish. She tilted her head to one side. "I need to wash my face."

Maire didn't follow as she made her way to the creek. The hammering in her head lessened, but she didn't know if it was from the leaves or her survival instincts kicking in.

When she returned, Maire stood in the tall grasses, purple and white wildflowers surrounding her. Her hair was back in its bun, and she cradled their food as she raised her face toward the sun. She turned her gaze to AJ. Her green eyes, so familiar, sparkled with adventure.

AJ sighed. "We need to get moving. Right now. I'm just not sure which direction."

"You remind me of my brother." Maire's melodic voice matched the twittering of the birds.

"How's that?" AJ picked up the calfskin.

"Always ready to jump to the next task. You've thought everything out just walking to the river and back."

AJ shrugged. "I never thought about it. I was a reporter back home. There's always research to do and a deadline. No one has time for planning." She turned around. "Which way to London?"

Maire pointed to the river. "That way is east. And I think we came in from that way, past that huge elm."

AJ nodded. "Maybe we can find their trail. It should take us to a road."

"See what I mean? You have it all figured out."

"I guess." AJ picked her way through the grass toward the spot where she'd seen the cart. She studied the ground for any sign of trampled grasses.

"I like to study things," Maire offered. "Learn people's motives, understand their passions."

"And then use them to your advantage." AJ stopped and twirled around. "I'm sorry."

Maire screwed up her face in thought. "For what?" Then she laughed. "You mean I know how to influence for my benefit?"

AJ blushed and studied her toes.

"Yes, I'm aware of that. I have been for as long as I can remember. I think from the first time I wanted something, and my da or mam said no." She grabbed AJ's hand and turned her back to their path. "I think this is your trouble fitting in. I don't know what it's like being a woman of the future, but here, we can't be as direct as a man. Unless you're a queen."

AJ squeezed Maire's hand and returned to her search for wheel tracks. "We have equal rights and the right to vote. There are still problems, but we have a great deal more than you have here."

"Which is why we must find other ways to get what we want. Most of the time without the other person knowing what they've given us."

"If I'm stuck here much longer, you'll need to teach me all you know." AJ stopped. "Here we go." She squatted and stared at the bent grass and noticed a faint trail. "I think they went along the river. I suppose that makes sense."

"Then we follow it until we get to a road."

"How far do you think we are from London?" AJ relished getting lost in the crowds of London. They could hide from the viscount until they found the earl. He was their only source to the stones. They had to stay focused.

"I don't know. It will take several days on foot."

"And probably longer because we need to find a less direct route. We need horses, or preferably someone with a coach headed that direction."

"Who are willing to pick up two women lost in the woods."

Their options were slim. Maybe they should try going back to Ireland. They could use Maire's home as their central base while locating the earl. That made more sense, keeping their distance from the viscount, but the trip would be difficult without money. She studied the trail the wagon had left behind, but it held no answers. She lifted her face to let the sun warm her as she concentrated on their choices. "Let's see where this takes us."

THE WOMEN EMERGED from the shadows of the trees a couple of miles from the Romani camp. They had slowed their pace before venturing onto the road, listening intently for signs of travelers or Dugan's men. AJ peered to the right then left before checking the position of the sun.

"The road appears to be running north and south. Don't we need to go east?" She pulled a twig from her frayed skirt before tugging at her sleeves. Her fingers ran over her hair, and an errant leaf fluttered to the ground. She glanced at Maire, who appeared to have stepped out of manor rather than a day in the forest. Only close inspection showed any wear in her dress.

"Yes, we should be going east. But this road must lead to another."

AJ strode down the road before turning to stalk the other direction. She focused on the ground, scratching at her head as she continued her pacing. Her lips moved, but no words could be heard. After a minute, she stopped in front of Maire and heaved a long breath.

"Feel better?" Maire's lips twitched, but she retained her stoic expression.

"Go ahead and laugh, but our situation doesn't seem to be improving."

"You give up too easily. We are still free of the viscount's men." Maire turned to her left. "I hear something. It sounds like a wagon."

The women returned to the shelter of trees and waited. Several minutes later, a cart with an old man appeared. AJ looked at Maire, but Maire shook her head.

"Why not?" AJ whispered, a note of frustration sneaking out.

"Why not wait and see if one shows up with a woman?" Maire leaned against a tree, resting her head along its trunk.

AJ bent her head and counted to ten. This patience thing was going to take practice. She waited for the cart to pass before speaking. "We could be here all day, maybe two, waiting for the perfect situation."

They started walking north for no particular reason other than to follow the direction of the cart. And perhaps to keep one step away from Dugan.

"The Romani helped us because they have no loyalty to the English. Nor do they care enough about money to take bribes to turn us over." Maire picked up her pace. "Let's try to reach a town before dark. Maybe we'll find a friendly face to at least help with our bearings."

They walked for a while before AJ heard horses—moving fast. She ducked into a thicket of bushes, dragging Maire behind her just before two men barreled down the road. They passed by in an instant, never slowing.

AJ's body shook, but she didn't know if it was from fear or adrenaline. She could feel the trembling from Maire, and when they glanced at each other, they tried a smile. "I need to wait for my heart to stop pounding."

Maire sipped from the calfskin before handing it to AJ. "That was close, but I don't think they were Dugan's men."

AJ ran a hand across her mouth and handed the calfskin back to Maire. "Maybe."

A few minutes later, AJ heard it first. "Another wagon?"

Maire perked her ears and peeked through the leaves. Then she moved out to the road, leaving AJ to scramble after her.

"What are you doing?" AJ tried to keep the hysteria out of her voice until she saw the cart. A man and woman perched on the bench of the aged wagon, drawn by a single draft horse. She shook her head. "I can't believe it. You're a regular Irish shamrock."

Maire smiled. "Aye, or just patient."

AJ rolled her eyes and stood next to Maire, letting her take the lead.

"Whoa, girl." The man pulled on the reins, and the wagon

slowed. He was on the other side of middle age, gray running like veins through his light brown hair. His sharp brown eyes examined them before he glanced at the woman next to him. When she nodded, he turned to Maire, who had moved in front of AJ. "What do we have here?"

"Maybe they're hurt, Henry."

The woman's clear, honeyed voice washed over AJ, and for a moment, she was overwhelmed by a flash of her mother's concerned brown eyes, her hands reaching for the string of pearls she always wore. AJ blinked and waited.

"We're not injured, but we are in need of assistance." Maire spoke to the man but slid a glance to the woman. "We were on our way to a friend's manor when one of our horses took fright and threw my lady's maid." Maire nodded toward AJ, who had the good sense to stay behind her, nice and quiet. "Both horses spooked when I got down to help."

Maire lowered her gaze. "We're not from around here. And we're a bit turned around." She lifted her head just enough to watch the woman, who had grabbed her husband's arm. "We're not sure who to trust."

AJ kept her eyes lowered so they couldn't see her rolling them again. If she didn't know Maire, she would have fallen hook, line, and sinker for this story.

But Henry sat back, reins held loosely in his hands as he studied them. He scratched his chin and ran a hand through his hair. His wife kept a firm grip on his other arm and gave it a squeeze. He responded with a long, slow breath.

"Then let's get you in the wagon. It's getting late, and I want to get to town and back before dark," the old man grumbled as he stepped down.

Maire grabbed AJ's arm and followed Henry to the back of the cart filled with vegetables and wool. Once they were settled, Henry gave them a sidelong glance before climbing back onto his seat. He gave his wife a slow shake of his head before clucking to his horse, who moved on with barely a twitch of the reins.

After several minutes, AJ leaned over to Maire. "What are we going to do when we get to town? What if they try to help us?"

"I think he'll be happy to be rid of us. We should lie down with the wool when we get to town and try to stay out of sight as much as we can."

"We should ask someone else where we are and the best way to London."

"I've been thinking about that." Maire reached into her collar and pulled out a gold chain with a small ring. She ran her fingers over the ring and clasped her hand over it. "I think we can get enough money for a horse with this."

AJ sat back and considered Maire, who suddenly became interested in a basket of cabbage. "You might as well tell me."

Maire shook her head and gulped some air. "It seems so silly after all this time. It's just a ring."

AJ opened her mouth and then closed it. Seeing a hole in the bag of wool, she pulled out a white lock and ran her fingers over it. After rubbing it several times, she rubbed the grease from the wool over her hands like spreading lotion.

"Where did you learn to do that?"

AJ laughed. "I once interviewed a woman who owned a sheep farm close to town. She ran her own yarn store, and part of her inventory came from her own sheep. She explained the process and let me put my hands into raw wool. I couldn't believe how soft my hands felt afterward."

Maire nodded and let a minute slip by. "My parents died when I was young."

"Yes, I remember you telling me that."

"My brother removed their *fede* rings before they were buried. He gave me one, and he took the other. It was his way of binding us, letting me know we'd always have each other." This time, she didn't fight the tears, and they trickled down her face before she wiped them away. "It's silly now that we're grown." She heaved a gasp and lifted her chin. "He'd understand."

AJ leaned her shoulder against Maire's and reached out a hand. Maire grasped it, and they watched the passing terrain as the wagon rolled on, still a long way from London.

The smell of warm wool mingling with the earthy aroma of vegetables did little to reduce the tightening in AJ's chest as she stared at the empty blue sky. The wagon reached the edge of town in a little over an hour, with both women snuggled together. AJ and Maire had asked to be dropped off at the local mercantile and provided their best docile smiles when the old couple lifted eyebrows at their request.

When the wagon slowed, AJ raised her head and scanned the town. It was bustling with activity: wagons parked in front of buildings, people scurrying about their day, a few stopping to talk with friends, their faces lit with smiles. She didn't see anyone that could be one of Dugan's men, but she couldn't stop the nausea growing in the pit of her stomach.

"We should get into the store as quickly as we can." AJ shimmied off the edge of the cart and helped Maire down.

AJ leaned against a wall next to a stack of crates, partially hidden from view, and waited for Maire to thank their transportation. After a minute that seemed like ten, Maire walked past her into the store. AJ glanced around, then followed her but lingered near the door as Maire spoke with the owner.

From her vantage point, her perception from her first scan of the town didn't change. Everyone appeared to be about their business, and though nothing seemed out of the ordinary, the hairs on the back of her neck signaled caution. She jumped when Maire stepped next to her and peered over her shoulder.

"I don't see anything to be concerned about."

"I know." AJ bit her lip. "Something doesn't feel right. I can't put my finger on it." She took another glance down the street before turning to Maire. "How did it go?" Then she noticed Maire holding a wrapped package. She sighed.

Maire passed the package to her before pushing AJ out the door. "It wasn't what I hoped for."

"For your ring?" AJ's face paled. The thought of trading her mother's ring for a meager amount of food increased her nausea.

Maire glared. "I thought you knew me better than that." She jingled a silk pouch, and AJ caught the flash of the ring on Maire's finger. "They wouldn't buy the ring, but I was able to sell the chain. It's not enough for a horse, but the owner suggested someone who might buy the ring."

AJ smiled. "Of course. So where next?"

"A little shop just a couple of doors down."

Maire led the way, and AJ stayed a step behind her like any good lady's maid until she heard someone behind her. As she glanced back, she bumped into a young man, the package tumbling from her hands. His work pants were stained and smelled of hay and manure.

"Sorry, miss." He bent and retrieved the package. "Have a good day" was mumbled from his lips as he scuttled off.

AJ brushed off the package and turned back to follow Maire.

She was gone.

Panic seized her, and she picked up her pace before stopping at the next store.

Before she took another step, arms as round as tree trunks and hard as granite wrapped around her. A sweaty hand clasped her mouth to cut off her scream. She struggled as the man hauled her into the store. Another man, who appeared to be cut from stone, closed the door and leaned against it, blocking any exit.

The fight drained from her, and she whipped her head around to find Maire, caught like a fly in the strong arms of Dugan. His face, a mixed bag of rage and jubilation, seemed in bizarre conflict to the calm, impassive face of Maire, her green eyes placid.

A movement on the other side of the room drew AJ's attention to a thin man, slightly bent and frozen in the shadows. He took another step back, head down, refusing to meet anyone's gaze. She had only a moment to feel sorry for him before she felt herself lifted like a rag doll and carried toward the back of the store.

AJ and her captor huddled by the back door as Dugan dragged Maire to the horses. He barked a command at a man sitting on a horse holding the reins of three others. The man who had blocked the front door appeared and retrieved the reins from the mounted man before he rode off to obey Dugan's orders.

Dugan lifted Maire onto a horse and mounted behind her. He turned to AJ, and she shriveled from the intense hatred. If he had the power, she would have turned to ash. But a smidgen of satisfaction snaked through her for their merry chase, even if it hadn't lasted long. But even the pleasure of that short success curdled at Dugan's words.

"There are only so many roads to London. We just needed to wait."

How stupid they had been. AJ grabbed for the pommel as she was lifted to the saddle. She stared down at the face of granite man, and his leer made the bile rise in her throat. Taking a cue from Maire, she lifted her head and turned to face front, dismissing him. She straightened her spine when she heard his menacing chuckle, the fear held in check by the thinnest of walls.

They left town in the opposite direction of Dugan's messenger. AJ arched forward, keeping space between her and her captor, once again trapped and out of options. Before long, her back hurt, and she grew tired. Giving in, she leaned back and stared into faded afternoon skies. And cursed the man who left her to this fate. *May Finn Murphy rot in hell.*

———

AJ WOKE to blackness when the horse came to a stop. Her stomach tightened when her vision adjusted to the darkness, and she spied the soft outline of the carriage sitting on the side of the road. She despised the coach as much as the hoard of men gathered around it. She swallowed a hysterical giggle. All these men for two little women. As dire as their situation was, she couldn't help but be proud of the chase.

Dugan led Maire to the carriage and helped her in. Once in, two men stood in front of the door as Dugan turned toward her, his face as menacing as it had been when he'd held Maire in his arms at the store.

Her captor dismounted and pulled her from the horse, almost dumping her to the ground. She gained her footing and shot him her best impersonation of Stella's blistering stare. A grin slipped into place when she saw her captor register shock before turning back to his stony glare. That should give him something to think about.

She turned without being told and strode to the coach, her back stiff and unyielding. Refusing assistance from the men, she grabbed both sides of the opening and hauled herself up. When she saw a man sitting next to Maire, AJ dropped onto the opposite bench and kept her face forward, matching Maire's silent countenance.

Another man climbed in and took his place beside her. She glanced at Maire, her blonde hair a continued ray of hope in the darkness. Even in the shadow of the coach, AJ swore she saw

300

Maire smile. They might not have gotten away, but they were dangerous enough to warrant an army.

After a mile or two, the exhilaration wore off. She hugged her arms around her, stared out the dark window, and conjured up the sounds of gulls. The gulls that called to her—the gulls of home.

AJ smelled the sea thirty minutes before the carriage rolled to a stop. The sound of men shouting orders and wagon wheels on cobblestone floated through the coach. Her gaze flickered to Maire, who pulled back the curtain to study their new surroundings. AJ remained where she sat, fatigue tugging at her.

Dugan stopped the caravan only twice on their day-long journey, and AJ dozed for most of it. From the moment she stepped into the coach, a bone-deep weariness took over, and it required every ounce of strength to lift her head. The swaying of the coach made her turn to see their chaperones climb out, slamming the door behind them. She had no doubt they posted a guard at the door.

She swiveled back, and, curiosity getting the better of her, she mustered the will to scoot closer to the window. Pulling back the curtain, she gawked at the flurry of activity. The town was twice the size of the one where the *Daphne Marie* had made port in England. Two ships floated at the dock, and her gaze swept over them. A quick stab tugged at her heart when she confirmed neither was the *Daphne Marie*, although there was no reason why it would be here.

Men scrambled over both ships, crates moving off one while trunks and stores were hauled onto another. More men worked at the rigging, untying ropes from the sails, and AJ's chest tightened.

"After all we went through." AJ pushed away from the window and folded her arms across her chest.

"We're not going to go through that whole 'Fate is a cruel mistress' tirade again, are we?" Maire pulled at her sleeves and ran her hands over her dress, brushing at the two-day-old wrinkles that weren't going away.

"That sounds more like my brother than me. Although today it may be fitting."

Maire leaned over, and her voice dropped to a conspiratorial tone. "You never told me you had a brother."

AJ barked a quick laugh. "I don't think of him that often. More now, I suppose. We don't get along."

"Really? Is he a bad person?"

AJ shrugged. "He's a lawyer. I think you call them barristers."

Maire's brows drew together. "Isn't that a worthwhile profession where you come from?"

"Not always."

The carriage door flew open, startling both women. Dugan stuck his face through the door with his usual glare. "Out. You first." He pointed at Maire and stood back.

AJ followed Maire toward the dock, her legs like lead, nerves scratching at her skin. Each of them had two men walking with them, their own guard detail. She almost laughed, but as they drew closer to the ship, an overwhelming need to make a break for it came over her, almost buckling her legs. One of her guards grabbed her elbow, steadying her before pushing her forward. She searched the passing faces, but everyone ignored her.

Maire glanced back once, but her gaze moved beyond AJ as if searching for something.

AJ turned but saw nothing that could help them.

By the time AJ's guard pushed her forward again, Maire had stepped onto the deck of the ship. She glanced back once more, her gaze sweeping the docks before she turned and disappeared onto the deck.

AJ slowed her steps, but all it gained her was another shove before boarding the ship. She turned as Maire had, glancing over the town. This was her last look of England. And the country had brought her nothing but pain.

She stepped onto the bustling deck. Dozens of men scurried about the crates and barrels waiting to be stored. She stumbled her way to Maire, and before she could say anything, her anger flared. Although she'd spent only a short time with him, she could tell from the way he stood, prissed up in his Beau Brummell finery, that she was staring at the back of the viscount.

He tugged at his sleeves and pointed at something as he spoke to the man next to him. He lifted his head, as if catching a scent in the air, or perhaps he felt AJ's glare boring into him. He turned toward them. When he gave Maire a slow, possessive appraisal, AJ slid closer to her companion. The viscount passed over AJ, his brows pinching together. The nausea returned as she waited to see if he'd have her stored in the hold with the rest of the cargo.

The viscount stared at them for several seconds before turning his back on them. He said something to his man and walked away. The man stalked toward them, and AJ took another instinctive step toward Maire.

"Your quarters aren't ready yet," the man barked. "The viscount has asked that you find a safe spot starboard and stay out of the way. We'll retrieve you after we've set sail." He gave them a withering sneer and marched off to his next duties.

"I thought he'd have me dumped in the hold," AJ said.

"Some men still think women are bad luck at sea." Maire tugged AJ's arm. "Come. Let's work our way to the bow."

AJ glanced back toward the dock. There was such a flurry of activity, she doubted anyone would notice them leaving the ship, until she spotted Dugan. The darkness simmering below the surface should have been a warning. He hadn't settled the score with her yet. That was all right. She had her own rage she kept stored for the right time. *For Ethan.*

She followed Maire along the starboard side toward the bow. The sun hovered low, turning the sea several shades of orange, and it took her breath away. The sunset would be spectacular set against the thin clouds. She wiped an errant tear as she watched three gannets skim the surface of the water, their white feathers a beacon over the gray of the sea. The sea would forever remind her of the home lost to her. Lost forever if they didn't recover the stones and figure out how they worked.

After several minutes, Maire took her hand as lines were cast off, sails unfurled, and the ship lurched forward. AJ tensed at the movement before relaxing her shoulder next to Maire's. But the comforting warmth of her friend couldn't stop her pounding heart as the ship gathered speed.

THE CLATTER of hooves on cobblestone echoed through the narrow street. Finn and Ethan had slept two hours before leaving to follow the carriage. *We should have caught them by now.* They'd wasted time resting, regardless how necessary. It was too late to do anything about it, but he couldn't swallow the lump lodged in his chest.

He glanced over to Ethan, who jaw was set, his eyes silver slits in the shadows of the passing buildings. The man had to be in pain, his bruised ribs taking punishment for almost two days of riding since leaving the glade. But he never wavered.

Finn turned his focus on the street, slowing as they reached the docks. The smell of rotting fish and salt spray grew stronger as they pushed their horses through the increasing crowd of carts and people. His heart sank when he spotted the one ship at dock, sails furled and stowed, and a handful of men milling over the deck. *We're too late.*

Ethan's horse nudged his own forward, forcing the crowd to let them pass. They turned their horses into an empty space at the dock where men tidied ropes and washed out buckets. In the distance, a ship made its way to sea.

"Is that them?" Ethan settled his horse next to Finn and leaned over, running his hand through his hair before reaching down to rub his side.

"Aye." Finn squinted into the setting sun, trying to make out the details of the receding ship. Men crawled across the rigging and sails like spiders across a web. If the women were on board, and where else could they be, they must be below deck. "We'll need to confirm it's the viscount's ship, but I can't see how it could belong to anyone else."

"When will your ship arrive?"

"I'm surprised they're not passing each other now. Jamie must have had an unforeseen delay. Or perhaps Hensley still waits for details to share with us." Finn spit the last sentence, and his hands turned to fists around the reins. He let the moment pass and shook his head. "Will your men arrive before we sail?"

Ethan shrugged. "If all went well with the earl, Thomas should be close. Even if the earl decided to send no men, he would send a messenger." He turned in his seat to scan the surrounding buildings. "Perhaps he's already here."

"Aye. Let's check the inns. If they're not here yet, we'll put out word." But Finn didn't move, his focus on the ship, observing the men on the rigging.

"How quick can we turn her back out?"

"Jamie should have full stores on board. Then it's just a matter of boarding men and readjusting sails."

"We won't be able to catch them."

Finn gave Ethan a wry smile. "All this time together, and you still doubt me?"

Ethan nodded to the open water. "He'll have a decent head start, and it's not a long sail to France."

"Perhaps." Finn glanced at the ship before turning to Ethan. His smile widened to his full signature grin. "Beckworth's ship rides heavy, and his men aren't setting the sails for best speed. Even if we don't catch a favorable wind—I can beat them to France."

"If we leave soon?"

"Aye, soon." Finn's grin slipped away as the ship faded into the glare of sun, carrying the two women who meant the world to him.

CHAPTER 35

The women stared into the open stretch of gray water, the wind unraveling their hair. With one hand, AJ tightened her grip on the railing as she entwined her other with Maire's.

"All will be well," Maire whispered into AJ's ear. Her fingers squeezed. "You'll see."

Maire's words washed over her like a cold rinse, leaving her chilled to the bone. Nothing would be well again. Finn had betrayed her, and Ethan lay dead in some meadow. Life as she knew it was blown away like petals in a summer storm. Even if the earl could mount an offensive for the stones, the viscount's men were formidable.

AJ gazed at the sky and watched the gulls circle. This time, their frenzied cries matched a quiet restlessness building within her, fanned by the warmth of Maire's touch. Her fate might have been set, but with this woman by her side, they could chart their own course. She would find home.

THANK YOU FOR READING

Thank you for reading *Keeper of Stones*. Follow AJ and Finn's journey in Book 3 of the series, *Torc of Stone*.

Stay connected to Kim to keep up with new releases, book signings and other treats through her website: www.kimallred.com. Join her newsletter at: https://www.kimallred.com/contact. Connect on Facebook: https://www.facebook.com/kimallredwriter.

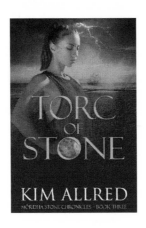

TORC OF STONE

CHAPTER 1

Present Day - Baywood, Oregon

The fog swirled. Ethereal tendrils stretched out like long bony fingers as they searched, poked, and prodded. Adam Moore blinked. The mist was so dense, he could see only a few feet in front of him. He stood on the dock at the Westcliffe Inn, amazed at how quickly the fog descended. It blanketed the ship, the dock, and everything around him. He squinted into the utter whiteness. Nothing.

"AJ, step away." Ethan Hughes' plea filled the void, full of concern.

Adam blew out a breath, relieved to hear another voice.

He took a tentative step. The waves slapped against the dock and confirmed where he stood. One step, and another. He stopped. The sound of the waves vanished, the surrounding air became denser, leaving him in a vacuum of space.

The fog continued its hazy swirl, and Adam ran a hand over his arm. No moisture. No chill in the air. *That's odd.* He turned in a tight circle, no longer sure how close he stood to the edge of the dock.

"Ethan." Adam croaked, and he cleared his throat. "Ethan?" Although he shouted the words, they sounded muffled and reverberated in the silence.

A splinter of fear crawled up his spine, followed by something disagreeable lodging in his stomach. He shook his head, closed his eyes, and heard nothing but his own heavy breathing. No birds. No waves. No sea.

The panic choked him.

His nausea increased, and an urge to sit flooded over him, a need to confirm his connection with the ground, anything to ensure he remained rooted in sanity. Uncaring what the others thought, he dropped to the dock, and though the dock's rough planks chilled him, he reveled in the tactile comfort they gave him. Something real.

Clearing his throat once more, he called, "Ethan? AJ? Is someone there?"

Silence.

When he'd arrived at the shore with Ethan, the man seemed crazed. He wasn't the even-keeled man Adam had known these past weeks. Ethan had never been out of sorts. But that changed when Ethan discovered Adam ransacking AJ's bedroom, searching for that blasted necklace. A momentary jolt of shame shuddered through Adam when he remembered his frantic search. When Adam told Ethan that AJ owned the necklace, it all went haywire.

Ethan had raced from the room, anxious to get to AJ, squawking about the necklace, a ship, and Finn Murphy. But Adam needed that necklace. He'd been scouring Baywood for weeks before learning AJ had purchased it. Finn offered money for it, and Adam still owed Victor for his gambling debt. He had no choice but to follow Ethan.

Adam shivered, but not from any chill. He remembered the death-defying drive to the coast, Ethan at the wheel, his expression crazed, and nothing Adam said slowed him down. Once at the coast, Adam couldn't piece together why they were at the Westcliffe Inn, where AJ had spent her childhood with their father talking about history and antiques.

A two-hundred-year-old ship appeared out of the mist, a ghostly figure as it softly nudged the old wooden pier. His jaw dropped, his heart beat faster, and his skin prickled, and for a moment he'd frozen in place.

As he'd chased after Ethan, the fog had grown denser. The ship still hugged the dock, and he'd spotted AJ next to Finn through the swirling murkiness. He hadn't known they knew each other. At first, he'd worried she'd learned of his gambling debt. But she had been in Finn's arms. Were they lovers? If there hadn't been terror in Ethan's call, Adam would have sneered at the scene.

Ethan's yelling increased before it cut off, like a door closing, leaving only the fog.

Adam inhaled a deep breath, closed his eyes, and counted to ten, an old trick his college roommate had taught him when practicing their mock trials. Adam scoffed until he found it worked. Now he used the trick before his opening statements when he was alone with the jury. The only other time he found it helpful was when his youngest daughter, Charlotte, had been deathly sick. Maybe it would help now.

He turned his head and listened. The flapping of wings and a screech from a gull. Adam's eyes popped open, but he snapped them shut. The piercing light blinded after the fog. The warmth of the sun touched his skin, and he laughed. After acclimating to the brightness, he stood, ready to put this behind him and demand an explanation.

But there was nothing there. No ship. No Ethan. No AJ or Finn.

He shook his head as if it would clear this deceptive vision. The rustle of the waves reassured him, the salty air tickled his nose, and the wind brushed his shirt. More gulls shrieked. Still alone.

He staggered back and fell, hitting the dock hard. The air rushed out of him, and, seized by shock and fear, he stared at where Finn's ship used to be. Had he lost his mind? A sharp jolt of pain from a splinter piercing his hand confirmed the reality. The emotional turmoil of the last two hours overwhelmed him. And for the first time since Charlotte's illness, he cried.

After ten minutes in a semicatatonic state, Adam wiped his face and stared at the empty dock. The fog, no longer visible, seeped inside him, dragging him down to dark places. He resisted the surge of dread, fighting to crawl out and deal with the unexplainable.

Perhaps his mind snapped when he didn't find the necklace, and he imagined everything else. Maybe Ethan never found him raiding AJ's apartment. He'd conjured it up over guilt for his out-of-character actions these past weeks, and hiding his gambling debt from Madelyn. He'd never kept a single secret from his wife before. And instead of developing an ulcer like any normal person, he hallucinated.

He had been the lunatic speeding to the shore, not Ethan. Good God, only luck got him here without killing himself or someone else.

He laughed. A two-hundred-year-old ship. Really? His imagination had taken over. Working for Finn for the last month, he would know if the man owned a ship.

Adam pulled himself up and brushed the dirt from his pants. He tugged at his shirt sleeves and glanced around. The sun slipped toward the horizon. Madelyn would wonder why he was late.

He strode up the path, stopping halfway to look back. It had all seemed so real. The ship and Ethan. Finn's arms around his sister. He smirked. AJ and Finn. No, that was an improbable match. Ethan he might believe, with his interest in history, but not Finn. He shook his head, shoved his hands in his pockets, and turned back to the path.

The farther he moved from the dock, the better he felt. What an imbecile. All because of his weakness for cards. He was better than this, and his family deserved more. As he reached the top of the path, he stopped in front of the inn. He barely remembered the last time he'd been here. His father had brought him when he was just a kid. The old man had tried so hard to get Adam to love the lore, but his interests ran elsewhere. It was AJ who'd caught the bug. He didn't know why he'd driven here of all places.

He shrugged and turned to the parking lot. And froze. Two cars sat in the lot, neither of them his. AJ's Subaru and Ethan's Escalade stared at him, soulless creatures from an episode of *Twilight Zone*.

And for the third time in his life, Adam fell to the ground and cried.

The day had been disastrous. Two failed real estate closings. All Stella Caldway wanted to do was immerse herself in a long, hot shower and call AJ. Once she had calmed her clients in the escrow offices, she sifted over the drama from the day before. With Ethan's irrational concerns over Finn Murphy, and AJ lusting after the same Mr. Murphy, she had fallen into a soap opera. She hadn't had this much fun in ages.

Stella laid her bag on the table on her way to the kitchen. She'd just finished pouring a glass of wine when someone pounded on the door, followed immediately by the doorbell pressed over and over again. The pounding increased. Her heart leapt as she remembered Ethan's warnings. Maybe she should have been more diligent in calling AJ.

She ran to the door, out of breath when she swung it open,

expecting the tall, lean form of Ethan Hughes. A butterfly could have knocked her over when she found Adam waiting for her. A flippant remark died on her lips as she took in the wild eyes, his tawny hair tossed about like a street urchin. Her stomach lurched. "What happened to AJ?"

"She's gone."

Thank you for reading *Keeper of Stones*. Follow AJ and Finn's journey in Book 3 of the series, *Torc of Stone*.

Stay connected to Kim to keep up with new releases, book signings and other treats through:

Her website: www.kimallred.com.
Join her newsletter at: https://www.kimallred.com/contact.
Connect on Facebook:
https://www.facebook.com/kimallredwriter.

ABOUT THE AUTHOR

Kim Allred lives in an old timber town in the Pacific Northwest where she raises alpacas, llamas and an undetermined number of free-range chickens. Just like AJ and Stella, she loves sharing stories while sipping a glass of fine wine or slurping a strong cup of brew.

Her spirit of adventure has taken her on many journeys including a ten-day dogsledding trip in northern Alaska and sleeping under the stars on the savannas of eastern Africa.

Kim is currently working on the next book in the Mórdha Stone Chronicles series and her upcoming new sizzling romance series—Masquerade Club.

To stay in contact with Kim, join her newsletter at https://www.kimallred.com/contact/, follow her on Facebook at https://www.facebook.com/kimallredwriter/, or visit her website at www.kimallred.com.